The Measure of His Grief

Lisa Braver Moss

NOTIM PRESS

First Notim Press Edition, November 2010

Printed in the United States of America

Cover design by Chloë Dalby
Typesetting by Mona Reilly
Author photograph by Deborah Braver

ISBN: 978-1-453-72025-7

The Measure of His Grief

For Marcy,

Best wishes, and thanks for a very memorable discussion.

[illegible] Braver Moss

3.7.11

Part One:
KADDISH

CHAPTER ONE

"*SHIVA!*" DR. SANDY WALDMAN EXCLAIMED.

Sandy had never entirely rid himself of his childhood impression that the word was really "shiver," something Jewish people habitually pronounced with a Brooklyn accent even in Berkeley. Of course he knew better; *shiva* was the set of religious services held at home following a death in the family, something involving covering up mirrors and sitting on low benches. But when his friend Zev brought it up, Sandy shuddered. He'd gotten the call from his sister Shayna only a few minutes before, and wasn't feeling any sense of loss or grief yet. A chill was, in fact, more like it.

Sandy was sitting on the black leather stool in Exam Three, Zev on the green bucket chair in the corner. Zev leaned forward earnestly, the buttons of his white lab coat straining over his pot belly. "*Shiva* will give you structure," he explained, "a way to help you through the trauma of losing a parent. It's not just a matter of demonstrating respect for the dead, Sandy. Compassion for the mourner is also built in. There's comfort in the fact that you're not alone in your grief. You'll take the week off—"

"A week?" Sandy imagined the reaction of Dr. Critchfield, the Chief of Medicine, who always seemed slightly taken aback by observance of Jewish holidays, as if their basis in the lunar calendar multiplied their power to disrupt. Critch's attitude was less of an issue with Zev, a cardiologist in the practice, than with Sandy, an endocrinologist who was also Assistant Chief. Critch wouldn't look kindly on Sandy's missing so much work when the quality reports were coming due, and Sandy had taken a day off just last week for Yom Kippur—and the week before for Rosh Hashanah.

"I'll get someone to take your patients," Zev assured him. "And someone to fill in for you when you're on call. Don't worry—I'll handle Critch."

Sandy felt the urge to bring air into his lungs, more air than could fit there. As Zev prattled on about *shiva*, Sandy took a breath, loosened his tie underneath his white lab coat. He was watching himself as if from above, noticing himself: the slight frame, the beaklike nose, the widening bald area at the back of his head that was just about average for a forty-eight year-old. He used to look young for his age. Sandy was acutely aware of his own rear end on the stool—the pelvic bone vertical, the thigh bones horizontal, the curved spine. As he straightened his back, he imagined its transformation as it would look on an X-ray. Before, after.

His father had died. Shayna's father had died, too. *How did the old man die?* Sandy asked himself, in a mild panic. *A stroke, probably*. He and Shayna needed to find out for sure; he should get on the phone right away and order a CT scan of the body... why did they need to know, again? There was a reason, but Sandy was left with an odd feeling, as if this were something he'd always wondered whenever anyone died. What *was* the reason for finding out all the particulars, anyway? He was almost soothed by the blank space stretching out in front of him where an answer should have been.

Though he and his wife, Ruth, belonged to a synagogue, Sandy wasn't religious. His Holocaust-survivor parents had reared Sandy and Shayna with very little in the way of Jewish education or practice. Yet Sandy was finding himself curiously unable to dismiss the idea of a traditional *shiva*. During the period when his parents were hiding in a cellar in Budapest with their three-year-old daughter, the child had died of a blood infection. From what Sandy could piece together based on stray remarks his mother, Belle, had made over the course of his life, her inability to mourn her daughter properly—Jewishly—was an ongoing source of anguish for her, despite her having given up Jewish practice almost entirely in the time since. It didn't feel right to deny Belle a traditional *shiva* for her husband if that were something that would give her comfort.

"And as far as prayer books go," Zev was saying, "I can put them in my car for after the funeral. I could even lead the *shiva* myself, if that would be helpful to you." He paused. "You okay, Sandy?"

He winced at this question to which one could only answer *yes*. "Of course."

"Have you spoken with Ruth yet?"

Sandy nodded absently, peering at Zev, the fading freckles, the pasty skin, the yellowish teeth that can go along with being a redhead. He supposed he should go home. But he couldn't quite bring himself to endure the concern on his wife's face, the smell of the kitchen as she ironed out the final version of—what was it, this week? A low-fat cinnamon-beef lasagne, for the pasta section of the high blood pressure cookbook. Sandy visualized Ruth layering the noodles, spooning in some fragrant sauce she'd invented, dipping into the container of ricotta cheese with a butter knife, using her fingers to help spread clumps of the sticky white stuff over the noodles and sauce, adeptly turning on the water afterwards with the back of her hand so as not to soil the kitchen faucet—just as he'd been taught to do on his surgical rotation at Hopkins. Wiping her palms hurriedly on her yellow cotton apron as the phone rang.

Gina, the administrator for their internal medicine group practice, knocked and poked her head in the door. "Sorry to interrupt, Doctor. Your sister is on the phone again. Line 2. And your patient is still here. Shouldn't I send her home?"

"Absolutely not." Sandy stretched his body upward toward the phone as Gina closed the door. "Shayna?"

"Hi, Sandy," his sister said, sounding pinched and distant. "I just talked to the funeral people again. I was thinking Thursday would give the out-of-towners a chance to get here."

"Thursday. What time?" Sandy grabbed his prescription pad out of his pocket and got his pen ready, then realized the absurdity of writing down the information as if this were an appointment he might otherwise forget.

"Two o'clock. I have to go to the funeral place and choose Daddy's coffin. Do you care what kind I get?"

"What kind of coffin," Sandy repeated. Seeing Zev prick up his ears, Sandy turned away, put the pen back in his pocket. "Whatever you choose is fine, Shayn. Thanks for handling all this."

"Did you talk to Ruth?"

"Yeah." He wondered whether Ruth had reached Amy, their eighteen-year-old daughter.

"I'll stop by the house later. Bye for now, Sandy. Love you."

"Wait. Shayna?"

He heard the faint *whoosh* as she brought the receiver back to her ear. "Yeah?"

"What about Mama?"

Shayna gave a long sigh. "I haven't called her yet. You want me to?"

"I don't know—maybe we should hold off. Break the news when we pick her up to go to the funeral."

"You're probably right."

Sandy hung up and turned to Zev. "Thursday at two. Our house afterward."

Zev grimaced, and Sandy remembered hearing somewhere that according to Jewish tradition, a body is supposed to be buried within a day. "There are practical considerations, Zev, like giving the relatives time to get here."

Zev conceded with a nod. "Do you need help with the coffin?"

"Shayna said she'd handle it."

"The simpler, the better, you know," Zev said gently, leaving Sandy to wish he'd never complained to Zev about Shayna's tendency toward ostentation, or the fact that Belle's care was causing major hemorrhaging of his parents' assets. "A plain wooden one is best, according to Jewish law. It's really a matter of respect for the fact that we're all equal in death, no matter how poor or rich we may be, how good or bad..."

Sandy had never known Zev in his pre-Orthodox incarnation, when he was Willy Marks from Brooklyn. He had reinvented himself as Zev before he and Sandy were put together as med school roommates in their first year at Johns Hopkins. By that time Zev had already shocked his assimilated parents by coming back from a teen trip to Israel announcing that he wanted to keep kosher; already stunned them by enrolling in an Israeli *yeshiva* for three years after finishing college, telling them he wanted to be a rabbi, not a doctor, and that he intended to live in Israel permanently. He had been transformed, he said, by having *tefillin* put on him by an old rabbi, and realizing that through this concrete act—binding a small leather box housing a passage from the Torah around his arm, and fastening another one to his head—he was connecting himself to Jews from many generations past. Though he did wind up at Hopkins a few years later, bowing, as Sandy had, to family pressure, Zev had retained his observant ways.

"I'm sure that whatever coffin Shayna chooses—" Sandy said vaguely.

Zev put his hand on Sandy's shoulder. "You sure you don't want me to take you home? I'm done for the morning."

"I'd still need to come back for the car. Anyway, I'm—fine."

"You're not fine. You've just lost a loved one."

Loved one. It sounded almost like an accusation.

"Sandy, would you stand up?"

"What for?"

"If it's okay with you, I'll rend your garment for you. It's a statement of mourning."

"Okay, sure. Yes," Sandy found himself saying. Weakly, he got up off the black leather stool as Zev reached into the cabinet above the sink, then tore open a packaged pair of scissors. Sandy felt the touch of the leather at the back of his knees before the wheels skidded a little across the linoleum. Maybe after this one last patient of the morning, he really should go home. He could have another cup of decaf, help Shayna with phone calls. He should try to catch Shayna before she went to the funeral home. He could easily imagine her ponying up excessive cash for a coffin to assuage some nameless guilt.

Zev stood in front of him, brought the left lapel of Sandy's light blue Oxford shirt out from under the lab coat, and snipped the lapel with the scissors. Then he put the scissors down and took each tiny half in his hands. "This represents the tear in your heart," Zev explained, and when he ripped the lapel, Sandy sat back down on the stool, hard, tears spilling onto his lab coat. There was something absurd in all this. Sandy suddenly recalled a Marx Brothers scene in which Harpo mischievously snips the long beards of three unsuspecting brothers as they sleep side by side in the same bed.

"*Ha makom y'nachem*," Zev pronounced. "May you find solace."

SANDY SAT IN THE exam room with the patient, skimming her chart to jog his memory. Like many diabetics, she'd been seeing her primary care physician to manage her condition, and had recently been referred to Sandy because she was having chronic crises. "So you've been doing the home blood sugar tests," he observed.

He squinted at the results of the A1-C blood test he'd ordered, comparing them against the blood sugar levels she'd reported. There was no way this patient had been sticking to the recommended diet; she had to be fudging her levels. He fingered his freshly snipped lapel. "I see here that you've reported that your levels are good," he said kindly, looking into her face.

The examination table paper crinkled as the patient shifted her weight. Her broad, lined face was wary, her ample shoulders rounded forward in resignation. She was black and in her mid-seventies, and seemed somehow permeable, as if she didn't have skin protecting her from the world.

"Well, your A1-C test came back with a level of 14. That's abnormally high, my dear. We have to make it a goal for you to achieve better control. You're going to need to keep track of your blood sugar levels more—accurately."

It was starting to sink in. Sandy's father was dead: not breathing anymore, not generating his mysterious clove-like scent. He wouldn't be eating or sleeping. He wouldn't be remembering, or forgetting, to take his blood pressure medicine. He wouldn't be smoothing back his glorious, thick white hair as he thundered on about Israeli politics, or Brahms, or the importance of a daily swim.

"You know," Sandy heard himself saying, "I think it might help you to talk with other people in your situation. See how they handle the challenges. Have you ever participated in a support group before?"

She shook her head.

"It's kind of like a class. You'd come once a week for a few weeks. Get to know the others, and learn from each other." He wheeled the seat a little closer, swallowing. *Call for a CT scan of the body.* "You're thinking diabetes isn't a reason to join a group, isn't that right?" he said softly. "You feel awkward about sharing your personal information with other patients whom you don't even know?"

The woman nodded.

"Well, listen, I can understand your hesitance. But this is not a therapy group. It's for just what it says—support. Most diabetics do much better when they attend one for awhile." Sandy's voice sounded false inside his own ears. He hadn't sounded that way, had he, just an hour earlier? During the follow-up with one of his "pale-and-frails," as he called them, to see whether six months on Fosamax had improved her osteoporosis? With the patient whose blood pressure problems were apparently being caused by her adrenal gland? With that weird guy whose thyroid was out of whack, probably from a calcium imbalance, who was on his way out the door when Sandy had gotten the call? *What was the reason for finding out all the particulars, anyway?*

Sandy wheeled over and reached for a yellow flyer from the counter. "You're in luck—there's a session tomorrow afternoon, up in the conference room on the eighth floor."

"Well, I have an eye test tomorrow at three—"

"Perfect. The group starts at four. Listen, I really think this will help you." Sandy helped his patient off the table, opened the door. "Now don't forget to study for that eye exam."

She looked confused. "I won't."

Sandy winked and patted her shoulder. He managed to get her out of the room before leaning back against the closed door and letting the tears come.

CHAPTER TWO

SANDY REACHED FOR another box of Kleenex from the stash Ruth kept in the hallway linen closet. Was this, his tissue consumption, the true measure of his grief? He thought of his gynecology rotation, when he'd been instructed to ask women to tell him how many sanitary pads or tampons they'd gone through in a given day as a way of determining the quantity of bleeding. It seemed such a dubious way to evaluate the situation—why was it assumed all women changed their paraphernalia after the same amount of blood had collected on them? Some women had to be more fastidious than others, and would thus report heavier bleeding. That a suspicion of cancer or other reproductive dysfunction could be based on such subjective observations had always struck Sandy as incredibly primitive.

Today was the last day of *shiva*, and this was the last service. Sandy wasn't surprised by how draining a time it had been. What he hadn't been prepared for was the physicality of his loss: almost a numbness in much of his body, yet a palpable dread in his chest cavity; a pervasive, deep fatigue. But now that the mourning week was drawing to a close, Sandy had to admit that Zev had been right. *Shiva* had been a time without distractions, during which Sandy had been free to do nothing but metabolize his loss. He'd never thought of freedom as something that could result from traditional observance.

He dug his thumb into the tissue box perforations and ran his fingernails around the edges. The closet door was still open, shielding him from the *shiva* guests for the moment. He folded the rectangle of cardboard in half and slipped it into his back pocket, grabbed a few tissues, and dried his eyes.

He came back into the living room past Belle, who was planted in her wheelchair at the side of the room next to Shayna. Lately, it had been a challenge to get Belle to understand that the Home for Jewish Parents was not a concentration camp just because everyone living there was Jewish and most were separated from their families. Sandy and Shayna had long since stopped trying to explain to their mother that her husband was in his late seventies now, living alone in the house they'd bought together forty-five years earlier. Sandy wondered, not for the first time this week, how much Belle was absorbing.

Retrieving his glasses from his shirt pocket, Sandy sat down heavily in the armchair he'd been using, next to Ruth. The chair was still warm. At first, Sandy had been apprehensive about leaving his seat during the various prayers. He'd assumed that traditional Jewish observance, even held in his own home, would be more prescribed than the Reform services with which he was familiar. But the atmosphere was much more casual than Sandy would have predicted. Zev milled around while leading, and when Sandy had questioned him about it, he'd explained that Orthodox services weren't very formal, even in the synagogue. It was a far cry from the experience at Sandy's Reform congregation, where people tended to hold still as if they were members of an audience—as if the rabbi and cantor were giving performances on a stage.

Sandy grabbed another Kleenex. It surprised him that Amy hadn't brought up the topic of handkerchiefs during *shiva*. Ever since she'd moved into a student co-op on the Berkeley campus—as an employee of the university, she was eligible for student housing as available—Amy had become preachy about recycling and energy efficiency. She'd been on Sandy's case about the pre-made trays of disposable tools he used in his group practice, wanting to know why he couldn't instead buy reusable ones that could be assembled into trays by hand. He'd explained that reusable examination instruments were labor-intensive—the sterilization, the inventory. She'd insisted that the practice's disposable examination gowns should be replaced with washable cotton ones. It wasn't so simple, he said. Laundry services were expensive, and used up natural resources, too—water, for instance, and heat, and the gasoline it took to deliver the clean gowns in a truck and haul the dirty ones away.

Sandy almost relished this kind of argument with his daughter, just as he was secretly pleased to be able to challenge her about the going-nowhere job at the Cal Botanical Gardens she'd taken instead of enrolling in one of the local community colleges. Whenever the topic *wasn't* Dr. Eugene Corrador, whom Amy had been talking about contacting ever since she turned eighteen last November, Sandy felt a certain relief.

Corrador was the Los Angeles obstetrician whose patient Brenda Sprig, waitress and part-time college student, had found herself pregnant and desperate some nineteen years ago. It was completely natural that Amy would want to get in touch with him, and as far as Amy knew, the reason for Sandy's aversion to the man was that he held Corrador partly responsible for Brenda's death during childbirth with Amy. Which was also true.

It had crossed Sandy's mind, when he and Ruth had composed the letter to his HMO colleagues about how much they'd love to adopt a baby, to exclude Corrador from the mailing list. But ultimately, Sandy had distributed the letter throughout Hyl (short for Hyllis, which was in turn short for Hyde and Ellis, the San Francisco intersection where the huge organization had set up its first, modest offices during the fifties). After all, what were the odds that out of all those contacts at all those branches of Hyl, it would be Corrador who would come through? And now Sandy couldn't help feeling he'd made some Faustian bargain, something about paying the devil back with one's first-born. Though that was clearly putting it too strongly.

"Judaism teaches us to understand death as part of the Divine pattern of the universe," Zev was saying to the crowd in the living room. "We wouldn't have our consciousness, our awareness, without our vulnerability. Mortality is the price we pay for the privilege of being human." Sandy felt Ruth's hand in his. This was the last evening service, the last time during *shiva* that they would be reciting *kaddish* for his father. Everyone rose, and voices in the room began to chant along with Zev: *Yit gadal ve-yit kadash shemei raba...*

Kaddish. When Sandy had first read its translation, he'd been surprised to find that the poem wasn't about death at all, but life. *Let God's great name be blessed for ever and ever; let the name of God be glorified, exalted and honored...* The prayer was in Aramaic, which made it harder to learn than the ones in Hebrew. The cadences were unfamiliar, and it was recited, not sung, making it harder to retain. But as Zev had promised, Sandy was able to follow along pretty well after having had the prayer repeated so many times all week, though there was still that one long phrase coming up that he knew he'd stumble over. *Yit barach, v'yish tabach, v'yit pa-ar...*

In truth, heartache and loss weren't the only things Sandy was feeling. His father had bullied everyone in the family for as long as Sandy could remember, while retaining his image, in social and professional spheres, as the ultimate compassionate liberal. Dr. Abraham Waldman had brought black colleagues home for dinner at a time when this wasn't done; he'd been the first male physician on staff at University of California San Francisco Medical School to jump on the equal-pay bandwagon for women physicians; he'd refused to use his privileged parking spot on campus. But it was a different story being the man's son. How was Sandy supposed to feel grief now, only grief?

Sandy stopped, dabbed at his eyes underneath his glasses. *He would have expected me to know* kaddish *perfectly, even though no one ever taught me. Well, if he thinks he can get anyone else to say it for him better, he's sadly mistaken, may he rest in peace... Shayna is stumbling more than I am, and as for Mama—oblivious, as usual...* He stuck his glasses into his pocket and grabbed another tissue. Nowhere in the *shiva* service did it mandate that you cry out of grief for the deceased. You could cry out of grief for yourself, if you wanted.

...slapped me across the face that time I asked him about his experience during the war. His hands were so big! I was only twelve. And he was always so belittling about the tears, when there were tears. God, if he could see me now. Weeping—he'd mock me, never mind that it's for him I weep!

Oseh shalom bimeromav, hu ya-aseh shalom... Damn it, the trickiest phrase had passed once again and Sandy hadn't been able to wrap his tongue around the syllables quickly enough to stay with the group. Here it was the last part of *shiva*, and Sandy still hadn't managed to master the central mourning prayer of a tradition about which he was, let's face it, ambivalent to begin with. Sandy was crying. *I'm sorry, Dad! I'm sorry!* He was suddenly weeping long, gushing sobs. He reached behind him to put his prayer book down on the chair, squatted down again to get more tissue. He felt Ruth's soothing hands on his shoulders, could sense the concern of relatives, colleagues and friends boring into the back of his head. He felt the cluelessness of Belle in her wheelchair, and the disappointment of a favorite student of hers from years ago who had flown in to offer support only to find she'd been forgotten. The tissues made a scratching noise against the cardboard as Sandy tore them from the box.

Tears were flowing, it seemed, from every distant corner of Sandy's body. They flowed from deep in his abdomen, from his groin, from his lungs, from his throat. He was a circulatory system whose grief carried through the blood vessels to every part of him. He was a musculoskeletal system whose tears racked his bones and joints and tendons and rattled his cartilage. He was an endocrine system, his thyroid overactive, his adrenal and pituitary glands knocked off kilter by his anguish. Everything was white with the purity of his grief. He began to see himself from a distance, weeping from his pores, weeping from his fingers and toes... His crying sounded like a song. He rocked back and forth as he stood.

Amy would leave them! She'd be disgusted, rightly so, if she ever found out that Sandy's discomfort with Eugene Corrador had more to do with covering his own butt than with the circumstances of Brenda's death. Sandy had no choice but to bank on Corrador's delicacy, but who knew whether the code of discretion of the typical illicit drug dealer applied to this boorish idiot?

Sandy could claim he was trying to protect Amy, but what it all really amounted to was his own panic. See? He had feelings, goddamn it. Ruth had said once, at the height of the tension between them over the fertility problems, that Sandy was more interested in talking about feelings than in experiencing them. He was an intellectualizer, she said—no more in touch with his emotional life than his distant, stoical parents were; he only deluded himself into thinking he'd broken away. Well, Ruth was wrong now, wasn't she! Sandy was scared of his own daughter's abandonment of him, and angry at his father, who'd been right all along; Sandy loved being a doctor!

Sandy's eyes were blurred, his throat full of tears, as he thought of how much his father had loved chamber music. Brahms, Schubert, late Beethoven. Old Waldman had been so appalled by the sound when Sandy took up the violin at age eight that after a few weeks, Sandy had compliantly put the instrument down and refused ever to play it again. By that time, Sandy was accustomed to being good at everything non-athletic that he tried. It was a shock to have hit a wall, though in retrospect, he realized violin required manual dexterity: being moved by music didn't mean you could be a good musician; being academically inclined didn't mean you'd grow up to be a surgeon.

Damn him! Why couldn't his father have noticed that it was little sister Shayna who was dextrous, Shayna who should have gone to medical school, if he wanted to pass down his scalpel? Shayna, who could make dolls' clothes with a needle and thread out of unlikely scraps of felt, unrelated bits of yarn? Shayna, who was like the Eveready Battery bunny, and could probably have made it through without ever putting anything up her nose? It was true that Shayna was more interested in shopping than studying, but judging from the fact that their father had never once hit her, shopping had apparently been less of an affront than Sandy's main skill, which was talk, introspection.

Sandy cried and cried, remembering his father's beautiful, authoritative hands. He would never see those hands again... Engulfed in a wave of exhaustion like the times he'd come crashing down after coke use, or the times when Amy was an infant and he and Ruth were up every couple of hours, Sandy felt about to pass out. Still standing somehow, he was almost in a trance, helpless, like a baby, a mass of needs and orifices. Protection; he needed protection. Those hands...

All at once, Sandy felt a sharp pain toward the tip of his penis. He collapsed backward into his chair, tears spilling out from the shock of—what was it? Not a twinge; much worse than that. Excruciating pain. Searing, white-hot pain like no pain he could remember ever feeling before. And it stayed with him. He tried bending forward, but that didn't work either. He was dying, or at least bleeding. Hemorrhaging, more like. He looked down at his tan khakis, but there was no blood. He tried to use his sobs to breathe through the pain, the way he'd been trained to talk women through labor contractions. Useless.

Ruth, still standing, had put down her prayer book and bent toward him in consolation. He could hear her thoughts: *poor Sandy, doubled over in grief...* Her hands were irritating on his shoulders, and hot, even through the light satin *tallit* that Zev had lent him for the week because he hadn't been able to find that wool one in the green velvet bag, the one that had been his father's.

A kidney stone! That was it. Men compared passing a kidney stone to giving birth. True, that was a description of the pain while peeing, not while *daven*ing. Kidney stones presented with pain in the back or lower abdomen, not in the penis. But what else could this be? Blood in the urine, that was what Sandy should look for... The pain was so intense that he thought he was going to retch. He writhed forward, trying to find a comfortable position. He heard murmurs from the back of the room. Belle was weeping, Shayna comforting her. Amy reached behind Ruth and put her hand on his arm, sympathetic with her father in his wave of bereavement. He could hear their thoughts, the thoughts of everyone in attendance. *This is to be expected. Dr. Sandor Waldman's father has died, and this is the last service of* shiva. *All two dozen of us here are witnesses: Sandy really let himself go at the end, was literally knocked off his feet by grief during the last recitation of the* kaddish.

But that wasn't it.

Sandy got up, managed a helpless "I'm sorry" to no one in particular, and dizzily made his way to the bathroom, hoping there was no visible evidence of his pain, no inappropriate bulge. People were stirring in anxious concern, or bafflement.

"Sandy?" Ruth called out.

"Where is he going?" wailed Belle.

Ruth was following him into their bedroom, but Sandy had locked the bathroom door. "Sandy? You all right?"

His penis was still quivering, and he was panting from the pain. "I'm fine, Ruth," he said thickly between breaths, massaging his groin through his clothing. He tore off Zev's *tallit* and the crocheted *kipa* from Amy's bat mitzvah that he'd been wearing all week, and threw them on the bathroom counter. Then he stripped off his clothes in such a hurry that his glasses fell out of his pocket. Ignoring the keys, the wallet, and the rectangle of Kleenex box cardboard that was still sticking out of his back pocket, he let all the clothing crumple on the floor and started the shower, more for noise protection than out of any intention of bathing. He picked his glasses up off the tile, put them on, and cautiously took hold of his member, examining it in front of the mirror and then going over to the heat lamp where the light was more intense. Nothing looked different. He turned it over, looked at the tip, turned it over again. Nothing. He was still panting.

"Sandy?" Ruth's voice was high-pitched. He heard other female voices, murmurs of consultation.

He took off his glasses and got in the shower. Hot water streamed over him. The pain was still fierce, and his head was pulsing, but the torrent was soothing, and Sandy realized he needed to pee. Normally he would have toweled himself off and used the toilet, but it was made of grey porcelain, and he was afraid he wouldn't be able to gauge the color of his urine. So he loosened his bladder right in the shower, expecting an orange stream—yellow mixed with red—against the white tub. But his pee was pale. He held the urine back; then he turned away from the water flow, not wanting to dilute what color there was, and peed some more.

No blood.

Without a concrete explanation, and without any dissipation of the pain, Sandy racked his brain. He supposed it was possible, with a kidney stone, to bleed in such small amounts that the blood could be detected only microscopically, but he couldn't help panicking about other possibilities. If this wasn't a kidney stone, what was it? *The patient complains of intense pain around the glans of his penis. The patient reports that it is unlike anything he has previously experienced. The patient reports no discoloration of the urine. The patient reports no recent trauma, other than the death of his father, whom he loved intensely, but also hated, for whom he is crying...*

He became a second-year medical student again, an ad-hoc hypochondriac, running the gamut of grandiose scenarios. AIDS. Syphilis. Gonorrhea—it couldn't be. He and Ruth had been faithful to each other for twenty-two years. Could Ruth have contracted something and not told him? He tried to imagine it, but it just didn't hold... Yeast infection? But that was itchy, not painful, and it didn't come on so suddenly. Besides, he avoided the tight underwear associated with that problem; he'd started wearing boxers years ago to increase his sperm count, even though that had nothing whatever to do with the infertility. Urinary tract infection? But the main symptom there was burning, and he'd just peed without burning. Whoa, cancer of the penis? Rare, especially in circumcised men, but possible, he supposed. No; pain wasn't a symptom. This had to be a kidney stone. He'd ask Zev. Or he'd get Vinod Sengupta, the urologist on the second floor, to run some tests for hematuria. There could be microscopic traces of blood in the urine.

Still in the shower, Sandy wasn't doing his usual cleaning of each body part in order, nor heeding Amy's voice at the back of his head telling him to conserve water. He let it flow hard, turned the dial further and further to the left as the hot water ran out. Finally, from under the lukewarm cascade, he pushed the knob off. He grabbed his towel, which was still damp from this morning's shower, and wrapped himself in it. Then he put the top down on the toilet and sat down and stared blankly at the grey-and-white tiles for a moment before wiping the fog off his glasses, putting them back on, and taking one more look. Nothing. The pain had started to subside, but his penis felt raw and vulnerable, as if he'd had sex too many times in one night.

He expected to hear Ruth calling him. He was cold now. He put on his terry cloth robe and used the sleeve to wipe away some condensation on the mirror. What stared back at him from the irregular patch was an outdated version of his mother's face. Then the image fogged over.

It occurred to Sandy that he should take a Xanax. He opened the medicine cabinet and noticed a digital thermometer, reminding him that he needed to rule out a systemic infection of some kind. Not wanting to cool his tongue with water before taking his temperature, he grabbed the thermometer and sat down on the toilet with the lid down. He'd never used this one before, and when he stuck the metal register under his tongue, he found its weight was mainly in the outer end, making it impossible to keep in place without using his hand to hold it there. Such a lousy design! Sure, the mercury ones were breakable, and not easy to dispose of responsibly, but at least they were sleek and had a reasonable center of gravity. Sandy tried to breathe deeply through his nose as he waited. His nostrils were pretty blocked.

Even having had the long, hot shower, which can raise the body's core temperature, Sandy wasn't feverish; in fact, he had the usual sub-normal temperature not uncommon in small, thin people.

He popped a pill, took a swig of water and opened the door to the bedroom. The jackets and sweaters were mostly gone from the white bedspread, other than a flamboyant sweater Shayna had knitted for herself, Belle's cardigan with the brass buttons, and Zev's tweed jacket. Sandy could hear people talking in the kitchen. He put on faded sweats that were nice and loose, a cotton turtleneck, and a wool vest Amy had gotten for him from the Global Exchange for his birthday last year.

"What are these?" Amy's voice as Sandy approached the kitchen.

"Chocolates from the Levinsons," answered Ruth. "The waxy kind, unfortunately. Barton's."

"Pure petroleum," Shayna declared. "Put 'em in your gas tank."

Ruth, Amy, Shayna, and Zev were crowded into the breakfast nook, Belle facing them from her wheelchair. Though their *shiva* guests had been bringing food all week and Ruth had supplemented with some of her own dishes, Shayna had also over-ordered from the most expensive Jewish caterer in the East Bay. The kitchen counter was groaning under the weight of the leftovers.

Ruth, sitting on the outside, got up and started rubbing his back. "You all right, Sandy?"

"I'm—just—" Later, Sandy would ask himself why he chose, in that moment, to extricate himself from the back rub rather than taking Ruth aside and telling her about the kidney stone the way he told her about everything else. Nearly everything else.

"Want me to do anything for you, Sandy?" Amy asked.

Sandy bristled. His daughter couldn't call him "Dad," even today?

"Can I make you a plate of food?" Ruth offered.

"I'm telling you, Sandy, this kugel!" Shayna chimed in. "I took one look at it and went, *screw* Atkins."

"I tried to save her," cried Belle, reliving the death of her little daughter for the millionth time.

"It's all right, Mama, you tried," Shayna murmured, rubbing Belle's bony forearm.

"Would you like to go for a walk, Sandy?" asked Zev. "It's traditional to take a walk around the block after the last *shiva* service is over—"

"That sounds good," Sandy said.

"What are we gonna do with all this food," Amy said to no one in particular.

"You see," Sandy heard Zev saying as he went back to the bedroom to grab a windbreaker and Zev's jacket, "the walk provides a kind of separation between the seven-day *shiva* and the rest of *sheloshim*, the thirty-day initial mourning period."

Sandy's pain was half gone, and the Xanax was kicking in. Whatever it was, at least things were moving in the right direction.

Outside, the twilight air was cool. Berkeley's traditional September heat wave often rendered the middays indistinguishable from summer, with morning and evening chill embracing the exaggerated warmth like parentheses. The days would be getting shorter now. Sandy zipped his jacket.

"So what happened there, Sandy?" Zev asked, resting his hand on Sandy's shoulder. "You okay?"

"You know, I had this—" Sandy hesitated. How to explain? Did he want to? "Thanks for leading services, Zev. And for suggesting *shiva* in the first place. It really has meant a lot to all of us."

"I'm glad I could help. And if you want to talk—"

Sandy groped for a topic.

"You know, I still can't stand the idea of Amy talking with Eugene Corrador. Overgrown frat boy."

"He was when we knew him," Zev agreed.

Sandy turned toward his friend. "Remember that stupid joke he kept telling during third year, about how the term 'bed*side* manner' shouldn't apply to gynecologists?"

"Right, because they work mostly at the—"

"—*foot* of the bed," they said together. Sandy could tell Zev was indulging him, that he would have preferred to be talking about something more fitting at the end of *shiva*. "Wasn't even his joke," Sandy added.

"Didn't he lift it from that petite Texas gal, on our Ob-Gyn rotation?"

"It was funny when *she* said it." Whether by means of a stolen witticism, the white late-model BMW he drove, or the vapid, leggy blonde with whom he lived, Corrador had constantly tried to impress. "I still can't believe he wound up going into Ob-Gyn. Remember his oh-so-eloquent description? 'You stick stuff up women's pussies all day long. You stick your latex fingers into their asses. What's so hard about that?' I mean, how offensive."

"To be fair, Sandy, he was pretty drunk at the time."

"And what about that reprimand he got just after starting his practice, for groping one of his patients? Not to mention during our rotations, that girl he—" Sandy stopped.

"Right, that young woman he got pregnant. The one who worked night shifts in the on-site pharmacy. Gorgeous, but—mildly retarded or something, right?"

Sandy nodded. He'd never told Zev that the night before the pharmacy girl's abortion, when, as a favor to Corrador, Sandy dropped by her apartment to deliver a gram, she'd tearfully—invitingly—begged Sandy for reassurance that Corrador wasn't with her just to secure a steady supply of Valium for customers wishing to come down.

Sandy hadn't so much kept secrets from Zev as not advertised them to someone so sincere and driven. In private, Sandy could rationalize: he had to stay awake somehow; it wasn't human, what was asked of them; everyone coped in his or her own way; Sandy had way too much self-control to allow himself to get addicted to cocaine. But cheap self-delusion would hardly go over with someone enduring the same hazing as Sandy, yet managing to keep his equilibrium through, of all things, religious practice.

Besides, if Zev was so oblivious as to be unaware at the time of Corrador's appalling little sideline, why would Sandy bring it up? If Zev thought it was marijuana for which Sandy got busted, why would Sandy correct him?

"In any case, Sandy, Eugene Corrador's bad behavior—that was years ago."

"I know, and I'm sure he's matured by now, but—"

"And he did give you Amy."

"Of course, of course. I'll always be grateful for that. More than grateful."

As they made their way back to the house, Sandy was ready to ask whether Zev thought a kidney stone could be passed without noticeable blood. "You know, what happened earlier, during *kaddish*—I suddenly had this intense pain. Like nothing I'd ever felt before."

Zev nodded sagely, put his hand on Sandy's shoulder again. "That's the beauty of *shiva*. There's no condescension to the mourner, no pretense. You're free to experience the full extent of your grief."

CHAPTER THREE

LATER THAT NIGHT the pain was gone. But even with another half a Xanax in his system, Sandy was anxious going to bed. When Ruth tried to comfort him, he turned away from her as if his grief were overwhelming him.

Sandy and Ruth were a physically close couple. They still hugged and kissed when they greeted each other after a day's work, when Sandy came into the kitchen for breakfast, when they turned out the light at night. After sex—generally once every week or two—they'd drift off either with his arm around her waist or, if they happened to find good sleeping positions facing opposite each other, with her butt against his. Why was it that now, when Ruth smoothed his hair lovingly before turning her reading light off, Sandy felt a pang of contempt for her good nature?

Slowly, Sandy's eyes adjusted to the dark. He fixed them on the blue vertical lines of the painting they'd bought in Israel, which hung above the bookshelf that housed his collection on geodesic domes and on Aaron Burr. Sandy had always had a tendency to become obsessed with one thing at a time, living and breathing each topic in a kind of serial monogamy of intellect. In freshman year of college, it was Gregorian chant. Then the Sacco and Vanzetti case. Then pre-Columbian erotic art.

In tenth grade, when Sandy wrote a paper about European Jews who had been in hiding during the war, his history teacher had taken him aside. "You have real talent for writing history, Sandor," she'd said in her thick German accent. At five foot four, Sandy was still hoping for a significant growth spurt, and he felt as if the teacher were towering over him, her wool cardigan smelling of cedar pellets. Then she'd grabbed a pen and a piece of paper and began writing down a list of books for him to read, stooping over a worn wooden desk in the front row, adding one more title, and one more, until there were nearly twenty. Sandy had stopped by the library on the way home and spent the next month devouring the literature, stashing the books under his bed. But one night, his father came into Sandy's room unannounced.

"Vat is this?" he roared. It might as well have been *Penthouse* his father grabbed, instead of *Night* by Elie Wiesel. And in knocking the book out of Sandy's hands, he also dislodged the bedspread, revealing the pile of library books on the floor underneath. The old man glared at Sandy for a long moment but, unaccountably, didn't take the materials away. Afterward Sandy was, if anything, more fascinated by the subject: the irrational regret of those who, like his parents, had been merely in hiding during the war, not in the camps; the irrational regret of those who'd been in the camps, but hadn't died. Sandy wanted to study the emotional experience of people who'd lived through the trauma in one way or another.

Later, it occurred to Sandy that it might be interesting to explore what happened in the next generation. His history teacher (who he later realized was herself a survivor) told him there had been a few articles already about the patterns—the pervasive sense of responsibility children felt for their survivor parents' happiness and, often, the familial code of silence about the war experience. Sandy visualized himself doing his own research, leading therapy groups, writing articles. He had plenty of his own material from which to draw. Like the time his father had slapped him across the face because Sandy had said that if his parents would allow him to become a Boy Scout, he could learn how to defend them.

Sandy had double-majored at U.C. Berkeley—pre-med and history—and as his undergraduate years drew to a close, he secretly put in an application to a Ph.D. program at Brandeis, where he'd be able to study Holocaust history more deeply and do his own research. He hadn't planned to mention this; he'd even intercepted the mail so that his father wouldn't know the acceptance packets had arrived. Why was it that that evening, Sandy had blurted out his conflict? *No Ph.D.*, his father had bellowed. *It's a vaste of your telents.* And Belle of course was useless, as ineffectual at putting father and son together as she was inept at timing eggs and toast to be hot at the same time. As Sandy and Shayna had often observed, the Alzheimer's-induced oblivion that now defined her was, in a way, just a distillate.

Really, it wasn't a question of whether Sandy's father would pay for graduate school. It never got that far, and if pushed, Sandy knew he could always take out student loans. The problem was that it had seemed impossible to address something as weighty as a career choice without his father's blessing. Sandy hadn't even been able to convince his parents to let him live in the dorms or student co-ops as an undergrad, no matter how many times he explained that most of the other native Berkeley kids got part-time jobs and moved out of their parents' homes while at Cal.

Separation from parents—let alone rebellion against them—was a luxury, something for other children.

You go to medical school, his father had pronounced, pointing at him. Later, he'd added that Sandy could always choose to specialize in psychiatry if he wanted to talk to people about their *feelinks*. *Feelinks*, he said, as if it were a cognate of *tiddlywinks*. Then of course, once Sandy started doing his clerkships, his father had told him in no uncertain terms that psychiatry wasn't the reason people went to med school—a sentiment echoed among his peers at Hopkins, where psychiatry wasn't considered real, hands-on medicine (this was in the days before psychopharmacology became so hot). One had to be squeamish of decision making, or a plodder, to choose such a specialty. In retrospect, Sandy understood that his father had been aware of the status of psychiatry among physicians all along.

Fortunately, by then, his fourth year, the new-and-rehabilitated Sandy had started working closely with an older endocrinologist. He'd decided he liked the complexity and variety of this specialty, the opportunity for true detective work—plus, he didn't particularly want to be around addictive psychiatric drugs. Not long after his training was finished, Sandy found a way to re-connect with his other passion, putting together a network for children of Holocaust survivors, a support and education group in which he was still actively involved. Whose existence he'd managed to keep a secret from his parents to this day.

And Sandy had found ways to distinguish himself as a doctor—notably, his support group idea, an innovation that had affected not only his endocrinology practice, but the practices of all seven other sub-specialists of internal medicine that comprised his group. Clearly his father never realized that because of

Sandy's vision, Zev had started a dietary workshop for his cardiology patients; other colleagues had followed with stress reduction workshops, stop-smoking clinics, and support groups for geriatric patients and their caretaking families. One could even make the case that Sandy had indirectly influenced other departments: Hyl obstetricians integrating midwives into their practices before any other HMO did so; Hyl surgeons providing comprehensive pre- and post-surgical documentation to their patients and budgeting their time to make human contact with them.

Ruth sighed in her sleep, and Sandy turned his body over. It was after one when he finally drifted off in the fetal position, facing away from the bookshelf, his hands cupped over his groin.

WHEN SANDY SLEPT through the alarm the next morning, Ruth woke him, made him an omelet, and sent him off for his first day back at work. He was glad to return, and relieved to realize that his state of turmoil would be attributed to mourning by anyone who noticed.

He started off the day with a woman whose serious weight problem he was monitoring on an ongoing basis. Of course he checked in with her about her arthritis, too, and gave her the usual gentle lecture about joining a weight-loss group. Her regular doctor was Brett Ingersoll, a young internist in Sandy's practice. But with many of his patients, Sandy wound up serving as the primary care physician, managing various other ailments—heart disease, kidney problems—as well as the endocrinological ones. It could be challenging, but along with Sandy's on-call duties as a regular internist at the hospital and the continuing medical education he was required to take, it kept him current in internal medicine.

When Sandy took a break and went to pee, there was no pain, and no blood. Later, just before lunch, he went down to the second floor, locked himself into a bathroom and peed again, this time into a specimen cup. Then he took it into the urology lab to examine it under the microscope, grateful that the tech barely looked up when he came in.

There were not even trace amounts of blood, and his pain was completely gone. Halfheartedly, Sandy smiled to himself as he remembered an adage he'd learned in medical school: "I don't know what it is, but it's nothing."

Grief. Grief was the source of the pain, and the sadness.

But as the days passed, Sandy still didn't want to go anywhere near Ruth. He found himself avoiding time alone with her, and he turned away from her each night, hoping she wouldn't try to make contact.

Around 4 a.m. one night, a week after *shiva* had ended, Ruth scooted over to Sandy's side of the bed in her sleep, hugging him close. Sandy tolerated it, feeling too awkward to extricate himself. But shortly after they fell asleep that way, Sandy had a terrible nightmare. He was trapped naked inside some kind of jail cell, and one by one, his organs were to be excised. "No!" he shouted, as an evil guard disguised as a wise old man approached, his eyes fixed on Sandy's penis. "No!"

Ruth shook him. "Sandy! Wake up!"

Sandy opened his eyes, but the rest of his body wouldn't move. He was sweating and panting—and the pain was back.

"Sandy! Are you all right? Sandy!"

Finally able to move, he kicked off the covers. He stumbled into the bathroom, shut the door, and sat on the floor, still panting, staring up at the ceiling with the light out, ignoring Ruth's tapping on the door, the crescendo of her concern. "Don't worry, Ruth," he managed finally. "Bad dream."

"Do you want to talk about it?"

"Holocaust," he said simply, turning on the light and keeping the door shut.

There was no blood in Sandy's urine, as far as he could tell. He decided not to take a pill, because he wanted to stay awake for the rest of the night. When he left the house, Ruth was still asleep, it was still dark. He stopped at the all-night doughnut shop to get a cup of coffee. Normally a decaf drinker, he knew he needed to produce more urine as quickly as possible. At 5:15, when he got to work, he peed into a specimen cup and took it into the lab. Still no microscopic evidence of blood.

Sandy called Vinod Sengupta at home—woke him up—and asked him to come in early, because he was passing a kidney stone but had somehow missed whatever hematuria there was. Forty minutes later, Vinod was squinting into the microscope.

"No hematuria," he enunciated under his breath, the "r" sounding like a "d." Vinod spoke in a clipped, rapid British English. One time during Grand Rounds, the continuing medical education program held at lunchtime every month, Vinod had asked the pulmonologist speaker a question about respiration. Sandy had thought it sounded eerily like "desperation."

Vinod was the only person Sandy knew who had an arranged marriage. He seemed to get along very well with his wife, a short, sour-faced woman of about thirty. More incredibly, his wife's parents were living with them at the moment, helping take care of their three small children. Vinod's in-laws didn't have a permanent address, rotating instead among their four children from Berkeley to Sacramento to Phoenix to Chicago, staying for months at a time and helping with chores, childcare and cooking. Vinod had told Sandy this was traditional in Indian families. He didn't seem the slightest bit ruffled by the setup.

"No hematuria," Sandy repeated.

"This means it is not a kidney stone." Vinod stuck a hand into his lab coat pocket, fidgeting with what sounded like a cellophane candy wrapper.

"But we can't really rule out a kidney stone until we check for obstruction. Right?"

Vinod peered into the microscope again.

"The weird thing is," added Sandy, "I have no pain now. It's completely gone."

"And yet you say this was more intense than anything you have experienced before."

Sandy nodded. "What about a CT scan?"

Vinod looked over at him. "You say you had this pain before?"

"I had it a few days ago. It came on suddenly, out of the blue."

"And describe this pain, please?"

"Well, it was—very intense. Like—"

"Like a burning, or more like this was bleeding?"

"I guess more like bleeding, now that you mention it."

"Hmm." The cellophane crinkled. "But you say there was no blood the first time, either?"

"No. I checked in the lab." Sandy paused. "Maybe an infection?" It didn't ring true.

"This is unlikely. An infection does not present so suddenly. It does not come and go. You had no fever, correct?"

Sandy shook his head. "What about some kind of neurological disorder?"

"This is also unlikely. The first thing we must do, you are correct. We must do a CT scan."

Sandy glanced at his watch. His heart was racing, he noticed; probably the caffeine. "It's 6:20. You think we have time before the Monday meeting?"

"We can do it, yes."

But the CT scan revealed no obstruction, and Sandy and Vinod had to conclude that whatever the mysterious pain was, it wasn't a kidney stone. "This is up to you now," Vinod told him. "I would suggest a watch and a wait. Perhaps this will go away. Otherwise, the next step I suppose would be hospitalization. For an extensive workup."

Sandy swallowed. Hospitalization seemed excessive, to say nothing of an incredible logistical hassle; he'd just had a week off for *shiva*. Besides, the pain was gone. "Let's watch and wait," he told Vinod. "But it's bizarre. I mean, it was excruciating."

"This is a mystery," said Vinod.

"I was *sure* it was a kidney stone."

"Hmm. Of course you know the expression, 'I do not know what it is'—"

"—but it's nothing," Sandy finished, forcing a grin.

CHAPTER FOUR

RUTH OPENED THE OVEN door and cocked her head, listening. Everyone talked about the smells of cooking, the delight of walking into a kitchen and being greeted by the hearty, authoritative odor of onions, garlic, rosemary, roast lamb. People didn't realize that part of the pleasure of cooking was the sound: the confident sizzle of fat that signaled that food was ready to be pulled from the oven, as opposed to the bland silence of something still underdone or the angry sputter of the overcooked. When it was perfect, food chanted to you.

Ruth grabbed the pot holders and took out her creation, a beef stew, robust and inviting. Her father's kind of dish. He'd been a restaurant critic and food columnist for the Chicago *Sun-Times*, and had died when Ruth was twelve of what she later realized was alcoholism. He was never a violent or angry drunk, just an absent one. He'd disappear for days on end, then come home with white paper bags filled with gourmet leftovers of all sorts that he would reheat, enabling Ruth to think of him as her primary parent. It was a fiction that comforted Ruth to this day, and was there any more harm in feeling sustained by it than there was in Amy's gripping those brightly colored plastic doughnuts to take her first steps, thinking they were keeping her from falling?

Ruth's mother, Nadine, was a monster, capable of berating teenaged Ruth for being scrawny and mousy, then in the same breath denouncing Ruth's younger sister, Ellen, for being overly seductive in her choice of clothes. Nadine had repeatedly told her girls that she would have preferred sons. As Ruth and Ellen blossomed, Nadine began to dress more and more provocatively. She'd worn a low-cut red mini-dress and spiked red heels to Ruth and Sandy's wedding. She'd mocked Ruth in front of others at their synagogue for the way she held the bottle at Amy's baby naming ceremony. She'd refused to attend Ruth's fortieth birthday party, saying it was selfish of Ruth to call attention to how old Nadine must be.

Nadine wasn't a drinker. Ruth and Ellen used to joke that if only their mother had graduated into alcoholism or drug dependency, they'd at least have been able to attend a program; there was no such thing as Adult Children of Raging Narcissists, was there? But that was before Ellen started attending twelve-step meetings for family members affected by alcoholism, and told Ruth that sometimes, the non-alcoholic partner caused more damage in a family than the drinker did. Ah.

If not for Sandy, Ruth would never have tried to include Nadine in her adult life. Ruth looked to Sandy for family normalcy the way an obese person notes the eating habits of a slender one—without considering the luck involved, the genetics. Despite all the issues with his parents, Sandy had always had a working relationship with them, the unspoken family contract being that they skimmed over anything remotely painful, like Sandy's getting busted for pot in medical school, and just plowed forward. Of course Sandy had difficulty with his father in particular—partly because Sandy didn't like the unspoken contract—but there was never any question of his cutting his parents off. The Waldmans enjoyed a basic level of respect and functionality that was foreign to Ruth, exotic. Perhaps it was inevitable that she would ascribe magical powers to it, as if just by adopting the Waldman approach, she could somehow transform Nadine from a black hole, anti-matter, into something resembling a mother.

So Nadine had been invited to Amy's birthday parties, Amy's bat mitzvah, Ruth's book signings (Nadine made it clear she would not be referring to Ruth as an author, since it was just cookbooks). Ruth got swept up into a kind of usualness with Nadine that, in retrospect, felt like a mortgage, a gigantic loan whose balloon payment she'd never be able to make but which provided a lifestyle so seductive that Ruth couldn't extricate herself. They were a family. Amy had another grandmother. There was someone to send snapshots to, across the country.

But now that Nadine was gone, Ruth couldn't honestly say she missed her. She kept waiting, this past three years, to feel some sort of grief over Nadine's death, some sense of loss similar to what she'd felt about her father's death, or similar to what Sandy was now freshly going through. Similar to what she herself was experiencing at the loss of her father-in-law. She'd never felt emotionally close to Abraham—you couldn't, really; he wasn't a warm man like his son—but his presence was in itself grounding, reassuring.

Of course Ruth had been shocked to her core by Nadine's death. It was shocking that a seventy year-old woman who'd smoked Virginia Slims for decades never contracted lung cancer, but was instead mowed down by a bus one Saturday morning while walking back to her car after going to the gym. Shocking—a cliche, even—that someone with such contempt for the people around her was ultimately felled by her own vanity: having undergone her second tummy tuck, still on narcotics for the pain, Nadine had insisted on going to her regular Jazzercise class too soon after surgery. She'd died in her black leggings.

Ruth tried to picture her mother putting on the leggings that morning instead of loose-fitting sweats. Did the waist band hurt Nadine's incision; did she decide it was worth it for the vindication of seeing her new silhouette in the mirror-covered wall at the gym? Or did the Fioricet mask the pain so well, she didn't notice? If she'd known, lacing up her white Reeboks, that this was the last time she'd ever tie her shoes, would Nadine have chosen other footwear? Did she skip breakfast that morning to look slimmer, tamping down a niggling thought that the narcotics might make her even less sure-footed on an empty stomach? Was she busy flirting with some muscular gay gym rat, or did she maybe run into her personal trainer after class and elected not to admit to him that after all that exercise, she was feeling a little spacey, and could he please walk her to her car?

But shock wasn't the same thing as grief.

Why did everyone assume, always, that it was better to be nice than not? Why didn't anyone ever talk about the price of extending oneself? Sandy, for one. He didn't seem to comprehend that Ruth's relationship with Nadine had cost her something more than the standard emotional tax one pays with family. Over the years, Ruth had expended effort on Nadine that she couldn't actually afford—the kind that couldn't be replenished with a good meal or a foot massage. She kept trying to tell Sandy that the effort was coming out of her bones; this was the only way she could think to describe the permanency of the expenditure.

And then, when Nadine died, instead of feeling grief, Ruth felt hollow, light, as if she had rickets. Bones soft, marrow mushy: Ruth could tell Sandy didn't really grasp what she was talking about. Slowly, Ruth was beginning to realize that the way she'd thought of it all along—that she'd been as nice to Nadine as she could—wasn't accurate. No, Ruth had been *nicer* to Nadine *than* she could.

If Sandy didn't understand the depth of Ruth's depletion, at least she could count on him for physical comfort. Which was why this past week and a half, since that last night of his father's *shiva*, Ruth had begun to feel deprived. She knew it was unreasonable to expect Sandy to be fully available to her while he was in the early stages of grief, but what she needed from him didn't cost him anything, so why was he withholding it? No wonder her thoughts of Oliver, with whom she'd had a flirtation for several years but little contact, had returned full force these past few days.

Twenty-four years ago, when she'd been a dietician at Hyl, Ruth had fallen hard for Sandy. He was really the first viable candidate: insightful, charming, articulate, accomplished and empathetic, nothing remotely like Nadine, and nothing like Ruth's first husband Russell. In that brief marriage, when Ruth was in her early twenties, she'd endured Russell's verbal abuse, alcohol abuse, and self-abuse (it was his habit to masturbate instead of having sex with his wife). If not for Josh, the older man with whom Ruth had had an affair, she might not have had the courage to climb out of the Russell pit. Ruth would always be grateful for the affair with Josh—it had been her lifeline—but she had no illusions about it. Until Sandy came along, no one had made any sense for Ruth.

And Sandy wanted her. In fact, within a week of their first date, he'd insisted on introducing her to Shayna. Ruth remembered being surprised that Sandy had a sister who wore too much makeup. Shayna was tan and had big boobs. Her fingernails were painted an alarming shade of coral which exactly matched her blouse. She had the kind of cheery, reassuring presence that probably made other customers in Macy's mistake her for an employee, asking her to direct them to the evening wear or the linens.

As soon as they met, Shayna peered a little too long at Ruth, at Sandy, and back at Ruth again. "You're essence twins!" Shayna squealed. "You know, like Eddie van Halen and Valerie Bertinelli. Or, no, John and Yoko—that's an even better example. You can tell they belong together just by looking at them. They're cut from the same cloth. Kind of like *entity*-mates."

Essence twins, entity-mates—whatever they were, Sandy and Ruth were very happy to have found one another. They both had an uncannily similar taste for irony in news stories, both thought Mozart brilliant but over-exposed on the radio. They discovered that for years, they'd both been frequenting a tiny hole-in-the-wall crepe place in Berkeley, in which the owner and cook, a French woman, sneered openly at the customers but created the most delicious food imaginable. Sandy and Ruth went there together, rolling their eyes during the meal and laughing afterwards, imitating the woman's accent and scowl. And a week later, when Ruth invited him over to her apartment for dinner, she surprised him with an amazingly authentic facsimile of the food they'd eaten—not from a recipe, of course, but from deducing what had been in those crepes. Sandy had come right out and said he was in awe of her.

Initially, he'd teased her when she'd said she thought that diet played a part in all disease processes. It was the first time Ruth disliked something about him. But Sandy had apologized, and within a few months had taken her idea and run with it, reading voraciously on the topic and then drawing on his experience creating the Children of Holocaust Survivors group to put together the first support groups for diabetic diet and lifestyle changes. Soon colleagues were commenting admiringly on Sandy's innovation. "It was Ruth's idea," he'd said more than once when they were at a Hyl function together. "They don't train you in nutrition in med school." Now, nearly two decades later, dietary awareness was an integral part of Hyl culture. Ruth, no longer on staff there, still did nutritional consulting work for Hyl. And Sandy was one of the most popular doctors in the Berkeley system.

Of course Sandy could be negative. He was cerebral to a fault, a perpetual analyzer of his inner life. He was one of those people with a permanent litany of woes, a catalogue of chronic complaints, from his digestion, to press coverage of Israel, to the obnoxious shriek of gardeners' leaf blowers. Sandy was right about lots of things, but that didn't make it any easier to be around him when he was spewing indignation. And it was neurotic, the way he wouldn't walk barefoot on the beach because he couldn't stand the lingering feel of sand between his toes afterward. The way he'd immerse himself in one obscure interest at a time, as if he'd previously been delusional not to have realized how intriguing it was. The overwrought, self-conscious manner in which he parented, on the one hand twisting himself into a pretzel trying to hide the fact that he'd flirted with drugs in the past, while on the other hand failing to conceal his narcissistic anxiety about Amy's academic abilities.

But then, what child of Holocaust survivors came out unscathed? Sandy was pretty damned functional, considering.

Pretty damned communicative, for a guy. And pretty passionate. Ruth loved the way he had to sit down and close his eyes while listening to his favorite passages of Brahms chamber music and Bach oratorios. She loved Sandy physically, too: the smell of his skin and his scalp, his generosity with physical contact, the way their bodies fit together. He not only wanted her to enjoy sex; he seemed to insist on it, relieving Ruth entirely of the moral burden of sexual pleasure. Sandy made it easy, telling her how her thrusting reminded him of the ocean, how her vulva was as sweet as gardenias and, toward the finish, how he wasn't going to be able to hold out much longer, how he was coming, Ruth, coming, right now, right now, now, now, my sweet Ruth... Ruth set the stewed meat on the range to cool and sat down at the kitchen table to jot down a few notes. She wondered what Oliver might say to her while he was coming. Maybe nothing. Maybe he'd just make long, low groans.

Low-Fat Organic Beef Stew, Ruth wrote at the top of the page, then tried to remember precisely what she'd done. These recipes came to her so intuitively that she often had trouble recreating her steps afterward, so she usually tried it a second time for any needed adjustments, following her own directions as scrupulously as if she were a college sophomore trying to impress a prospective boyfriend.

The cookbook writing dovetailed nicely with Ruth's Hyl consulting and her teaching duties in the Department of Nutrition at U.C. Berkeley. While she loved the interactive nature of the classroom, she also needed time to herself to create. Her first collection of recipes, *Diabetes Eaties*, which had evolved out of a modest pamphlet she'd written as a Hyl dietician, had been published before she'd even found an agent. After that she'd written *Nourish*

Your Joints and *Heart-y Meals* within three years, followed by a slim volume entitled *Eating For Fertility* (though she'd been quietly ambivalent about the project, since the diet clearly hadn't been effective in her case). Now she was finishing up a low-sodium cookbook whose working title was *Hypertension Life Extension.*

The cutesy names made Ruth wince, but ever since she'd realized that titling was strictly in the publishers' domain, she'd tried to preempt them by dreaming up the most trite titles she could think of, reasoning that they could only improve it. Ruth had roped Amy, who didn't have much interest in cooking, into the habit of naming potential books, then potential recipes. Hot Flash Succotash. Gout Sauerkraut (low-salt, of course). Psychotic Break Chocolate Cake (it's positively therapeutic!).

One lb. organic beef stew meat, Ruth wrote. She'd sauteed it, drained the fat, then paper toweled the chunks to get rid of even more fat. Then she'd added some cinnamon—about a teaspoon and a half, she guessed. And some fresh garlic, finely crushed and lightly fried in a little olive oil (a tablespoon?). A small can of low-sodium tomato paste, for consistency and extra sweetness. A couple of cubes of low-sodium beef bouillon. Water—two cups, maybe. A dash of vinegar to make it less obvious that salt was missing. Two or three ounces of sweet blackberry wine from the Manichewitz bottle she kept in the fridge.

The Manichewitz was left over from Friday nights, when Ruth used to put together a little informal *shabbat* service at home, braving Amy's monosyllabism and Sandy's mute tolerance as she lit the candles and chanted the blessings before serving a nice meal. Things like that, things she'd done when Amy was still living in the house, took effort. But it wasn't the same kind of effort Ruth had spent on Nadine. Nadine had been a drowning woman thrashing around in the water, willing to take down anyone and anything just to find something solid to grab onto. Ruth was a flotation device.

Everyone bandied about the term "sandwich generation," people Ruth's and Sandy's age who had to care for elderly parents and rear their own young children at the same time, while juggling work and other commitments. Sure, Ruth had something in common with her peers who were challenged by increasing life spans of the elderly while having waited longer to have children in the first place. Of course all that was taxing in many ways, but at its heart it was just work, just logistics. The real killer was the emotional "sandwich"—middle-aged people dealing with toxic parents while trying heroically (making a mission of it, in fact) not to poison the next generation.

In the Christopher Reeve movie, Superman flies Lois Lane through the skies, reassuring her, "It's okay, ma'am, I've got you." "You've got *me*?!" Lois shrieks. "B-but—who's got *you*?" Yes, Ruth "had" Amy. But who "had" Ruth? Except Sandy, of course?

It wasn't that Amy had been difficult. Not at all. Sometimes Ruth had felt nearly giddy with the ease of being Amy's mother; it was as if all she'd had to do was just not breathe too loudly, and Amy had kept tooling along, unharmed. Ruth marveled at how well it had gone, how effortless it had been for her not to destroy her daughter. Even the things that Ruth would have expected to set off some hideous core of Nadine-ness within herself had slid off her back. Like the fact that Amy was strikingly beautiful while Ruth was not, or that Amy preferred Shayna to Ruth for clothes shopping and, who knows, maybe confided in Shayna more about boys.

No, it was other things that made Ruth feel destitute, unmoored, missing a mother even when Nadine was alive. Things that inexplicably broke Ruth's heart. Eleven year-old Amy tearfully asking Ruth to take away the Game Boy that Shayna had given her, because she knew she was using it too much. Six year-old Amy bursting with anxiety because she'd bumped up against a boy at school after snack time, and a girl had said touching a boy made you "not a version." Four year-old Amy giving up an unopened box of beloved Junior Mints to a younger child at a street fair, someone she didn't know, who wasn't even crying.

Ruth had shared these things with Sandy each time. And he had understood, hadn't he, mostly? She loved that so much about him, that he made time to know her. There had always been things he didn't grasp. But at least he wanted to.

CHAPTER FIVE

AMY SAT ON THE PADDED folding chair with the toaster oven on one knee and her bike helmet on the other. Her kitchen supervisor at the co-op told her about this place, but Amy already knew about it because Sandy always came here. Enigma Repair. Sandy always kind of emphasized it in this way that was just really annoying. *Enigma*, he said, like he was the only guy in the world who ever thought of repairing stuff.

The kitchen supervisor told Amy that the owner of Enigma was the best repair person in the East Bay. He called himself Ocean. It took Ocean a long time to fix stuff, and he charged a lot. For money, you'd be better off if you just tossed whatever it was and bought a new one. Plus you had to call before going down there, because Ocean sometimes took these backpacking trips. One time Sandy got really pissed because all Ocean did to explain why he was closed was this sign he hung in the window that said *GONE FISHIN'*.

At the student co-op where Amy was living, they always tried to fix things. It was their way of fighting a society where people just throw stuff out when it stops working. You didn't have to be a student to live in a student co-op, if you worked for Cal. You had to share a room, work five hours a week on site, and not mind noise, messiness, or random mouse infestations. The co-op was cheap, and way better than living at home while she was making up her mind about what to do next.

At first, she was thinking of signing up at Cal Extension to take a class in philosophy. But then she decided philosophy was kind of pointless.

Amy looked around. Enigma Repair's dirty white wall board had these metal hooks jutting out of it at weird angles. There were dusty, yellowish packages no one would ever buy, like these boxy night lights that had probably only been cool during the seventies, and these kind of depressing pull chains for ceiling fans. Repair places all looked alike. It wouldn't matter if the electrical packages were shoelaces, Dr. Scholl's pads, or those squat round jars of shoe polish instead.

Amy really needed to figure out what to do about Cedric, because she was feeling really guilty. Cedric was a graduate student in ecology at U.C. Santa Cruz, and he was the first person Amy had sex with. They met when she was in a summer program a couple of years ago, between sophomore and junior year at Berkeley High. She and Cedric kept having sex after that, every time she visited, right after her period, because he said you couldn't really get pregnant that way. Her parents and Shayna and all Amy's friends thought she went down to Santa Cruz every month to hang with people from that summer program, to smoke or whatever.

Cedric taught her about going down. She'd heard about it at school but it didn't sound like something she'd ever want to do—it sounded really annoying. Cedric was really glad she liked doing it to him, and she liked it because he liked it, and he hated condoms, and she was scared of getting pregnant.

He called again this morning to find out when she was going to visit. She hadn't seen him in two months, because she was trying to get away from him.

It was way worse than just missing Cedric. Everything she did, she felt like she was doing it because of him. Sometimes it was almost like the pores in her skin were open, and he was the air around her. If she ate an apple, she wondered, would Cedric think it's crisp enough? When she wrote e-mails, she had to force herself to write them the way she wrote, not the way he wrote. When she got a migraine, the images of mini-soldiers on the left side of her vision all looked like him, even though she remembered when she was younger, they had no faces. Like in some old song, Cedric was underneath Amy's skin. Kind of like a tattoo. Something permanent that you end up wishing you hadn't gotten.

She knew it wasn't cool that he cheated on his wife, and she was getting more and more sketched out about letting it happen. Cedric even had a baby daughter now, which made Amy feel extra shady. But she couldn't help how Cedric loved persimmon trees in the fall. The way he smiled out of one side of his wide mouth.

Sometimes when Amy was getting into Cedric too much, like sitting here now, she made herself think about Dr. Eugene Corrador instead, so she wouldn't be totally bored. Corrador was her only link to Brenda, her birth mother. Amy had his number memorized, even though she'd never used it.

Sandy was still trying to get her to not call Corrador, even though he was way too much of a tool to admit that was what he was doing. He said Corrador had fucked up and that was why Brenda had died. (Of course he was too much of a retard to say *fucked up*, but that was what he meant.) For one thing, Brenda's boyfriend Mick was the reason she was dead, not Corrador. Plus, if Brenda hadn't been pregnant in the first place, she wouldn't of died from bleeding in childbirth, so in a way, it was Amy's fault too. All the nice-nice talk Amy learned in therapy wouldn't change that.

Sandy told her how when he and Corrador were in medical school, Corrador had hooked up with this kind of pathetic girl who worked in the hospital pharmacy, and he got her pregnant, and she had to get an abortion. Sandy got all intense when he talked about it, like if Corrador was this total tool, Amy wouldn't be able to handle it.

Maybe this guy named Mick, who her parents told her was her birth father, really wasn't. Maybe he was jealous of Corrador and that was why he beat Brenda up. Or, maybe Mick didn't really exist and that was why her parents said he'd gotten this reduced charge of voluntary manslaughter after being charged with second-degree murder, and he'd been in prison for a lot of years somewhere in southern California, and they weren't sure where he was now. So it would sound more real. Maybe Corrador knew Brenda before he was her doctor, from the place where she was a waitress, near his hospital, and he was a regular customer and he still liked young girls, and maybe Brenda was like Amy, liking older men. Maybe that was why her parents made this big deal out of how Mick was such a badass. To take attention away from the Corrador part.

Amy's parents were obsessed with stuff like "psychological damage" and "guilt reactions." Like those were some kind of wild animals that you could tame if you talked enough. The real problem was her parents, how pathetic they were, especially Sandy.

Like the way Sandy had handled Amy's, quote, drinking problem during her junior and senior years of high school. She still remembered that stupid conversation she'd overheard from the bathroom floor one night, in between the times she was hurling into the toilet. It was practically the only time Sandy's suspicions were right. Amy had drunk eight beers that night before a friend finally drove her home.

"How do you know it's alcohol?" Ruth said. "She could have the flu."

"Come on, Ruthie. She was reeking, didn't you notice? Anyway, that Kenny kid is widely known as a drunk. That dermatologist down on the second floor told me. He lives right across the street from them."

"The party wasn't even at Kenny's house. Anyway, how did you happen to be talking about—"

"I don't like that kid."

"Sandy, you can't legislate who she's interested in."

"The point is, if she's hanging out with those kids, she's probably drinking herself."

"Guilt by association."

Amy was starting to feel like hurling again.

"You have to face it, sweetie, it's the most likely explanation. It's not just this kid Kenny. It's that whole jock crowd. It's the drinking crowd."

"We can't control things like that. Besides, I don't think Kenny is a jock."

"You're missing my point! You want her to turn out like Denise?"

Amy leaned over the toilet for another hurl while they argued about Denise, who was Brenda's mother, which made her Amy's birth grandmother. *"That's hardly the point!"* she heard, in between hurls. *"And I don't want her to turn out like my father, either, Sandy."*

Hold up. Ruth's father drank a lot? Amy never knew that. She didn't want to make noise, so she didn't flush the toilet. She just put the lid down, rinsed her mouth out and listened for more.

"You're only going to alienate her if you keep this up. What are you going to do, give her a breathalyzer every time she comes in from a party?"

"You think it's a coincidence that she's in there right now puking? She needs treatment."

"Treatment? Are you nuts?"

"A program. A support group."

"For God's sake, Sandy, that's ridiculous. You're over-involved. There's no *pattern*. Anyway, she's already seeing a therapist. She needs to work through the psychological issues underlying—"

"You think she can just overcome her heredity? It's not that simple."

"Look, Sandy, even if you're right, if we make a big deal of this, it could backfire. Besides, it's probably a phase—as *you*, of all people, should understand."

Sandy didn't say anything for a minute. He probably realized Ruth had a good point, since he studied stuff like teen development to become a doctor. Supposedly.

"Anyway, it's normal for kids her age to experiment."

"I tell you, Ruthie, between this and her getting her driver's license—"

"Come on, Sandy, she's a very safe driver."

"—that teen trip to Israel is looking better and better."

"Israel—are you crazy? It's a war zone over there."

"At least she wouldn't be behind the wheel."

Amy couldn't believe Ruth's father was some kind of drunk and Ruth had never said anything about it before. She was like, *bite me*. But then after a few minutes, Amy didn't care that much. When her mom was being totally unfair, Amy got over it pretty fast. With Sandy, it was more like the stupid stuff he did made you realize how stupid he actually was.

Amy was in therapy. The therapist was really sincere, and Amy didn't want to tell her what she thought about the Dr. Corrador thing, because what if the therapist thought it was all in Amy's imagination? Or, if she believed her, she might think Sandy and Ruth should come in for a therapy meeting, all of them together. Yuck.

So Amy told her about things like her grandma Nadine getting run over when she was fifteen, and her zayda dying, and the Barbies her aunt Shayna gave her when she was little. Plus, Amy told her how fake Sandy was about the whole college thing, acting all, "hey, it's outrageous" because she wasn't in college, when he didn't really believe in her—he just pretended to, with all that crap about how genes don't determine stuff. And his being totally condescending, like, "you're just as smart as we are" without saying it. And then also, this thing about how Zayda pushed Sandy too much and Sandy was all obsessed with not doing that to his kid, and how Sandy used the whole not-pushing thing as an excuse, because he didn't really think Amy was smart.

Therapy was boring, and Amy didn't want to tell the therapist about Cedric. So she talked about what it felt like to be adopted, which was kind of pointless, because talking wouldn't change anything. Amy was taller than her parents. She weighed more than either of them. She had this thick, wavy hair, kind of reddish-blonde, and she was tan. She had a square jaw, big teeth, and blue eyes that were kind of too deep in her face, and the kind of nose that didn't say anything about her, the kind that was just boring. Plus, her parents were super intense, and she wasn't. And she did stuff differently.

Like last week, when she took her boss's van to pick up the new Botanical Gardens brochures from the printer's. The way she parallel-parked. She turned the steering wheel hard, so the tires were faced outward and it would be easier to get out of the parking space later. No one taught her that—she just liked to not have to back the van up when she was ready to go. Amy imagined Brenda being good at things like campfires (stuff her parents sucked at), and parking her car the same way as Amy somewhere in southern California. Or, a tall man, maybe a doctor who was really coordinated, with big shoulders, backing his stick-shift pickup truck into a tight spot, no power steering or anything. All confident, just wrestling with the wheel to turn it outward, so he could get out easily when he was done at the hardware store. And, not the kind of guy who would of made rude comments while he was teaching her to drive, the way Sandy did, all clenched up, telling Amy, "Honey, you're giving me enough isometric exercise to last me a lifetime."

Amy kept waiting until she turned eighteen. But then, ever since she did, last November, it felt like calling Corrador was something she should put off. Not like homework—more like how Sandy said you had to put off giving steroids to a person with arthritis. A last resort. Now she was almost nineteen, and she still hadn't done anything.

Maybe it was better to just have the phone number. Like that time Grandma Nadine had sent her a ruby ring to wear to her bat mitzvah and she lost the ring. Amy thought it might be in the secret compartment of her jewelry box, but she was afraid to look, in case it wasn't there. As long as she didn't check, she could keep this idea that the ring *might* be in the box.

Amy could hear Ocean poking around in the back, kind of ignoring the guy at the counter, who kept talking about how long he'd had this one electric shaver and how he was still using a typewriter.

A guy was coming in. Tall and skinny, with a scraggly beard, wheeling his bike onto the grimy grey linoleum floor. He was wearing ankle clips, the kind that gather the bottoms of long pants so they don't get caught in the bike chain. When he took off his helmet and put it in the carpeted window inset, Amy recognized him, but she wasn't sure from where. Then she remembered—it was from that retreat she went on a few years ago. The one that put the kids from local synagogues all together. It was Cantor Jeremiah Traub. He used to be just a tutor at Temple, a helper with the kids, and now he was the regular cantor there.

He opened a green canvas backpack that was all faded, and he pulled out a toaster oven. Then he saw the one sitting on Amy's lap. "Great minds," he grinned. "How about a *toast*?" She smiled a little, and he lifted up his toaster oven and said, "*L'Chaim*. To life."

"You're Cantor Traub, right?"

"I am," he said in surprise. "And you're—"

"Amy Waldman." He wasn't her tutor for her bat mitzvah. She'd gotten stuck with the old cantor right before he retired, the one with the fat fingers that were stained from cigars. "From that youth retreat a few years ago?"

"I'm terrible with placing people," he said.

Ruth and Sandy were always saying Jews come in all shapes and sizes. They said that looking "mainstream-Jewish" wasn't important, because it was on the surface. But how did they know it was on the surface for someone else? Even something like a sweatshirt, which lots of people would say wasn't important, might be a big thing to someone else. Maybe at the sweatshirt factory, one of the workers touched that sweatshirt and realized something really important at that exact moment, or they joked with another worker about how much they hated that color, and then those two people ended up getting married. Or, maybe some rotten orange is the first thing someone sees when they wake up from a coma, and they take a really great photo of it and get famous. Or the kind of toothpaste you like—that seems trivial, but maybe it's the only sweet thing you ever get because your parents are obsessed with no sugar.

Amy didn't feel comfortable at synagogue. Rabbi Weinstein was boring, and she didn't like the organ music, plus it just seemed way too formal. She would rather be in one of those churches where black people clapped and rocked back and forth and sang really loud. The reason Amy liked Jeremiah Traub, besides the fact that he was kind of cute, was that he brought his guitar to that retreat and told everyone to sing along with spirit. *Ruach*, he called it. Not the way they sang at regular services, or during those *shiva* services they'd had at the house a couple weeks ago for her zayda, which were *so* boring.

All the way from the time Amy was a baby, Ruth and Sandy did all the Jewish stuff, like Ruth lit candles every Friday night and made a nice dinner. They had a naming ceremony for Amy when they got her, and told her about it a lot of times. They thought baby girls should have as big a welcome as a baby boy had with his *bris*. None of it made her feel Jewish.

Cantor Traub grabbed the cord of his toaster oven and squashed it into his hand so it wouldn't dangle. "Well, it's heartening that other people like to have things repaired," he said. "It's all part of *tikkun olam*. Healing the world."

"It's a waste, throwing things out. Plus, the landfills."

"I'm glad whenever I meet someone who understands that." He peered at her. "So are you in school, Amy?"

"I graduated."

"From—" He was looking at her like he was trying to figure out how old she was.

"Berkeley High. I'm working up at the Botanical Gardens. At Cal."

"Ah. You're involved in maintenance, not just repair."

She shrugged. "I guess."

"So what retreat were you on?"

"The one a few years ago. Where we went to Camp Tikkun. I don't think they go there anymore."

"Ah yes, the notorious Camp Tikkun. It rained all weekend, and the cabins leaked."

"And the food kind of sucked." Probably she shouldn't use the word "suck" to a cantor.

"You know, speaking of food, I'm trying to put together—are you at all interested in food distribution?"

"Me?"

"I'm trying to get a project off the ground with Berkeley Potluck. See, usually, when a family has a celebration at Temple Beth Isaac, it's up to that family to deal with any leftover food afterward."

"Yeah?" He was all sincere. Amy wondered if he liked girls to go down on him.

"We always encourage families to think of homeless shelters for the leftovers, but half the time, with everything they have to do in planning a *simcha*, they forget. And it's too chaotic to make a phone call on the day of the event. Anyway, I had this idea that the families could sign up in advance to have Berkeley Potluck come and pick up their leftovers, if there are any."

"Cool."

"So we're trying to coordinate with Berkeley Potluck, and get some volunteers to drive leftovers from parties and restaurants to the various shelters, using the temple van. The thing is, I need to find people who are energetic and strong, but a little more mature than high-school age."

She shrugged. "I guess I could help."

"Great. Can I get your phone number and give you a call?"

She pulled a random piece of paper out of her backpack and a pen out of her jacket pocket, and wrote down her cell number. The guy with Ocean finally turned around to leave, and Amy got up and gathered up the dangling cord so she could bring the toaster oven to the counter.

"I'm sorry about not remembering you," the cantor said. "I really am bad at that. Not exactly a useful quality in my line of work."

"No problem."

"Next?" Ocean called loudly, looking right at Amy, but like he didn't even see her.

❧

AMY GOT HOME FROM work early, because rain meant she didn't need to do the afternoon watering. Her roommate, Rebecca, was still in class. Amy didn't really have anything to do between now and dinner, besides filling out the community college application that'd been sitting on her desk for the last two weeks.

Time was always the reason for not calling Dr. Corrador, right? That she didn't have time during the week? First because of school, and now because of work. Well, she could call early on any weekday morning, before work. She could leave a message with a receptionist. But she wouldn't have any privacy if he called back, or time to talk, so what was the point?

And what would she say?

Hello, my name is Amy Waldman—

How do you spell that?

W-A-L-D-M-A-N. Anyway, I'm calling about a patient of Dr. Corrador's.

Are you the patient, ma'am?

No—her name was Brenda Sprig—S-P-R-I-G. This was about nineteen years ago—

We don't keep records that far back, ma'am.

Wait, I was—she was pregnant, and Dr. Corrador was her doctor, and then she died in childbirth...

We would have to access the microfiche, ma'am, and Doctor doesn't generally order that unless there's a compelling medical reason. Are you a current patient?

It's not really a medical reason, it's more like—

Can I put you on hold, ma'am?

Didn't you hear me? She DIED, you pathetic bitch!

Amy loved those stories about identical twins who got separated and grew up in different families. How they eventually met and it turned out they liked the same beer or wore the same type of blue jeans. Or they brought each other the exact same gift when they went to meet each other for the first time.

One time a few weeks ago, on a Saturday night, Amy walked into the bathroom in the co-op. Rebecca was cutting her own hair in front of the mirror. She already had short hair, but she was cutting it more. There was a shaving mirror hung across from her on the shower door.

"What are you *doing*?"

"Giving myself a trim," Rebecca said, all matter-of-fact. It was late, and she was kind of fucked up, probably drunk and high. She moved her head so she could see in the hand mirror. There were newspaper pages on the floor around her, and there was hair all over them. Some hair had landed on the orange tile by mistake.

"Do you always do that?"

"'Course. Been doing it since I started high school."

"*Why?*"

Rebecca turned toward her and shrugged. "Well, it's always, like, midnight when your hair gets too long. You know."

Amy didn't know. She wore her hair long, with no bangs. She never felt like getting a haircut was some kind of emergency.

"Like, you're just desperate for a trim," Rebecca said. "You can't stand the idea of waiting until the next day."

The guy down the hall who kind of stank from always wearing the same black Radiohead T-shirt came in to take a leak. When Amy moved in, Sandy and Ruth were weirded out by the co-ed bathrooms. Amy didn't tell them it was the one thing she hated about the co-op.

"So that's why I just cut it myself. It saves money, too. And time. Hey, did you go to that party at Guevera House?"

"For awhile," Amy said. "I don't really know anyone. Plus, everyone was on E and I'm sick of E." Amy hadn't actually tried E. Someone offered it to her one time, and she kind of wanted to try it, but she flaked at the last second because she didn't know if she was ready for this really intense experience. Plus, she heard it made people get dehydrated, and getting dehydrated was what gave her migraines sometimes. "I have to get up early tomorrow and go to work, anyway."

"I love parties." Rebecca pulled some hair to the side and trimmed.

"I bet you haven't even tried E," the Radiohead dude said to Amy, then flushed.

"Fuck you, Jesse," Rebecca said, "we weren't talking to you."

He jiggled his pants back in place and left without washing.

Amy was blushing, so she turned away from the big mirror and picked up the shaving mirror and spun it around so she could look at herself distorted. "Shit. A zit."

"Hey, put that back." Rebecca turned around. "That is not a zit, Amy. It's a sunburn, just in one little place."

Amy laughed and put the mirror back up the way it was. She stared at Rebecca in the big mirror. It was weird, how people's faces looked different in the mirror, not exactly the way they looked *not* in the mirror. Like the real face and the mirror face were twins, but just a tiny bit different. So that meant you didn't really ever know what your own face looked like, because you always only see it in the mirror. Except in pictures, and that wasn't the same thing as just looking at yourself, because pictures weren't up close enough so you could really see the difference between yourself and your backwards self.

Amy looked at her own reflection. See—nothing weird about the backwardness. Except for she was always kind of surprised by how she looked. Amy didn't have the personality of a blondish-reddish-haired girl with blue eyes. She always thought she seemed more like the type that would have dark, curly hair and brown eyes, and a straight, regular nose, bigger than her real nose, which was kind of small for her face. But she didn't imagine herself with a Jewish nose. The way she thought she should look—it wasn't like Sandy or Ruth. Like, her personality matched someone with big bones, which she already had, and which wasn't very Jewish-looking. Also, the way Amy thought she should look wasn't prettier. Amy was already pretty, but it just wasn't the kind of pretty that fit her. She wanted to look more like how she would look if she were a character in a book.

Rebecca was saying, "How I do it is, I judge from the ends of the hair, not from the scalp. That's how you know how much hair to cut."

Amy had to pee, but she wanted to keep watching. "But I mean, what made you try it the first time?"

Rebecca shrugged. "Drunk, prob'ly. My older sister does the same thing. Hey, wanna hold the mirror closer for me?"

"Wait. Your *sister* does that?" Amy unhooked the shaving mirror from the shower door.

"Yup. I never even knew about it. I found out when she was, like, already in college." She burped, a loud cloud of invisible beer that Amy could smell from behind.

"You mean, you started cutting your hair and you didn't know your sister did the same thing?"

"Yup. Some people just do the bangs. But my sister and I, we do the whole thing. She cuts hers at night, too. Hey, hold it up more."

The haircut turned out great, all professional, like someone else did it, not like a girl all fucked up on a Saturday night did it to herself. Amy peed and helped clean up, and then she took a shower because she felt sad, like she was getting her period, and the shower was a good place to cry, even though she didn't like to waste water so she didn't stay in very long.

Now, sitting at her desk, Amy decided it was totally pathetic, being obsessed with not upsetting Ruth and Sandy. Maybe she had the wrong number for Corrador. Maybe he wouldn't call her back. Maybe he was dead.

Amy had to pick between the two things, being scared of his not being there, and being the type of retard who hadn't called him. There was this slippery feeling on the pads of her fingers.

She punched in the number and sat down on the chair in front of her desk with the phone next to her ear. Her heart beat fast, and she waited.

CHAPTER SIX

ON SUNDAY MORNING, while Ruth puttered around in the kitchen a little more noisily than seemed strictly necessary, Sandy sat on the living room couch working the *Times* acrostic and listening to an LP of Bach's *Passion According to St. Matthew*. His favorite part was coming up, and he closed his eyes as he heard Ruth come into the room.

"Sandy, we need to talk."

He kept his eyes closed.

"Sandy?"

"Shhh! I'm thinking of converting."

She went over and snapped the needle off the record, sending a loud scratch through the speakers. "Sandy, you're shutting me out."

He sighed. That was a relatively new stylus. "I'm not trying to shut you out, Ruth."

"You barely talk to me anymore." She plunked herself down next to him.

"Look, I'm just not myself."

"I know you're grieving, Sandy, and I'm here for you. But that doesn't mean you can go AWOL on me."

He cleared his throat and looked straight ahead. It wasn't that she wouldn't understand a phantom kidney stone. Or a phantom sadness, for that matter.

"Come on, tell me."

He sighed slowly.

"*Tell* me."

"Okay, look." He turned toward her. "You know how, toward the end of that last *shiva* service, I kind of lost it?"

"Yeah. You came in and took a shower."

"You probably thought I was overwhelmed by my emotions."

"Weren't you?"

"Of course. But—I was also—I had this intense physical pain."

"Pain? Where?"

"My dick," he said quietly.

"Your dick?" She paused. "What, some kind of urinary tract infection?"

"Kidney stone. At least, that's what I—"

"Jeez! No wonder you haven't wanted to have sex. Why didn't you tell me?"

He shrugged. "It just seemed—too raw, somehow."

"Did you check it out with Vinod?"

He nodded. "There was no blood in it."

"Well, that's a relief." She leaned back on the couch.

"But see, Ruth, if it wasn't a kidney stone—"

"Then what was it?" She sat upright again.

"Right. It was this incredibly intense pain. More intense than anything I could have imagined. Anyway, since there was no hematuria—no blood in the urine—I was stumped. And so was Vinod. And then you know how I woke up with a nightmare a few nights ago?"

Ruth nodded.

"Well, it happened again."

"You mean, you passed *another* kidney stone?"

"I just told you, there was no kidney stone in the first place."

"Right. Sorry."

"There's really no rational explanation." Sandy shook his head, shifted his weight. "I'm stumped."

Ruth paused. "Sandy, maybe you should go back into therapy. I mean, you've just lost your father."

"You might be right."

"You want me to get you an appointment with Ezra Kohn? I know how crazy it gets for you during the day. I can call for you."

"Nah. I'll take care of it."

She took his hand. "Sorry I interrupted your music like that, earlier."

"I know you don't like Bach on Sunday mornings. Too churchey."

"Want me to rub your feet for you?"

"I'll do yours first," he said.

"Twist my arm," Ruth said.

TWO WEEKS WENT BY without another attack. Sandy talked several times with a woman who was new to the area and wanted to know about the Children of Holocaust Survivors group. He cursed the TV commentators who declared that the inept George W. Bush had done better than Al Gore in the presidential debates. He saw Kohn twice, occupied himself with work, bought a set of the complete Bartok string quartets on CD.

But there was an underlying sadness that Sandy couldn't shake. He held it together at work, but would fall apart in the car on the way home or weep in a shower stall at the gym after working out. Sometimes he'd go about his business, then suddenly, out of nowhere, remember the pain as if it were a forgotten obligation.

A month after *shiva* had ended, Ruth found him sitting on the floor of their walk-in closet one Saturday morning, in tears. "Honey?" she ventured.

"Leave me alone!" he shouted, from among the shoes. Moments later, he scrambled up and apologized, then looked frantically at his watch, wondering where he was supposed to be.

He muttered something to Ruth about his digestion and shut himself in the bathroom, closed the toilet lid and sat down. All he had to do was say the word *grief* and Ruth would be there for him, the way she'd talked Sandy and Shayna through dozens of upsetting incidents when Belle was exhibiting early signs of Alzheimer's, the way she'd given delicate motherly support when Amy had a crush on that boy Kenny in high school. Ruth had attended to Sandy so thoughtfully in the last month. In retrospect, Sandy had probably been cavalier about Nadine's death.

He got up and washed his face, looked at himself in the bathroom mirror. Was he a good husband? He hadn't behaved particularly well after Ruth's ectopic pregnancy twenty years ago. It probably would have been kinder if he'd come out and told her that her incisions and bleeding turned him off sexually, made him feel overly responsible for her, because, medical degree notwithstanding, when it came to the bodily functions of loved ones, he was squeamish. The needier Ruth became at that time, the less he wanted her. But, that was ancient history. They'd been back to normal for ages.

Sandy wasn't the world's most honest spouse, he supposed. Eugene Corrador, for instance: not that it was a big deal, but as far as Ruth knew, Corrador had been Sandy's pot connection. Sandy had never explained to her that on the night of his bust—the only time he'd done any kind of distributing, other than that one gram to the pharmacy girl—Sandy had just left Corrador's apartment complex with an eighth-ounce of coke, having already lined up three other med students at a gram each so that he'd be able to keep a half a gram for himself for free.

Of course he'd told Ruth the cute part—that while driving, he'd recognized Prokofiev's *Alexander Nevsky* on the radio and, wanting to savor that doleful, transcendent mezzo-soprano solo toward the end, he'd cranked the volume way up, and that was why he never heard the siren behind him until he noticed the lights in his rear-view mirror. What Sandy left out was that when he pulled over and snapped the radio off, he was so out-of-his-mind with terror that he completely lost control of his bladder. The bemused older cop, who'd been following him because one of his back tires was visibly low on air, became suspicious because of that. Because of Sandy's peeing.

And Ruth didn't know the extent of Sandy's humiliation: the tearful phone call to his father, who demanded to know what drugs, and where Sandy had gotten the money to spend on them. The split-second decision Sandy made to tell him the provocative lie that he'd cashed in the savings bond (his parents' gift to him when he'd graduated from U.C. Berkeley) and the provocative truth that it was cocaine. But the worst part was the strings that a quietly enraged Abraham had pulled: he'd phoned the Hopkins dean, with whom he'd attended medical school, and got him to agree to talk to the D.A.—whose son, as luck would have it, was in the process of applying for an Orthopedics fellowship at Hopkins. The upshot was that Sandy would be allowed to stay in medical school, that there would be no jail time. He just had to do community service at a local free clinic and attend twelve-step meetings for a year.

Sandy had never been sure he'd redeemed himself in the old man's eyes—whether his dogged professional devotion all these years, and his redoubled effort never to give his parents a moment's trouble again, had made up for his father's mortifying rescue of him. Or made a dent in his father's basic opinion of him. He sometimes wished he could talk with Ruth about that.

Chillingly, all Sandy's father had asked of him (besides the obvious: be a different son, a worthy son!) was that he never let Belle find out it was cocaine. His father would tell her Sandy had borrowed someone's car without realizing there was a stash of marijuana in the trunk. He'd gotten in trouble with the police because he'd been in the wrong place at the wrong time.

Wouldn't his father have expected this—that Sandy would protect not just his mother, but his wife?

SANDY PRESSED THE ELEVATOR button, then pressed it again, as he and Zev waited to be transported up to the twelfth floor for Grand Rounds. Today's lecture, delivered by internist Brett Ingersoll, was about support services for spouses of cancer patients. It was a topic with which Dr. Ingersoll himself had unfortunately had personal experience, but Sandy suspected Ingersoll wouldn't be arguing for liberal use or expansion of such resources. More likely, he'd come up with some data questioning whether these services were really cost-effective.

Sandy didn't like Dr. Ingersoll, who seemed more interested in cozying up to Dr. Critchfield than in improving patient care—more interested in lobbying for a better vacation package for his colleagues than in, say, finding ways to decrease typical waiting room times for patients. Ingersoll had been so charming in the talk interviews, and so affable during the working interview—even Sandy had been taken with the fact that he and Ingersoll shared a passion for Hungarian composers—that most of Sandy's group had been all too happy to have him when he'd joined a little over a year ago in July, convincing themselves that Ingersoll, though not a perfect match with the prevailing culture of the department, would breathe new life into it. Besides, Ingersoll's wife had been battling ovarian cancer for some time, and no one wanted to deny him the job. Sandy hadn't been able to admit to his colleagues that he'd had nagging doubts about their choice almost from the start, that he wished he'd listened to his instincts: there was something too slick about Brett Ingersoll.

At first it had seemed like coincidence, but lately it had become clear to Sandy that Dr. Ingersoll was filling his panel with as many easy follow-up visits as possible, taking on practically no time-consuming new cases while generating the illusion that he was "churning" patients. Of course, he'd pay later for that tactic by not having spent the time to establish relationships with patients over a long period; already, despite his charm, he wasn't one of the more popular doctors on staff. But he definitely knew how to make his numbers look good.

It was a sad statement about medicine these days, but it *was* all about numbers. At Hyl, doctors were constantly being measured and monitored, and their popularity with patients was only one criterion. Their patients' health (the desirable state, since health is more profitable to an HMO than illness) was measured by various objective criteria; the doctors' conservatism in use of lab resources, diagnostic imaging and pharmaceuticals factored into their ratings too. Sandy was convinced that the reason Dr. Ingersoll often referred his internal medicine patients out to his specialist colleagues was that he knew Critch was monitoring the total expenditures of each doctor. By seeing to it that it was other doctors who ordered the necessary workups, Ingersoll was artificially trimming his own spending while making his colleagues look a little worse—in short, gaming the system. Sandy would have to bring this hidden inequity to the Chief's attention.

Sandy's stomach growled. He was glad food would be provided upstairs at Grand Rounds. For the past few days, feeling vaguely undeserving of Ruth's bag lunches, Sandy had made up some nonsense about a new vendor in the lobby who was offering half-price gourmet items all week. Too busy to hit the cafeteria, he'd been grabbing yogurt, a Payday bar and an orange juice from the vending machines and eating the sugary repast at his desk, fighting nausea afterward. He missed Ruth's thoughtfully balanced packed food. Egg salad with some curry and Dijon mustard in it, on thick slices of New York rye from the bakery next to Till's. A container of vanilla-flavored soy milk, a Washington Delicious, a little bag of home-roasted almonds that Ruth seasoned with rosemary and garlic granules and sea salt.

"You okay, Sandy?" Zev asked as they stood by the elevators.

Sandy shrugged.

"Give yourself time. It's the most intense part of the grieving process. You're barely out of *sheloshim*."

Sandy pressed the elevator button again. "What the hell is taking so long?"

Zev was right that Sandy was struggling to assimilate his father's death. Sandy had loved the old man, of course; but to say that he was suffering from the loss wouldn't have been the most precise description. Rather, it was as if Sandy's center of gravity had shifted and he had yet to relearn balance. *I'm next* was the thing that kept coming to mind, even though in reality, it was Belle who was next. But if his mother's existence were any kind of cushion between him and eternity, it was one of those broken vinyl air cushions that look as if they're inflated but reduce down to nothing the second you squeeze them. There was really no longer anything separating Sandy from his own demise. That was reason enough for feeling disoriented, wasn't it?

"Sandy, is it something more than—is everything okay at home?"

Sandy dropped his voice to a near-whisper. "Well, I haven't—umm. Ruth and I haven't had sex in a while," he blurted.

"Oh."

"But Ruth has been great about it. Really."

"Sandy, do you think you should be seeing someone?"

"I've gone back to Kohn," Sandy said. Elevators were ridiculously distractible. Why couldn't the damned things be programmed to "remember" pushed buttons while stopping on other floors? "Totally A.D.D.," he muttered.

"A.D.D.? Are you having trouble concentrating, Sandy? Because that could be grief, too."

"Of course not. I was just—"

"Ezra Kohn can't prescribe," Zev said in a low voice. "Maybe you should go talk to someone in Psych."

Vinod rounded the corner and came toward the elevator with Anne Padway, an Ob-Gyn who had been a good friend of Sandy and Ruth's for years, and who was married to a younger cousin of Critch's wife. Neither Anne nor Vinod was headed to the Grand Rounds that Sandy and Zev were attending, which was just for sub-specialists in internal medicine. The two were probably going upstairs to one of the small meeting rooms to work on the paper they were co-writing on the repair of urethral injuries following hysterectomy. Anne was bogged down with a stack of journals and a huge notebook.

Sandy nodded to them as the elevator finally arrived and the four of them stepped in, Anne pulling her materials toward her and flicking back her long, thick, dark hair. Sandy remembered the shock of seeing her in the parking lot one day with an attractive bob, but that didn't last. After enjoying exceptionally high patient satisfaction ratings for years, Anne had experienced a precipitous drop in those ratings as soon as she cut her hair. Apparently Critch had scoffed when Anne confided to him at a family gathering that she thought there was a connection between her hairstyle and her numbers. But when she grew her hair long again, sure enough, her patient satisfaction ratings went right back up.

"We could have chosen circumcision as our topic," Anne complained to Vinod. "At least we'd have a ton of data at our disposal."

"This is an unfortunate fact about circumcision, yes," said Vinod.

"Unfortunate? That there's a wealth of data about circumcision?"

Vinod looked annoyed. "Surely you are not in support of the idea that we should circumcise each boy who is born, without regard for his particular situation?"

"Come on, Vinod," Anne said. "Circumcision is a harmless procedure that prevents UTIs and all kinds of other problems—" she turned toward Sandy and Zev in exasperation. "*You* tell him what they've found in Africa. Risk of HIV cut in half in circumcised men."

Zev spoke up. "Well, certainly with infant circumcision there's less of a chance of spreading STDs later in life. Fewer UTIs, and better hygiene. And it's a low-risk procedure."

"And now that we're using the nerve block, it's painless," Anne added. "Two injections at the base of the penis. That's how I'm doing all my hospital circs now."

Sandy was on the verge of remembering something, as if a record player were repeating one phrase over and over and he was expected to make meaning of it. He felt uncomfortably confined in the small metal box traveling upward.

"But you do not mention the illogic of performing routine surgery on all male infants for preventive reasons," said Vinod. "Surgery should not be done as a preventive measure."

"Look, I don't want to fight with you, Vinod. All I was saying is that you and I would be having a much easier time right now if we weren't scrambling for data."

"Routine circumcision is wholly unnecessary," Vinod went on. "It does not make sense to excise a perfectly healthy piece of skin, just because it is possible that something might go wrong in the future. There is no other country that is civilized that performs, as a matter of routine—"

"Sandy? Are you all right?" Anne slammed her journals and notebook into Zev and bent over to Sandy, who was now slumping toward the floor of the elevator. She was in front of him, loosening his tie and undoing the first button of his shirt. Her hair fell forward, and her feminine breath had an almondy, slightly bitter undertone. Sandy was hyperventilating. He was sweating. He could feel his own pulse in his neck.

And the pain in his penis was back.

"You look like you're going to pass out," Zev said, squatting next to him, hugging Anne's journals. "Put your head down. Between your legs."

Sandy was afraid he'd vomit if he put his head forward. He had an urge to get into a fetal position on the elevator floor, protect his groin. He felt Anne's hand on the back of his head, trying to force his head downward. The hand felt hot.

Vinod and Zev were now both squatting as they continued up, and Sandy grabbed Anne's hand, trying to tell her to stop the elevator. Out of the corner of his eye, he saw Vinod glancing up at the lighted panel that showed "8" and apparently deciding it would be quicker to go all the way up than to try to stop anywhere sooner. There was no air. Suddenly the elevator gave a jolt, and the doors to the twelfth floor started to open. That was the last thing Sandy remembered.

RUTH POUNDED THE SLICE of boneless, skinless chicken breast, trying to get it as thin and even as possible, the way Sandy liked it. She knew his behavior these last few weeks had nothing to do with her. Some aspect of his grief, some ambivalence about his father, and of course those weird pain events, had scared him off sex for now.

When Nadine had offered wisdom to her newlywed daughter, it had been easy for Ruth just to roll her eyes. Every woman has to work hard to overcome her natural bodily odors; don't wait too long for the first facelift; men never look at women over forty. Sandy was Ruth's ally, the neutralizer of the venom, but it was hard these days to remember that feeling of emotional protection by him. She found herself slipping back into her compulsion to change her underwear three or four times a day.

Ruth gasped. Could Sandy have found out somehow about Oliver? But how? Oliver hadn't participated in their *shiva*. Besides, why now? Ruth hadn't seen Oliver in nearly a year, since that last work cocktail party, right around the time she was starting to put *Hypertension Life Extension* together, when she'd told him once and for all that his advances were inappropriate and unprofessional. "Arguably unethical," she remembered saying, which was as ridiculous under the circumstances—his nose nearly touching hers, her mouth quivering—as it was accurate. She was flattered, she'd told him, backing away and almost tripping on a chair, but she couldn't go through with this. On top of everything else, he was, after all, her husband's boss.

Flattered—really, dizzy would have been a better description. Neither was exactly an approved feminist reaction. But wouldn't any woman be disoriented by having a man like that tell her how moved he was by her brightness, her goodness, and how much he wanted her—even if he was under the influence of God knew how many highballs? Besides, not everyone would have had the brains to protect herself, enjoy the attention but never let her guard down enough to succumb.

Someone was turning a key in the front door. Amy? Occasionally she rode her bike down the hill from work and dropped by during lunchtime, though now that Ruth thought of it, Amy hadn't come over since Sandy had talked to her about not wasting a vote on Ralph Nader. Ruth poked her head out of the kitchen as the door was opening.

It was an ashen Sandy, alongside Zev, who had one hand on Sandy's shoulder.

"Sandy?" Ruth gave Zev a quizzical look, wiped her hands on her apron as she came out into the living room.

"He passed out." Zev guided Sandy toward the couch.

"I'm fine now," Sandy put in irritably.

"Passed out? How?"

"Just some anxiety, maybe a mild panic attack." Zev put Sandy's keys down on the coffee table. "He'll be fine. Needs to be hydrated."

"Of course. Thanks so much, Zev, I'll take it from here. You go back to work."

Zev let himself out as Ruth went over to Sandy and unlaced his wingtips. "Breathe," she coaxed, putting the shoes under the coffee table. "In through your nose, out through your mouth."

He sniffed a breath in.

"Slowly," she commanded. "Good. Let it out on four long counts. One-thousand one, one-thousand two..."

The color began to return to Sandy's face.

A little while later, Ruth and Sandy sat at the kitchen table, sipping iced green tea. "So you want to tell me what happened?" Ruth asked.

Sandy paused. "I got the pain again," he said quietly.

"That same pain? In your penis?"

He nodded.

"That's so weird."

Sandy hesitated. "You know, this time when it happened, I noticed—"

"What?"

"Well, it was kind of like—" He looked into her face. "A cutting, I guess."

"A cutting?"

"Like my dick was being cut."

Ruth's jaw dropped. "Oh my God, Sandy."

"What?"

"You think you were molested? Like, as a child?"

He leaned back in his chair and grimaced.

"Seriously, Sandy. It could be some kind of primitive memory."

"Wouldn't I know it by now if I'd been molested? I'd recognize the signs in myself."

"You could have psychological defenses about it. Just like anyone else."

"I don't have the profile of a molestation survivor. There are certain—"

"It's not as if you haven't had issues, Sandy. I think Ezra Kohn would want to explore this with you. Do you want to call him?"

Sandy shook his head.

"At least have yourself worked up physically," Ruth added. "It could be anything."

Sandy played with the lemon wedge floating in his drink. "Hey, for all I know," he said, not looking up, "I could be reliving my own circumcision."

"Yeah, right."

Sandy laughed too loudly. "Why don't I go in and say to Kohn, 'Hey, dude, I think I remember my own *bris*.'"

Ruth gave up. "Yeah, and then tell him you need to talk with him about one or two of your past lives—"

"—which are wreaking havoc on my karma."

Ruth rolled her eyes, smiled in spite of herself. "You are some piece of work, Sandy Waldman." She brought his stockinged feet onto the edge of her chair and massaged them, basking in the familiar moans of his appreciation.

CHAPTER SEVEN

"MAVIS? COULD YOU GRAB the Sprig file?" Dr. Corrador's voice boomed. Amy had to move the phone away from her ear a little, he was so loud. Why did people always shout when they were on speaker phone?

It was kind of weird, how this person she was finally talking to wound up being just some retard who obviously didn't know the "hold" button from his ass. Who yelled at his assistant instead of figuring out how to work his phone. Amy was starting to wish she'd gotten his voice mail and hung up, the way she did a few weeks ago.

"Sprig?" Amy could hear Mavis's voice getting nearer. "Isn't that the girl who died like, twenty years ago?"

"Right."

"It's too old, Doctor," Mavis said. "Those files are all in storage. I'd have to phone—"

"No no, it should be pretty current. Look under 'S.'"

"Oh, right. You had it out a couple years ago when the birth father contacted you from prison, isn't that the one?"

"Right." Dr. Corrador picked up the receiver. "Are you still there, young lady?"

"Um, yeah." *The birth father. Prison.* It was really annoying to hear strangers talking like all of that was just a way of identifying who Mick was, as opposed to some other guy. Of course Amy knew Mick had been arrested after she was born, and did time someplace in L.A. Mick was a coke user and dealer, and he'd beaten Brenda up and that was a big part of the reason she wound up dead, besides her being pregnant in the first place. But Mick had probably gotten out of prison for that awhile ago, because even though he got like eleven years, you could get out early for good behavior even if you did something that bad, which was kind of pathetic.

Without realizing it, Amy had always imagined that if she called Corrador, she might end up connecting with Brenda's mother, Denise. She'd never even thought of Mick trying to contact anyone. She'd never thought much about him at all. He was a bad guy, and that was it.

"Well, I'm glad you got in touch. Brenda's—boyfriend called me, must be, what, a couple years ago now, said he was clean, hope he still is. Sent me a letter for you, in case you ever contacted me."

"Oh." A letter? Amy kind of wanted to hurl. She could hear her heartbeat, in her ears, and it felt like her pulse was trying to jump out from the insides of her wrists. There was a letter, and Corrador just hung onto it, waiting for her to call?

She heard Corrador cover the receiver with his hand. "Mavis? I don't have all day?" He came back to her. "Here we go. Yep, it's right here. Where should I send it?"

Amy hesitated for a sec, because he was just really annoying. Then she gave him her address at the co-op.

"Well, it was nice talking to you," he said when he was done writing. "You say hello to your parents for me, okay?"

"Sure, I guess."

"You know," he gave this lame little pause, almost with a laugh in it, like he wanted to show he wasn't in a hurry. "Brenda was a fine young lady. Had her nose in a book or magazine every time I saw her. She was a bright girl."

Amy's fingers felt slippery, like someone was rubbing against them too lightly. Brenda was none of Corrador's business.

After she hung up, Amy wanted some time to deal with the conversation, pick at it, kind of like what you would do with a favorite scab. Why didn't Corrador call her Amy, instead of "young lady"? And why did he call Mick "Brenda's boyfriend," instead of "your birth father"?

Even if it made some kind of sense that Corrador held onto the letter before Amy turned eighteen, why didn't he try to get hold of her as soon as she did turn eighteen? Maybe he was too much of a retard to do the math and figure out when that was. But he was a doctor, so he was probably pretty good at math. No, he should of called Sandy and Ruth as soon as he'd gotten the letter. But then, maybe he thought about it and decided not to because Sandy was such a tool. Sandy and Ruth always tried to make it seem like it was Corrador's fault that they had no relationship with him, but that didn't mean it was true.

When were Sandy and Ruth going to really talk to her, when she was thirty? She should go over to the house and just scream at them. Or wait, this was even better: she should act all calm, and then, when she got the letter, tell them in this really casual way that she'd heard from Mick. Plus she'd be in their face about Nader. They didn't have to know that at the last minute, she'd voted for Gore.

⁂

AS FAR AS AMY KNEW, Shayna had never found out what Amy had done to the Barbies. Every time Shayna would give her one, like for a birthday or Chanukah, she said thank you really nicely. Later that day, maybe, she took off the clothes. Then, maybe the next day, she pulled off the head, and then the arms and then the legs. She stuffed the legs, arms, torso, and head with hair coming out from it into this white plastic purse she had from preschool. Then she took the purse outside into the back yard and threw the pieces, one at a time, up onto a part of their roof that was kind of inverted.

When she first started doing it, the bits of plastic along the ridge looked random. The work of a crazy person, or maybe a hurricane. But then after awhile, the pieces kind of built up, and the roof became like art in progress. Or like some kind of statement.

Amy loved Shayna. Shayna gave her a kind of attention that Ruth never did, the kind where the main reason for it was to have fun. Shayna never mentioned the missing Barbies, even though she must of noticed, because she liked to hang out with Amy in her bedroom. Plus, Sandy and Ruth had a barbecue out in the back yard one time and Shayna must of seen the "decoration" on the roof. She was cool, not saying anything.

Shayna called Amy's cell on Saturday from Bubba and Zayda's house to say she'd wrecked her favorite black skirt and she needed a new one, plus she wanted to see about some cute sweaters, and there was a sale at Nordstrom.

"I thought you said shopping is fun only if you're not looking for anything specific."

"Sometimes in life, you make an exception," Shayna said. "Besides, I'm dying to get out of here."

Amy was totally bored anyway. "Okay. I'll go."

Amy and Shayna started going to Nordstrom together when Amy was eight or nine, around the same time Shayna had stopped giving her the Barbies. It had started with back-to-school shopping, which Ruth hated. Plus, Shayna respected stuff like when Amy was ten and only wanted to wear that sweatshirt-grey color, anything out of grey stretchy sweatshirt material, like sweats and T-shirts and socks, because to Amy, it was the most comforting color ever. Putting it on was like biting into hot buttered cinnamon toast. Shayna totally got stuff like that.

Shayna acted like shopping was kind of creative, instead of materialistic. She wasn't embarrassed to totally love it—it was almost like she thought it was a really important subject. She said stuff like, "the current Macy's is what Emporium used to be," like she was one of those super-enthusiastic history teachers explaining how Strasbourg was kind of French and kind of German. "Nowadays, if you want Macy's, you have to go to Nordstrom." Shayna worked as a residential real estate broker, so she was always looking for clothes that *conveyed an aura of success*.

Shayna had no kids of her own. Marrying Chris made her the stepmother of these two teenage boys who never talked, practically. Shayna hardly ever saw them now that they didn't live at home anymore. Amy got the feeling Shayna kind of relied on spending time with her. Plus, Chris drank a lot, so she was probably lonely.

As soon as they got to the first round sales rack at Nordstrom, Shayna got all excited. "That is so *cute*!" she said in a loud voice. She held up this tiny, short top with sequins that had one brown three-quarters-length sleeve and one blue one.

"Pretty," Amy said. She looked at the price tag. $165 on sale—what was Shayna smoking? Sandy and Ruth said Shayna acted like she had a lot of money, but she didn't, really. All the stuff Amy bought when she was with Shayna, Ruth paid Shayna back for. Amy wasn't sure if Shayna knew that she knew that.

"Try it on," Shayna said.

"Yeah, right, maybe I could fit my hand into it."

"Don't be silly. It stretches."

"*You* try it." Amy went through the stuff hanging between the white plastic "L" doughnut and the "M" one. She and Shayna were kind of the same size, but they usually went through the carrels because Shayna said there was a lot of variation in sizes, plus Amy liked things loose and Shayna didn't. Amy pushed stuff aside. The hangers squeaked, metal against metal. The noise was annoying, and she realized the left side of her head was starting to pulse. Out in the distance, she already saw a few white soldier-shaped spots. She should of eaten more today, eggs or something. Which was worth a whole lot more than those pathetic biofeedback exercises from the workshop Sandy made her go to, taught by some narologist.

"It's too young for me," Shayna said. "Anyway, I need some practical stuff. Things I can throw in the washer."

Amy saw a red sweater that looked like Shayna. The tag said sixty bucks. "What about this?" She checked the label. "It's all cotton."

"Lemme see." Shayna looked at the label underneath the main one, and frowned. "Dry clean only."

"I thought cotton was washable."

Shayna shrugged.

"I don't get it." Amy hadn't ever thought of it before, but something bugged her about the label. "I mean, people have been wearing cotton for hundreds of years, right?"

"Thousands, I think."

"Whatever. For a lot longer than there's been dry cleaning."

"Dry cleaning started maybe in the forties."

"So what did people do before there were a bunch of toxic chemicals that supposedly clean things?"

Shayna shrugged. "Maybe you're right, maybe it is washable. I'll try it on."

"I bet there's, like, a kickback," Amy said. "I just bet the dry cleaners pay the companies that make clothes to put in labels saying 'dry clean only' even when they don't need it. The companies already use sweatshops, so hey, no big deal, just add one more shady thing."

"You know, you're starting to sound like Sandy."

There were more of the ghosts, the Cedric-soldiers. She *so* didn't need this. Visual distortions, the narologist had called them. Amy was glad when she finally got the diagnosis two years ago, plus pissed off. Sandy had been accusing her of drinking for years. He was sure it was hangovers, Amy's hurling, her not being able to stand light or noise, and the totally fucking unbelievable pain on the left side of her head. What a jerk. He was a doctor, so he should of known better, and plus, fathers are supposed to believe you.

Amy had even heard of migraines when she was in middle school, but she never thought of them for herself. It was like, *My headaches really suck. Lucky I don't get migraines, 'cause I've heard those are REALLY bad.*

"What about this lacy top for you?" Shayna was saying. The red sweater was hanging over her arm. "All it'd need is some cute buttons. Or, I know, we could put a fringe on the bottom."

Amy had left the Imitrex tablets in her desk drawer. Probably she should always make sure she had them with her, but the thing was, Imitrex didn't really cure a migraine. It just made you not feel it quite as much. Like when you take cold medicine and you feel better even though you still have a cold. With Imitrex, you still had the migraine, underneath.

"Hey Shayna, I need a cup of coffee."

"What? We just got here."

"Advil, too."

Shayna asked the sales lady to hold the things she wanted to try on. As they started walking, Shayna's purse bumped up against Amy. That thing was so big, she probably had a hair dryer in there.

At the café, Shayna bought two pieces of quiche that cost way too much and a salad with ranch dressing for her and Amy to share. They sat down and Shayna messed with the pill box she kept in one of the like zillion zipper-things in her purse, and handed two little brown tablets to Amy. Amy suddenly thought her aunt looked gross, this lady with fake-looking coppery hair and gold bracelets, who was obsessed with carbs. Trying too hard. That was one thing where Shayna was just like Sandy.

Amy put the Advils next to her plate, waiting until she had some food in her so they wouldn't hurt her stomach. "I can tell there's nothing here today."

"What do you mean—at Nordstrom?" Shayna scooped quiche out of the crust with the side of her fork. "How do you know?"

Amy shrugged. It was like that book *Bee Season*, where the burglar lady knows right away if whatever random thing she's looking for is there or not. Only she doesn't even know what it is, at least she doesn't think she knows.

"Whatever," Shayna said. "I'm just glad to have a break from sorting through all that shit at Bubba and Zayda's. Hey, if you ever wanna help me out over there, I'd love the company."

Amy ate the extra crust and a bite of the quiche. She thought it was kind of weird how much time it was taking her parents and Shayna to move stuff out of the house, almost like the more people were working on it, the longer it went on. "How come Sandy doesn't help you and Ruth more?"

"Who knows. Too busy. Anyway, no real hurry. It's the wrong time of year for us to sell the place—spring is best." Then Shayna talked for awhile about how the house was paid off years ago, so there was a huge amount of equity tied up in this big, "rambling" property that no one was using, how that money could be used to help keep Bubba in the Home for Jewish Parents.

Amy rubbed her left temple, picked at the salad. The ranch dressing reminded her of something. Sunscreen, that was it, when you accidentally get some of it in your mouth.

"Lemme get you a brownie," Shayna said, all passionate. "Did you see them? They look *fabulous*."

"I thought you didn't eat sugar."

"I don't."

"You said you don't even miss it."

"That's true," Shayna said thoughtfully, "but it's funny—I still have an opinion. I guess it's like if you're a gay man, and you're completely into Cher. Or Judy Garland."

Shayna was a retard, but Amy kind of knew what she meant, because Amy sometimes had these really strong ideas about stuff like what Sandy shouldn't wear, even though she was planning on ignoring the way he looked anyway.

"I talked to Dr. Corrador."

Shayna blinked. "Dr. Corrador? In L.A.? When?"

"Two weeks ago."

"Wow. Why didn't you tell me before?"

Amy popped the Advils in her mouth and took a swig of water. Her saliva tasted sweet, the kind of sweet that you feel right before hurling, but then the Advils went down okay. "He sent me a letter from Mick in prison."

"Mick is still in prison?"

Amy shrugged. "I don't know if he's still there. He sent this letter two and a half years ago."

"What?"

"Corrador didn't forward me the letter. He was waiting for me to call him, I guess."

"Why didn't he just send it to Sandy and Ruth?"

"What*ever*."

Shayna looked worried, like she thought Amy might not be able to handle something so adult. "So what'd the letter say?"

"Iono," Amy shrugged.

"Wait, you didn't get it yet?"

"I got it. I just didn't open it."

"Why? Aren't you curious?"

"I guess." She knew Shayna meant that *Shayna* was curious.

"Did you tell Sandy and Ruth?"

"No, and I don't want you to, either, Shayna."

"Why not?"

"Why should I? They obviously don't want to have anything to do with Corrador. Even if that means I don't get an important letter until two and a half years after it was sent." The Cedric-soldiers had become an army, and the pain wasn't the main thing any more. The main thing was wanting to hurl.

If Corrador were her real father, wouldn't he of talked to her differently when she called? Wouldn't he make more time, want to get to know Amy more, like it was really a cool thing that she called? Instead of blabbing at the top of his lungs about Mick? Or, wouldn't he at least take Amy's number? No way he was the kind of guy who knew how to check his phone to get the numbers of people who'd called, after they'd hung up.

"Aren't you being a little hard on them?" Shayna was saying.

"Shayna, I was like, seventeen before they told me Mick beat Brenda up and that was what made her start having labor. And how that was the thing that made her bleed too much and then die. And the whole thing about Mick bargaining for a plea and getting voluntary manslaughter for a reduced sentence. Like I was some baby before then. I mean, what else did they decide to not tell me?"

Shayna looked miserable. Her mouth was this mess of smudged orange lipstick with wet pink lip tissue showing through underneath. "They just didn't want to—they thought—"

"What?" Amy glared.

"They didn't want you thinking about how you yourself had been beaten up. As a fetus," Shayna said in a whisper.

Amy had to get up, because she didn't want Shayna to see anywhere in her face that she'd never thought about Mick beating her up as a fetus, which was a *sickenating* thought. *Sickenating*—that's what Amy would of said about it when she was younger.

The lights were too bright and she was dizzy. She ran to the women's room and had just enough time to lock herself in a stall before hurling.

CHAPTER EIGHT

SANDY AMBLED WEST ON University Avenue toward the biodiesel station, the one place in the East Bay where he could get 100% recycled vegetable oil, reclaimed from fast food places, to put into the tank of his burgundy 1983 Mercedes Turbo Diesel. Shayna had owned an Audi for years, but for most of his life, Sandy had felt it would be a betrayal of his parents to drive a German car. It was only because of the beauty of the biodiesel solution that he'd gotten over his lifelong aversion a couple of years ago and bought the Mercedes used from one of the docs down in Radiology. Besides, he liked the idea of driving around an older car. He'd read that forty percent of the impact of the average vehicle on the planet, over the course of its lifetime, took place in its manufacture.

Sandy loved his car's sturdiness, its elegance, its workhorse reliability even at 190,000 miles, but he wasn't in the mood today to deal with it. He'd been feeling nauseated lately by the chronic French fry smell. Plus, the biodiesel place, a one-pump establishment with odd hours, had more in common with a rural gas station from the 1930's than with anything resembling an efficient modern filling station. Instead of green glass bottles of Coca-Cola, there were organic juice drinks and vegan granola bars. People parked their old Mercedes and VW Rabbits along the sidewalk and sat waiting their turn at the outdoor picnic table or the beat-up old couch inside, discussing the relative merits of corn, soy and algae as fuel sources or, more recently, speculating about what was going to happen with the Florida recount. Only a few weeks earlier, Sandy had been a willing participant in such conversations. But lately he'd become focused on the circumcision controversy, and he'd been so busy reading, picking Vinod's brain, and expressing to his colleagues his growing disdain for the practice, that nothing else seemed as compelling.

There was a pledge drive on the local NPR affiliate, and Sandy reluctantly pressed the car radio button to KALM, a station that, in bending over backwards not to offend, managed to offend deeply. Sandy grimaced as he heard that they were playing Mozart's *Eine Kleine Nachtmusik*—again. These programmers constantly pandered to the lowest common denominator, airing the most uninteresting Haydn and Mozart snippets or, in the case of Bach, only the Brandenburgs, it seemed, over and over, until Sandy swore he hated them. He had no idea why he even kept KALM programmed on his dial, never mind that it was the only classical music radio station still available in the Bay Area.

Last night Sandy had had that nightmare again about being in hiding, needing surgery and not having anesthesia available—on one level, he knew, a Holocaust dream, or something related to the loss of his father. Yet, several months having passed since the incident in the elevator, Sandy had been unable to shake a creeping awareness of the absence of his foreskin. It was as if he'd been deaf from birth and was just becoming conscious of what it was he'd been living without. That had to be adding a layer to his dream life.

Sandy remembered when he'd suddenly found himself wondering if Ernesto, a classmate in high school, was gay. It was a question, wasn't it?—is Ernesto gay, or is he straight?—yet it wasn't really a question. In reality, Sandy was reviewing his entire knowledge of Ernesto, reliving each exchange they'd ever had, each thing he'd ever observed about him, to make the new, intuitive premise fit: because he'd never thought about Ernesto's sexuality before in the first place. Though Sandy would have characterized the idea as a possibility, what had really happened is that it had been transformed almost instantaneously into visceral knowledge, pieces fitting together into a puzzle.

He glanced at his watch. Damn it. The pump was closing in twenty minutes and wouldn't be open tomorrow. He'd been stuck behind a bus for the last two blocks in the right lane, knowing that the other lane, with the lack of left-arrow lights at intersections on this street, was worse. *Eine Kleine Nachtmusik* was almost over, and Sandy wondered what condescending slogan they'd be using at the upcoming break. "KALM—we take you away from it all!" *Yes, like a lobotomy.* "KALM—your fortress of tranquility!" *If it's so goddamned tranquil, why do you always have that guy shrieking about a mattress sale?* "KALM—you feel so different here!" *Why yes, I feel homicidal...* Sandy could always fill up with petro-diesel at a regular pump, but that would defeat the whole purpose, wouldn't it? It would transform the Mercedes back into an immoral car.

The bus nosed in vaguely toward its stop at a diagonal, instead of pulling over into its designated zone and allowing vehicles behind it to pass. Ordinarily Sandy would have just cursed, but this time, he landed on the horn and stayed there. As passengers got on and off, the driver glared at him in his side mirror, but Sandy gleefully kept his hand down, registering his outrage at the volume and duration it deserved, letting up only when the bus finally started moving again. It was an exhilarating act of defiance. Why, then, was Sandy weepy a minute after it was over?

If he'd been close to Ruth, the way he usually was, she would have said he was sublimating his sexual urges and, of course, grieving for his father. But then, if he and Ruth were close enough for him to tell her about the bus incident, he would have been confiding in her about his nocturnal experiences. The nightmare he'd been having; the painful erection and burning sensation with which he often awoke; that one wet dream that had been singularly devoid of pleasure. And probably worst of all, the feeling of *nakedness*.

Sandy pulled a Kleenex out of the glove compartment and dabbed at his eyes underneath his glasses, watching the road as he crept forward. *Trust your body*, everyone said. But Sandy's body seemed to be telling him he'd had a memory of his own *bris*. It was outlandish, if not insane. It was, at the very least, fringey, as Kohn's quiet tolerance had confirmed. Anyway, what did it mean to trust the body? That his crazy intuition carried more weight than, say, a sexual urge, or the appetite for red meat? Why did people say to trust the body when the body wanted things like Doritos? And cocaine?

Ruth left a library book on Sandy's bedside table about recovered memories of abuse. She plied him with rich foods—baked enchiladas, potato-leek soup to which she added heavy cream. She sat on his lap, whispered in his ear. But Sandy remained far too agitated about his penis to use it.

Without noticing, Sandy had driven three blocks. The bus had lumbered across the intersection on a yellow, and a new Toyota Camry was in front of him at the red light. Suddenly realizing he was about to plow into the Camry, Sandy slammed on the brakes, managing to slow the car down to the point where the impact was reduced to a tiny tap. Sandy jumped out of his car to check the damage.

Goddamn it! The Camry bumper was the painted kind, and was definitely now maimed. Why the hell were new cars made this way? Were rubber bumpers really so expensive that manufacturers had to cut corners like this? Or could it be that the parts departments had gotten together to give some kind of incentive to the car manufacturers to produce bumpers that would be ruined at the slightest impact?

As the driver climbed out of her Camry, glaring at Sandy, the cars behind them unleashed a bitter chorus of honks. It was a green light, but they all had to wait.

∞

BESIDES SANDY'S FULL patient load, drop-ins, the residents he was teaching, and his on-call duties, he had lectures to give, and quality reports to do for Critch. More and more, though, Sandy found himself heading up to the twelfth floor Hyl library in his spare moments to pore through the archives, or closing his office door and surfing the net.

Outlandish as they were, the online first-person accounts of men who claimed to have had recovered memories of circumcision fascinated Sandy. One of these men was suddenly struck with an intense penile pain while in a state of deep relaxation during a massage. Another had been suffering for years, starting in adolescence, from a recurring nightmare in which his penis was cut. Yet another had awakened from a hernia surgery a few years ago weeping about his foreskin having been torn away. None of these men had been more than cursorily aware of circumcision or the controversy surrounding it until the memories flooded them.

As if that weren't weird enough, one of the men had become involved in some kind of foreskin "restoration" society in Oregon, through which he met regularly with others to discuss techniques and to lend each other emotional support as they tried, over periods varying from months to years, to stretch their foreskins and thereby cover the heads of their penises. Sandy smirked as he pictured these obsessive men holding meetings in some conference room ordinarily used for a heart condition workshop or a smoking cessation clinic.

But not all of the information Sandy found could be dismissed so easily. Some studies showed that infants are affected by their early experiences and may be able to recall them later. Sandy read about a young child who was in a neonatal intensive care unit from age four months to eight months, and remembered the room intimately when he returned to visit a few years later. Another young child, who had been in the hospital only during his birth, never since, asked why there was such bright light in that big room he remembered, and why the lower halves of everyone's faces were green. Sandy was left to wonder whether all those alien-abduction fantasies, what with the green heads and the sterile rooms and the mysterious surgical agendas, were in fact echoes of baby boomers' pre-memory experiences on modern labor and delivery wards.

There was ample evidence that circumcision conferred health benefits, but with Vinod's opinion shoring him up, and despite the skepticism of others in his group, Sandy began to question the faulty premise on which the studies were based. Why was routine surgery being performed for preventive reasons in the first place? It went against all medical precedent. You didn't remove healthy tissue in *every* patient just because something might eventually go wrong in a *few* of them.

Sandy should probably have been concentrating on his existing projects, but he couldn't seem to shake his new interest. Besides, why was Dr. Ingersoll the only one who deserved a break? For two weeks in a row now, Ingersoll had entirely avoided seeing drop-ins by scheduling four-hour blocks for teaching rounds in the hospital—something that should have taken him a little over an hour. Sandy could snatch a few moments to indulge his fascination.

He kept reading. Even in women who were at high risk for breast cancer, most gynecologists and surgeons discouraged prophylactic mastectomies. And that was a decision made with fully informed, adult patients facing a life-threatening disease—something that was considered on a case-by-case basis. Where was the analogy in the various annoying penile conditions like chronic urinary tract infections among the few? Certainly the threat of penile cancer, only 1 in 100,000 in the U.S., wasn't enough to justify routine surgery on healthy infants who had no say in the matter.

He talked more with the other docs, especially Vinod. Why were health insurance providers—Hyl included—still covering a procedure that was almost always unnecessary and arguably harmful? Why weren't the risks and drawbacks of circumcision discussed with much seriousness in the literature? Why was the penis shown in some medical textbooks as circumcised, without any explanation?

Then there was the pain issue. Well into the 1970s, open-chest surgeries were still being performed on infants without anesthesia—a practice that had been brought to light only by the lawsuits of outraged parents. Why, then, were most circumcisions still being done without local anesthesia? The American Academy of Pediatrics had stated in 1987 that infants' pain response to surgery was similar to that of adults. A 1990 issue of *Pediatric News* had explained that neonates feel pain at least as acutely as adults; another study concluded that infants could remember pain both short-term and long-term. And there was research showing that recently circumcised babies had demonstrably different crying patterns from others, and were noted to shriek sympathetically when they heard other babies in distress.

Oddly, obstetricians, not pediatricians or urologists, were generally the ones who performed the procedure on newborns. So it was Anne with whom Sandy found himself discussing the pain aspect of the controversy.

"Fewer stress hormones are released in anesthetized babies than in unanesthetized ones," she explained as they walked back to the office from their Quality and Utilization Management meeting one morning. "That's why I use a local when I do a circ."

The term "circ" made Sandy wince. *Cirque du Soleil.* "So what do you use, exactly?"

"The dorsal penile nerve block. Two injections at the base of the penis. Some OBs use EMLA cream—that's a mixture of locals used as a topical. And I read something recently about the subcutaneous ring block. But, a lot of OBs don't see the point of using a local when the whole thing is over in a minute."

"Wait a minute, they've read the studies on infant pain."

"One presumes so, yes."

"And they don't change their practices based on the new data?" Anger rose in Sandy's throat. "They should call themselves *obstinate*-tricians."

"Sandy, you sound mad."

"Well, maybe I am. We used to think the neural pathways aren't fully formed in infants—fine. But we know better now. There's no excuse." He pushed the "walk" button for emphasis.

"I wonder how many OBs use a local," Anne said thoughtfully. "Have you thought of doing an informal poll within the Hyl system? It shouldn't be hard to send out a mass e-mail."

"Not a bad idea." He made a mental note to compose something. "But why is circumcision still being done in the first place? That's what I've been asking myself."

"Yes, and others, I've noticed." Anne's black pumps clicked along the pavement as they crossed the street.

"Well, yeah, I've been asking around. It seems to me the whole premise is based on a fallacy."

"It's a preventive health measure, Sandy," she said patiently. "Like childhood immunizations."

"Immunization doesn't involve the surgical removal of any body parts. Besides, immunizations are for protecting the public against the spread of infectious disease."

"Yeah? So?"

"I mean, deadly diseases that anyone could contract by unwittingly coming into contact with an infected person. When you urge individuals to be vaccinated against smallpox, TB, measles, typhoid—that benefits society at large. But circumcision—where's the analogy?"

"Sexually transmitted diseases, Sandy. AIDS."

"Those are the result of certain behaviors. They're preventable. Anyway, the research is incredibly flawed, Anne. Science at its most dishonest. They've retrofitted the data to fit the pro-circumcision model—I mean, *designed* the studies to show a causal association between circumcision and cancer, UTIs, STDs—"

"You think there's a conspiracy of pro-circumcision doctors? Believe me, Sandy, no one is that well organized in this line of work."

Sandy sighed, holding the door open for her as they entered the main building. This was one of the most unattractive elements of the medical fraternity—the kneejerk protective instinct toward other doctors. Maybe circumcision advocacy wasn't so well coordinated as to be a conspiracy, but that didn't mean there weren't incentives to keep things as they were. Doctors made money on circumcisions. And since 1975, hospitals had been quietly selling foreskins to labs for research purposes, as well as using them for burn grafts.

"Look, Sandy," Anne went on, "you're sounding a little hysterical. You don't want to be like that nutcase Pickett."

Sandy reddened. He had, in fact, read Dr. Noel Pickett's work—that's where he'd gotten the comparison between male breast cancer deaths and penile cancer deaths. A urologist, Pickett was probably the most outspoken circumcision critic in the medical profession. "Pickett has the guts to say what no one else dares to say. And he has the facts to back it up."

"Too bad his credibility is nil."

"Look, just because his ex-wife was convicted of drug dealing doesn't mean—"

"Sandy, he has psychiatric problems himself."

"That's a rumor, Anne," Sandy corrected as they stepped off the elevator. Funny—the instinct to protect other doctors didn't seem to apply to the ones who spoke out against circumcision. "Anyway, what does that have to do with the content of Pickett's arguments? He was an anti-circumcision activist for years before any of the other stuff came to light."

Anne gave a tolerant sigh. "Sandy, all I can say is, if you associate yourself with people like Pickett, you won't be listened to. Besides, don't you realize he's widely known as an anti-Semite? You remember that junior urologist, from the convention in Atlanta? The one who gave the paper on UTIs in elderly men two years ago? He told me Pickett humiliated him in a staff meeting one time for wanting to take off for one of the Jewish holidays."

"So? Critch has ribbed me about the Jewish holidays."

"That's different. He does it for egalitarian reasons."

"And that makes it different?"

"Besides, it's in private. Pickett publicly gives Jews a hard time. Is that the kind of person you want to affiliate yourself with?"

"That is not the point, Anne."

"Bottom line, circumcision has benefits. And it's a safe procedure."

Sandy followed her into her office, where she draped her cardigan over the back of her chair, stuffed her purse into the bottom desk drawer, and put on her white lab coat. She gave a quick look into the mirror to make sure her long hair was neat, then glanced at Sandy as if wondering what he was still doing there. "Look," she conceded, "you have some good points. But this is not an earth-shaking priority."

"How can you say that?" Sandy exploded. "Circumcision is the single *most common surgery* performed on males in this country!"

"Let's talk later. When you're less upset." Anne opened the door and went out into the hallway, leaving Sandy alone in her office to realize it was exactly this kind of condescending treatment that women were forever complaining about.

CHAPTER NINE

AND IT'S A SAFE PROCEDURE. But how safe? Online, Sandy found nothing about how doctors measured, recorded or reported complications. The risk was claimed to be low when circumcisions were performed by experienced practitioners, but that assumption wasn't based on hard data, and besides, lots of circumcisions were done by medical students. There were no studies comparing the complication rates for so-called experienced doctors with those for inexperienced ones. Plus, what about all the circumcisions performed by *mohels*?

Sandy also wondered why the scant risk information that was available didn't seem to factor in death as a possibility. It took some digging for him to discover that if a baby died following a circumcision, the death was generally attributed to other causes, like sepsis, hemorrhage or kidney failure. And as with other surgeries, it was up to the doctor who botched the operation to report the problem, something clearly not in his or her best interest. Nor was it in the interest of the hospitals, which always wanted to present themselves as having low mortality rates.

Late one afternoon, his last patient a no-show, Sandy went up to the 12th floor library to poke around. Dr. Critchfield was sitting at one of the tables facing the door. Half a dozen open journals were spread out in front of him; probably he'd carved out a block of time for his current research on hypertension, between his afternoon patient load and the four or five dinnertime cases he still insisted on scheduling twice a week.

"How are you, Critch?" Sandy knew better than to extend his hand; the Chief decried handshaking as a primitive and unsanitary practice.

"Waldman," Critch sneered. He squinted and jotted something down on a yellow notebook pad, then clicked his pen off and put it back in the front pocket of his lab coat without looking up.

Sandy had had too many experiences like this with the abrasive Chief to take it personally, or even to worry that Critch would begrudge Sandy a little break if he knew what Sandy was up to. He and Critch had enjoyed a long, mutually admiring history, going back to the days when Critch had hired Sandy to replace Berkeley Hyl's retiring endocrinologist, a well-loved, paternal type who'd been anything but experimental. At the time, Sandy's insistence on better monitoring of his diabetic patients had been controversial. Critch alone had supported Sandy when, for example, he'd pushed to make the A1-C blood test standard operating procedure.

Ignoring Critch's gruffness, Sandy decided to lay it out to him about Dr. Ingersoll's AWOLism, which was affecting the ten internists and various other sub-specialists in the practice. Sandy would start with Ingersoll's reluctance to help in the clinic—how he had every excuse in the book, and it wasn't just a matter of attending to his wife, either. He was off doing Grand Rounds at another hospital; he was writing up a clinical series in which a handful of patients had tried some expensive, hyped-up new medicine that wasn't significantly different from what was already available. The rheumatologist, gastroenterologist, nephrologist and two of the internists had all begun to grumble. According to Gina, the pulmonologist had literally rolled her eyes last Monday when she'd seen the schedule, wondering aloud why Dr. Ingersoll had signed up for a class in new blood pressure monitoring techniques when he wasn't the one who took his patients' blood pressure in the first place. Did Ingersoll really think his colleagues would be fooled by his recent group e-mail comparing the doctors' salary increases with those in similar departments at other HMOs?

"I'm glad you're here," Sandy began, pulling up a chair. "I've been wanting to—"

"So," Critch boomed. "Whaddya think of the idea of a Chief of Quality?"

"You mean—?" Sandy was confused. He sat down across from the Chief.

"As another Assistant Chief position," Critch clarified. "D'ya think it would make things more efficient around here?"

This was odd. Sandy was already essentially serving the function of a Chief of Quality, doing all the quality reports for Critch and generally helping monitor the department's ratings. Was Critch trying to acknowledge, in his brusque way, that Sandy needed support?

"The Department is growing," Critch said, "but things are going to hell. Five-thirty, you could fire a cannonball down the hall and never hit a physician."

"Well," Sandy quipped, "I'm sure the docs *would* be here at five-thirty, but they're trying to avoid those cannonballs." His smile faded. "Critch?"

Critch narrowed his eyes. "So. If a carpenter carries a tool kit, and a publicist carries a press kit, then what does a *mohel* carry?"

Sandy stared at him. This was the result of Sandy's conversations with colleagues about circumcision these past few weeks—a *mohel* joke? Critch had never been one to tell jokes, certainly not Jewish ones. Aside from the fact that he was a WASP with a tin ear who couldn't have imitated Jewish inflection if he tried, Critch wasn't the type to illustrate anything with a story.

"Go ahead, guess."

Sandy gaped.

"A *bris*-kit!" Critch guffawed unpleasantly. "Get it? *Bris*? *Brisket*, like that meat in Jewish cooking? *Bris*-kit? You knew it was made of *foreskins*, right?"

Without being aware of it, Sandy had gotten up out of his chair, his legs shaking, his cheeks on fire. Never mind Critch's mockery of Sandy's recent interest; something much uglier was going on here. Sandy was a Jew being taunted with a variation on the blood libel from 12th century England—the assertion that Jews kill non-Jews in a religious ritual in order to drink their blood.

Critch had never pulled anything like this before. Had he? Frantically, Sandy did a backward mental search through their relationship. Certainly Ruth didn't like him, and she tended to be a good judge of character, maybe better than Sandy. But had Critch been a closeted bigot all along?

"*Doctor* Critchfield," Sandy managed in a low voice, "why would you tell that joke?"

Critch was blustery. "Never mind," he said loudly, waving his hand. "Siddown."

He stayed standing. "You've offended me, Critch."

The Chief put his head back and snorted. "It's just a joke!"

"I take offense as a Jew." Sandy glared at his boss.

The levity drained from the Chief's face. "So let me get this straight. You turn your back on your own faith, and then accuse *me* of being offensive?"

"Critch," Sandy seethed, "not that it's remotely your business, but I'm not turning my back on my faith. I'm simply—" Sandy paused. What was he, simply, doing? Trying to be a responsible doctor, a thoughtful human being. In his own way, a good Jew. Without realizing it, Sandy had always operated under the assumption that anti-Semitism was a thing of the past, at least among sophisticated people. Would he have acted differently over these past few months if he'd realized that he couldn't take for granted others' good will toward him as a Jew?

Critch squinted at the notes he'd written on the yellow pad. "I should think it would be considered conduct unbecoming," he said without looking up. "Going against your—*people*."

Okay, that was undeniable. *Your—people.* It was condescending, nasty. "Now where do you get off telling *me* how to be a good Jew?"

"Well, I can certainly tell you how to be a good doctor." He stared into Sandy's face. "And Waldman, you're becoming a laughingstock. You were a bit of a troublemaker from the start—"

He means I'm Jewish.

"—which I can accept, fine. But you're over the top. You're jeopardizing the credibility of this whole department with your reckless claims. I won't have it."

"You won't have it?" Sandy exploded. "We're spending thousands upon thousands of dollars every year on an unnecessary, possibly harmful, surgery, based on what? The concern that someone might get a UTI in the future? Or penile cancer? More men die of breast cancer than penile cancer."

Critch had adopted a patronizing smirk. "I suppose you're not aware of the evidence that circumcision has been shown to be an effective way of preventing AIDS in Africa?"

"Oh, I see, education is too much trouble, so you're advocating surgery?" Sandy was unable to contain himself. "You want to encourage circumcised men to think of themselves as immune? *Hey, I'm circumcised, I don't need a condom? I can use dirty needles*?" He sat down and looked his opponent in the eye. How could Critch turn on him like this? Sandy Waldman, with the wonderful patient and colleague relationships built up over years, with the brilliant vision, the impeccable work ethic, the leadership? The one whose colleagues routinely sent their spouses and parents and children to him? The one whom Critch himself had appointed Assistant Chief of Medicine eight years ago?

"Patients have made comments, Waldman."

"Patients? What patients?"

"Patients overhearing you talking about this issue, which I don't need to remind you is not in your area of expertise."

"Slow down. Please. What patients?" He had the strong feeling that the Chief was bluffing. Certainly if there had been any kind of formal complaint, Critch would have mentioned it specifically. He would have called Sandy into his office instead of waiting for a chance encounter. At most, maybe Sandy had failed to notice a raised eyebrow; but who could have overheard him? He was generally pretty careful to keep conversations with his colleagues away from patient areas. Could Critch be making it up?

Anne, that was it! She'd been irritated with Sandy about the whole issue. And being Critch's cousin-in-law, she had access to

Critch in a way most people didn't. She could easily have told him how annoying Sandy had been lately. She could even have said it affectionately, not imagining that he was on thinner ice with Critch than either one of them realized.

"Brett Ingersoll told me a patient of his said something to him."

Ingersoll? Surely Critch had to see through that lizard. "Oh. So it's *one* patient," Sandy managed. "Not plural."

"And frankly, it's affecting the morale of the group."

"The *morale*—who told you that?"

But of course he already knew—Ingersoll. Ingersoll! Talk about never being hit by a cannonball. How could Critch be so blind? Stung to the core, Sandy mumbled something about having to get back to his office and walked out with what grace he could muster.

In the hall, he pressed the "down" button three or four times. Ingersoll, that worm. Practically new to the department, and some kind of self-appointed expert on their working conditions and raises. Now that Sandy thought about it, Ingersoll had been in Critch's office a lot lately, offering to go to meetings for Critch and to help him on various projects—generally trying to make himself look like God's gift. Thinking he could compensate in schmoozing for what he lacked in areas that really mattered, like patient care. Teamwork.

Sandy couldn't believe how offensive the Chief had been, but he knew he wouldn't be filing a complaint. Critch, if confronted, would insist he'd been joking. And he'd claim it was his right, indeed, his duty, to tell Sandy he was behaving recklessly with both patients and staff. Besides, Sandy would never be able to demonstrate a consistent anti-Jewish pattern on Critch's part; it was under Critch, after all, that Sandy had been promoted to

Assistant Chief. And as far as Sandy knew, Critch had never once harassed Zev about his Jewish observance. Then he realized why: the Chief saw no ambivalence in Zev. There was nothing negotiable about Zev's Jewishness.

Jewishness—was that what this altercation had been about? Sandy's head was spinning. On the one hand, Critch had mocked him for "turning his back" on his faith; on the other hand, he'd denigrated the faith in question. Which was it? It reminded Sandy of the Holocaust deniers who have no problem saying Jews bring upon themselves whatever ill comes to them. So, were these crazies trying to deny that Jews were mass-murdered? Or acknowledging that they were mass-murdered, and claiming they deserved it?

The truth was, Sandy had never been all that much of a defender of the faith. More than once, he'd let anti-Jewish nuance slide in the name of liberalism when he should have stood up for himself. Like that time during lunch at Grand Rounds when Critch had grumbled some remark about the Israelis' treatment of the Palestinians. While Sandy didn't disagree with the criticism per se, he resented the smug, Berkeley-style armchair liberalism, the reinvention of Palestinian terrorists (and, by extension, Arafat) as the obvious underdog in the situation. Why hadn't Sandy pointed out that Israeli policies had resulted directly from the Palestinians' avowed purpose of destroying the state of Israel, and from their embedding of terrorists within their own civilian population? Why hadn't he said that while it isn't inherently anti-Semitic to criticize Israel, it is clearly anti-Semitic to single Israel out for criticism without proportionately scrutinizing other parties in the Middle East? But Sandy had let it go. And now, he couldn't help feeling that the Chief's intentional offense was in some way the result of that lost opportunity and others like it.

Back in his office, Sandy closed the door and stared absently at his computer screen. Where *did* Sandy stand, finally, as a Jew? It wasn't enough to know where to buy the best lox, or to grasp all the nuances of a Woody Allen movie, or even to have redeemed the lie he'd told his father about the savings bond by founding the Children of Holocaust Survivors group with that money.

Sandy understood, when he and Ruth had adopted Amy, that if he really wanted to inculcate Jewish values in his daughter, he was going to have to engage in his own Jewishness in some meaningful way. Ruth did her part, making challah every week, leading an abbreviated *shabbat* service before their family dinner each Friday night that Sandy found very grounding. Ruth had told Sandy that when she was little, Nadine had made sure the family joined the wealthiest (i.e., most programming-heavy) congregation in Skokie, then signed Ruth and Ellen up for all the activities she could so they'd be out of her hair. After Ruth's father died, synagogue had become her lifeline, and she still embraced the comfort and familiarity of Jewish affiliation and observance. But what had Sandy brought to the table, really, besides second-generation Jewish trauma?

Sandy had hoped that when he and Ruth joined Temple Beth Isaac (largely so that Amy could attend the preschool there), his enthusiasm would follow. He didn't advertise the fact that he thought synagogue was tedious, saw Rabbi Weinstein mainly as a fund raiser, found the fat old cantor uninspiring. To Sandy, services were boring, an endless stream of Hebrew and English prayer and blessings that made his eyes glaze over, followed by events in the social hall consisting of cloying sweet wine and dismal, institutional honey cake to end yearly fasts in which he didn't even participate.

Sandy stared at the screen, avoiding his e-mail, which he planned to deal with before the four-day Thanksgiving break next week. He appreciated the convenience of the Internet, and especially the speed of access on the Hyl computers, but sometimes it was annoying to have one more means of communication, one more pile of correspondence to answer. Thank God Gina had the foresight to decide early on, before Sandy and the others were even Internet-literate, that the doctors in the practice would never give their e-mail addresses directly to patients.

Listlessly, wanting a distraction but not in the frame of mind to draft the e-mail he wanted to send out to OBs about the use of local anesthesia, Sandy moved the cursor over to the browser bar. "PubMed.gov," he typed, to access the web site of the National Library of Medicine.

The first time he'd entered "circumcision" into the search box, he'd neglected to precede it with the word "neonatal." He'd been greeted with the first of 136 pages of listings of published articles. *Neuroma of the clitoris after female genital cutting... Attitudes of Pacific Island parents to circumcision of boys... Appearance and culture: oral pathology associated with certain "fashions" (tattoos, piercings, etc.)... A prospective comparison of tissue glue versus sutures for circumcision... Carbon dioxide laser circumcisions for children...The need to address female genital cutting...* Out of curiosity, he'd clicked on the latter article, and information had flooded onto the screen. He winced.

Female genital mutilation has been perpetrated on at least 130 million African women. Though African women's opposition to the practice has caused a decline over the past thirty years or so, various forms of mutilation are still being done, without anesthesia, in parts of Egypt, Sudan, Somalia and Kenya, most commonly to girls between the ages of four and eight—at the rate of about two million girls per year. The radicalness and timing of the rite vary somewhat from culture to culture, from mere removal of the clitoral foreskin to the extremely radical practice of infibulation. Infibulation consists of clitoridectomy (removal of all or part of the clitoris), excision (removal of all or part of the labia minora), and cutting of the labia majora to create raw surfaces which are then stitched or held together to form a cover over the vagina when they heal. Complications include infection, AIDS transmission (if non-sterilized instruments are used), hemorrhage, abscesses, small benign tumors of the nerve, damage to surrounding organs, chronic extreme pain, and death...

No one would dispute that female genital mutilation was much more disturbing than male infant circumcision. And yet—Sandy had to question the kernel of self-righteousness within his own revulsion, his feeling of moral superiority to have come from a tradition that was clearly more humane. That female genital mutilation was more horrifying than male circumcision was hardly a justification for the latter.

If only it weren't Noel Pickett who was leading the charge against male infant circumcision. Sandy didn't think Pickett was entirely straightforward in how he presented the anti-circumcision case; his exaggerations, while small, tended to cast doubt on his objectivity. And as Anne had said, Pickett wasn't exactly a friend of the Jews. He had publicly questioned Israel's right to exist. On the circumcision front, Pickett blatantly attributed its routine practice to a conspiracy of Jewish doctors in this country when, in fact, it had more to do with cereal magnate John Harvey Kellogg, who had published a very popular and influential book in 1888 entitled *Plain Facts for Old and Young* in which he recommended circumcision as a cure for masturbation. And it was Kellogg who had first advocated its practice without anesthesia—not because infants don't feel pain, but because of the pain's supposedly curative effect on the child's mind. As much as Sandy was struggling with Jewish tradition, he resented Pickett's blaming Jewish doctors for widespread medical circumcision—as if it automatically followed that Jews would push a medical procedure on the public because it had religious significance within Judaism.

But the fact remained that Pickett was asking questions that needed to be asked. In one of his articles, he claimed there was value to the foreskin itself—that it wasn't just "extra" tissue covering the glans of the penis, but sexually sensitive tissue in and of itself. If that were true, why weren't more people concerned about it? And why hadn't Sandy seen any information about the foreskin's positive function in any medical textbook?

Sandy moved his cursor across the screen. There had to be information about the foreskin's inherent value. But how to frame a search specifically to address the foreskin's significance? If he typed in the word "foreskin," it would result in an excess of matches. He frowned, trying to come up with a way to narrow the search.

"Neonatal circumcision drawbacks," he typed finally into the browser space.

No items found, PubMed responded, in a cheery horizontal pink bar.

SANDY POKED HIS HEAD into Zev's office half an hour later, still rattled about Critch, but not at all sure he wanted to talk about what had happened.

Zev's last patient had just left. "Another of Dr. Ingersoll's," Zev remarked.

"He can't keep getting away with it," Sandy said, referring to the fact that once again, Dr. Ingersoll had palmed off on a specialist a patient in need of some basic tests. "That's why—I confronted Critch," Sandy blurted.

"About Ingersoll? What happened?" Zev grabbed his jacket and they started toward the parking lot.

"Well, I—" Sandy couldn't bring himself to correct Zev. "Let's just say it didn't go well." Sandy hoped his face didn't look too red. "Zev, do you honestly think a sip of Manischewitz is sufficient anesthesia for an amputation?"

Zev sighed as one would at a bright child who still remembers, after a long nap, a casual mention of cookies earlier in the day. "Sandy, when you use the word *amputation*—"

"Because I certainly don't."

"—it's inflammatory."

"Great. Maybe I should go on steroids. For the inflammation."

"A good *mohel* works so fast, it's all over in an instant."

Sandy threw up his hands in exasperation. "So is a tooth extraction! No one suggests going without anesthesia for *that*."

"Well, that's a good point. Sandy, you seem upset. What happened with Critch?"

Sandy shook his head miserably.

"I mean, why bother with the issue of anesthesia at all?" Zev said after a minute. "Why not abandon the entire ritual?"

"Good question."

"You don't want to see that happen, Sandy."

"Why not?"

"History. Tradition."

"If it's unethical, we should be strong enough as Jews to admit it."

"It's not that simple, Sandy," Zev said, straightening his *kipa*. "Jews through history have made great sacrifices to be able to fulfill the covenant of circumcision. It's the central promise between God and the Jewish people."

"I'm not a religious Jew, Zev. I'm Jewish—culturally. Politically."

"Well, the rest of the world doesn't make such distinctions—that's how Hitler was able to annihilate assimilated Jews, not just observant ones. Anyway, there's really no such thing as a 'cultural' Jew, Sandy. You're either Jewish, or not, according to *halacha*—that's Jewish law. And the main *halachic* criterion for being Jewish is whether your mother was Jewish or not."

A UPS truck was parked smack in the middle of the street. "Would you look at that?" Sandy exclaimed just as a car was honking at the truck.

"What?"

"There's a perfectly good yellow right next to that truck, but the driver insists on blocking traffic. Look at that—at least ten cars that can't get through. Can't they cite these guys?"

"The parking enforcement staff probably isn't big enough." Zev scratched at his beard.

Why did people offer these lame explanations when what was appropriate in moments like this was for them to agree—*you're absolutely right, that is colossally stupid*? "I just realized what it is! The truck drivers want to feel important, that's what."

Zev gave him the you-need-to-go-get-Zoloft-from-someone-down-in-Psych look.

"I think it's fascinating, that's all. Sociologically."

"That doesn't mean you should have an MI over it."

"I'm *not* having an MI, and even if I were, hey, I hear rumors you're a decent cardiologist." He turned to Zev. "Wait a minute. You just said your mother being Jewish automatically makes you Jewish."

"Right."

"Then you're saying circumcision is not a requirement." Sandy was grinning.

Zev put his hand on his friend's shoulder as the UPS driver started his engine. "Sandy, there have been times through history when Jews didn't practice circumcision. When we wandered for forty years in the desert, for instance. And there are individual exceptions, like Theodor Herzl refusing to have his son circumcised. But *brit milah* is at the heart of our modern practice, and has been for generations. You have to tread lightly here, Sandy." He paused. "So what did Critch say about Ingersoll?"

"Oh! I almost forgot. I spoke with Gina about the disposable instrument trays. They're costing us somewhere between thirty-five and sixty bucks a pack. Of course it'd be expensive to purchase sets of re-usable instruments, plus there's the sterilization. But I'm sure it'd be cheaper in the long run." Talking about the trays made Sandy feel connected to Amy, in the same way that a young boy gets a secret thrill at the mention of a girl he has a crush on.

"Probably better for the environment, too."

"Zev, look, I'm not trying to be offensive. But I thought it was Jewish to question the status quo. I thought it was Jewish to have an opinion. What's that joke about asking ten Jews a question and getting eleven answers?"

"Of course there's a long rabbinic tradition of intellectual inquiry. The interpretation of texts, and so on. That's not the same as destroying tradition."

"But what if the tradition is wrong?"

Zev shook his head as they reached his car. "You're only going to alienate people."

CHAPTER TEN

"THERE'S SOMETHING ABOUT the whole penile cancer argument that's *off*," Sandy said to Ruth that evening, to avoid talking about his day.

"How so?" she asked patiently, tearing off a piece of minted dental floss and setting to work in front of the bathroom mirror.

He put down the photocopied article he was reading, capped the orange highlighter pen, and sat up straighter in the bed so he could see her. "The first mention of it, as far as I can tell, is an article by some doctor named Wolbarst in 1932 tying circumcision to prevention of penile cancer. But the thing is, Wolbarst never did a study."

"Nnnh," Ruth murmured, her mouth open.

"In fact, there doesn't seem to be any original research on this point."

Ruth turned to him, the green thread dangling in midair between her thumb and middle finger. "I don't get it. Then how can they claim circumcision prevents penile cancer?"

"Beats the hell out of me."

He watched her ball up the used floss and throw it in the wastebasket, then rinse her hands. Even with dental floss in the mix, Ruth was an attractive woman, compact and vivacious, with salt-and-pepper hair and an alabaster body that was unusually young and taut for her forty-seven years. She was hardly the picture of seduction in her faded blue flannel nightgown, but Sandy felt himself getting an erection. Then it subsided.

In just a short time, they'd created a pattern of guarded affection: a chaste kiss good-bye in the morning, another one when Sandy came home in the evening, none at bedtime. They didn't brush up against each other; even in their sleep they were vigilant. Ruth had stopped so much as hinting that she wanted sex. Instead, she'd been quietly encouraging him to "delve into his past."

Ruth got into bed carefully next to him. "Maybe it's like that spinach thing."

"What spinach thing?"

"Some guy in the 1870s tested the level of iron in spinach and wrote it down wrong, and ever since then, we think of spinach as the be-all, end-all cure for anemia. All because of a misplaced decimal point."

"Wait, you mean there's no merit whatsoever to the Popeye business?"

Ruth shook her head. "Spinach has about the same amount of iron as other veggies. Which is not much."

"You have got to be kidding me."

"Nope." Ruth sighed. "So I spent the day copyediting. You know, I'd forgotten how unappealing this phase is. A lot like childbirth, I guess. I mean, don't women talk about how they forget the pain afterwards?"

"I've heard that."

"Because if they remembered, they'd never want to do it again. I know I must have gone through this with the other books, but it's just grueling. Line by line corrections, enough to make my eyes glaze over. I'd much rather be teaching or consulting or trying out new stuff in the kitchen. Hey, I'd rather be over at the house going through your parents' desk drawers."

"Well, you'll be done with it soon, and then we'll be talking about a pub party." They'd had a reception at the house celebrating the publication of each of Ruth's books. "Speaking of the house, how's it going over there?"

"Shayna's dragging her feet, as usual. Every item, there's a justification for keeping. Maybe you could come help speed things up."

"I'll put in some time next weekend. Four days off."

Ruth picked up her *New Yorker*.

Sandy uncapped his highlighter pen and returned to his article, wondering how much resentment Ruth was feeling about his not spending more time in the trenches, making decisions at the house. He hadn't intended to let Ruth handle all of it for him. He re-capped his pen. "You know about that pot incident at one of the co-ops?"

"No, what happened?"

"I heard it on the radio. Some kids baked pot brownies and got really sick from them. They had to be taken to the ER. I just hope Amy wasn't—" His pen was suspended in mid-air.

"Come on, Sandy. You don't honestly think Amy would—"

"Set foot in a kitchen?"

"We would have known if she'd gotten that sick."

"You're right."

"You're too worried about Amy and pot," Ruth observed. "It's a projection." She took up her magazine again, then put it down. "I do get the feeling she's avoiding us."

"We haven't been seeing her all that much, other than during the *shiva*."

"I don't know. There's something—" Ruth paused.

"What?"

"Well, I called Shayna a few days ago to talk about Thanksgiving, and she acted kind of cagey. Then she wanted to know whether Amy had phoned or come by."

"What did she say, exactly?" Sandy asked.

"Just that Amy got a migraine when they went shopping together a couple weeks ago. It was more the *way* she said it that seemed odd."

"Hmm."

"So I called Amy and left a voice mail on her cell asking what she'd like for her birthday. That was yesterday. She never called me back."

"That's uncharacteristic."

"Then I tried her work number today. You know how her cell doesn't work well at the Gardens. Anyway, I'm sure she was there, because her boss happened to answer, and went to get her, and then came back and kind of self-consciously said Amy was up in a tree with a chainsaw, and couldn't come to the phone."

"Well, she could have been in some far corner of—"

"But I told you, her boss said it in this self-conscious way."

The phone, which was kept on Sandy's side of the bed, was ringing. Ruth stared at him; it would be unlike Amy to call so late unless it was urgent. It was nearly eleven. Sandy picked up. "Hello?"

"Wha—?" The voice at the other end was male, but he didn't identify himself.

"Hello?" Sandy repeated.

"*Waldman*?"

It was Critch, sounding surprised and vaguely underwater, as if he'd been drinking. Having to get drunk to call and apologize—pathetic. "Critch?"

"Isss not you I wanted!" he boomed, and hung up.

"What an asshole," Sandy exclaimed, hanging up the phone. He didn't want to explain Critch's inebriated mis-dial, or mis-apology, or re-provocation. Whatever it was, Ruth seemed very annoyed by the intrusive phone call, her face flushed. Sandy went back to his article, then turned to her again with a new, awful thought. "You don't think Shayna told Amy about my—dealings with Corrador?"

"Sandy, this isn't about you."

"I can still wonder, can't I?"

"Besides, does Shayna even know Corrador was your pot contact?"

Sandy relaxed. Of course Ruth was right; he'd never given Shayna the specifics. "That shithead," Sandy muttered. "He should've gotten Brenda to a shelter. It's not like he was unaware of what was going on."

Sandy went back to his reading, Ruth to hers. Then she left the bed. He heard the back porch door slide open, then shut, then open and shut again after awhile. She came in again and slid back into bed.

"Make love to me," she whispered, her body rigid.

He reached over and took her hand. This was unlike her. "Ruthie."

"Don't 'Ruthie' me," she said, but she didn't remove her hand.

"You know I can't." He was getting an erection.

She got up on her elbow and propped her head up. Her scent was dark, unfamiliar, like a forest. "No, I *don't* know it. What I know is that you seem completely unwilling to figure out what's really going on with you. And it's made you incredibly self-absorbed and—neglectful."

"Ruthie, I'm so sorry. Really, I am. My digestion has been—"

She reached over and touched his penis, looking him straight in the eye.

"No, please," he begged as his erection grew. "Please don't do that."

"I'll be gentle," she said, almost harshly. She kept her body apart from him; only her hand was on him, a step removed, as if, having pushed aside any avowed concern about an unremembered trauma, she were giving him a demonstration of a hand job.

He moaned, even more conscious than before of the denuded state of the head of his penis, yet unable to remove himself. "I'm afraid," he panted.

She kept going, first lightly but insistently, then harder and harder, until he cried out in relief and pleasure: "Ruth, Ruth, ahh!"

Ruth said quietly, after a moment, "You *can* do it, see?"

He got up to wipe himself off, then turned out the light and came back to his side of the bed, saying nothing and making no bodily contact. From the rhythm of Ruth's breaths, he could tell she was awake. He lay still for awhile, like a child hiding in an obvious spot and hoping, through careful, slow breathing, not to be seen.

He didn't actually hear Ruth crying as he lay in the dark next to her. What he heard was the scratch of the Kleenex tissues as they came out of the bedside table box, one by one.

CHAPTER ELEVEN

SANDY WAS PROBABLY the kind of congregant a rabbi would find frustrating—the kind who participates when his child is studying for bar or bat mitzvah but who, once that milestone is over, slips back into showing up only on Rosh Hashanah and Yom Kippur, or, worse yet, lets his family membership lapse. Of course Rabbi Weinstein was aware of Sandy's work with Children of Holocaust Survivors, but that had little to do with the synagogue itself. Up until Weinstein had performed his father's memorial service and then made that one obligatory *shiva* call, Sandy had only had personal contact with him at the time of Amy's bat mitzvah—what was it, six years ago now. And that hadn't gone particularly well.

At the family meeting for all the bar and bat mitzvah kids beforehand, the parents had been warned not to micro-manage their children's preparation. They were told it was important to let the child work with the cantor for the required blessings, prayers, and chanting, and with the rabbi for the *d'var torah*, the interpretive speech about the assigned week's Torah portion.

Sandy had assumed this meant Rabbi Weinstein would engage Amy in some level of Jewish thought or inquiry. However important it was for Jewish children to feel connected to their community, this was all the more so for adopted children. There was even an added layer in Amy's case as the grandchild of Holocaust survivors. All that would be obvious to a rabbi, wouldn't it? So Sandy had restrained himself from coaching Amy about her speech or asking to see it beforehand. The result was a hackneyed, shallow interpretation of the Torah portion, with a phoned-in quality to Amy's delivery that made Sandy cringe.

After the service, while they were milling around the social hall getting ready to eat, having had most of a glass of red wine on an empty stomach, Sandy sidled up to Rabbi Weinstein while Ruth was busy with guests. He'd remarked to the rabbi that Amy could have used a little more guidance in preparing her *d'var torah*. He'd couched it in humor, but the truth was, Sandy probably seemed like an ass. Afterward, he worried (and couldn't admit to Ruth) that instead of conveying disappointment in the institution, he'd come across as insecure about Amy's abilities.

But none of that was an excuse for the condescending way Rabbi Weinstein had treated Sandy a couple of weeks ago when he'd gone in to talk about circumcision. Weinstein barely gave him ten minutes, fiddling with his hearing aid and saying he was late for a Sunday morning lecture. To get Sandy off his case, he'd given him the name of some feminist rabbi who led a Reform congregation in west Berkeley, who had an unusually liberal policy about intermarriage between her Jewish congregants and non-Jewish partners, and who was one of the first rabbis to do commitment ceremonies for gays and lesbians. Though a little resentful that Rabbi Weinstein would lump in Sandy's circumcision stance with every other non-traditional issue he could think of, Sandy set up an appointment with the feminist rabbi.

Sandy had to admit to a prejudice against hyphenated last names, especially when its components were multi-syllabic. What kind of person would make the rest of the world stumble awkwardly just to address her? There was something decidedly irritating about it. So when Rabbi Elizabeth Kupferman-Adelstein opened the door to her office the first week in December, Sandy was already a little annoyed.

She was a large woman, tall and somewhat overweight, with a greying dirty-blonde page-boy haircut and dangling silver earrings. "Nice to meet you, Dr. Waldman," she said.

"You can call me Sandy."

"Come on in, Sandy. It's a little chaotic, but hey—it's a living." She plunked herself down heavily behind her desk and gestured toward a wicker chair with a faded floral cushion.

Sandy sat. A beam of Sunday afternoon light fell across a jumble of too many framed pictures on the bookshelf behind the rabbi's desk, from which he gathered that she had two sons and a daughter, all elementary school age. Something about the clutter, or maybe the dust on the photo frames, depressed Sandy, sapped his hopefulness. He glanced at her, gauging the amount of grey in her hair, the sallowness of her skin. She must be fifty. What was it that made women think they could wait and wait before having children? Sandy knew it wasn't very feminist of him, but secretly he found the delayed childbirth trend ridiculous. Women nearing forty before getting around to it! Of course Ruth wasn't young when they got Amy (and Belle was on the older side by the time she had Shayna). But that was because of circumstances beyond their control, not because of some lofty delusion that one could defy biology simply by aligning oneself with the women's movement.

"So Rabbi Weinstein gave you my name? And you're doing research on *brit milah*?"

"Umm, kind of."

"It's a fascinating topic," she said, sitting down at the desk facing him and giving her watch a quick glance. "Are you mainly interested in the Jewish aspects, or are you coming at it from a medical point of view? You said on the phone that you're a physician."

"I'm trying to find out what alternatives are out there, that are accepted. And how feminists within Judaism address the problem—"

"—of the inherent inequity of the ritual," she finished for him, nodding sagely.

"Iniquity, more like."

She looked confused. Then an indulgent half-smile crossed her face. "You're expecting a grandson, aren't you?"

Involuntarily, Sandy touched the crown of his head; was he that bald? "No grandson just yet," he said irritably, watching her smile fade. "The truth is, Rabbi, I've just been realizing recently what a primitive ritual this is."

The rabbi paused. "Of course you know the significance of the circumcision *mitzvah* in Judaism?"

"Wait—*mitzvah*? I thought circumcision was a commandment."

"The word *mitzvah* means commandment, Sandy."

"I thought it meant good deed."

"That, too. It's both. A *mitzvah* is something God commands us to do, but it's also a good deed."

"Interesting," Sandy said thoughtfully. "Commandment or good deed, though, I don't think any of that enters into it for most people. It seems to get jumbled into this soup of confusion about things like sexual identity, medical issues—"

"From a Jewish point of view, Sandy, the medical aspect isn't relevant. Circumcision isn't done for cleanliness or health. It's strictly a sign of the covenant between God and the Jewish people, the physical manifestation of Abraham's message of ethical monotheism."

Sandy was getting impatient. "What I'm really here to discuss with you, Rabbi, is the current Jewish-feminist perspective on the whole thing."

"Right. This is a very interesting topic for Jewish feminists. Now, do you know about the covenant of the washing of the feet?"

"Foot washing? That sounds like christening."

"It's called *brit rechitza*, and it's a beautiful ceremony that we've been doing for little girls. We encourage the family to invite everyone they would if it were a *brit milah* ceremony. We don't believe boys should be welcomed with any more fanfare than girls."

The characterization of circumcision as "welcoming" irked Sandy. He glared down at the beige wall-to-wall carpet, which looked as if it were vacuumed regularly by one of those monstrous machines that can't quite get into the corners.

"Anyhoo—the *brit rechitza* can be held eight days after birth, as with *brit milah*, or sometimes a little later," she went on. "It just depends on when the family can all attend. The parents bring the baby up on the *bimah* during services, and we say a blessing over her and acknowledge her with her Hebrew name—"

"Yes, we did that with our daughter. That was nineteen years ago, Rabbi. What I'm asking is, what changes have been made in the last twenty years that address the *sexism* of circumcision?"

She paused. "Well, one change I can think of—are you aware of the certifying process to become a Reform *mohel*?"

Sandy shook his head.

"It arose as a Reform alternative to the Orthodox practice of *brit milah*. It's for Jewish physicians who practice circumcision—urologists, pediatricians, obstetricians—to be certified religiously. It's open to women as well as men. So now, women are being ordained within the Reform Movement to perform *brit milah*."

"There are women *mohels* now?" Sandy was aghast.

She beamed. "*Mohelot*, we call them in the plural. Instead of *mohelim*."

"Such progress," he croaked.

"Actually, that goes back further than you'd think. Zipporah set a precedent when she circumcised her second son, Eliezer, while on their trek through Sinai—"

"Rabbi, let me be blunt. What's being done among progressive or feminist Jews to *abandon* circumcision?"

She blinked. "Abandon it? Most Jews still feel—"

"In the *feminist* movement? Modern Jewish feminists feel that chopping off a part of the baby's God-given anatomy is a tradition worth keeping?"

The rabbi paused a moment. "As a feminist, Sandy, I would never interfere with the male aspect of our faith. But also, there's some mysterious power to circumcision. In exchange for fulfilling this one commandment, God gives the land of Canaan to Abraham and his descendants, for generations to come."

"Rabbi, with all due respect—only the most fundamentalist Jews interpret the Torah literally. And even the Orthodox don't follow commandments like putting to death a 'wayward' son." Sandy was glad he'd been boning up on all this. "I think as Reform

Jews, we look a little silly defending something on the basis that it's commanded. Isn't *choice* the whole point of Reform?"

"Choice based on knowledge, yes. We must educate ourselves Jewishly, and then make decisions accordingly. Some call it 'pick-and-choose' Judaism." She laughed loudly.

He grimaced. Was she one of those women of exhausting, forced cleverness, whose pleasantly sarcastic tone seemed designed to say, *look at me, see how witty I am*, possibly in an attempt to compensate for having been unpopular in high school?

"Rabbi, I just want to know—there are studies out there, credible pieces of research, that document the pain response in infants. A lot of babies might look like they're sleeping through circumcision, but they're actually in a state of neurogenic shock."

"I don't know anything about that. But—"

"So, doesn't Judaism need to incorporate that new information? The same way it's changed its unenlightened treatment of the *kheresh*, the deaf-mute?" The *kheresh*, Sandy had read, had been classified with the mentally incompetent in Talmudic times, unable to partake fully in Jewish life. Deaf men couldn't even be counted toward a *minyan*. But nowadays, even the ultra-Orthodox acknowledged that the *kheresh* should be considered an equal Jew in every respect.

"You make a good argument." The rabbi paused thoughtfully. "Thing is, you're going up against a tradition that's thousands of years old."

"So what? Women have been subjugated for thousands of years, too. I can't imagine you'd defend *that* convention for its own sake."

The rabbi pressed her lips together, then got up suddenly and fluttered her fingers in search of a volume on the shelf behind her. "Let's see what the Rambam has to say about all of this."

"The Rambam?"

"It's a Hebrew acronym for Maimonides," she explained. "Rabbi Moses ben Maimon. The Jewish physician and scholar from the twelfth century." She grabbed a book entitled *Guide for the Perplexed*, found the page after a minute, and began to read aloud.

"'*No one, however, should circumcise himself or his son for any other reason but pure faith; for circumcision is not like an incision on the leg, or a burning in the arm, but a very difficult operation.*' So you see," she said, sitting back down, "Maimonides doesn't claim that *brit milah* is easy or painless."

"Well, that's certainly honest."

She looked at her watch. "Yikes, I'm late. Hubby's turn to cook the family din-din. Roasted chicken and garlic mashed potatoes—don't wanna miss that."

Sandy's chair made a wickery creak as he got up.

"It's great talking with you," the rabbi said, shaking his hand. "You sure have done your homework on this thing. By the way, Sandy, do you want to borrow this Maimonides book? I haven't used it in a while."

"Oh. You sure?"

"The Temple library has a copy of the same edition, so I can get a hold of it in the meantime if I need to. Look it over and then bring it back when you're done. Although, hey, Sandy, that could take a lifetime."

"Well, thanks." He took the paperback volume from her and opened the door. *Ffffft*, went the bottom of it along the carpet.

"Here's my card, too," she said. "E-mail me if you have any more questions."

Any more questions. Was that what he was doing, asking questions, getting her answers? Sandy tucked the card into the book, wondering whether the rabbi's husband was using fresh or granulated garlic for the potatoes. As he made his way down the carpeted stairs, Sandy felt vaguely unsettled, as if he'd left something in her office by mistake.

CHAPTER TWELVE

AMY CAME UP THE PATH with the wheelbarrow in front of her and rounded the corner. She liked the crunch of gravel under the wheels and under her hiking boots. Like the sound Grape Nuts made in her mouth. She wiped sweat from her forehead. It was clear and sunny today, but they were still in the middle of the rainy season, so they had to hurry up and repair the railroad ties underneath the paths and steps. Then they had to re-pave them with gravel.

There was a frost over the weekend, so today she and this other guy dug a few ditches to expose the pipes and try to figure out which ones were leaking. Amy liked having her own section of the garden so she could get away from the guy, who was hot for her but too scared to hit on her. Super-nice, but such a retard. Even their boss noticed, and it seemed like she thought it was funny. It wasn't sexual harassment or anything, so it could be funny. To someone else. Amy *so* didn't need this.

She came up to the steps on the hill and kneeled down. Her back kind of hurt, which was really annoying. She started drilling, one hole a couple of inches in from the left side and another one from the right. Then she grabbed an iron rebar from the wheelbarrow and pounded through it to secure it into the ground. She dug out the area and grabbed a railroad tie. That copper solution, the one she'd soaked the ties in so they wouldn't rot once they were put in, hella stank. She fit the tie in and pounded the rebar again. Then she filled the hole with road base, which was this mix of gravel and clay that would harden really well when it dried. She tamped it down hard so it wouldn't wind up wavy as soon as water hit it. It was like her muscles knew how to do things there was no way her parents could do. Amy felt *adopted*, all the way on the insides of her bones.

Amy was still pissed about Mick's letter, just that it existed, even though she didn't know what was in it. She decided to not see Sandy or Ruth for a long time, even though she knew that if she helped Ruth at Bubba and Zayda's house while Shayna was gone, they could get a lot more done than with Shayna around. Shayna was good at buying stuff, but not at getting rid of it.

Amy didn't call her parents back on her birthday, either. Instead she spent the day at work and then getting fucked up on pot and vodka with people at the co-op. Late that night someone came up to her with a package that Ruth had dropped off, and Amy didn't even open it for two days. It was this expensive-looking backpack made specially for riding a bike, pretty cool, but Amy was like, *bite me.*

So her parents were jerks, duh. And Mick was a total tool, a manslaughterer plus a cokehead and a dealer. Nothing new. But all this stuff that Amy always kind of tried to not think about kept coming up, like did Mick try to get Brenda on coke? Was she on coke while she was pregnant, or drunk maybe? Plus, if sperm came from a strung-out guy, did that affect the fetus? Meaning, when the sperm got together with the egg, was the sperm basically coked-out at the time?

But Amy was kind of over it. She was doing a lot of stuff. She started going to visit Bubba on the way to work in the mornings. She always made sure it was after eight so she wouldn't run into Sandy or Ruth, because usually Sandy was at work by seven-thirty, and Ruth was either on campus or at Hyl, or at home figuring out her stupid recipes.

Cantor Traub had called her and she'd started helping deliver leftover food from the Temple. She'd been at Temple three out of the last four Saturdays. Weird, how she felt more comfortable in the social hall than in the sanctuary. Plus, she met with Cantor Traub a couple times. He told her how he was trying to get all the East Bay synagogues to donate their leftover food too. He asked her which plants would grow without much water in the new garden that the synagogue was planning. In the first meeting, it seemed like he kept her there longer than he had to. In the second meeting, he definitely did.

Cantor Traub was cute in this way where he didn't know it, and he was really enthusiastic, like about his work, and *tikkun olam*. He always asked Amy about herself and didn't just automatically take Sandy's or Ruth's side, which is how it seemed like he would be, since he seemed kind of old, even though in years, he wasn't. Cantor Traub really paid attention to what Amy said. He even offered to help her with figuring out the whole college thing, like what would be some good options, and how to fill out the applications, stuff that Sandy and Ruth would of been *way* too happy to help her with. So Amy kind of started talking to the cantor, on the phone and stuff, which was cool, because he kind of took her seriously.

But somehow Amy knew she wouldn't ever be about it, with Cantor Traub. It was weird, how his scraggly beard didn't seem to match his big white teeth. Every time he laughed, it went upwards, and sounded like "loop." He looked sort of sloppy the day she saw him at Enigma Repair, but even at work, in a suit and tie, the cantor was just kind of messy. Like he was the first one in his family to not go into the family's business of moving furniture, or owning a paint store, or whatever.

When Amy talked to her roommate Rebecca about Jay—that was what the cantor wanted her to call him, Jay for Jeremiah—Rebecca said, "Amy, duh, you're just not that into him. I mean, you can hook up with him or whatever, but basically, you like that guy down in Santa Cruz. So go for it." Amy hadn't told Rebecca that Cedric couldn't ever be a real boyfriend.

Rebecca was right, the main trouble with Jay Traub was, he wasn't Cedric. *Cedric*. Amy even loved the sound of it, the cedary, pine needley way that word was. A sound that kind of surprised you but then you really liked it.

He'd called again this morning, before seven. "Amy?"

Like anyone else would be answering her cell.

"I dreamed about you last night."

She felt her pussy get warm. Shit. "Hey, Ced."

"When can I see you?"

"You could always come up here," Amy said. It wasn't like she was trying to suggest that. It was just really annoying that he always thought she should come down there.

"You know I can't do that."

Yeah, right. His wife would want to know where he was for dinner. His two year-old little daughter would ask for her daddy. "Look, Ced, I've been thinking maybe—"

"You're not hooking up with anyone, right?"

"Not really."

"What do you mean, not really?"

She sighed. "Not anyone. I'm not hooking up with anyone. It's chill."

"That's my girl."

His voice sounded like one of those springs, up in the mountains.

"Because I definitely wouldn't be happy about that."

"It's not your business, Cedric." *That's my girl.*

"Well now, Amy," he said, all teacher-like. She was glad to not be with him. There was something too intense about him. Too much like he thought, *hey, of course I should be the one to control things*.

They hung up, and nothing was figured out except he said he'd call again. And even that was figured out only because Amy hadn't told him to *not* call.

She kneeled down and pushed aside some gravel in this one really bald spot. The wood had gotten dislodged from the perpendicular length of iron. Sometimes it seemed like maybe she was into men like Cedric because Brenda would of been. Like if Amy could just force herself to get interested in Jay, or her co-worker, or whatever, things would make a lot more sense.

Fuck, she thought, trying to get her mind off Cedric. Screw her parents. All that bullshit about communication and openness. Sandy wanted her to think *he* thought she was smart, kind of bending back to make her think that and not wanting her to notice the bending back. But then he gave her mixed messages, like why didn't she go to community college? He never told her she should apply to Cal or whatever, or even S. F. State, even though her grades were pretty good. But then at the same time, Sandy acted all disappointed that she wasn't going to medical school or something. You could get whipped lash just trying to figure him out.

Or like that night at Kenny's party. Sandy still thought he was just doing what any good father would do. He said Amy gave him no choice, because he'd been so worried. He said he was sorry, but it was the kind of sorry where he was just trying to show how cool he was for being able to ever notice anyone else's perspective.

Things were going great at Kenny's before Sandy showed up. Amy was sitting next to Kenny in his living room on a brown couch. It was the first time Kenny had sat with Amy. The first time it seemed like he even noticed her. There were about twelve people at the party, half in the kitchen, half in the living room. They were watching MTV with the sound off and listening to Porcupine Tree on a boom box. Kenny played air guitar and sang along. His breath smelled like beer. To Amy it was sweet, like bread, plus it made her stop thinking about Cedric.

She'd never liked a hot boy before. Actually, she hated paying attention to boys who other girls thought were hot. Especially if their reputation was that practically every girl in the class had gone down on them or wanted to. The thing was, though, Kenny wasn't just hot; he was *cool.* After school, he did these incredible raps across the street from Berkeley High, at Provo Park. He believed in individual revolution, not organized revolution. He was always saying things like if you took a stand, that was better than wasting time trying to get a bunch of people to agree on anything. Kenny had thought about stuff. He went to poetry slams all around the Bay Area. He didn't win any of them, but everyone said that was because he was white.

He wasn't afraid of what anyone thought of him. Like, one time they all had to go to this stupid assembly about safe sex. Afterwards, the speaker asked if there were any questions. Kenny shouted, just to freak people out, "Yeah, what's the best lubricant to use for anal penetration?"

He had super-long, dark hair and thick eyebrows. He still had these strong arms and torso from being a rower, even though he'd been kicked off crew in sophomore year for drugs and he hadn't done anything athletic since. He told everyone he didn't respect his parents, because they'd never gotten married but they didn't correct people when people called them married. Parents lied all the time, he said. Whatever you think you know, it's bullshit.

His parents were never around, so Kenny drank and smoked blunts whenever he wanted. Which was a lot. He told everyone pot was the best way to get through a hangover.

The air in Kenny's living room smelled sweaty. It was kind of depressing how the furniture didn't match, and the walls were this kind of icky avocado-green. Plus, there was this teeny but intense light from the piano lamp blaring out into the room. The light made Amy's head hurt. Or maybe that was from the five Henry Weinhards she'd already had. Or the six or seven hits she'd taken off a blunt. But she didn't want to get up and re-aim the glare toward the wall. She was afraid that when she got back to the couch, Kenny would forget to put his thigh right next to hers again.

"Hey, Amy," Kenny said loudly into her ear, over the music. He had socks on, but no shoes. When he toed her through the side of her sandal, she wondered how even in a thick sock, his foot could make this electric kind of excitement go up her legs.

Amy said, "Hey." She was going to play it cool. Finally! She'd had the hots for Kenny for two years, from even before she was with Cedric. She was in Literary Magazine with Kenny, and Ecology Club. And, she knew about him from his reputation. People respected him, even though he was kind of an asshole. Amy tried to forget about that one time when he got totally fucked up on vodka at a party and shouted that he had no use for virgins, and looked straight at her.

Amy wasn't going to act all desperate now, just because Kenny had gathered some strands of her hair and was rubbing them back and forth in his fingers, and it made her scalp tingle.

It was weird, but she almost couldn't focus on Kenny. She felt turned on, and also, she felt like she'd won something. But there were other things. The legs of the couch, which were really chewed up from when Kenny's black Labrador was a puppy. Chipped white paint on the front door where the dog had scratched it. Kenny called the dog Fat Fuck, and his parents let him. Which would be kind of a problem if the vet ever wanted to know the dog's name, like for identification purposes. Maybe they just used his initials. *F.F.* Amy grinned.

The brown carpeting under their feet was worn out. Plus, one of the girls reminded Amy of a fish. Had she always looked like a fish, like, in Chem? She was even wearing fishnet stockings. A fish, caught in a fishnet.

Kenny let go of Amy's hair to take the bong from Ashley, a girl with this curly long hair and big brown eyes that made her look like she thought about stuff a lot. Amy suddenly realized Ashley looked smarter than she really was. Whereas with Amy, it was probably the opposite, because she was just regular-looking, kind of American-looking.

They were talking about Sublime's guitar tracks, versus tracks from more established bands like Nirvana. "And they both committed suicide," Ashley said.

"The Nirvana guy and the Sublime guy?" Kenny's little brother looked up from his XBox. He was thirteen and he didn't know anything.

"Duh," one of the other girls said.

Kenny held the bong for Amy, waited for her to take a hit, and then got up and passed it to a girl she knew from English. A major-league stoner who was like, *I only wear black*. "Brad Nowell may be dead, but he's still alive," the girl said.

"What does *that* mean?" asked Kenny's little brother.

"It's like, I can feel his being."

The fish girl rolled her eyes. "*Feel his being*. Jesus fucking Christ, the guy's *dead*." She took a long hit off the bong and handed it back to Kenny.

"That's hella dumb," Kenny's brother agreed.

"Shut the fuck up, or I'll tell Mom you've been selling pot." It sounded funny, because Kenny was pinching his voice to try and hold the smoke in while he was talking. He let his breath out and said, "Anyway, they weren't both suicides. Kurt *Cocaine* killed himself, and Brad Nowell died of an overdose. Didn't he?" He turned to Amy and she shrugged. He held the bong for her. She took another hit.

Ashley said, "Know what's hella dumb? My mom's dating this guy named Dick? She went to high school with him and they, like, met again at their reunion? Anyway, he makes us all call him Richard, 'cause he hates being called Dick. But my mom always messes up and calls him Dick, 'cause that was what he was called in high school. So I mean, what's the point?"

"That's so pretentious," the fish girl said.

"Well, what would you do if you had a name like Dick?" Amy said to the girl.

"I know what I'd do," Kenny said. "I'd change it to Penis. Or Cock."

Everyone was laughing so loud, Amy didn't hear the knock at the front door. The dog waddled into the living room and started barking, not very enthusiastically. "Whoa, Fat Fuck," Kenny said, from the couch. "It's open," he shouted. "Whoa, boy."

Another knock.

Amy sat next to Kenny feeling happy and hot. Even if she had thought, *that sounds like Sandy's knock*, she was pretty sure, when she thought about it after, that she would of just figured it was that paranoia thing people said sometimes happened when you get stoned.

"Come on in," Kenny shouted.

Sandy was in slacks, deck shoes, and the brown leather jacket that he thought made him look cool. Amy could tell from his expression, kind of guilty but trying to look all concerned, that there was no emergency. The jacket, that was what really pissed her off.

"Who's the host of this party?" he wanted to know. He looked around the room.

Kenny had gotten up off the couch to turn down the music. "Sir, I'm Kenny." Kenny really knew how to suck up to people at first. It always took new teachers a while to figure out he wasn't a suckup, he was a fuckup. "If we're making too much noise, we can—"

Amy said, "Sandy, what the hell are you doing?"

"Noise?" Sandy said. "You're not making too much noise. I'm just here to—"

"You know him?" Kenny turned to her.

"Uh, he's—" Amy glared at Sandy. "What are you doing here?"

"Look, Amy, you don't realize you're playing with fire."

"Jesus Christ, Sandy! You are being a total tool!"

"Who's *he*?" the fish girl wanted to know.

"Look—Kenny, I'm really not happy about your exposing my daughter to alcohol and drugs. It's particularly dangerous in her case, because—"

"*Sandy!*" Amy shrieked. She didn't know what pissed her off the most. Was it just Sandy's being there in the first place? Was it the way he talked to Kenny, like he was Kenny's sixth grade teacher or something? Or was it how he said, right in front of all these people, that Amy was the main one there who shouldn't drink or take drugs? Or maybe the thing that was so pathetic was how upset she was getting, and how hard it was to hide that.

"It's not right for you to influence—"

"Get *out* of here!"

Mostly the other kids' mouths were open, but out of the corner of her eye, Amy saw Kenny's little brother smiling.

"I know you hate me right now, Amy," Sandy said. He said it so calmly, it made her want to kill him. "But I really don't care about that. What I care about is your safety."

"*Fuck!*" Amy yelled.

"Sir, I can explain—" Kenny tried.

"*Explain?*" Sandy snorted. "You're going to *explain* to me how you've gotten my daughter drunk and stoned?" He turned to

Amy, but he seemed a little shaky. Like someone who knows he's losing. "Come home with me, now, Amy."

Amy didn't move. Then, after this really long, quiet minute passed, and no one said anything, Sandy turned around and left.

After, like right after, Amy wished she *had* gone home with him. There was this silence, and then Kenny said to Amy in a loud voice, across the room, "You're adopted, right?"

"Y-yeah, so?"

"And Mr. Tight-Ass there, he tells you he loves you just like if you were his real daughter?"

Ashley said, "Come on, Kenny."

Amy's chin was trembling. "I *am* his—"

"No, I'm serious." Kenny walked away from Ashley and toward Amy, and it was totally quiet in the room. "He probably told you you were some kind of a clean slate when he got you. But how do you know your birth mother wasn't retarded? You can't do anything about that. Or, how do you know she wasn't shooting up while she was pregnant?"

"Shut *up*, Kenny," Ashley said.

Amy kept trying to say something, but she couldn't, because it was like she was in one of those dreams where you need to run and your legs don't work.

"You *can't* know any of that," Kenny said, right to her face. His voice was all calm. "Because your father doesn't know that. And even if he did, he wouldn't tell you. He'd just show up at some random party and act like a fucking twit."

Amy shouted, "Fuck you, Kenny!"

She ran into the kitchen to find her jacket, and Kenny put the volume back up on the CD. People started laughing. "Did you hear that guy?" "*What I care about is your safety.*" Laughing. "I know!

I know you hate me right now." More laughing. In the kitchen, there was this girl who'd promised her parents she'd babysit her little sister from 10 p.m. on. Amy didn't really know her, but she made the girl give her a ride home even though it was totally out of the way.

It seemed like everyone at school knew on Monday that Kenny had hooked up with Ashley, but no one said anything to Amy about Sandy or Brenda or anything like that. Amy never talked to Kenny again after the party. She went down to Santa Cruz to see Cedric the next weekend.

AMY HAD GONE HOME for Thanksgiving dinner last week, and even though she was still really pissed at her parents, she felt bad when she saw how pathetic they both were. So now she sent Ruth a "hey" e-mail. Kind of like a bookmark, holding her place until she was ready. And she sent Sandy an e-mail and asked him, how's life as a radical? He wrote back a few minutes later, like he'd been just waiting to hear from her. Even though that was totally annoying, Amy still felt a little sorry for him.

Hi there, Amy, so good to hear from you, sweetheart. I hope you're getting the space you need. To answer your question, I like life as a radical. Unfortunately it's a little like mania. Fun for the manic person, but apparently not much fun for the ones around him... More later, Much love, xoxoxoxoxo Dad.

Amy would of been glad to just keep sending e-mails back and forth and never see her parents. But then Ruth left a voice mail this morning that was all desperate. "I'm making that spicy vegetarian stew tonight, sweetie. The one you like. Why don't you come by after work? You can shower here. You don't have to call—just show up."

Amy looked out over the north side of the Gardens. The guy who was hot for her was bent over in his plaid work shirt. He had to redo a stone path, because some of its pieces had come dislodged from all the wheelbarrow traffic. Later this afternoon, they were going to make a stairway to connect the path she was on to the upper path near the oak trees. Amy tapped at her back pocket and felt the crinkle of the index card. That was where she'd copied down the formula for rise and tread, which would make the stairway easy to climb.

She wiped sweat from her brow again, then tilted the wheel barrow toward the hole where she was working. Road base came spilling out, like it was a liquid. Its dust rose up, like it was a gas.

CHAPTER THIRTEEN

RUTH HAD STARTED SMOKING out on the back porch, after Sandy was asleep. She told no one, not even her therapist. It was only occasional, so she didn't see that it was relevant. Plus, there were more pressing things to talk about these days.

Ruth didn't know why she started with the cigarettes, exactly: something to do with choosing one's poison, she supposed. Or a way to connect with Nadine? Someone had left a gold packet of Benson and Hedges one time after she and Sandy had hosted a party, and they were still sitting in one of the drawers of the living room coffee table. *Why the hell not?* Ruth thought unaccountably one night as she wandered around the house, unloved and unable to sleep. So she'd taken them out the back door with a box of wooden kitchen matches that was considerably larger than the cigarette pack, and situated herself in her favorite cushioned chair on the sheltered porch, looking eastward at the view of the Berkeley hills. Oliver popped into her head; he'd understand this impulse. Chief of Medicine, and he'd understand.

Ruth had never smoked before, unless it counted that she'd tried pot half a dozen times while at U of I. She knew how to light a cigarette only from having watched other people do it. She pulled one of the slender cylinders out of the golden box, put the filtered end in her mouth, and struck the match, surprised by the loud noise it made. She took a puff. She coughed, became dizzy, and dropped her head between her legs, shook the match violently to put it out. She held the lit cigarette at arm's length, her head still down. When she composed herself, she took another puff. She coughed some more.

But she was overcome with a sense of well-being and relaxation she hadn't felt in what seemed like years. It undulated through her body, reminding her of movie scenes in which a junkie finally gets his fix, the expression on his face turning beatific in recognition as the drug begins coursing through his veins.

What harm could it do to start smoking occasionally in one's late forties? Ruth tried it again the next night. She found that she enjoyed the sensations so much that she resolved not to smoke often; she knew that if cigarettes became a habit, she wouldn't get the powerful feelings of tranquility any more. Miraculously, as the weeks went on, Ruth found it easy to keep her intake to two or three cigarettes a week. Though she operated in secret, she didn't really care whether Sandy found out. What was he going to do, stop sleeping with her?

She would put her cigarettes out in the potted plant next to her cushioned chair, and camouflage the ashes (in case Amy ever dropped by) by rubbing them into the soil. Sometimes she'd push the stub into the soil to hide it; or she'd take the butt inside with her and flush it down the toilet. Other times, when she was angry, she'd throw the dead stub into a bald spot in the rosemary bush from which she picked tiny, pungent green branches for her roasted meats. Sandy would probably throw a fit if he knew she was littering.

It was the Friday night after Thanksgiving, and Ruth sat on the porch, thinking of the snapshot that Sandy loved so much that he'd taken a pair of scissors and trimmed it down to fit into his wallet (a major break from his usual anal approach to family photos, which involved meticulous cataloguing and, of course, the maintenance of pristine condition). It was a picture Ruth had taken at Amy's high school graduation. Sandy and Amy stood together, both beaming, Sandy's arm around Amy's gowned shoulders. Sandy regarded the shot as evidence of how close they were, father and daughter, both joyous at precisely the same moment. The truth was, Amy was only smiling at that instant—laughing, really—because Sandy had just delivered his standard joke, wanting, no doubt, to seem cool to some of Amy's friends who were hanging out nearby: *This won't hurt a bit, honey, but if you want, I can administer an anesthetic before we take the picture.* Sandy had entirely missed Amy's eye rolling. He had no idea that her gaiety, and that of her friends, were at his expense.

You got plenty of leeway as a parent. True, you couldn't undo the damage you did while rearing a child, but you could capitalize on the fact that the most recent way you did things was how the child seemed to remember them. While Amy was learning to drive, for example, Ruth always made a point of coming to a full stop at stop signs, leading Amy to conclude that Ruth was "obsessed with traffic laws." In reality, Ruth had taken the rules much less literally when Amy had been younger and wasn't watching so closely. All Sandy would have to do now is start establishing a different kind of relationship with his daughter, and pretty soon, that would be how Amy thought about him.

Ruth peered out into the cold sky, pulling a plaid wool blanket over her shoulders. She lit a cigarette. She even liked the sound of cigarettes, the tiny crackle of tobacco as she dragged smoke desperately into her mouth. It occurred to her that her back yard in Skokie when she was growing up had also faced east, and that like her childhood home, her house was just a few doors south of the nearest corner. If she looked straight ahead and not to the sides, she could imagine the corner park of her youth on her left.

It was noisy out here. Why was it that on some evenings it was perfectly quiet, while on others, at the very same time of night, there was a loud white roar of distant traffic? Suddenly feeling hot, Ruth let the blanket fall from her shoulders.

Shabbat dinners. Ruth had stopped even pretending they were a regular thing—tonight, for example, she hadn't even lit candles. Instead, she'd slipped into letting Amy determine whether Ruth would make the effort for the three of them. If Amy didn't join them, there was no ritual any more. How would Amy remember the many years when family dinners happened like clockwork, every Friday? Why did it all depend on Ruth?

She and Sandy had always made the parenting decisions together. They agreed, before key conversations with Amy, what her bedtime should be, whether they should insist that she take Latin at Berkeley High. Most of all, they'd always discussed issues related to the adoption *ad nauseam* behind closed doors before bringing them up with their daughter. But Ruth no longer cared whether Sandy thought they should tell Amy. *They*. Was there a "they" any more?

A marriage certainly was a strange organism. You had to take its pulse to know what was going on, but you had to do it with your own hand, and so while you were assessing its rhythm, you were also experiencing it from within. It reminded Ruth of the monthly breast self-exams Anne Padway had taught her to do.

There were really two pieces to it: what Ruth's probing fingers felt as they palpated the tissue, and how her breast felt from the inside during the palpation. She had to ignore the way the breast felt from the inside—tender—in order to evaluate it objectively from the outside—squishy, lumpy, God forbid spiky. But was such a separation of sensations truly possible? One time, after years of faithfully doing the self-exams, Ruth had failed to find a thickening that Anne happened to notice during an office visit. Luckily it turned out to be nothing, but the experience drove home for Ruth that there were limits to one's ability to be objective about one's own tissue.

Ruth drew another puff into her lungs and let go with a soft "khhh" sound, remembering Corrador's explanation. Mick had not only punched, but kicked Brenda's abdomen repeatedly. The trauma had caused the placenta to separate from the uterus prematurely.

"The bleeding from the placental abruption consumed all the factors needed for the blood to clot," Dr. Eugene Corrador had explained to them as Ruth held the tiny, fragrant newborn close to her and wept for Brenda. Ruth was sitting on a padded hospital bench with Sandy on her left and Shayna, who had flown down to be with them, on her right. Corrador was standing in front of them. There was a bright fluorescent light right behind him, and Ruth kept moving her head as he spoke, trying to get a sense of his facial expressions. "The consumption of all the clotting factors is called DIC—disseminated intravascular coagulation. The beating caused the abruption, and the abruption caused the clotting problem." There was something canned about his words, and Ruth realized he'd probably offered Brenda's poor drunken mother, Denise, the exact same measured, overly technical narrative in the same patronizing near-whisper.

Sandy and Ruth couldn't help feeling that if Dr. Corrador had been doing his job, he would have intervened earlier on. He'd told them during the pregnancy that things were "kind of volatile between the birth mother and her boyfriend," which in retrospect indicated that he must have been aware of what was going on. Sandy was absolutely right that Corrador should have called Family Services, urged Brenda to get herself to a shelter, talked to Denise—something.

Sandy and Ruth hadn't known Brenda, hadn't even met her. She hadn't wanted any relationship with them during the pregnancy, and had told Dr. Corrador that she didn't want to be contacted by them as the child grew up. No 4 x 6 reprints of the baby blowing out candles, no missing-tooth kindergarten shot, no graduation photo. Still, Ruth and Sandy mourned Brenda's death as if she were a dear niece they didn't see often. Brenda might have changed her mind at some point. She might have ultimately wanted contact with Amy.

Maybe Amy could contact Denise someday, but who knew whether that was remotely a good idea? The first time they'd met Denise, at the hospital, just after Brenda's death, she'd been on a bender and had barely made it there. And even if she were sober now, would Denise be open to contact with Amy? She hadn't wanted the baby when she'd had time to consider the possibility, during Brenda's pregnancy. And she'd apparently told Dr. Corrador after Brenda's death that she was relieved the baby was going to a doctor and his wife; she certainly didn't want to care for it. *It*, Denise called the baby. At the time, it didn't even occur to Ruth how wildly inappropriate that was, Corrador sharing that detail with them.

Ruth and Sandy had agreed early on that there was no reason to burden Amy with extraneous information. What parents in the world would want their daughter to know she'd been so unwanted in her extended biological family, or that she'd been beaten and kicked before she was even born?

Even after all these years, Ruth remained haunted by thoughts of Amy *in utero*. She remembered one of the first times she'd gone with Sandy to a cocktail party with other doctors there. The new Lennart Nilsson photography book was lying on the hosts' coffee table. Ruth was familiar with Nilsson's pictures of embryos and fetuses from *Life* magazine. It was groundbreaking work, and she was as fascinated as anyone—the tiny creases of skin, the albino-looking eyelashes on closed lids, the miniature thumb being sucked by a veiny, inchoate mouth.

As all the guests had stood there oohing and aahing, Ruth was suddenly seized by a disturbing thought. Nilsson had to be using extremely bright light to achieve the level of resolution and detail for which he was now famous. What were these fetuses like once they were born? Did they have an abnormal fear of concentrated beams of light? How were they to get over the intrusion they'd undergone before coming into the world? Ruth was afraid to bring it up at the party, though, thinking she'd come across as sentimental, possibly even an anti-abortion sympathizer. So she'd excused herself and gone into the kitchen to talk food with the caterer.

Ruth shivered, pulled the blanket back up on her shoulders, flicked the ashes into the potted plant. Why was it that the nurture-nature argument never seemed to take into account what happened *in utero*? Experiences that a baby had before it was born didn't really count as nature, since they weren't genetic. But they weren't nurture either; they had already taken place by the time the baby emerged.

Ruth stubbed the cigarette into the potted plant soil. The moist earth opened up to accommodate it.

ꝏ

"SO THE CRAZY CONTRACTOR dude finally came over," Ruth said as Amy came into the kitchen. "That's fresh grout you smell."

"Random. I thought I smelled oatmeal chocolate chip cookies."

"That, too. Your favorite."

"Thanks."

"I doubled the recipe," Ruth added. "Put 'em in a 700-degree oven."

"Hah."

Ruth took a sip from a pink Italian wine glass. She was suddenly teary. "It's been so long since I've seen you, sweetie."

"Thanksgiving was last week," Amy protested, picking up the entertainment section of the *Times*.

Ruth began slicing peeled carrots at an angle, bright orange pointy ovals accumulating on the white cutting board. "So yeah, the guy finally showed up after standing us up three times." An elderly patient had begged Sandy to give work to her grand-nephew, an aspiring sculptor who was desperate for some odd jobs. Ruth liked him immediately—he had competent hands and a sweet manner—but they'd been exasperated every time they counted on him, and Sandy quickly reached his limit. "Anyway, so now he's re-grouted the counter and some of the tub tile in the big bathroom, and did the measurements for the new cabinet doors in there. Barefoot, of course."

"Whatever," Amy said.

"I mean, at first we just thought he was a little unreliable. Possibly on drugs. Or, *should* be on drugs. So today, I finally confronted him. 'I waited for you all afternoon Monday,' I told him. 'You told me you were going to come over at two.' And he told me he'd tried to call."

"But you have call waiting," Amy pointed out.

"I know. I was ready to pop him, it was such bullshit. 'What do you mean, you tried to call?' I said. 'I was here all day.' But there was something about the way he looked at me, and this odd gesture he used, as if he were picking up the receiver of a phone—I had this sense that he was trying to tell me something. And I looked at him for a minute, and he looked back at me kind of sheepishly, and his hand was suspended in the air, reaching for an imaginary phone receiver—well, it suddenly occurred to me."

"What?"

"He meant he had *tried* to pick up the phone and dial, but couldn't bring himself to do it. I think he's phobic about it."

"Random."

"Because then he said something really lame like, 'I have trouble with the phone sometimes'—and it was totally clear he didn't mean his line was defective." Ruth shrugged. "Oh well, the tile is done, and he'll be back with the cabinet doors in a couple of weeks. At least, he'll *try*."

Amy came over and popped a slice of carrot into her mouth. "So where's Sandy?"

"Talking with some feminist rabbi about circumcision." Ruth stirred the onions in the pot, then picked up the garlic press and began squeezing, using the back of a table knife to coax the fragrant pulp off the surface.

"It's not even related to endocrinology," Amy said, tearing open the inner package of a box of Wheat Thins. "Wouldn't that be—like, pediatrics? Or urinology, or something?"

"Urology," Ruth corrected. "Hand me the olive oil, would you? And don't spoil your appetite. And actually, the specialty is obstetrics."

"Huh?"

"Obstetricians are usually the ones who perform newborn circumcisions."

"Random."

"Amy?"

"Huh?"

"The olive oil."

"Oh. Sorry." Amy handed the bottle over and opened the oven door. "Why does Sandy care what a rabbi thinks? He doesn't even like synagogue." She grabbed a pot holder and set the two cookie sheets down on the range.

Ruth stirred in the golden-greenish liquid. "Your dad is an iconoclast in some ways, but he's always felt his Jewishness very keenly. And it's always been important to him to change things from within the system. When I first knew him—I've told you this story, right?"

"You mean, how you met?"

Ruth nodded sentimentally.

"You were a dietician on the staff at Hyl," Amy said rotely, closing the oven door. "You had to write this pamphlet about a diabetes diet. So you interviewed Sandy." She pulled the cookies off the sheets one at a time and put them on the cooling racks Ruth had set up on the counter, sneaking one while she thought Ruth wasn't looking.

"He was so skeptical at the time. They don't exactly train med students about diet and nutrition at Johns Hopkins."

"Yeah, but then you won 'im over. And he started using your pamphlet in his groups or whatever."

"Right. And he was up against a very strong establishment at Hyl. They hadn't realized yet how much money they'd save if they set up diet groups and support groups for people who were diagnosed with various illnesses." Ruth started clearing the sink of the vegetable peelings, putting the waste into the mulch bag she was collecting for the compost heap in the garden. Not that she ever grew anything besides a few herbs here and there. The truth was that Ruth had always done composting mainly to set an example for Amy. "Anyway. Your dad does get kind of obsessed with whatever he's interested in. Hey, cut it out with the cookies."

Ruth washed her hands, wiped them dry on her apron, and stirred the onions, then picked up the cutting board and eased the sliced carrots into the pot. She stirred the mixture, cleared the spoon, lowered the heat and wiped her hands on her apron before bringing her wine glass over to the table and sitting down. "You know, sweetie, I haven't told you lately how much I love you and how proud I am of you."

"I know."

"Remember when we used to watch Hitchcock movies together?"

"Uhh, I guess."

"Your favorite was—"

Amy shrugged. "I guess I kind of liked *Vertigo*."

"Oh. I thought you liked *Rear Window* best."

"Grandma Nadine is the one who liked that."

"Oh, am I mis-remembering? Was that Grandma Nadine's favorite?"

"Whatever. She's the one who was totally into Hitchcock."

Ruth was teary. "I'd love to rent some movies and watch them with you, sweetie. Doesn't have to be Hitchcock."

The front door slammed. "Well, *that* was enlightening," Sandy shouted out from the hallway. His keys clinked on the entry table, and he walked into the kitchen. "So I just met with Rabbi what's-her-name. Bergensteiner-Overholzerman-Rabinowitz."

"Wasn't it Kupperman-Edelman or something?" murmured Ruth.

"What*ever*," Sandy shrugged and winked self-consciously at Amy, who winced. "Wow, that guy finally showed up? I smell grout. On top of whatever yummy things you're making." He opened the fridge, peered inside, and closed it without taking anything. "So what's new around here? Hey, you okay, Ruthie?"

"We were just talking about Hitchcock movies," Ruth said sadly.

Sandy came up to her, kissed the side of her head. "You're thinking about Nadine," he said, then grabbed a glass from the dish drain and filled it with filtered tap water.

"I must be. I guess maybe I'm feeling—something—"

"Maybe you miss her," said Amy.

"They weren't exactly close," Sandy said. "So anyway, this rabbi was supposed to be some radical Berkeley feminist, right? But it was pretty much the traditional party line: circumcision is a given."

Ruth's eyes filled again. Why would grief about Nadine come flooding in now, after all this time? And why was Sandy so dismissive? She got up to check on the food.

"If I had a baby, I'd protect it," Amy declared.

"You mean, you wouldn't let him be circumcised?" Sandy asked.

"Nope."

"What if your husband insisted?" Sandy asked.

"Dude. I'd *never* marry a guy like that. Someone who pushed me around."

Ruth looked up narrowly, remembering a family from when she was growing up. The woman was a friend of Nadine's, and had three daughters, then a son. Nadine had gone to the *bris*, and said the woman was hysterical before, during and after. Apparently she never forgave her husband. They'd gotten divorced a couple of years later. "Why isn't that a feminist issue?" Ruth said.

"Why isn't what a feminist issue?" Sandy asked.

"A woman's emotional reaction," Ruth answered icily, banging the wooden spoon against the pot to force the stray bits of vegetables back in. "I mean, if she's unhappy about the circumcision, no doubt she's patted on the head and told she's *not* feeling whatever it is she's feeling."

"She's patronized," Sandy nodded. "As in, *father*-ized! Ruthie, you're right."

"Yeah," Amy said, "maybe if the woman wants to protect her baby, they tell her she's stupid. Like, that she wasn't getting enough sleep, or she was, like, bitchy from being pre-menstrual. Or—you know what I mean. Post-"

"Post-partum," Sandy finished.

"Yeah. I mean, that's totally unfair."

"Amy," Sandy said slowly, "you're really onto something here. All the welcoming ceremonies there are for baby girls, all the female *mohel*s they want to certify—none of that addresses the new mother's experience when the baby is pulled away from her for the circumcision."

"They *so* don't need that," Amy said. "After the birth pains and everything."

Was it the wine talking, or did Sandy routinely masquerade as a person sensitive to feminine concerns, while being oblivious to his own wife? Even seeing Sandy connect with Amy, which Ruth ordinarily would have savored, seemed irritating.

"Right," Sandy went on. "Just beefing up ways for females to participate—that doesn't address the dominance of circumcision. I mean, if we beef up our Chanukah observance, does that 'address' Christmas? Making it out like Chanukah is a big deal—that's just reactive."

"Good point, Sandy," Amy said.

"All these baby naming ceremonies for girls don't change the basics about circumcision. That it interferes with the mother-child bond."

Amy nodded vigorously.

Sandy paused. "But then, maybe this rabbi can't afford to go to bat for something as emotional as a woman bonding with her infant."

"Really?" Ruth said, loudly cutting up the snap sugar peas, which would go into the stew at the very end so they remained crisp. "She's fashioning herself as a feminist, as a champion of women's rights. Doesn't that include the right to have emotions?"

"You've got a point, Ruthie," Sandy said. "But you know how there are people in minority communities who fight against affirmative action? Maybe she doesn't want to use up her credibility on issues she considers to be on the fringe."

"The mother-child bond is hardly on the fringe," Ruth said.

"I guess it's not easy being out there on the forefront as a feminist," Sandy said, "whether the context is equal employment or domestic violence or religion."

Ruth shrugged irritably. "Glad you're an expert."

"The *politics* of it, is what I'm talking about."

"Okay, whatever, you guys," Amy said. "This is getting really annoying."

CHAPTER FOURTEEN

SANDY HAD A HUNCH that the amenorrhea and resulting infertility of his 8 a.m. patient was being caused by a prolactin imbalance, but he'd have to check. Sitting at his desk with the chart in front of him, he picked up the phone. "Gina? Where are the labs for my 8:00?"

"Not in the chart? I'll see if they came in after I left yesterday. She's here, by the way."

"Already?" Sandy looked at his watch. He'd begun to come in early to spend some of his most alert time on private research and reading. Though he didn't like keeping his patient waiting, he wasn't about to see her thirty-five minutes early, either. "Don't send her in until it's time," he told Gina. He hung up and straightened the stack of charts on his desk, then pushed it aside in favor of the pile of books he'd gotten out of the Berkeley Jewish Center library yesterday.

Since his meeting with Rabbi What's-Her-Name a few days ago, Sandy had been ruminating about the question of why infant circumcision was considered more humane than the circumcision of older children and adults. It was one of those assumptions that seemed incontrovertible until you actually thought about it. Online, he'd begun to read everything pertaining to Jewish law that might shed light on the issue, such as *responsa*, which were rabbinical opinions on a wide variety of issues. Sandy had never realized that an entire body of literature, the thousands of volumes of *responsa*, had evolved for the sole purpose of examining contemporary questions related to Jewish law. He was awed by the diversity and, in some cases, the arcaneness of the questions: Is it permissible for a Jew to own stock in a company that sells unkosher food? Should a person who has converted to Judaism say *kaddish* for his dead non-Jewish father or mother? What does Judaism have to say about violent video games?

Sitting at his desk, avoiding his e-mail, Sandy picked up the book the rabbi had lent him. Could Maimonides have been the first to posit the concept that circumcision was easier on babies? Sandy remembered that *Guide for the Perplexed* included some rationale for doing the circumcision at eight days. He flipped through the index and turned to the page, then re-read the passage:

> The parents of a child that is just born take lightly matters concerning it, for up to that time the imaginative form that compels the parents to love it is not yet consolidated. For this imaginative form increases through habitual contact and grows with the growth of the child... The love of the father and of the mother for the child when it has just been born is not like their love for it when it is one year old, and their love for it when it is one year old is not like their love when it is six years old.

When they'd first gotten Amy, Sandy remembered, the lawyer and the support group leader insisted with a little too much enthusiasm that adoptive parents' attachment to the baby was every bit as strong as if the baby were biologically theirs. But then, they also stressed that men were just as capable of emotional attachment to their children as women were. Yet even without breastfeeding, it was Ruth, not Sandy, who seemed immediately sensitive to every nuance of the baby's experience. Sandy was competent but awkward, approaching the infant's incessant demands with the cool professionalism he'd picked up in medical school.

Of course Sandy had immediately adored Amy, had felt fiercely protective of her—all the more given her experiences *in utero*. But he didn't *know* Amy yet, not the way he would come to know her. As Amy grew, the stakes seemed higher: now, if he did something inept or insensitive, Amy could glare at him, hold a grudge. One careless mention of his own high SAT scores, a few months before Amy took the exams, would be remembered—never mind his frantic attempts at damage control after the fact, his overly earnest *you know, quite often, intelligence doesn't show up on standardized tests. Some of the brightest people...*

Sandy grabbed a Post-It from his middle drawer, marked the *Guide for the Perplexed* page, and sat back in his chair. It had been such a shock six or seven years ago when, over a period of a few months, Amy had grown out of her flattened-dirty-hair stage and turned into a bewitching young woman, with bountiful strawberry-blond waves and fierce blue eyes, deep-set within the perfectly proportioned square face. More than ever before, Sandy had felt overwhelmed with the need to see to it that no harm ever came to her. He'd suddenly grasped the etiology of fairy tales in which beautiful princesses are locked in towers, or forced to sleep for an eon or two until the right prince comes along: how else to address such staggering magnificence but to put it away for safekeeping?

He took his wallet out of his back pocket and flipped to his favorite snapshot, a picture of Amy and himself at the Greek Theater, looking so happy together just after her graduation from Berkeley High. He allowed his thumb to graze the photo lightly before closing his wallet and returning it to his pocket.

He glanced at his watch. It was 7:46; just enough time for him to dip briefly into his e-mail. He logged in and scanned the return addresses and the "Re:" fields of his new messages without opening them. There was a save-the-date announcement for the Children of Holocaust Survivors annual dinner (fortunately, one of the women in the group had stepped forward as secretary a few years ago), a reminder from the Hyl Quality and Utilization Management committee chair about the upcoming meeting, an item from Gina responding to his inquiry about re-usable instruments, one from moveon.org about the Supreme Court's upcoming decision, and one from Shayna whose subject line read *decisions—at the house?* Post-Thanksgiving e-mails that were meant to capitalize on the brief period in early December before the insanity started.

There was another e-mail from Cantor Traub, whom Sandy had contacted last week to find out about adult bar and bat mitzvah studies at Temple, it having occurred to Sandy that a more solid grounding in Jewish studies would make him more effective in talking about circumcision. It turned out the class for this year had started meeting in October. *Makeup work*, read Cantor Traub's e-mail in the subject line.

There was also an item from Vinod regarding a study on the pathology of the prepuce, the anatomical name for the foreskin.

Subj: pathology of prepuce
Date: 12/08/00 5:06:42 PM Pacific Standard Time
From: vinod.sengupta@hyl.org
To: sandor.waldman@hyl.org

Sandy, do you know of this study? It was done by a Canadian pathologist, John Taylor, who has concluded that the prepuce is not at all extraneous, not at all the way we were taught to think of the appendix. In fact the prepuce contains far more sexual nerve endings per square inch than the glans of the penis. I attached the file for your perusing.

Also, there is a related question. I have been reading that the skin of the glans keratinizes after circumcision. I cannot help wondering regarding a man's sex drive declining as he gets older. Does a glans with a thin covering (i.e., the prepuce) allow him more sexual sensation than a thick-skinned one? Perhaps men are walking around today without fully the awareness of what they have lost?

Vinod

Sandy gritted his teeth and downloaded the file. He was curious, primed for outrage, yet in some way, Sandy didn't want the foreskin to have a function.

The paper, which Noel Pickett had referred to in one of his articles, had been published in the British Journal of Urology in 1996 by John Taylor, a pathologist at the Manitoba Health Sciences Centre. After examining the foreskins of 22 deceased adult men, Taylor concluded that the inside of the foreskin contained highly specialized nerve endings, and that anatomically, the foreskin was very similar to the lip. Taylor explained that the inner lining of the foreskin contained a band of ridged skin, the ridges comprised of a number of round nerve endings which massage the penile shaft during intercourse. This anatomical discovery led Taylor to postulate that the foreskin's purpose was to encourage the ejaculatory reflex. Sandy saved the file for later.

Sandy saw that his next e-mail was from "junglejim," also known as Jim Horovich, a man with whom Sandy had become acquainted online in the course of his circumcision research. *Foreskin restoration group*, junglejim's e-mail said in the subject box. Should he open it?

When Sandy had first become aware of the phenomenon known as foreskin "restoration," it had made him snicker. But now, after glancing through the Taylor study, Sandy felt more nauseated than anything else. Wait, wasn't there a passage in *Guide for the Perplexed* in which Maimonides had discussed the sexual sensitivity of the foreskin? Sandy picked up the book again, found his Post-It bookmark and scanned for the reference:

> ...the use of the foreskin to that organ is evident... circumcision simply counteracts excessive lust, for there is no doubt that circumcision weakens the power of sexual excitement, and sometimes lessens the natural enjoyment; the organ necessarily becomes weak when it loses blood and is deprived of its covering from the beginning...

What if junglejim was a weirdo? What if he thought Sandy himself wanted to "restore" his foreskin? Sandy had made it clear from the start that he was a physician interested in the issue of recovered infant memory as a research question. Maybe he'd fire off a quick note saying thanks-but-no-thanks.

Sandy had decided not to open any more of his messages when he saw a return e-mail address he hadn't noticed before. Did it pop up just now, or while he was looking at *Guide for the Perplexed*? Sandy held back briefly, then clicked on it.

Subj: your informal poll
Date: 12/08/007:56:15 PM Pacific Standard Time
From: eugene.corrador@hyl.org
To: sandor.waldman@hyl.org

hi sandy, good to hear from you. yes i do use a local for clrcs, the dorsal penile nerve block. so do at least half the obs here at the los angeles hyl, and i'm sure up there. i think it makes a difference, baby doesn't cry as much. are you planning a study? what's the connection w/ endocrin, though? enjoyed talking with your daughter a few weeks ago, she sounds lik a fine young lady. give my best to your lovely ruth, keep in touch. regards, eugene

Sandy became aware that his hand was on the telephone receiver and was shaking. He took it away. He needed a minute before calling his "lovely Ruth."

Amy had contacted Eugene Corrador, and not said anything? What had Corrador told her? Sandy shuddered. He guessed it had to happen at some point, but did it have to be now, when she was still so young, when she still seemed to be in a state of adolescent rebellion? Or was that unfair? Maybe that was unfair.

Sandy would forward the message to Ruth electronically; even if she didn't check her e-mail before teaching her class, at least the time stamp would indicate Sandy had forwarded it as soon as he'd received it.

"Hi Ruthie," he typed, carefully forming the words that would come next. "I got the attached from Eugene Corrador. I forgot about the e-mail questionnaire I sent out to all the Hyl OBs—of course he's part of that group. Funny, most of them haven't even answered me yet." He paused, pressed the return key, then added: "Think we should ask Amy about this? I guess I'm a little freaked out. Love, S."

He pushed the "send" button just as Gina was knocking at his door, labs in hand.

"Thanks, Gina," he said quietly. "Show her in, OK?"

WHEN SANDY GOT HOME, he found Ruth sitting on the couch sipping a glass of Merlot, reading the *New York Times Book Review* and listening to a CD of Brahms' second piano concerto. The open wine bottle sat on the coffee table.

Since the copyediting was done and the cookbook was finally in the printing phase, Ruth had taken some time off. Once the book was out, in May, she'd be busy promoting it, doing readings and signings and radio talk shows and possibly even some TV. It made sense for her to take advantage of these few quiet weeks when all she had to do was finish the quarter at Cal and be available to the Hyl nutrition department. Still, Sandy felt something was off when he walked in. Then he realized what it was. Instead of the aroma of dinner cooking, there was that faint foresty odor he'd been smelling lately.

Cigarettes, that was it! It smelled like cigarettes. Sandy could hardly believe his nose. How could Ruth be smoking? It was entirely unlike her. When had she started? He took off his jacket and hung it up in the hall closet. "D'you get my e-mail?"

"Uh-huh."

He sat down opposite her in his reading chair. “Dr. Corrador. Can you believe that?”

“What part of it?”

“What part of it? The whole thing! She didn’t even tell us! And who knows what Corrador told her?”

Red wine jostled in Ruth’s glass. “You’re ridiculous, Sandy. Corrador isn’t going to let on about you. And even if he did, do you honestly think Amy gives a damn if you smoked pot when you were in your twenties?”

“I got busted,” Sandy reminded her, swallowing, “and Johns Hopkins didn’t find it amusing.” *Neither did my father.* “Anyway, the last thing Amy needs is to have that reinforcement. About drug use. I mean, look at what she’s got going against her genetically. A coke-head father, and then an alcoholic maternal grandmother—”

“And you think nurture is her only chance? And that we’ve blown it?”

“Well—”

“My God, Sandy. You don’t even know how offensive you are.”

How many glasses have you had, by the way? Sandy peered at the bottle, but it was hard to gauge the level of the red liquid in the dark green bottle.

“I, for one, am going to talk to Amy. Tell her that last beating Brenda suffered wasn’t the first one. I think she has a right to know.”

“Come on, Ruthie. It isn’t like you to act unilaterally like that.”

“You’re a fine one to talk—you’ve unilaterally decided our sex life is over. As you did once before, if you recall.”

Sandy swallowed. “Ruthie.”

“Don’t Ruthie me.” She glared at him, holding the wine glass out at a distance. “Don’t you *dare* Ruthie me. The only time you can Ruthie me is when you're screwing me. And since you're not, that name is off limits. From now on."

"R—sweetie. I've neglected you," he said. He got up from the chair and sat down next to her on the couch, folding his leg under himself to face her, but not quite daring to take her hand. "I haven't been attentive. I've been in so much turmoil myself that—"

"Well, Sandy, how about addressing the turmoil? Instead of behaving like a self-absorbed idiot?"

He winced. She would never say something like that if she were sober. "Look, Ruth, I am so sorry. You've been patient with me, and I really do appreciate it. I'm trying here."

"In the immortal words of some comedian or other, Sandy, you're trying, all right. *Very* trying." She plunked her wine glass down on the coffee table.

Desperately, Sandy scooted over toward her. Ruth seemed too surprised to protest, nor did she fight him when he began alternately to kiss her neck and to scratch it gently with the stubble on his chin. This had always excited her. It certainly excited him. Commingled with the smoky smell was the sweet, fruity odor of her neck. He had missed this so much, her faintly apple-like scent. He felt himself start to get hard. *I can do this*, he thought to himself. *I have to do this.*

Ruth remained impassive, and it was only when he reached up for a tentative touch of her breast that he felt her soften. But it wasn't the kind of softening he was hoping for. She was crying. Then she was sobbing, loud, anguished sobs. "You hurt me!" she wailed, rocking back and forth.

He held her as she rocked. "Ruthie," he murmured, then pulled away from her to look into her face. "Please understand. I just haven't felt—whole."

"You haven't felt *whole*," she mimicked.

"I mean, I feel as if I've—lost something."

"You have. *Me!*" She started crying again, loud and gushing. She wiped her face on the sleeve of her cotton cardigan.

"Ruthie, don't say that."

"I told you not to call me that."

"Please, Ruth," he begged. "Don't say I've lost you."

"Goddamn it, Sandy, can't you see I need a tissue?" She got up to grab the box of Kleenex from the book shelf, then sat back down, noisily blowing her nose as if in a deliberate attempt to seem unfeminine.

He touched her shoulder as she wadded up the used Kleenex, threw it on the table next to the couch, and took a fresh one. "I want to make love to you," he whispered in her ear.

Ruth blew her nose again.

"Come, Ruth. Come to bed with me."

She threw another tissue into the pile and faced him, still crying. He took this as an opening. He covered her hand with his, stood up, and tugged.

In the bedroom, he unbuttoned her cardigan as she stood still in front of him, weeping. He couldn't remember the last time he undressed her; the most he usually did was to open the top buttons of her nightgown before she cooperated by pulling the garment over her head. But now she waited stiffly, crying into another Kleenex as he undid the last two buttons. She let him take it off a sleeve at a time, then impatiently slipped out of her loafers and the rest of her clothing herself. He hugged her naked body, kissed her ambivalent, smoky mouth.

It had been many weeks since Sandy had had sex with her, and he felt ashamed and awkward. He was worried about the pain returning at the crucial moment. He caressed Ruth's delicate, milky skin, her remarkably perky breasts. "You are lovely," he murmured as she wept. "You are so lovely."

Moments later, he was inside her. "I feel—my p—I feel so naked in you," he breathed, as if it were a statement of intimacy, when it was really an expression of the way he was experiencing his penis.

"You mean—" Ruth, under him, looked up quizzically.

"Never mind." He saw comprehension register on her face but was quickly distracted by the fact that he was coming. It was only when his orgasm died down and he was sure he was out of the woods that he felt any relief.

Still inside Ruth, he reached down and massaged her clitoris. She had stopped crying, and when she came, she shuddered in the way a child does following a bout of hysteria. He held her close, not saying anything, and eventually her dry breaths became long. Sandy's stomach growled. He lay there in the dark, holding his sleeping wife, feeling remiss that he hadn't lasted longer.

It occurred to Sandy to wonder what had happened to the foreskin following his circumcision. Had it been buried in the ground long ago, as is the custom among some Jews?—but where? In the back yard? How had his parents decided on a location?

Would his father have approved of Sandy's anti-circumcision campaign? The old man had been wholly opposed to unnecessary medical intervention. And he'd always fought for social justice. He'd been completely matter-of-fact regarding homosexuality, viewing it as a natural state for some people. He'd refused to refer to the offspring of unwed mothers as "illegitimate." He'd held his opinions without warmth, certainly without self-congratulation.

Or maybe Sandy had had a hospital circumcision. Maybe his father and Belle didn't want a traditional *bris* for their son. Maybe the old man had had a friend of his at the hospital do the procedure. In that case, Sandy's foreskin had probably been thrown away as medical waste... Sandy's eyes widened. *Could his father have done the deed himself?* Certainly that was consistent with Jewish tradition; it was a father's responsibility to circumcise his son, or have it done. Not that Abraham Waldman would have concerned himself with tradition. No, more likely, his surgical expertise would have been the explanation.

Sandy hugged Ruth close. She was so helpful, nothing like his father, the way she plunged fearlessly into the emotional subtext of everything they discussed—feminism, infant bonding, adoption issues. She made him think. Where had he heard that a soul mate was the person who challenged you? Sandy could talk to Ruth about anything, and probably should. He stared at the wall next to her, ruminating, enveloping her, until he could sense from her breathing that she was awake. At one point he thought he heard the muted, crisp sound of her kicking off the down comforter to get up, but it turned out to be only the wind outside.

Then, abruptly, Ruth did get up out of bed, and padded out to the kitchen. Sandy listened for the sounds of her preparing something to eat, but he heard the back door slide open. She was headed out to the porch.

CHAPTER FIFTEEN

Subj: maimonides
Date: 12/09/00 7:06:42 AM Pacific Daylight Time
From: sandor.waldman@hyl.org
To: rabbielizabethk-a@yahoo.com
Bcc: zev.marks@hyl.org

Dear Rabbi Kupferman-Adelstein,

Thank you for meeting with me last week. I've been thinking a lot about our discussion. Also, thanks for lending me your copy of *Guide for the Perplexed*.

I noticed that in the book, Maimonides touts the benefits of doing the circumcision when the baby is an infant—i.e., before our growing love for him interferes with what is commanded. Maimonides says that the more we come to know the child, the less we will want to fulfill this *mitzvah*.

Yesterday I happened to come across some information about the Torah's commandment to love the stranger—which, as you know, is so important that it's part of the "holiness code." As the Talmud points out, the precept of treating the stranger with kindness occurs dozens of times in the Torah. And, as an "ethical *mitzvah*," it trumps all "ritual *mitzvahs*."

So here's the problem I'm having. If Maimonides defines the baby as someone we don't know well yet—a "stranger," if you will—then aren't we Jewishly obligated to treat him exactly as we would treat an older child or adult?

In other words, let's say we find adolescent circumcision abhorrent. Shouldn't we then find newborn circumcision equally so? Wouldn't that be consistent with Jewish thought?

Regards,
Sandy Waldman

Subj: circumcision/aids
Date: 12/09/00 7:21:02 AM Pacific Daylight Time
From: sandor.waldman@hyl.org
To: vinod.sengupta@hyl.org

Vinod, I need to let off some steam. This morning I read another piece of research touting the benefits of circumcision in AIDS prevention. Do you have any idea how these studies keep getting funded?

I went on the World Health Organization web site just now and it quotes the HIV infection rate in these circumcision-happy United States at around 16,000 cases per 100,000 population. That's the largest proportion in the developed world. What a colossal waste of research dollars, to suggest circumcision would help! To say nothing of the ethical issues.

Sandy

Subj: revolution
Date: 12/09/00 4:24:06 PM Pacific Daylight Time
From: awaldman@botgarden.berkeley.edu
To: sandor.waldman@hyl.org

hey sandy, i started thinking, after you saw that woman rabbi. if you're planning a revolution, maybe do it one person at a time. why does the whole jewish world have to decide at the same time to get rid of circumcision? that just isn't gonna happen, because i think the whole religion is too men-dominated for that. anyway, i think good revolutions are grasp-roots. like, if one family decides to not do it, and then another and another. that way, the whole thing might happen, you know? but if the leaders are deciding for the whole religion, no way they'll all agree. because it's too controversial, right?

Re: revolution
Date: 12/09/00 5:20:44 PM Pacific Daylight Time
From: sandor.waldman@hyl.org
To: awaldman@botgarden.berkeley.edu

Hi Amy,

You give me something to think about here. What a good insight. You may be right—it may be too much to expect the Reform Movement as a whole to rethink this issue, let alone all the other branches of Judaism. Maybe one person at a time can have more of an impact.

Realistically, it's probably hard for individual parents to feel comfortable doing something iconoclastic that no one else is doing, especially when the issue is connected with sexuality.

But I wonder whether there are some Jewish parents out there "just saying no," regardless of what the Reform Movement or any other branch of Judaism has to say about it. That could be a springboard, right there. You are so smart.

Love you lots,
xoxoxoxo
Dad

Re: circumcision/aids
Date: 12/09/00 1:06:29 PM Pacific Daylight Time
From: vinod.sengupta@hyl.org
To: sandor.waldman@hyl.org

Sandy, your e-mail made me want to let off my steam, too. Yes, if the foreskin really did increase the risk of HIV infection, Europe would be expected to have the highest rate of HIV. And yet Sweden, Norway, Finland, Poland and Hungary, which are countries that do not circumcise, have some of the lowest numbers. That claim is not very scientific, to say the less! Vinod

Subj: your circumcision research
Date: 12/10/00 7:18:49 AM Pacific Daylight Time
From: sandor.waldman@hyl.org
To: shersh@drs.wisc.edu
Bcc: zev.marks@hyl.org

Dear Dr. Hersh,

My name is Dr. Sandor Waldman, and I did an online search that linked me to your e-mail address. Apparently you're doing post-doctoral research on the ways in which the practice of *brit milah* has changed over the centuries?

I am a Jewish physician who is questioning circumcision. I have done a little medical research on the function of the foreskin and am trying to get a more complete picture of what is lost during circumcision. I understand you believe that the procedure as practiced at the time of Abraham is quite different from what is standardly done now, in terms of the amount of tissue removed. Could you explain?

Many thanks.
Sincerely,
Dr. Sandor Waldman
Hyl Health Maintenance Group
Berkeley, California

Subj: question, medical procedures
Date: 12/10/00 7:33:18 AM Pacific Daylight Time
From: sandor.waldman@hyl.org
To: goldfarb@templebethamrochester.org
Bcc: zev.marks@hyl.org,rabbielizabethk-a@yahoo.com

Dear Rabbi Goldfarb,

My name is Sandor Waldman, and I'm doing research on the Jewish laws pertaining to *brit milah*. I read your *responsum* on hazardous medical procedures and learned that they are strictly forbidden according to *halacha*.

Since your article doesn't mention *brit milah* specifically, I wanted to ask you whether you were aware of the risk of death from *milah*. You probably already know that during Talmudic times, a third infant son in a family would be exempted from circumcision if two of his brothers had already died from it. (It seems likely that this was made into a law following disastrous results in hemophiliac families.) Anyway, since *brit milah* deaths were common enough during the rabbinic period to warrant this special exemption, I can only conclude that scholars have known for a long time that the *milah* carries certain risks.

Circumcision deaths have also been documented recently. There was that baby who died in New York of a herpes infection passed to him by his *mohel*. And I know there was a case documented in Israel in the 1980s, and another in the 90s. However, to my knowledge, there is currently no mechanism in place for follow-up and documentation of *brit milah* cases gone awry. So it seems likely that there are more deaths than we hear about.

Are you aware that even in modern times, *milah* deaths do occur?

Respectfully,
Dr. Sandor Waldman
Hyl Health Maintenance Group
Berkeley, California

Subj: from sandy waldman (friend of anne padway)
Date: 12/12/00 6:50:39 AM Pacific Daylight Time
From: sandor.waldman@hyl.org
To: marthaberg@netscape.net

Dear Mrs. Berg,

I really appreciate your agreeing to have Dr. Anne Padway give me your contact information. It sounds like your decision not to circumcise your son Seth a couple of years ago was very difficult for you and your husband, so I am most grateful for your openness. I think for those of us who are Jewish and who are questioning circumcision, it is better to have a feeling of community. You and your husband are certainly not the only ones who feel this tradition needs re-thinking.

I was curious mostly about your experience since the time you made the decision to leave Seth uncircumcised. Anne mentioned that you belong to a synagogue in San Leandro. Has anyone there given you a hard time—has it been an issue?

Again, thanks so much for your openness.

Sincerely,
Sandy Waldman

Subj: penile cancer data
Date: 12/12/00 7:33:39 AM Pacific Daylight Time
From: sandor.waldman@hyl.org
To: vinod.sengupta@hyl.org

Vinod,

Do you have any idea where the penile cancer data actually comes from? I am having trouble getting to the bottom of it. The Kern claim that circumcision is 99.9 percent effective in eliminating penile cancer has always sounded fishy to me—it's just a little too perfect.

I've been looking into this, and I haven't been able to find any actual positive research associating circumcision with penile cancer prevention. There are a lot of references to the work of Wolbarst, but you and I both know he didn't actually do a study.

By the way, I just looked up the rate of penile cancer in the U.S. and it's 1 in 100,000 males. Then I looked up the rate in other industrialized nations—places that *don't* practice routine infant circumcision. Countries like Denmark, Finland and Japan have two to three times *fewer* cases than we have here. What's wrong with this picture?

Sandy

Re: maimonides
Date: 12/12/00 7:36:42 PM Pacific Daylight Time
From: rabbielizabethk-a@yahoo.com
To: sandor.waldman@hyl.org

Dear Sandy,

Back now from the Reform rabbis' convention. You can imagine what Washington, D.C. is like at the moment, with what the Supreme Court did yesterday. (Is it just me, or was that a coup d'etat?) Oh, and there were also rabbinical matters to attend to. So, I am just catching up. Drowning in paperwork—the eleventh plague.

You make an interesting connection between the baby and the *halachic* admonition to treat the stranger kindly, but it's a bit of a stretch. Why do you view the bond between parent and infant as incomplete? I, for one, bonded instantly with my children when they were born.

So, no, I don't think the baby would qualify for protection as a "stranger" under Jewish law. (Nice try!) But Sandy, you definitely have a feel for *halacha*. I think you would find it very fulfilling to study more.

By the way, as for the pain issue, the graduates of the Reform *mohel* training program all use local anesthesia.

B'Shalom,
Rabbi Elizabeth

Re: penile cancer data
Date: 12/12/00 8:33:59 PM Pacific Daylight Time
From: vinod.sengupta@hyl.org
To: sandor.waldman@hyl.org

Sandy,

I agree with you, the 99.9 percent figure is like fish. I have been delving into the literature since your e-mail and I cannot find the research verification of these statements anywhere, either, and perhaps this is why you have had trouble getting to the bottom.

The whole argument about circumcision preventing penile cancer seems to be based on an editorial by Kern. In that editorial, he refers to an article by Dr. Wolbarst. This Dr. Wolbarst had personal communications with four hospital officials in India in the 1930s. But the data in those communications, if there was any, was never published.

As far as I can tell it, I know this sounds not to believe, the origin of the association between circumcision and lower rates of penile cancer is unpublished, and unverified.

I had always assumed: there is such a low incidence of penile cancer in the first place that preventing it doesn't justify the risks of routine infant circumcision. Now, after I have been delving into the origins, it seems to me that the data on which the penile cancer prevention argument was based is invalid to begin with. The whole premise of this argument is simply off the base. Vinod

Subj: baby as "stranger"
Date: 12/15/00 7:49:02 AM Pacific Daylight Time
From: sandor.waldman@hyl.org
To: rabbielizabethk-a@yahoo.com
Bcc: zev.marks@hyl.org

Dear Rabbi Elizabeth,

Happy Chanukah, and thanks for the vote of confidence. Now that you mention it, I am studying with a group at my synagogue for an adult bar mitzvah in June.

Re. my idea that the baby is a "stranger" and should be treated with kindness—here's what I mean (and what I think Maimonides means): our bond with the infant, however strong at birth, is incomplete compared to what it will be later. So I think it's perfectly legitimate to think of the baby as a "stranger." It's the best explanation of our capacity to hand him over to be circumcised a week after birth.

Ruminating about all of this, I keep thinking about that famous ethical dilemma known as the "trolley problem," in which most people are confident that they could pull a lever to kill one person on a train track in order to save five on a different train track. But change the circumstances so that, in order to save the five, you'd have to kill the person standing right next to you—well, the vast majority couldn't do it.

I know that in my own case (and I only have a daughter, so I never had to face the decision), I would have found it a lot harder to subject my kid to circumcision when he was five or six than to circumcise him at birth. A six year-old could hold something like that against me.

Best,
Sandy

Subj: ethics
Date: 12/17/00 8:46:02 AM Pacific Standard Time
From: awaldman@botgarden.berkeley.edu
To: sandor.waldman@hyl.org

hi sandy, you know that quote, "what is hateful to you, do not do to someone else." this guy told me that is the most important part of judaism, and all the rest is just comments, did you know that?

Re: ethics
Date: 12/17/00 1:02:08 PM Pacific Standard Time
From: sandor.waldman@hyl.org
To: awaldman@botgarden.berkeley.edu

Good point, sweetheart, the Rabbi Hillel quote. You are so insightful, making that connection. Love, xoxoxox Dad

Re: question, medical procedures
Date: 12/18/00 9:49:38 PM Eastern Standard Time
From: goldfarb@templebethamrochester.org
To: sandor.waldman@hyl.org

Dear Dr. Waldman,

Thank you for writing to me and I'm glad I can clear up some confusion. If babies were dying of *milah*, rest assured, I would have heard about them! The risk of fatal complications is so infinitessimal as to be a non-issue in comparison to the imperative to carry out the *brit milah* commandment.

I assume you're worried about such a remote possibility because you are expecting a son? It is natural to be nervous, but believe me, there are far worse dangers out there! Anxiety is part of becoming a parent, and it settles down after awhile. Parents often have to make decisions for their children that involve temporary pain for a purpose—immunizations, for example.

Let me just reassure you that the Jewish practice of circumcision at eight days is very humane. The baby is too young to understand what is happening to him. Most babies sleep through it, and they certainly have no memory of it afterward. Much better to do it, for the baby's own good, before he has a choice in the matter, and before he has complexity of thought or the ability to experience pain.

Best wishes for a happy Chanukah.

Regards,
Rabbi Goldfarb

P.S. Regarding the Talmudic exemption you mentioned for a third son—we're lucky! Today's *mohelim* (and doctors) are aware of hemophilia and also, they provide much more sanitary conditions than were available back then. Of course as a physician you are probably already aware of this.

Subj: penile cancer, more
Date: 12/19/00 5:19:30 PM Pacific Standard Time
From: vinod.sengupta@hyl.org
To: sandor.waldman@hyl.org

Sandy,

I have been looking into the origin of the penile cancer prevention argument, and it is interesting like a mystery novel. A thriller. I found an article in the 1995 issue of *American Family Physician* which cites several studies that supposedly prove that infant circumcision prevents penile cancer. Here is what I found.

One of those studies is retrospective, and as you know, it goes against epidemiological protocol to draw conclusions from retrospective studies. Another one uses a 1963 textbook article as its basis for claiming that circumcision prevents penile cancer. You have guessed it, I traced the basis for that article back to the 1932 correspondence of Dr. Wolbarst.

It seems that nearly everything regarding this issue traces back to Wolbarst. The 1977 literature review by Persky, the one that claims Jewish are immune from penile cancer, has significant flaws when you dig in his references, which are mostly opinion pieces, textbook articles and retrospective literature reviews. Not research work.

Persky relied heavily on a 1965 literature review by Auster, and so I followed up on the references in the Auster review. It is not surprising to you, most of them could be back traced to Wolbarst.

I think the penile cancer argument does not withstand the most basic epidemiological scrutiny. The whole thing is like a vicious circle.
Vinod

Re: question, medical procedures
Date: 12/20/00 6:58:33 AM Pacific Standard Time
From: sandor.waldman@hyl.org
To: goldfarb@templebethamrochester.org

Dear Rabbi Goldfarb,

Thank you so much for writing back. I am not expecting a son. I am researching *brit milah* because it is an area of interest for me as a person, as a Jew and as a physician.

I'll concede that *brit milah* deaths are most likely rare nowadays, but I assure you, they do happen. Speaking medically—and a lot of Jewish babies are circumcised by doctors, not *mohelim*—circumcision deaths occur every year. Often these fatalities go unreported, due to the fact that they can be attributed to secondary causes—such as septicemia (a systemic blood infection), liver failure, and kidney failure—instead of being linked directly with their actual cause.

Also, frankly, there is an incentive for the botching doctor not to come forward. Nor does the hospital want it advertised that a baby died following a routine elective surgery. I can't imagine it is any different with *mohelim*.

I know that according to Jewish law, every life is of infinite value. Doesn't it follow that every death must be considered an infinite loss? In other words, regardless of how frequently or infrequently circumcision deaths occur, aren't they of concern *from a Jewish perspective?*

Sincerely,
Sandy Waldman

Subj: the pain issue
Date: 12/22/00 9:39:21 AM Pacific Standard Time
From: rabbielizabethk-a@yahoo.com
To: sandor.waldman@hyl.org

Dear Sandy,

I happened to be at a *bris* this morning and was chatting with the *mohel* afterwards about the pain issue. (See, you got me started...) I came back to the office and checked out what he had said, and I thought you might be interested.

The first person to write about the issue of pain during *brit milah* seems to have been Meir Arik of Galacia (1855-1926). In his *Imre Yosher* (II:140), Meir Arik says the early rabbis were aware of anesthetic options, and that their not recommending them suggests that the pain serves a purpose from a Jewish perspective. Talmudic scholars, too, apparently believed the infant should not be numbed during this holy event.

However! Later authorities ruled that pain is not a necessary element of *brit milah*. So there you go. Another example of how Jewish law does shift over time in some respects.

Still no answers over here about trolleys and levers, though...

Happy last-night-of-Chanukah to you and yours, Rabbi E.

P.S. Question: What's another way to say Reform, Conservative and Orthodox? Answer: Lazy, Hazy and Crazy!

Re: question, medical procedures
Date: 12/22/00 10:31:44 AM Eastern Standard Time
From: goldfarb@templebethamrochester.org
To: sandor.waldman@hyl.org

Dr. Waldman,

Are you seriously accusing *mohelim* of botching circumcisions and then covering it up? It is widely known that *mohelim* practice circumcision with more skill than anyone else in the world, doctors included. That is why Queen Elizabeth hired a *mohel* for her sons' circumcisions. I will make every effort here to provide you with some much-needed information.

First of all, are you aware of the nasty history of the anti-circumcision perspective? Greco-Roman culture saw circumcision as a marring of the perfect body, and as an act of hostility against Gentiles. Then in Christian times, Paul proposed that real circumcision was that of the heart. Paul viewed the flesh as the enemy of the spirit, and advocated a kind of metaphorical circumcision to reject sexuality. From a Christian point of view, actual bodily circumcision is evidence of the Jews' alienation from G-d.

Brit milah is the son's birthright, Dr. Waldman. Talmud teaches that Jerusalem fell to the Romans and the Temple was destroyed because the Jews failed to circumcise their sons and thereby broke the covenant. There is a Talmudic saying "But for the blood of the covenant, Heaven and earth would not endure." The Talmud also says, "the commandment of circumcision is so great that it equals all of the other *mitzvos* of the Torah."

A history lesson might help you here. Jews throughout the centuries have made great sacrifices to circumcise their sons; some have *died* for the right. After King Antiochus decreed that Jews must leave their sons uncircumcised, the women who followed the tradition anyway were put to death, as were the babies and other members of the household.

In Soviet Russia, *brit milah* was forbidden. Jews faced immediate layoffs from work, possible criminal charges and a trial, and even jail time. Some parents waited until the baby was up to six months old to do it in secret. And even in modern times—some people circumcised their eight-day-old babies in the trains on the way to the concentration camps.

All that should give even you a sense of how deeply important this ritual is to the Jewish people.

To deprive a Jewish son of the privilege of *brit milah* would condemn him to a life without *shayachut*, without belonging. As my *mohel* friend Jeffrey Solomon says, *brit milah* should be regarded as a "spiritual life insurance policy." Frankly, Dr. Waldman, your thinly veiled attack on *brit milah* under the guise of concern about Jewish law is deeply offensive.

Yours Truly,
Rabbi Goldfarb

CHAPTER SIXTEEN

IT WAS THE FIRST WEEK of January, and Sandy had set aside this Saturday to work at his parents' house. Ruth and Shayna had dealt with most of the furniture. All that was left, Ruth told him, was boxes of handwritten letters and snapshots, his parents' personal papers, some medical texts and other volumes, the classical LP record collection, and his father's clothing.

When Saturday came, Ruth stayed in her chenille bathrobe, sipping her black coffee and absorbing herself in the *New York Times* while George Bush gesticulated idiotically on the silent kitchen TV screen. "You'd have to be bulimic to want to watch that guy," Sandy said.

"Our president-elect?" Ruth didn't look up from the *Book Review*.

"Our president-*select*," Sandy corrected. "Not even inaugurated yet, and already he's given me an eating disorder."

"Huh?"

"I'm saying the only response to him that makes the slightest bit of sense is projectile vomiting."

"So turn it off."

Sandy grabbed the remote control and pressed the Power button, but the television went off and the cable stayed on. "Why can't they make this damned thing easy to use?"

"You have to press the Power button for longer," she murmured.

"No, I mean why are things like this designed to be difficult? I don't want more features. I just want something usable!" Sandy pressed the button on, then off again, longer this time. He glanced over at Ruth as he zipped up his windbreaker. He'd assumed she'd be going over to the house with him. "Sorry I'm a little cranky, Ruthie."

"It's okay." Ruth kept reading.

Much as Sandy had hoped his marriage would start to return to normal now that he'd managed to have sex a couple of times, Ruth clearly hadn't snapped back. Her wine consumption, which had in the past always been minimal, was alarming, though more for the increase in frequency than for any concern he could objectively have about the amount. And she continued not to cook. Evenings were a depressing matter of takeout cartons, scrambled eggs, sandwiches Sandy put together haphazardly for the two of them. They didn't discuss her strike any more than they discussed her pointed lack of response to the e-mails he forwarded her about his research. After eating, while Sandy pored over articles on various aspects of the circumcision controversy in the living room, Ruth would silently read a book or the *New Yorker* in their bedroom. Every night Sandy felt gratitude and relief when Ruth chose to sleep next to him, apparently not having thought of moving into Amy's old room. He wistfully recalled the time a few months ago when Ruth was so worried about his weight loss that she'd prepared special foods for him.

He'd have to start making more of an effort with her. Make love with her again; last longer this time. But, how to shake his creeping awareness that the head of his penis was intended to be an internal organ, that instead it had been forcibly denuded? That what had felt perfectly natural to him all his life suddenly made him squeamish?

He kissed Ruth on top of her head, making sure his cell phone was in his back pocket since he was on call today, and got into the Mercedes. His brooding mood ping-ponged around, looking for a place to land. Though Amy had been reaching out to him lately, he couldn't entirely tamp down his worry that she'd perceived some inconsistency in the way he'd spoken of Dr. Corrador, and the entire father-daughter relationship was going to come crashing down any minute. And work! Things had been going fine patient-wise, but Sandy fretted over Ingersoll and worried that Anne had betrayed him. She'd been his friend for years. She'd been Ruth's gynecologist. Sandy and Ruth had had dinner parties with Anne and her husband on countless occasions. Still, Sandy couldn't imagine Critch having become so disenchanted with him just because of that upstart Ingersoll.

It was insecurity, Sandy told himself, that made him imagine Critch was grooming Ingersoll to take over for him. The Chief wasn't a favorites-player; he was committed to cultivating leadership in the department to ensure a smooth transition when he left. His job was for someone with vision and a proven track record, someone who could team-build, someone well thought-of by his colleagues. After all, ultimately it was colleagues who selected the Chief to serve for a five-year period—a term that was often renewed if everyone was happy with the choice (and that was interruptible mid-term if necessary).

Sandy pulled into his parents' driveway. *Okay, in and out.* He'd be done by this afternoon.

Resolve crumbled the moment he let himself into the front foyer and saw the massive mirror-backed coat rack he'd loved so much as a child. What should be done with it? Neither Ruth nor Shayna liked it, Amy didn't have space for it in her co-op room, and Sandy couldn't fit it in his office. And what about the hallway's awful orange and mustard-yellow still life of flowers, from when Belle had taken up oil painting one summer? Belle had been so proud of that thing. Sandy felt himself sinking into a quicksand of indecision.

Heavily, he trudged up the stairs and went into Shayna's old room, running his hand over a garish acrylic blanket Belle had crocheted years ago that still covered the twin bed. Sandy had never given much thought to *shabbat* observance, but now guilt tugged at him. Why hadn't he arranged not to be on call today, planned a nice relaxing day with Ruth instead, and come over to the house to work tomorrow? He'd fashioned a sabbath for himself that was the antithesis of relaxing or spiritual.

He took off his windbreaker and snapped on a dusty black radio with a broken antenna that flopped around instead of staying wherever he put it. The radio was tuned to KALM, on which the smarmy female announcer was reminding listeners to go online and participate in the KALM Listeners' Top Twenty Pieces poll (as if they actually *aired* more than twenty pieces on this station). "Stay tuned now as we hear from another *B* composer—Beethoven!" the announcer gushed, having no doubt just played a movement from one of Bach's Brandenburgs. "It's the first movement of Symphony Number Five!"

When Sandy was a child, there had been two classical stations, both decent, though his father complained they weren't as good as they used to be. They'd play entire pieces, not just short movements or excerpts. They'd play lesser-known works of great composers instead of sticking to the most insipid or familiar. The ads in those days, while pretentiously presented—an announcer with a mannered British accent talking of fine dining at Katha's India Palace or a concert series on the Berkeley campus—were at least marginally tasteful, not loud or crass or absurdly frequent the way they were on KALM. The stations would give air time to esoteric works, and the announcers were knowledgeable. Sandy and his father would play a guessing game (his father always won, of course): which period was the piece from—baroque, classical, romantic, impressionistic, or contemporary? Then, which composer was it? What type of piece? Specifically which one? Often his father would skip over everything and identify the piece straight away. He could sometimes even guess the performers.

Now classical radio was all about commercial profit. It had nothing to do with responsible stewardship of public airwaves, nothing to do with broadening the horizons of those who wouldn't otherwise have access to classical music.

Sandy switched the radio to NPR and peered into Shayna's closet, which in recent decades had been a repository for Belle's crocheting and sewing supplies as well as wrapping paper and gifts she would amass during the year for special occasions. He glanced at the shelves and at the floor and decided he'd have to come back to this later. Maybe Amy could help.

He opened the filing cabinet next to the bed. His father had been a great organizer of his paperwork. There were meticulously labeled folders with brochures from museum exhibits his parents had gone to, flyers explaining how to become a volunteer for the literacy project through the Berkeley public library, records of his parents' charitable contributions going back decades. Files stuffed with articles about various political candidates, Berkeley Jewish Center swim schedules—these were easy, going immediately into a makeshift recycling pile on the bed. But that barely made a dent. Of course Sandy should keep copies of the articles his father had gotten published in medical journals, but where? And where should he put the original copy of Belle's teaching credential, or the folders jammed with loving letters from her former students?

Belle. Sandy still found it remarkable that she'd wound up in a classroom; she'd always been in a little over her head when it came to the American school experience. He remembered the time his kindergarten teacher had told the children each to bring an apple to school the next day, which was Halloween. Knowing that little Sandor wouldn't eat the whole thing, Belle had quartered a Washington Delicious and put two of the slices in a waxed paper bag, saving the other two for herself and toddler Shayna. When Sandy got to school and compared his lunch with his deskmate's, as they always did, Sandy's apple slices were already brown and a little fuzzy.

"You were spos'ta bring a *whole* apple, dummy!" exclaimed the deskmate, who had an older brother and knew the ropes.

Sandy started to cry, humiliated that the apple slices his mother had given him were such an ugly color. It was only when the teacher rushed over to him with a small green Pippin from her own lunch bag that Sandy learned the reason for her request the previous day: right after the parade, the children were going to bob for apples in a large metal can filled with water. For the first time, Sandy had felt ashamed of his mother, who would surely never understand such wasteful, unsanitary customs.

Sandy got up and went over to the dresser, where a rectangular tin of lavender furniture polish was sitting on top. He opened it, losing himself in associations—his mother in a floral print on a windy day; his violin teacher's strangely yellowed grey hair and orange-ish fingertips. Sandy put the lid back on and opened the top drawer. Inexplicably, a necklace of bright green and blue beads that Shayna had strung for Belle when she was just a teenager brought a lump to his throat. How had the necklace ended up back in Shayna's room instead of with Belle's other jewelry? Had Belle been planning to give it away to someone as a gift? Or had she absent-mindedly taken it off in this room one day and left it there?

This was ridiculous; he had work to do, and he could wind up having to go into the office. He shut the bureau, went back to the filing cabinet and resolutely started going through more folders. When in doubt, he shoved things into the recycling pile, starting another pile when the first one began to tip over. He made his decisions hastily, as if each folder would begin to emit poisonous gas if he handled it for too many seconds. Mission: impossible.

He stopped in his tracks when he got to a folder labeled "Children of Holocaust Survivors." Sandy pushed the piles of recycling toward the wall, turned down the radio, and sat at the edge of the bed. When he opened the folder, a yellowed newspaper clipping and some canceled checks fluttered to the floor.

In the eighties, when it was clear there was adequate interest in a support group for Holocaust survivors' children, Sandy had approached the Berkeley Jewish Center to see whether the idea could be incorporated into their regular programming. His original seed money long gone, he'd been operating the group under BJC's auspices ever since, and Sandy had assumed it was handled as a line item in their budget. Of course he'd always encouraged participants to contribute to the Center to help support the group and other important projects. But it had never dawned on him that earmarked contributions had been coming in anonymously from his parents, from whom he'd taken great pains to hide what he'd started. Sandy shook his head in wonder. The Center's programming director had never breathed a word to him.

Sandy squatted down to pick up the newspaper clipping. It was an article from the *San Francisco Chronicle* in which Sandy had been featured and quoted. "Support groups are beneficial to the next generation of any ethnic group that had been the victim of genocide," read the pull-quote under Sandy's photograph. He gathered the canceled checks off the floor. Each one had "Children of Holocaust Survivors" written on the memo line in his father's perfect European script. It looked like there was a hundred-dollar check for each year.

Sandy put everything back in the file and walked it to the little mahogany table at the top of the stairs, then found himself wandering into the bright, airy master suite. His father had always needed a lot of light—probably from the months of subsistence in that dark cellar—and he'd loved this room, with its perfect view of the Oakland and Berkeley hills and the elegant magnolia, which bloomed twice a year, right outside the window. Sandy sat in the oversized blue armchair and took in the eastern panorama for awhile. Since his father's death, he realized, he'd been haunted by his father's disappointment in him, worried that he'd never fully been forgiven for the cocaine bust and the subsequent hoop-jumping Abraham had done to keep his wayward son at Hopkins. Relief washed over him now.

Sandy got up and went into the walk-in closet and stood amid the suits and expensive silk neckties that weren't his style. On an upper shelf, he could see a brown cashmere cardigan the old man had had since the sixties, wrapped in a clear plastic sweater bag with cedar pellets for moth protection. Sandy reached for it, unzipped the bag, and pulled it out, losing himself in the lush, multi-ply softness. It would be too big for him, of course—his father had been large and barrel-chested—but he tried it on anyway. In the pocket he found a clean white handkerchief. Lucky thing, because Sandy began to weep.

It wasn't so much his father specifically for whom he cried; it was something about the gentility that made men of that age walk around with fastidiously folded handkerchiefs in their sweater pockets. What was taking over was a generation of Ingersolls, men whose social conscience was something to be called attention to, men whose convictions were in place as long as they didn't interfere with golf, whose handwriting wasn't the elegant European kind, but a hurried, self-important scrawl: *fuck you, I haven't got time to explain*. Men who, if they owned a cashmere cardigan, had purchased it because it was expensive, not because it was an item of quality to be enjoyed and cherished over decades. Such a sweater would be given away or lost within a few months without a thought, another one bought in a different color simply because it could be afforded. There would be no handkerchief in it, ever. Sandy wiped his face, put the hankie into his own back pocket with his cell, and kept the sweater on until he was ready to go back to the files.

Many hours and two work-related phone calls later, hungry and exhausted and certainly not finished with the task at hand, Sandy brought the file folder, the sweater, and some books he wanted out to the car, along with the green velvet bag he'd found containing the velvet *kipa* and the wool *tallit* that his father had worn at Amy's bat mitzvah—the set Sandy had wanted to use for his father's *shiva*.

Ruth would grasp the poignancy of all of these things. That was Ruth.

CHAPTER SEVENTEEN

AMY STROKED BUBBA'S messy white hair back from her forehead. "Bubba, can you try some Jell-O? They just want you to eat. So you can keep up your strength."

"I can't." Bubba was whining like a little girl. She reached up and started pulling at the tube in her nose.

"Okay. Okay." Amy grabbed her hand and gently put it back to her side. "Don't get all upset. We can try again later." Amy swivelled the food tray away from the bed. She should ask the nurse who she should talk to in the kitchen about food donation, for leftover wrapped foods like bread slices and squares of butter that should be sent to shelters.

Bubba had emphysema and was in the skilled nursing place. It didn't seem like she knew Zayda was dead, but she did seem extra sad, plus confused. Maybe she thought she was still sad about her first daughter dying in the war. An old student of hers had stopped by earlier, and she told Amy that Bubba seemed like she was depressed.

"I brought you some new yarn," Amy said. She pulled four super-bright acrylic yarns out of a white plastic bag and put them gently on Bubba's tiny stomach. The orange one was the exact same color as the Jell-O. There was also a bright yellow, a bright green, and a purple. They were butt-ugly. Amy chose them because she knew Bubba would like them.

Plus, the yarns were so fake, they were practically shiny. Shayna would of said, "pure petroleum," because that was what Shayna always said about acrylic stuff, or polyester. "Save a trip to the gas pump." Bubba and Zayda's whole house was filled with stuff Bubba had crocheted, like pillow covers, blankets, and pot-holders. They were all hot pink and bright yellow, colors like that. It was weird, because the whole reason Bubba used acrylic was, "Vool iss too expenseev. End you ken't vash it." But all the stuff she crocheted, she never washed anyway.

"Beaut-ee-ful," Bubba said. She petted the yarns like they were a cat or something. "Beaut-ee-ful, d'you know?" Then she looked up at Amy and started talking Yiddish. She was crying a little. "*Shayna punim, shayna maydeleh.*" Amy had heard it like a million times. Beautiful face, beautiful girl. "Beautiful" was what Shayna's name meant.

The purple yarn fell on the floor and rolled under the table next to the bed. Bubba grabbed Amy's hand so hard that it hurt. "You're zee best nurse off all off zem."

"Thanks, Bubba." She got her hand out by putting her other hand over Bubba's. Her idea was, crocheting would keep Bubba's hands busy and she'd stop fucking with her nose tube. "Bubba, do you want to make something with the yarn?"

"You start eet for me." Bubba lay back on the pillow. "My ars-a-ritis."

"Sure. Okay." Amy picked up the purple yarn and sat down again. The vinyl made a "Sssss" sound as her butt settled on it.

She looked through the bag, grabbed the crochet hook and tried to start on the purple, but then she couldn't remember how to do the first stitch. She forgot what Shayna had taught her. She made a loop. She tried to make another with it. "How do you do this again, Bubba? I forget."

Bubba sighed. Her eyes were closed like she was sleep-walking, only this was sleep-talking. "I tell you about my cheel-dren. Leetle Sandor alvays reminds me off my daughter, d'you know?"

Amy knew Bubba was talking about her first daughter. "Sandy reminded you of Klari?"

"So senziteev. He cried all zee time as a baby. My husband, he couldn't stand zee sound, d'you know? I had to hold zee baby, all off zee time. D'you know, he looked just like Klari, until zee blond curls vent avay."

"Sandy was blonde when he was little?"

"Now, he grew up. He ees a doctor. He made a group for younk people like heemself, d'you know? He vants to talk to ozzer younk people about zeir parents surviving zee var."

Amy put the crochet hook and purple yarn back in the white plastic bag. This was the kind of crap Sandy was such a retard about, warning Amy all the time to not say anything about his kids of Holocaust survivors group in front of her grandparents, like it was some big secret.

"He got into zee trouble."

"Wait, Sandy got into trouble?" Yeah, right. He probably got an A-minus in one of his classes. "What kind of trouble?"

"Leetle Sandor. Zee blond curls vent avay. Hees hair grew dark, so dark." Bubba began to cry. "Klari never grew dark. She vas fair. She died. I vas holding her, end she died."

"I'm sorry, Bubba." She reached out to rub Bubba's hand.

"Such feelth ve lived in, viz rats," she cried. "Such cold. She stupped her toe and it vas bleedink, and then she got seek. An infection. Ve should take her to ze hospital, d'you know?"

"You couldn't risk it," Amy said.

"I veel inzist!" Bubba started thrashing around, pulling at the nose tube. "Ve take her in!"

"Bubba, you couldn't." Amy said it firmly, like Shayna would. She took Bubba's hands and held them, and forced Bubba to look at her. "You had fake papers. You were in danger."

"I tried to save her! I begged my husband, d'you know? He vouldn't change his mind. He vasn't a doctor, yet. And ve didn't have ze medicine. Eet vas too risky, he said."

"He was right, Bubba. They could of killed all of you."

"I vish zey had."

"Bubba, don't say that. Then, you wouldn't of come to this country and, like, tasted freedom or whatever. You wouldn't of had Sandy, and Shayna."

Bubba sighed and twisted her body away from Amy. "Sree cheeldren I had, d'you know, and only von grandchild. Can you imagine?"

Amy wasn't really surprised that Bubba didn't think of Shayna's stepsons as grandchildren.

"A beaut-ee-ful baby." She turned back toward her.

"Baby—?"

"Sandor and his vife. Vat's her name?"

"Ruth."

"Rute, yes. Lovely voman. They got a beaut-ee-ful baby, d'you know?"

"Bubba?"

"Ze pregnant girl, her own mozzer didn't vant ze baby, ken you imagine? Alc-a-hol, I sink. Too much alc-a-hol." Her eyes were closed again.

Amy already knew about Brenda's mom being a total drunk, but she didn't know anything about Sandy being in trouble, ever. "Belle, you said Sandor got into trouble. What trouble was it?"

Bubba didn't open her eyes. Instead, she sighed. "My husband died, d'you know?"

Amy was surprised. "I know, Bubba. It's really sad."

Bubba didn't seem to hear her, like maybe she was going back out of reality. "Vee are so vorried he might not feenish his train-ink. Eef he goes to jail. My husband ees too hard on him, d'you know?"

"Jail?" Amy tried not to breathe too loudly. "Wait. Belle. Are you talking about Sandor? Did Sandor go to jail? When he was in medical school? He got kicked out?"

"Zee blond curls vent avay." Bubba looked up at the ceiling, like she was trying to remember.

"Belle! Did Sandor get kicked out of medical school and go to jail?"

"No more drugs!"

"Belle, are you talking about Sandor? Did Sandor take drugs? And Zayda got all mad at him?"

"Drugs, nowadays people get meexed up vis drugs."

"But is that why Sandor got in trouble? Because of drugs?"

Bubba was all alarmed. Her eyes were wild. "Drugs! Zey von't let me out, d'you know? Zey keep me here. Zey force me viz drugs."

This was totally annoying. "It's okay, Bubba, I won't let them." Amy touched Bubba's arm. It was thin and rough, like the skin was made of that coarse kind of colored paper that felt like it was giving you splinters when you moved your hand across it. Construction paper.

"My husband—he died, now." Bubba sighed slowly and closed her eyes just as the door was opening. It was Shayna.

"Hello, Mama. Hi, Ame. I brought your perfume," she said to Bubba.

Bubba lifted her head up suspiciously. A clump of white hair jutted out toward the pillow. "How do you know vich perfume I like?"

"You told me," Shayna said, all patient. She was reaching into her purse. The purse was so big it looked more like an overnight bag. "L'Air Du Temps."

"L'Air Du Temps," Bubba nodded. "I need a leetle shpritz, d'you know?"

Shayna pulled the bottle back out and took off the cap, and then sprayed a tiny bit on Bubba's arm. She made this "pshhh" sound with her mouth. "See? Doesn't it smell good?"

Bubba nodded and closed her eyes.

Shayna sat down at the far end of the bed. "This place is hideous."

Amy was staring out the window. She must of not understood Bubba. Bubba was pretty fucked up right now. Even though, saying her husband was dead meant at least she was kind of aware of stuff.

"Reminds me of Oscar Wilde's last words," Shayna was saying. "He's lying in his hospital bed, right? And he looks around? And he says, 'Either this wallpaper goes, or I do.'" She laughed really loudly.

"Whatever," Amy said.

Amy and Shayna went down the hall and sat on a bench next to the elevator. Shayna pulled her makeup bag out of her purse and looked in a little mirror that was part of a compact.

"Shayna, did Sandy get kicked out of medical school?"

"Jeez, what a mess." Shayna patted makeup onto her nose and forehead. "Why didn't you tell me how closely I resemble a corpse?"

"Shayna!"

Shayna looked at Amy, and looked back in the little mirror. "He didn't get kicked out, no."

"But what, he got busted?"

Shayna's makeup compact hung in the air, open, like her jaw.

"Was he in jail, Shayna?"

"Of *course* not," Shayna said, turning toward her. She was using her thumb to make sure the powder puff thing didn't fall out. "Amy, sweetie, there are a lot of pressures in medical school, and—"

"He is so full of shit!" Amy didn't care any more about the cool stuff Sandy was doing, going against the circumcision thing. He was back to being a complete tool.

"Amy, come on, that's overly dramatic. And anyway, it's not my place to—you should have this conversation with Sandy."

Amy felt like grabbing the compact out of Shayna's hand and chucking it across the hallway.

"Look," Shayna sighed. She quietly zipped the compact into her makeup bag, then put the bag into her purse. "He got busted for pot. It was a wrong-place-at-the-wrong-time kind of thing."

"You better tell me what happened to him, Shayna."

"Nothing! He wound up with just a slap on the wrist. Had to do community service, I think, and that was it. Frankly, I think the worst part for him was that your zayda had to pull some strings so Sandy could stay in medical school. Called in a favor in the medical community, or something. Amy, please don't judge your father. It's ancient history."

This whole thing was so pathetic that for a second, Amy actually felt bored. Bubba's nurse was passing by, and Amy thought about how she should ask her about the wrapped leftover food.

"Hey," Shayna said, "you never told me what was in that letter from Mick."

"Why?" Amy stared at her meanly. "You want something to blab about to Sandy and Ruth, so they can know secret stuff about me? When I don't know secret stuff about them?"

"Amy, come on. I haven't talked to them about that letter. You asked me not to. So what'd it say?"

Amy still hadn't opened the letter. Shayna probably wanted to make some stupid connection that wasn't even there, between Mick the coke-head prisoner, and Sandy the moron getting busted in medical school. And then, for some random reason, Amy suddenly got the Oscar Wilde joke. She started laughing, and she couldn't stop.

"Are you OK?"

Amy was folded in half with laughter. She heard the squeak of the nurse's shoes way down the hall. Shayna kept asking her, "What's so funny? What'd the letter say?"

CHAPTER EIGHTEEN

JEREMIAH TRAUB SEEMED TOO young to be a cantor, let alone teach a class of grown men and women studying for their adult bar and bat mitzvah ceremonies. But then, Sandy had this sense more and more with each passing year. When he did teaching rounds at the hospital, he was alarmed by the residents' resemblance to teenagers: some even had acne. And when he passed women waiting in the pediatric wing as he made his way to the snack machines, it was never their infants or toddlers who struck him as childish; it was the mothers themselves. They didn't look that much older than Amy.

But if the cantor seemed inordinately young for his position, there was also something ancient about him, archetypal. He was like an old-fashioned *yeshiva bocher*, the sort of studious, disheveled person whose most serious adolescent rebellion might have been to help himself secretly to a little extra ice cream after dinner, washing the bowl and spoon off quietly afterward so as not to be heard by his parents watching *Jeopardy!* in the living room. Cantor Traub exuded an earnestness that was almost off-putting, even as it was reassuring.

Sandy shifted on the child-sized vinyl chair and looked at his watch. Cantor Traub was supposed to meet briefly with Sandy to give him the study materials and explain what he'd missed so far. The cantor had no office at the moment—the old cantor's office had been under renovation since Cantor Traub had been formally hired a few months ago—and he'd asked Sandy to wait for him in the one cheery, primary color-decorated temple classroom that was not in use by the after-school program this evening.

During the day, the room was used by the preschool, and it was easy to imagine runny-nosed little boys and girls doing finger painting, singing songs in a circle on the floor, being told to use their words instead of hitting. That latter lesson made Sandy smile as he thought of the time two year-old Amy had been in an agitated state, crying at the dinner table, and Ruth had tried to calm her down by urging her to explain her feelings. "Use your words, Amy," Ruth coaxed.

Amy swallowed. "I am crying," she explained.

The pleasure of that incident washed over Sandy once again. He and Ruth had gotten so many laughs out of it and similar episodes. They'd lie in bed and retell one adorable Amy story after another, holding each other and talking in shameless self-satisfaction, as if they were the only parents in the world equipped to appreciate such charm.

Sandy looked around the room. When Amy had attended the preschool, it had been held in a depressing space in the basement, with dark old carpeting and poor access to the outdoor playground. Sandy was glad he and Ruth had made a donation to help ensure that the new wing could be built over the summer when Amy was entering kindergarten, even though she'd never had the benefit of using it. This kind of improvement helped bring young families in.

In one of his e-mails, Cantor Traub had recommended that Sandy start going to services on Friday nights as part of his training. Last Friday, wishing Ruth were by his side, Sandy had attended, chanting *kaddish* for his father and taking special interest, because of Amy, in that one part of the service that urged, "What is hateful to you, do not do to your fellow person."

The service he'd attended hadn't made Sandy warm to Rabbi Weinstein, but Sandy did respond to the inviting voice and attitude of the young cantor. For someone who seemed ineffectual on first glance, Cantor Traub had a surprisingly authoritative singing voice, yet an unpretentious, inclusive way about him on the *bimah* that was worlds apart from the cold soloism of the old cantor. Instead of feeling as if he needed to keep still during services, Sandy had found himself swaying back and forth to the music, sometimes clapping his hands with others in the congregation. Cantor Traub used a guitar, and Sandy had overheard a young couple talk after the service about how the cantor had amused both the preschoolers and the preschool staff with his Groucho Marx imitation during the toddlers' lunchtime that day. Of course, neither the preschoolers nor the staff nor, indeed, many of the parents, were old enough to know it was a Groucho Marx impression. It made Sandy respect Cantor Traub more to imagine him deriving inspiration from old black-and-white classics.

Now, finally, Cantor Traub burst into the classroom where Sandy was waiting, holding a binder, a prayer book, a stack of photocopied materials, and a few cassette tapes, and what looked like a deck of flash cards. With his white shirt slightly untucked and his hair a little wild, he almost looked like Groucho. Sandy stood up. "I'm Sandy."

"You're Amy Waldman's father," Cantor Traub announced with a grin, dumping the materials on the low table and pulling up another tiny chair.

"Uh—yes." Sandy was delighted to be known as Amy's father. It used to happen all the time when she was younger.

The cantor sat down. "You know, I didn't make the connection until this afternoon when I was photocopying these materials for you."

"How do you know Amy?"

"She's the one who helps me with the new food distribution program here."

"Food distribution program," Sandy repeated.

"There's food that goes to waste after *simcha*s. We couldn't distribute those leftovers without a responsible driver. And Amy's been such a help with the new synagogue garden—she's made some great recommendations for water-saving plants. You must be so proud of her, Sandy. I work with a lot of young people, not just in bar and bat mitzvah training, but with the teen group. Amy's one of the most focused, committed people I've met."

Sandy thought Cantor Traub seemed a little over-involved in how focused and committed Amy was. There were strict guidelines about relationships between clergy and congregants, especially young ones. But then, Amy wasn't that young any more, and besides, Sandy realized, technically, she wasn't a congregant, hadn't even attended services with them on the High Holidays this last fall. She was the adult daughter of congregants with whom she didn't share an address.

"So you work with all the bar and bat mitzvah kids?" Sandy asked.

"Yeah, there are like fifty this year. The congregation has really grown under Rabbi Weinstein. He's brought a lot of young families in, with the help of the preschool." The cantor began handing materials to Sandy, leaning forward in the chair. "So I've photocopied everything you need to get started. Use these flash cards to learn the *aleph-bet*. When you're comfortable with that, you can start reading the words that comprise each of the blessings and prayers."

"What are those cassettes?"

"Oh. I've taped the blessings you'll need to learn for the Torah service. There are special prayers to be said before the weekly reading of the Torah, and after, within the main service. Then there are the *Haftorah* blessings—again, before and after. There's a melody for each one that you'll have to learn. You won't be able to do it without the tapes."

Sandy swallowed. Somehow he'd made the assumption that singing what was essentially a solo in front of the whole congregation was a humiliation reserved for Jewish children—not an indignity foisted on squeamish adults with years of complacency under their belts. "I thought I was just going to be reading from the Hebrew," he whined.

The cantor gave a disconcerting little whoop of a laugh. "You'll be chanting, Sandy."

"But I thought that was only during the actual Torah reading."

"All the blessings and prayers have melodies. Some of them are probably thousands of years old."

"I—I'm not very musically talented. I mean, as a listener, I love music—"

"Don't worry," the cantor reassured him. "Some really amazing bar and bat mitzvah ceremonies are led by kids who aren't musically inclined. Anyway, this second tape has the specific lines you'll be chanting within Korach—that's the name of the Torah portion for your group's bar and bat mitzvah service." The cantor looked at him and gave that little laugh again. "Trust me, Sandy—by the time the service rolls around in June, you'll be a pro."

Sandy figured he could always take the materials and then e-mail Cantor Traub to tell him he'd changed his mind.

"So Amy says you're on this anti-circumcision campaign," the cantor said.

"Amy mentioned that to you?"

"She says you've been doing some really interesting research on the topic. You want to tell me about it?"

Tentatively at first, Sandy gave the cantor a brief rundown of the issues he'd explored thus far.

"So this week," Sandy concluded, "I've been ruminating about the whole issue of faith."

"Faith?"

"Well, just that circumcision is supposed to be done as a sign of religious belief. But there are so few Jews who do it for that reason any more."

"Hmm." The cantor paused. "You know, Sandy, in Judaism, doing good things is more important than having faith. You work actively toward *tikkun olam* by fulfilling the *mitzvot*."

Sandy still had trouble thinking of circumcision as a good deed, though he could now adopt that perspective as necessary to frame his arguments Jewishly. "But what about all the young Jewish couples who fulfill this *mitzvah* just to throw a big party, to please their parents or impress their friends?" he pointed out. "Or because of the aesthetics of circumcision?"

"Well, it's not for us to judge that couple's sincerity," the cantor explained. "That's between them and God."

"Come on, Cantor, doesn't Judaism demand a certain level of commitment to its ideals?" Sandy felt ridiculous, suddenly, sitting at the kiddie table discussing Jewish ethics with an old soul in the body of a young man.

"It's true that in Judaism, you're supposed to perform any *mitzvah* with sincerity."

"Exactly! Otherwise, what would be the point?"

Cantor Traub tugged at his scraggly beard. "Well, you're right in the sense that *halacha*—Jewish law—literally means 'the way.' There's a lot of discussion about how making the *way* into an *end* is a mistake."

"Right. That's what I'm saying."

"You know, when I was in cantorial school, I heard this lecture by a Jewish scholar, and his big thing was condemning the blind following of ritual. I remember he quoted some Chassidic rabbi, Menachem Mendl of Kotzk, I think it was—something about how sometimes, a *mitzvah* can become idol worship."

"Exactly," Sandy said excitedly. "You really understand what I'm—"

"The thing is, though, Sandy, a person may not have spiritual intent at the time he does a *mitzvah*, but even without it, he should still do the commandment."

"But why?"

"Okay. Let's say there's some fat real estate developer, and he donates money to a homeless shelter. And the only reason he does that is that he thinks it will make him look good, or that he'll get something in return. Well, that's OK in the eyes of Judaism. Because he's still feeding the hungry."

Sandy groaned.

"The idea is, sometimes the intent follows after the *mitzvah* is done."

"The spiritual cart before the horse."

"I guess so, if you want to see it that way." The cantor paused. "Sandy, listen, I can tell you're not sold on this bar mitzvah deal."

"It's a little intimidating," Sandy admitted.

"I just have to tell you—you're going to love Korach. Your Torah portion."

"Why?"

"Because in a way, Korach asks whether there are situations in which God wants us to look into *ourselves* and ask whether something is right."

"Well—"

"There's a sense that when we go to bat for the values that are at the heart of Jewish ethics, God may actually approve of our stubbornness," Cantor Traub added. "Even if we do it at the expense of established practice."

CHAPTER NINETEEN

ON FRIDAY, AFTER SHE'D taught her first morning seminar of the new quarter and then dropped by briefly to see Belle, Ruth was ready for some time alone. Lately, interactions with people left her feeling drained. She found it hard to imagine how she'd kept up a social life all these years, throwing dinner parties and attending them, chatting affably with strangers on planes, keeping up with her literary agent Honora as to how her aging Lakeland terrier was doing. Ruth kept thinking about the chaotic intersecting networks of people of which she'd ever been a part. The exercise exhausted her, the way it's exhausting to go through last night's garbage, looking for a missing fork amid the coffee grounds and worn-out Rescue pad and olive pits and soiled napkins. Elementary school; her neighborhood growing up; a classmate with Tourette's. Sisterhood at the Temple. Neighbors. Amy's friends and their families and step-families and cats and neighbors. Ellen's friends. Nadine's. Shayna's. Her own. College dorm life. Graduate school. The adoption support group. Colleagues. Sandy's colleagues; the families she and Sandy met when Amy was in preschool; the medical staff on Belle's floor; the guys at the Volvo service shop. Russell. Josh. Sandy. Oliver. It all made Ruth long for order.

Belle had been especially agitated today, going on about some phone call Abraham had made to keep Sandy from getting kicked out of medical school, and how Abraham had come down hard on Sandy about the whole thing, too hard. Why hadn't Sandy ever mentioned anything about his father's having had to lobby to keep him at Hopkins after the pot bust? He claimed to be all about honesty and openness, but the truth was, Sandy was like anyone else, secretive about whatever might trigger his shame. And his shame always seemed to be about the wrong things.

Food, Ruth thought as she hesitated in the entryway of Till's Market on the way to her car. Till's carried a wide variety of organic produce which, while overpriced, was some of the best around. Maybe she'd wander in for a few minutes.

It was unnatural, not cooking. Where else in her life did she have such an outlet? The yard? Hardly. That was Amy's domain. Compost heap notwithstanding, Ruth didn't really know what she was doing outdoors. She enjoyed her sometime herb garden, but that was all in service of a larger purpose. Ruth was not a flower gardener. She was pragmatic to the bone. Her teaching? Somewhat, though it didn't offer the concrete satisfaction of food. Her consulting? Fun, but not all that creative. Her writing? That, too, was a means to an end. She didn't mind pulling out her spiral-bound notebook, its cover stained with the red and brown residues of long-forgotten concoctions, to jot down notes at the kitchen table. But when she had to sit down at her laptop and craft introductions to each section, or explain in plain English how to do what she herself did without thinking, like staggering the different vegetables that are added to a stew so that the delicate ones don't get overcooked—that took effort. It certainly wasn't something she'd do if she didn't have to.

"Mrs. Waldman!" the butcher exclaimed from behind the counter. "Haven't seen you around here for awhile."

Ruth managed a warm smile. The butcher always gave her special cuts. She'd even thanked him in the Acknowledgments section of two of her books.

"How's the book?"

"Done. Being printed even as we speak."

The butcher grinned. He had the kind of inviting, fat face in which it was easy to see an eight year-old boy who was constantly being kissed by his mother, grandmother, and whatever other female Italian relatives happened to be around. "So when's it coming out?"

"Early to mid-May, I think. I'll bring you a copy. I'll sign it for you."

He gave her a nod, glancing sideways, taking in another woman who had edged toward the meat counter just after Ruth got there. "So what can I do for you today, Mrs. Waldman? An organic chicken?"

Ruth asked him for a pound of grass-fed, organic stew meat, then milled around the store. She selected a head of fresh garlic and some carrots, potatoes and onions for the stew; some sweet frozen peas to put in at the very end: the kind of basic staples it was easy to take for granted if you cooked often. Then she put some flour, eggs, oil and yeast in her cart, and found a bottle of Cabernet that could flavor the stew but wouldn't be bad to drink, either.

One of her neighbors was in line at the checkout stand, and Ruth took a detour to the sanitary products aisle. After all these years, tampons still gave her a tiny thrill. Nadine had kept tampons in the house, but only for herself, telling Ruth and Ellen they were for real women, not girls. Girls got bulky, uncomfortable Kotex pads. Ruth put the tampons into her cart, then pulled out her cell and put it to her ear, engaged in an imaginary call in case her neighbor got the idea of approaching her.

After checking out, Ruth got into the Volvo and drove for awhile before realizing what she was doing: making the turn toward the rambling brown-shingle on the south side of campus that had belonged to Belle and Abraham since the late fifties. She pulled into the driveway and sat for a few seconds, ruminating with the car still on. The last time she and Shayna had been over, Shayna had taken the silver tea set, Ruth the good China. Suddenly the idea of using the dishes for Passover in a couple of months seemed distant, implausible.

Ruth cut the motor and lit a cigarette. She'd been here so many times over these past four months since Abraham's death that she'd begun to feel intimate with the house, even in its nearly vacant state. Or maybe it was just that Ruth had always relied on her in-laws for a certain kind of orientation, and the house had become the stand-in. Suddenly, sitting in the car, Ruth was flooded with grief. In his crusty, limited way, her father-in-law had loved her, too. He'd called her *Ruti*, sometimes even *Ruteleh*.

Ruth sat in the car, visualizing what was inside: the cheerless floral wallpaper, the oppressive plain dark wood. Other than musty old furniture and piles of items that she and Shayna had already sorted through, the house had been largely stripped of its former personality, reduced to piles of giveaway, recycling and garbage; yet there was a residual, palimpsestic Waldman-ness. What a contrast to the shocking sterility of Nadine's condo in Rogers Park, which she and Ellen had seen for the first time when they'd gone to pack up the place. Nadine had a compulsion to "buy up" every few years, and had moved into that high-rise, for its view of Lake Michigan, within six months of her death. Sandy's parents' place, on the other hand, had housed her in-laws for so many years that even in their permanent absence, it seemed incontrovertibly theirs.

Ruth loved older homes, though she'd never been able to figure out why the gloomy paneling that characterized Craftsman architecture was unthinkingly equated with good taste. She suddenly imagined herself sneaking in to paint the cabinets in oil-based eggshell and to put black wrought-iron pulls on them. Probably Shayna would thank her; the house would almost certainly sell better if it had a livelier, more inviting feel to it. But no one dared paint plain hardwood that was in beautiful condition; it was as if that would be immoral.

She put out her cigarette, pulled the keys out of the ignition, picked up the grocery bag, and let herself into the house, greeted by a nasty stench that got worse as she headed toward the kitchen. Passing the hall coat rack, then making a quick detour into the little bathroom to jiggle the handle of the leaky toilet, she put her keys, purse and groceries on the yellow Formica and chrome table in the kitchen, opened the refrigerator and tried not to gag. A few weeks ago, she'd stashed half a burrito in there when she'd come over to do some organizing. The beans in the forgotten lunch must have gone bad since last weekend.

After putting the rotten food down the garbage disposal, Ruth opened the two kitchen windows and, for cross-ventilation, the back door. She washed her hands, then sat down heavily at the kitchen table and rifled through her purse for her cigarettes again. She thought of Oliver, who'd called her twice in the last week, saying he'd missed talking to her over the holidays. It was alarming how often she thought of seeing him, but she couldn't figure out how to make that happen safely. She wondered when "safely" had started to mean without-being-found-out, as opposed to without-giving-Oliver-undue-encouragement.

As Ruth lit a cigarette and took a puff, using a stray glass coaster as an ashtray, an absurd idea presented itself: what if Oliver visited her here? *It's not as if Sandy is going to show up unannounced*, she thought. It was only after a moment that *Are you crazy? In your in-laws' house?* kicked in.

She took another puff. She was up to half a pack a day, and Sandy still hadn't commented, or perhaps even noticed. Granted, Ruth usually smoked outdoors, and Sandy hadn't exactly kissed her lately. He kept his distance, as did she, so she supposed it was possible he hadn't detected anything, though that seemed unlikely for someone as fastidious as Sandy. Smokers stank; everyone knew that, with the possible exception of the French. Could Sandy really be that self-absorbed, that oblivious? Amy would certainly think so.

Ruth knew it wasn't the answer, contact with Oliver. It was a childish notion, like making a meal out of a Snickers bar. On the other hand, if you were starving, you'd be hard pressed to refuse the Snickers, let alone denounce it.

Ruth wasn't normally one to second-guess herself, but she couldn't help looking back now to see whether maybe there had been ominous signs of Sandy's selfishness even before the ectopic pregnancy. Some character flaw whose likelihood of becoming a character canyon would have been perfectly apparent if only she'd been more tuned in to the warnings—if only she hadn't been so overcome with gratitude to Sandy for some kind of perceived normalcy that she'd overlooked what was right in front of her.

Sandy seemed to think his big crime was withholding sex after the ectopic. But there was more to it than that. He'd robbed her of her privacy by relentlessly talking to his colleagues afterward, sharing every detail like a teenaged boy describing some astonishing conquest of a teacher or an older cousin. Ruth had fainted in the kitchen; that was why he'd brought her to the ER; the Fallopian tube had probably gotten blocked as a result of the emergency appendectomy Ruth had had as a teenager; she'd had vaginal bleeding for days but hadn't thought much of it. Why was this anyone's business? It wasn't as if Sandy were picking co-workers' brains for information in their field of expertise. He should have limited such sharing to conversations with Zev, or Shayna.

Ruth took a long puff, reliving the ectopic. Her menstrual cycle had always been somewhat unpredictable (another thing for which Nadine had mocked her), so Ruth hadn't even realized she was two months along, hadn't allowed herself to hope she was pregnant after nearly two years of trying. But after a week of irregular bleeding and pelvic tenderness which she'd mentioned to Sandy, reluctantly, only because it was making sex painful, she began to experience dizziness and intense pain in her left shoulder while preparing a late dinner. That was the last thing she remembered before Sandy was guiding her into the car.

At the ER, the on-call physician, whom Sandy didn't know, suspected "an ectopic." *An ectopic*—they were on a first-name basis already. Sandy had insisted on phoning Anne Padway at home and asking her to come in. He didn't want some amateur making the diagnosis or proposing the treatment.

Twenty minutes later, Anne had confirmed the ectopic. Ruth's shoulder pain indicated that she'd already bled substantially into the peritoneal cavity, and that she needed an emergency laparotomy to remove the embryo and control the bleeding. So, without having even had time to contemplate the pregnancy, Ruth was now facing major surgery. In her tight-lipped agony, she had just wanted Sandy to hold her, comfort her, or at least smooth things along somehow with medical savvy. Instead, he paced the room, berating himself for not having picked up the clues days ago. Then he slipped into irrationality, cursing that there wasn't any way with current technology to remove the embryo from the tube and implant it into the uterus—apparently having failed to absorb the fact that the embryo was already dead.

Anne had been reassuring after the surgery. In similar situations in the past, obstetricians generally removed the entire Fallopian tube, but during Ruth's procedure, Anne had managed to salvage the tube for future pregnancy, as was now becoming standard practice whenever possible. Ruth needed to realize, though, that once a woman had had an ectopic, she had a somewhat elevated risk of having another one, in addition to an increased danger of infection. About a third of ectopic pregnancy patients experienced difficulty in getting pregnant again, and those who did become pregnant had to be monitored carefully.

Sandy was kind and solicitous when they got home, and for the first few days of her recovery, Ruth gave him the benefit of the doubt. He was trying to protect her by not hugging her or holding her close. He knew her incisions hurt, and he was busy keeping a chart of her pain medication and antibiotics and bringing her reading material and herbal tea. The reason he wanted her to change her own bandages was that she was in a better position than he was to know what would hurt and how tightly the bandage should be put on. Gradually, Ruth came to understand that there was something off-putting to Sandy about her wounds, something that for him was irreconcilable with sexual contact or even physical affection.

But weeks later, with the bandages retired and the wounds healing nicely, Sandy still didn't return to his role as sexual initiator. Ruth flirted, coaxed, confronted. Sandy said he was worried about impregnating her prematurely; Anne had recommended—didn't Ruth remember?—that they wait a few cycles before trying to conceive again. Ruth pointed out that they could go back to the diaphragm and spermicide jelly method they'd used before they'd started trying to have a child. Sandy said he didn't like the idea of Ruth putting chemical substances into her body when she was still healing and was more susceptible than usual to infection. Ruth suggested condoms. Sandy refused, invoking the old saying about how using a rubber was like taking a shower with a raincoat on.

Showers, in fact, became Sandy's nightly ritual, enabling him to avoid going to bed at the same time as his wife. Ruth bought condoms and left them out on Sandy's side of the bed. Her cycle came and went, and came and went again. One night, discovering that her third period had started, she went into the bathroom to get a tampon while Sandy was in the shower, and heard him panting. Concerned, she drew the shower curtain.

"What are you doing!" she exclaimed ridiculously.

His hands went up suddenly as if in self-protection from an oncoming blow. "I just—I—"

"*This* is what your showers are all about?"

He didn't say anything, just stood there open-mouthed with the water running, his penis limp now.

Ruth threw him a towel. "Dry off. We're going to talk." It was Sandy's misfortune to have pissed her off on day one of her cycle.

The ensuing conversation didn't change anything, other than that it enabled Ruth to vent, a mortified Sandy to apologize (unlike Ruth's first husband, Russell, who had tried to make it seem as if Ruth were to blame for his habit, at least Sandy was contrite). Ruth cried, Sandy held her, and it solved nothing. But luckily, they had a follow-up appointment two days later with Anne, who wanted to know whether they'd been trying to conceive again. Sandy became flustered, blurted out something about not being sure Ruth was fully healed yet. Not wanting to call attention to Sandy's obvious squeamishness, Anne recommended quietly that they start again as soon as they could. When it came to fertility problems, time was of the essence.

Anne had shamed Sandy into it, but Ruth didn't care. He made love to her that night, and the next night, and two nights after that, and soon Ruth forgot about the deprivation and just enjoyed the return of sex into her life.

A year later, Ruth still hadn't conceived, and agreed to Anne's suggestion that they give in-vitro fertilization a go. Sadly, two IVFs failed to take, and the third ended in miscarriage. Two days after the miscarriage, while Ruth was still bleeding—before she'd begun to mourn the loss—Sandy had put the word out among his colleagues that they were looking to adopt. That was a bit faster than Ruth would have liked.

But it had all worked out, hadn't it, when they'd gotten their precious Amy? Ruth stubbed out her cigarette. Yes, until now, she and Sandy had been pretty much in sync since their daughter had come into their lives. They'd wanted another child with the forced casualness of people who couldn't bear being disappointed, so that when none came up for the next six years or so within Sandy's network, neither of them really minded giving up on the idea. Amy was perfect. They were totally, utterly in love with her; their sadness was behind them.

Ruth got up and started rummaging around for the trash bags and Lysol spray she and Shayna had bought, and paper towels, of which there were none. She grabbed a kitchen towel.

The fridge was full of condiments, some, it seemed, dating from the 1970s. She and Shayna hadn't even thought about cleaning it out. Urgently now, as if creating order and space in this one small enclosure might offer her some relief, Ruth set to work. She chucked a jar of encrusted Gulden's mustard, a half-eaten jar of pickles, and an empty sauerkraut jar into the garbage. *Aged* cheese, she mused, tossing a moldy piece of Jarlsberg in. *Pickled* herring. Strawberry *preserves*. What was the word for the nearly unrecognizable lemon at the bottom of the vegetable bin? Penicillin, she supposed. And the half-dozen opened, barely used jars of pink horseradish from as many Passovers? The History of Our People.

The more Ruth threw out, the better she felt. Amy would have been appalled: Ruth didn't even bother to recycle the food jars. She also threw in two of Belle's crocheted potholders, charred along the edges and filthy beyond salvation, that were hanging on a magnetized hook on the side of the fridge.

Ruth worked until there was nothing left, surprised that the contents of one small, basically empty fridge could fill a large trash bag. She grabbed the towel and the spray disinfectant and set about making the refrigerator shelves look clean and inviting. Afterward, she thought of opening the bottle of wine, but she'd been drinking more than usual lately, and was sort of sick of it. She put the white-paper-wrapped beef and the carton of eggs into the center of the fridge and closed the door. She opened and closed it once more just to enjoy the look.

Ruth washed her hands again and got out a huge stainless steel mixing bowl, and started putting together the ingredients for a *challah*. Belle was a horrible cook, but she'd always been a competent baker, possibly because for most people, there was no mystery to it. Baking was chemistry; you followed the instructions and wound up with something yummy. Ruth pulled a big wooden spoon and a whisk for the eggs and oil out of a drawer, and located a loaf pan that was a little rusty but still serviceable.

It was when Ruth was stirring the dissolved yeast into the mixture of oil and eggs that another radical thought came to her. She could move in here. She could get away, clear her head.

Sandy's preoccupation with the state of his penis—how was it resolvable? The way he'd framed the problem, it was intractable, permanent, no different in impact from his suddenly having realized he was gay. Sandy was a victim of an abhorrent practice, yada yada yada, and as a result of having had that realization, his sexual landscape was no longer the same, and he didn't feel sexually comfortable with Ruth any more. Even that story—the bullshit story—had taken therapy time for Ruth to unravel; Sandy's fixation wasn't exactly on the list of the hundred most common signs of male grief over the death of an emotionally unavailable father.

The real story: if Sandy didn't have sex anymore, he didn't have to feel so guilty about being alive when his father wasn't. What else could it be? Who ever heard of a man being fixated on his penis, yet deriving no pleasure from it? Who but Sandy could come up with such a perfectly lose-lose proposition? Not that Ruth should have been using her own therapy sessions to analyze Sandy. But what was she supposed to do? She had to understand him in order to figure out where she stood. He certainly wasn't collaborating with her on how to move forward.

It struck Ruth that moving out would be a way of calling Sandy on his craziness. *OK, Sandy, if this is really all about your dick, how is our relationship ever going to change?* It wasn't as if Sandy let go of an obsession, once he got started; he simply made room for the new one among his many others. Relentless, that's what he was. Just not about the right things. Ruth could certainly make a case.

But then there was also a part of Ruth that was too tired to make a case. Too tired to do anything but remove herself, try to refuel.

What was the big urgency about clearing out this place? Homes didn't get gussied up for sale in January; it was much better to wait until the spring, when the residential real estate market picked up and they'd get a better price. Anyway, she and Shayna had already done a lot of the work, and Sandy had lately started putting in an appearance on weekends. Shayna had told Ruth that it wouldn't take more than a couple of weeks to get the house ready. Ruth stirred in the flour, covered the *challah* dough with some ancient waxed paper and, cigarettes and lighter in hand, climbed the stairs to the second floor as if a browse around might reveal something more about the possibility.

It was a little warmer up here, and she unzipped the top of her gray cardigan and wandered through an obstacle course of books, boxes and debris. The hallway and the bedrooms all had the chaotic look of work partly done, the kind of organizational mess that only an involved party would recognize as evidence of accomplishment. In the master bedroom, Ruth put the cigarettes and lighter down on the table next to the blue armchair and opened the window. Then she sat on the chair, leaned forward for the smokes, and lit up, using the planter for an ashtray. She looked out over the barren magnolia and smiled a little, out of spite. Sandy would be furious if he knew she was smoking in his parents' house, let alone in their bedroom. She took another puff and leaned back in the chair against a crocheted headrest, thinking about the first time Oliver had approached her.

It was mid-December three years ago, a couple of months after Nadine's death, and Ruth and Sandy had gone to a Hyl holiday party at one of those touristy water-view restaurants at the Berkeley marina. Sandy was in the middle of an animated conversation with Anne Padway about France's failure to stop French-trained Hutu forces from slaughtering Tutsis in Rwanda, and Ruth didn't feel like mingling, nor would it have been appropriate for her to indulge her impulse to huddle in the kitchen and talk shop with the staff.

She went outside onto the deck and inhaled the bracing pungency of the San Francisco Bay, editing out the thread of decay. She was wearing her only pair of black evening shoes, the left one of which pinched a little at the outside of her foot, and her only black cocktail dress, which was a little tighter around the waist than it had been last year. It was a flattering outfit, but felt unnatural, like a party dress on a ten year-old tomboy. Ruth wished she were home in bed, reading.

She took a sip of her Chardonnay and glanced out across the bay, pulling her favorite silk shawl more tightly around her shoulders. The shawl had been a birthday gift from Sandy (Shayna had seen it in a local shop and told Sandy she thought it was perfect for her), and Ruth had been dismayed to discover during dinner that she'd somehow gotten a big brown spot on it. Shivering, she wanted to rub each arm with the other, but there was nowhere but the planks below to put her wine glass, and it was too windy for that. She could put the glass between her two feet, but she was a bit wobbly in her high heels. It occurred to her that she was tipsy. She was trying to calculate whether she could keep the wine glass upright if she put it down when Oliver sidled up, smiling broadly as if he and Ruth were old friends.

The truth was, Ruth had never really liked him. He was old-school, not at all someone with whom she felt comfortable. She could easily imagine him using the word "Negro" in the sixties and seventies, long after "black" had been adopted—or, in more recent times, using the word "gay" only with a sarcastic edge. "Merry Christmas, Mrs. Waldman," he enthused, putting a tumbler down on the nearest table and grabbing her hand in both of his.

"Actually, please call me—" Ruth began. His right hand was freezing from holding his drink.

"Yes, yes, I know. It's Hanukkah."

"No, I meant—"

"Or should I say, Chhhanukkah," he corrected, grinning. He wouldn't let go of her hand.

Taken aback by his childish over-pronunciation, Ruth forced a smile. "It's funny, in Jewish tradition, Chanukah isn't even a major holiday, and yet—"

"Holiday, that's it. It's a *holiday* party! That covers it, right? Christmas, Hanukkah, Kwanzaaaaaa?"

"Well—"

"Fine. Winter solstice, then." He winked. When he let go of her hand, Ruth felt relieved until suddenly, outrageously, he put his arm around her.

He had never behaved like this before, and there was some underlying off-ness about it that inebriation alone didn't explain. Ruth stepped out from under his embrace, racking her brains for something to say. Maybe something that would counter Critch's insensitive remarks, challenge him in a nice way. "You know, I once got off jury duty by telling the judge during *voir dire* that I found his questions offensive."

"Ruth." He leaned in toward her, too close. His skin was grayish, almost as if his time in Korea had permanently altered his coloring as well as his world view—as if he'd been dipped in lye. His jaw was square, his hair thick and silvery, with hardly any balding. His teeth were small but well-proportioned, and very yellow. There was something reptilian about him, she realized.

It struck Ruth that this strange behavior reminded her of Belle's period of early Alzheimer's symptoms, during which Belle had done such uncharacteristic things—yelling at a waitress, bragging about how rich she was. Of course most of Belle's symptoms were related to forgetfulness, but the neurologist who shared Sandy's practice had told them that poor judgment, changes in behavior, and even personality transformations were not uncommon in Alzheimer's patients. "Uhh, where's your wife this evening, Oliver?"

"Lorraine? Touch of the flu, I'm afraid." He waved vaguely toward the hills, then leaned in toward her again.

Ruth took a large gulp of her wine and stepped back a little, shaking her head. Her dangling pearl earrings bounced back and forth as she searched wildly for a topic. Though she wanted just to walk away, she had the strange sensation that she needed to stay and talk him down—as if he were on a bad acid trip and she couldn't abandon him. She was a little fascinated by his behavior. And, she would have to admit to herself later, she was flattered. She remembered she was in the middle of a story. "I mean, during *voir dire*, the judge wanted to know if I belonged to a church."

"And—?"

"Well, we don't call it a church. We call it a synagogue."

He scoffed. "Semantics."

"No, no. He should have asked whether I was affiliated with any religious institution," Ruth explained. "That wouldn't have offended me."

"But 'church' did," he said quietly, looking at her so kindly and with such genuine curiosity that in that moment, an unlikely thought crossed her mind: she'd been entirely wrong about him; this was, in fact, the real Oliver, sweet, and educable. But if that were the case, then what was he doing flirting with her?

"Well, yes," she nodded. "The word 'church' is inappropriate, and he should have known better. They're dealing with a cross section of the population, so they should at least—"

"You know, Ruth, you're enchanting," he breathed. "And so beautiful. I think *more* beautiful than when you were younger. When you were first on staff."

Ruth blushed. She knew she wasn't beautiful; he was drunk. But that he'd noticed her years before—why would he make that part up? Suddenly self-conscious about her shawl, she adjusted it over her shoulders to hide the stain, the wine glass tipping precariously as she grasped the silk fabric.

"You were always lovely," he went on, "because your intelligence shows through. And there's an inner goodness about you. That's what I see. Your goodness." He covered her hands with his.

"Oliver—I don't think this is appropriate. Though I'm flattered."

He stared at her. "Ruth," he whispered, her name an incantation.

"Very flattered," she conceded, trying to extricate herself.

"Ruth," he said again, just as Sandy was coming out onto the pier. "If you ever decide—"

"There you are! I've been looking all over for you." Sandy kissed Ruth on the side of her head, and Oliver loosened his grasp. "Isn't she great?" Sandy beamed at his boss, just as Anne barreled out to say goodbye to her cousin-in-law before leaving to catch her midnight flight to Guatemala.

Later, Ruth would wonder why Sandy hadn't noticed Oliver's palms enclosing hers that night. Everyone knew Oliver Critchfield hated to shake hands.

❧

OLIVER WAS NOT RUTH'S type. He wasn't witty, or handsome, or particularly moral, other than his work ethic. She was a little repelled by his cockiness and his pot belly, to say nothing of his booziness. And she wasn't at all sure he wasn't showing early signs of dementia.

Why, then, was she unable to stop thinking about him in the weeks and months after their encounter on the deck at the marina? She kept replaying the event, like a teenager. No one had flirted with her like that in years—since she'd first dated Sandy, and before that, since Josh had pursued her while she was married to Russell. But it wasn't just Oliver's flattery that had been pleasurable, or his audacity; it was also his vulgarity. His blunt lust for her made him the responsible party.

At first, Ruth called up the Oliver encounter every day, many times, getting a thrilling sensation from her loins up through her abdomen. Guiltily, she'd even thought of it on several occasions during those first weeks while having sex with Sandy. But by the time she found herself alone with Oliver again a couple of months later, in the elevator at Hyl, she had almost entirely forgotten how he looked, or sounded, or why she'd been moved by his behavior even as she was disgusted by it. When she saw him, her body seemed to know that its blood pressure should go up and that its heart rate should quicken, but Ruth couldn't remember why with any precision.

She'd gone in for a brief consultation with the Nutrition Department on one of the pamphlets that needed updating, and had stopped by to say a quick hello to Sandy before heading over to campus to teach her afternoon class. But then on her way down in the elevator, along with two young interns, there was Oliver.

"Mrs. Waldman," he intoned, as if contemptuous of her.

"Dr. Critchfield." Absurdly, she felt rejected by his coldness, then humiliated by the feeling of rejection. As she blushed, she felt the spread of a hot-flash across her chest. Damned hormones! She pushed up the sleeves of the thick ivory turtleneck, a wool-cashmere blend, which Shayna had given her years before but which was still in pristine shape because she didn't wear it often.

He smiled at her obvious embarrassment, and as soon as the two interns got off on the third floor, he turned to her. "Ruth," he said tenderly. "How are you?"

"Uhh—all right. Fine." Ruth found herself thinking she was glad she'd dressed simply but elegantly today—slimming black slacks and the turtleneck. She was not a makeup wearer, not her mother's daughter, but she had added a simple silk scarf and silver hoop earrings on a whim this morning. Had she dressed up a little more than usual, without even being conscious of it, in case she might run into him?

"What a pleasure to see you," Oliver Critchfield breathed, moving closer toward her. "You're a sight for sore eyes."

She was shaking. "Look, Oliver, you're my husband's *boss*. It's not that I'm not flattered. Really. It's—" The elevator jiggled a little as it moved downward.

"You move me, somehow," he said thoughtfully. "I can't even explain it."

"What, I'm not your type?" It came out sounding bitter.

He looked at her lightly, narrowing his eyes. "Actually, you're not. I seem to have a penchant for WASPs, mostly. And, of course, Korean women." He paused. "But Ruth, if you think this is something I *do*—"

She turned her face to his. Her chin was trembling, partly with excitement, partly with rage. She bit the inside of her bottom lip to steady it. She felt like crying.

"It's not," he insisted. "I've been a good boy for years. Ask my wife. And in any case, the way I feel about you—it's different, Ruth."

She was melting. "Look, Oliver, even if I believed you—"

"All I'm asking is that you consider—spending a little more time with me. I can be the perfect gentleman, if you like. Or not. Your choice."

She tugged at the neck of her sweater. The elevator jostled them as it arrived on the first floor. When the door opened, she and Oliver both hesitated for a moment. People began piling in. "Let me know," Oliver pleaded urgently under his breath, pushing Ruth gently forward through the crowd with his fingertips. Her heart raced at the whisper of his hands on her body.

What was it that made her consider Oliver's offer, even become obsessed by it? She wasn't sure, but she sensed it went something like this: Ruth was good. Sandy was also good. Oliver, on the other hand, wasn't good. But that was what enabled Oliver to see Ruth, and treasure her, in a way that Sandy, being so thoroughly good himself, could not—never mind that Oliver wanted to corrupt the very thing he cherished in her.

He began calling her occasionally at home every few weeks. Never, of course, when he knew Sandy wasn't at work. True, there had been that one terrifying recent time he'd called late at night within a day of their last conversation, and Sandy had answered. But that was probably from his having hit "redial" by accident while under the influence of multiple highballs. And Sandy didn't even seem to notice Ruth's wild blush; that's how preoccupied *he* was. He'd mistaken it for annoyance at their having been disturbed by a phone call so late in the evening.

Ruth knew she should put an end to the calls, but she was almost hypnotized by Oliver's attention. He was genuinely interested in her. Was she close with her daughter? Why had she become a nutritionist? Did she prefer teaching, or writing? Being a professional, was it hard for her to enjoy restaurants? What was her childhood like? And did she miss her mother?

It was only natural that Ruth ask him about himself, too. Eventually, Oliver told her about his two sons, both of whom were doctors also, and about how he felt closer with the younger one than the older one, who was kind of a mama's boy and had purchased a home just a few blocks away from them. Oliver also filled Ruth in on his war experience, though without much in the way of emotional detail. He had gone to Korea before attending medical school, and had been in the 38th Artillery Battalion, 2nd Infantry Division. He'd been marched along with eighty-two other men to Camp #5, where he'd remained a prisoner of war for ten months. He recited the facts with a detachment familiar to Ruth from her having learned from Belle and Abraham of their war experiences.

At times, Ruth was sure Oliver was losing it. He'd be talking about the day during their trek to Camp #5 that his best friend collapsed and died; then he'd jump without warning to what made him miserable in his marriage, or the corn fields around his childhood home in Iowa. Other times, he was completely lucid, and Ruth was left to wonder in which category, crazy or lucid, the flirtation belonged.

"You know, Ruth," he confided one day on the phone, "since that evening at the marina, I've felt more alive than I have in years. Sexually."

Ruth sat down warily at her kitchen table, moved the receiver a little away from her mouth so that Oliver wouldn't be able to detect that she was breathing more quickly than normal. All bravado aside—all bragging about it being her choice as to whether or not he was a gentleman with her—Ruth suspected Oliver Critchfield was more bark than bite in the sex department.

"I wish you were here right now," he went on. It was late afternoon, and Ruth wondered whether he'd been drinking at work. "You know, we wouldn't have to have sex. We could try—"

Ruth winced, thinking he was about to suggest oral sex. She'd read somewhere that men who had trouble with sexual functioning sometimes became fixated on blow jobs, since oral sex is less psychologically and physically demanding than intercourse, an easier way for some men to come to orgasm.

"—phone sex," he finished.

Ruth's jaw dropped. She tried to hang up, but she couldn't. It reminded her of being on the couch, very tired, and feeling that she couldn't get up. Of course she could if she had to. She could—but she couldn't. "I feel you're overstepping," she managed. Her entire vulva was pulsing.

"I become erect just hearing your voice."

This was getting out of hand.

"Ruth, if you ever change your mind—"

But Ruth knew then, with a certainty she couldn't quite summon now, that she wouldn't change her mind. Whatever betrayal of Sandy she was engaging in, phone sex was a step further down the road than she could conceivably justify. "Oliver," she said confidently, "I want you to stop this right now, and never mention it again."

And so he backed off. But he still called sometimes, asked her about herself, her classes, her aspirations, and Judaism. She didn't feel he understood the latter at all—in fact, it seemed to her she needed to educate him. She approached the task with the grace of someone trying to talk to a homophobe about gay rights. She knew he had some deeply embedded distrust of the Jews, and saw it as her calling to get him to see things differently. She felt she was making progress.

A few months ago, when Oliver had phoned her at home (come to think of it, it was the day before that time he mistakenly redialed her at night and Sandy had answered), Ruth had mentioned that she was concerned about the intensity with which Sandy had immersed himself in the circumcision issue. She was careful, of course, not to betray the slightest information about her marital sex life. When she said she was a little exasperated—and that it was a delicate matter, going against a tradition that was thousands of years old, as she was sure he could imagine—Oliver couldn't have been more kind or understanding.

∞

WHAT WOULD IT BE LIKE to live for awhile in limbo, here at the house? She could pretend she was back in the dorms at Champaign-Urbana, with a handful of record albums, three pairs of jeans and assorted shirts and sweaters, plenty of underwear of course, plus her winter clothes. The prospect of living in a makeshift state was appealing, somehow. Ruth hadn't realized how bogged down she'd been feeling by the familiarity of the physical objects all around her at home, the complicated histories of all the furniture and dishes and art and books she and Sandy had acquired together over the years. To say nothing of the cruel daily reminder, now the chronic condition of their lives, that Sandy was more interested in his own genitals than in hers.

Ruth stubbed out her cigarette and got up, ready to go downstairs and check the dough, start the stew. To air out the house after smoking, she went into both bathrooms and the rest of the bedrooms and opened all the windows. That was the good news about natural, unpainted wood: even windows that hadn't been opened in years glided up with relative ease. Nadine, though, wouldn't have had the slightest hesitation about getting the trim painted in eggshell.

CHAPTER TWENTY

Re: from sandy waldman (friend of anne padway)
Date: 12/23/00 9:18:44 AM Pacific Standard Time
From: marthaberg@netscape.net
To: sandor.waldman@hyl.org

Dear Sandy,

Hi, thanks for writing, no problem. It's actually been a lot easier with Seth being intact than we thought it would be. No unpleasantness from anyone at our synagogue. Maybe it's because we're in a big congregation and people don't know about our decision, but even the rabbi and cantor have been cool about it.

Seth will be starting preschool at Temple next summer, and the issue didn't come up when we talked to the preschool director, and they didn't refer to it anywhere on the enrollment forms. The kids don't have to be toilet trained to start preschool, so there might be comments once Seth enrolls and it's really "in their face." I guess we'll cross that bridge when we come to it.

There's a lot of intermarriage at our synagogue and I'm pretty sure we're not the only ones there with an intact son. Also, I've been in touch with a number of other Jewish families in the Bay Area and across the country who've made the same decision. Their boys range from newborn to college-age. None of the families has experienced any Jewish ostracism that I know of, other than pressure from family and friends at the time the child was an infant. Eddie has talked openly with several of the intact boys, too, and none of them feels weird or "other." They all feel comfortable with the way they look. It's strange—we worry so much about the ostracism factor, the idea of a child looking like his father, etc., etc., but when it comes down to it, so much of it is attitude, the way a child is taught to look upon himself and his intact penis.

(By the way, we use the word "intact," not "uncircumcised." Do we say "unmastectomized" to describe women with two healthy breasts?)

It was an incredibly difficult decision at the time—mostly, Eddie and I were worried about turning our backs on Jewish history—but we're completely comfortable now with our decision, and it feels like the only one we could have made. If anything, we are more determined to be active members of our shul and in other aspects of Jewish life, to show that circumcision has nothing to do with being committed Jews. We are very much involved in the feed-the-homeless project, and while Eddie used to play golf on Saturdays, he now attends Torah study group instead.

Did you know that in the 18th century, Moses Mendelssohn passionately argued that Judaism had to change if it was to survive and remain meaningful—yet he personally led a life of strict traditional observance?

Anyway, even our parents have relaxed about it and haven't really been on our case. Eddie's dad had been very hostile about our decision, but he shaped up quickly when we told him that if he continued to be disrespectful, we wouldn't let Seth near him.

By the way, check out my new web site about alternative ceremonies—www.alternative.bris.ceremonies.org—you'll probably find it interesting.

Take care,
Martha

Re: question, medical procedures
Date: 12/27/00 12:44:55 PM Pacific Standard Time
From: sandor.waldman@hyl.org
To: goldfarb@templebethamrochester.org
Bcc: zev.marks@hyl.org

Dear Rabbi Goldfarb,

I am sorry that you find my inquiry offensive. I assure you I am only trying to reconcile Jewish law and ethics with the circumcision tradition.

I have read your e-mails carefully and hope you will bear with me and allow me to provide you with some information in return. It is not just fatal complications that are of concern from a Jewish point of view; circumcision can lead to non-fatal complications as well. For example, there's a report from 1997 documenting two cases of necrotizing fasciitis of the penis following circumcision. (Necrotizing fasciitis is an inflammation of fibrous connective tissue leading to the death of that tissue.) More hair-raising, a 1996 study documents seven cases of accidental amputation of the head of the penis during circumcision. Six of those cases were at the hands of *mohelim*.

When an accidental amputation occurs, the boy is generally subjected to more surgery and then reared as a girl. To my knowledge there has been no long-term study on how these children cope with their gender assignment. However, current research about "hermaphroditic" children (i.e., those with characteristics of both genders) who feel they've been forced to identify as the wrong gender suggests to me that this is an extremely complex issue, one that at the very least cries out for further study.

As I understand it, unlike tattoo artists in this country, *mohelim* are not regulated. And truth be known, circumcision falls through the cracks somewhat in the medical world too. If a patient goes into the operating room for surgery, there's an established protocol so that any complications during the procedure are meticulously documented. But that doesn't apply in the case of circumcision, which, while clearly a surgical procedure, isn't performed in the OR.

It is not only wrong to ignore the risks of circumcision; it flies in the face of Jewish law. In light of the *halachic* prohibition against hazardous medical procedures, shouldn't the Jewish community take a leadership role in addressing the possibility of both fatal and non-fatal complications of circumcision?

These days, computers enable us to keep detailed medical records and to collect data easily and efficiently. Shouldn't we be a light to the medical world by seeing to it that all results from this elective procedure, whether perfect or not, are properly followed up and documented?

Best,
Sandy Waldman

Subj: yetzer hara
Date: 12/30/00 8:27:29 PM Eastern Standard Time
From: goldfarb@templebethamrochester.org
To: sandor.waldman@hyl.org

Dr. Waldman,

What exactly are you suggesting—that we give up our tradition because of some obscure risks? This would be preposterous, and frankly, Dr. Waldman, your manipulative arguments will do nothing to alter G-d's plan for us. In fact, in my opinion, the path you are going down shows *yetzer hara*, evil inclination.

Sartre suggested that Jewish identity is a matter of being labeled by the outside world as Jewish. *Brit milah* challenges this notion—it is an identity that we proudly confer upon ourselves. Also, as Maimonides tells us, circumcision counteracts excessive lust, ensuring the humanity and restraint of Jewish men's sexuality. Unchecked, the human sexual drive is *yetzer hara*. Circumcision therefore represents a kind of *tikkun*, a healing of nature.

I have tried to be patient and open with you, Dr. Waldman, but you seem to be deliberately blocking yourself from spiritual fulfillment.

Regretfully,
Rabbi Goldfarb

Subj: ethics
Date: 01/16/01 11:52:25 PM Pacific Standard Time
From: awaldman@botgarden.berkeley.edu
To: sandor.waldman@hyl.org

hey sandy, this guy i know said something about how ethics is more important in judaism than rituals. i just thought, if you want more ideas for your revolution. also, i was wondering what does hyl do about leftover food in the hospital? another words, do they donate it. sandy why are you letting ruth stay at bubba and zayda's? i know you guys are having problems but dude. get it together. i know its not my business and everything.

Re: ethics
Date: 01/17/01 6:17:20 AM Pacific Standard Time
From: sandor.waldman@hyl.org
To: awaldman@botgarden.berkeley.edu

Hi sweet Amy, thanks for the e-mail. I know you don't want to get in the middle of things. Your mom and I are trying to work things out and you're right, getting it together would be a really good idea right about now. The situation is temporary, don't worry.

I'll think about what you said about ethics (who's the guy?), but I'd bet that from the perspective of Jewish law, individuals shouldn't be deciding what's ethical and what's unethical; otherwise there'd be chaos.

I'm trying to come up with arguments that can't just be dismissed as emotional or incendiary by observant Jews and Jewish scholars. I seem to be pissing people off, but I really am trying to go about this in a way that's true to the spirit of Judaism and Jewish law, and that's respectful of tradition. But, I'm going to read up on ethics and see what I can come up with. Thanks for the great idea!

I'll look into what the hospital does with leftover food. Probably if it's wrapped and untouched, it could be donated—not sure about prepared leftovers.

Can we get together soon for dinner? I hope so.
Love and hugs, Dad

Re: your circumcision research
Date: 01/26/01 10:14:04 PM Central Standard Time
From: shersh@drs.wisc.edu
To: sandor.waldman@hyl.org

Dear Dr. Waldman,

Sorry for the delay—I just found your e-mail in a bunch of unanswered ones. Sure, I can give you brief accounting of my research. But I am trusting you not to misuse this information, or publish it.

I respect your desire to question this tradition within a Jewish framework—I'm trying to do the same thing. However, there are a lot of weird, anti-Semitic web sites out there that are against circumcision, and I don't want my research to end up on one of them. I am sure that as a scholar yourself, you understand my concerns. So please be responsible with how you use the information.

To answer your main question, yes, there is historical evidence that the type of circumcision undergone by Abraham and other early Jews was considerably less severe than what is currently being done.

Let me give you some background. Originally, *brit milah* was a fairly minor procedure in which only the end of the foreskin, the part that hangs down over the penis in its flaccid state, was severed.

During the Hellenic period (500-300 B.C.E.), Jews were heavily taxed, and were denied access to education at the Aphbia and physical training at the Gymnasium (where nudity make it easy to tell who was circumcised and who was not). At that time, many Jewish men began stretching their foreskins with weights in an attempt to "pass" so that they could avoid persecution and gain their civil rights. These assimilationists learned how to restore the foreskin to its original look and function over a period of months. Some of them even underwent surgical procedures in pursuit of the same goal. "Stretching," then, was fairly widespread among Jewish men.

Not surprisingly, the rabbis of the period were outraged by this corruption of the sign of the covenant. So they legislated a far more radical operation for male Jewish babies—one that couldn't be reversed—i.e., a full amputation of the foreskin all around the edge of the glans, instead of just what's hanging down. Additionally, they mandated the removal of the thin protective membrane underneath (this severing is called *p'riah*, and refers to the part of the under-skin that Orthodox *mohelim* remove with their sharp fingernail). In other words, the Talmudic rabbis demanded a completely denuded glans.

So, that's it in a nutshell. Please write back if you have any more questions. I would be glad to correspond.

Sincerely,
Stephan Hersh, Ph.D.
Department of Religious Studies
University of Wisconsin at Madison

Re: your circumcision research
Date: 01/28/01 7:12:21 AM Pacific Standard Time
From: sandor.waldman@hyl.org
To: shersh@drs.wisc.edu
Bcc: zev.marks@hyl.org

Dear Dr. Hersh,

Happy New Year, and thanks for your e-mail. It's kind of you to refer to me as a scholar. Really, I'm a dilettante. I am an endocrinologist by training, but I have been delving into the circumcision issue in some depth lately.

Are you saying that the original form of circumcision left a truncated, but functional, foreskin? One that afforded protection to the head of the penis? This is most interesting. I read Maimonides' description of circumcision in *Guide for the Perplexed*, and he certainly makes it sound like a difficult operation. As one translation puts it, "for it is not like an incision in the leg or a burn in the arm, but is a very, very hard thing."

Now that I have your information, I can see why he describes it that way; by Maimonides's time, circumcision involved the total severing of both types of tissue.

Just so I can really have a clear idea what you're saying: is it this same total severing that is still in practice today?

Many thanks.
Sincerely,
Sandy Waldman

Re: yetzer hara
Date: 01/29/01 7:31:20 AM Pacific Standard Time
From: sandor.waldman@hyl.org
To: goldfarb@templebethamrochester.org
Bcc: zev.marks@hyl.org

Dear Rabbi Goldfarb,

Current medical research tells us that there are definite risks associated with circumcision. I would think this would be of interest to you as a *halachic* expert on hazardous medical procedures. In other words, the risks are of concern from a *Jewish* point of view, not just from some vague moral or even medical perspective. Simply denying the risks, without regard for the evidence, doesn't erase the reality.

I'd like to pose that one of the beauties of *halacha* is its capacity to evolve over time. Certainly even observant Jews such as yourself acknowledge that *halacha* can change in light of new information—the case of the *kheresh* is perhaps the best example. Thus, it is perfectly legitimate for me to be asking how we should address *in a Jewishly ethical way* the current data about circumcision risk, as well as related issues such as the fact that infants have now been shown definitively to be capable of experiencing pain.

You are not suggesting, are you, that *halacha* cannot withstand the integration of new information?

Sincerely,
Sandy Waldman

Re: yetzer hara
Date: 02/04/01 2:27:21 PM Eastern Standard Time
From: goldfarb@templebethamrochester.org
To: sandor.waldman@hyl.org

Dr. Waldman,

I am appalled by your assault on the ritual of *brit milah*. Worse than that, you use *halacha* to justify your attack. Dr. Waldman, you can't just twist Jewish law into whatever pretzel you want to suit your own personal agenda. This is offensive, and a violation of what is meant by Jewish scholarship. That is why I am taking the time to write back to you in detail before you go further down this destructive path.

You seem to disregard the direct link between *brit milah* and Torah learning. The external circumcision activates an inner commitment to G-d and the *mitzvos*, as is evident in the striking similarity between these two quotes:

"If not for *Torah*, G-d would not continue the world's existence." (Nedarim 23a)

"If not for *milah*, G-d would not have created the world!" (Nedarim 32)

It is also important to note that a Jew who lacks commitment to the covenant is described as "uncircumcised" in Jeremiah 9:25 and 6:10, Ezekiel 44:7, Deuteronomy 70:16, and Exodus 6:12. In other words, if a person's heart and mind are blocked, he cannot grasp or fulfill G-d's commandments.

In having had his foreskin removed, a Jew bears the sign of the covenant upon his body. It is no accident that this sign is on the organ responsible for procreation.

Midrash relates that Abraham waits at the entrance to hell and refuses to let in all who are circumcised. It is the highest honor, and a Jewish father's most important obligation, to bring his son into the covenant. The importance of *brit milah* is signified in our daily prayers and in the prayer for the naming of the newborn infant when we recite, "Remember forever His covenant, the word that He commanded for a thousand generations." We are the seed of Abraham, Isaac and Jacob, and we must remember forever that we are bonded to G-d. And according to Jewish law, he who doesn't fulfill the commandment of *brit milah* is subject to the severe punishment known as *karet*, being cut off from the community.

Your concern about the pain caused to the infant is misplaced, Dr. Waldman. When *halacha* is followed to the letter regarding the carrying out of the *mitzvah* of *brit milah*, I assure you, it is absolutely painless. In my observation, *halacha* is more concerned about the child's suffering and trauma than the medical world. For example, the medical profession will go ahead with circumcision when an infant is jaundiced or has an eye infection, whereas *halacha* prohibits *brit milah* under those conditions.

I am baffled by your attempt to reduce this beautiful commandment to a medical procedure. Regarding anesthesia, of course you as a physician are aware that the use of anesthesia involves a chance of infection and allergy. Why risk it?

But perhaps the most important argument against these misguided alterations to the tradition is best summed up by the Hatham Sofer: "Innovation is forbidden in the Torah."

With regret,
Rabbi Goldfarb

Re: more about penile cancer
Date: 02/16/01 7:49:30 PM Pacific Standard Time
From: sandor.waldman@hyl.org
To: vinod.sengupta@hyl.org

Hi Vinod, just a thought—should we form some kind of professional group opposing circumcision? Call ourselves Docs Against Circumcision, or something, and try to get Hyl to come out on our side? Also, we could try to get Medicaid to stop reimbursing practitioners, and try to get the other insurance companies to stop reimbursing patients. What do you think? S.

Re: your circumcision research
Date: 03/13/01 10:13:09 AM Eastern Standard Time
From: shersh@drs.wisc.edu
To: sandor.waldman@hyl.org

Dear Sandy,

Sorry again for the delay. Yes, all my research indicates that what is practiced today, both Jewishly and medically, is much more radical than the comparatively mild cut Abraham probably made on his own penis. In other words, it is the full circumcision mandated in the Hellenic period that is still in modern practice. Many contemporary

Jews think we're going back to the Bible in practicing circumcision, but that's a bit of a fallacy. Or should I say, "phallus-y"?

What we don't know is whether the rabbis were aware that they were legislating the removal of extremely sensitive erogenous tissue.

Have you heard about those men trying to "restore" their foreskins? Pretty difficult, if they've been circumcised any time within, say, the last 1500 years. The way circumcision has been done for centuries, there's practically nothing left to work with.

Makes you wonder if eventually we'll be using stem cell technology to regrow foreskins...

Stephan

Part Two:
TIKKUN OLAM

CHAPTER TWENTY-ONE

JIM HOROVICH, A.K.A. JUNGLEJIM, had assured Sandy that the East Bay Foreskin Restorers weren't a bunch of crackpots or anti-Semites. They were just half a dozen circumcised guys in the process of stretching their residual penile shaft skin so that, over time, new tissue was formed to cover the head of the penis. Although no amount of stretching could make up for the sexual sensitivity of the foreskin itself (that was gone forever), Jim said there was comfort in having the glans "tucked in"—essentially, restored to being an internal organ, as nature intended—so that it no longer rubbed against the underwear or was exposed to the air. It was in this way, apparently, that the men in Jim's group were steadily regaining lost sensation.

There was something decidedly fetishistic about the whole business, Sandy thought. It was one thing to be anti-circumcision, quite another to be so preoccupied with one's lost prepuce that one was willing to join an unlikely fraternity of men who gradually stretched their penile skin the way members of African tribes stretched their lips or necks or earlobes. But then, it was not the remediation of circumcision that was bizarre and tribal; it was circumcision itself. Besides, Sandy was hardly in any position to be judgmental.

As a child, Sandy had realized at the pediatrician's office one day that his tetanus booster was a matter of a fluid being forced into his body, while a blood test, however unpleasant, wasn't, in concept, nearly as invasive. Later, Sandy administered plenty of shots during his training, and he was of course a huge advocate of childhood immunizations. But on a gut level, after that early insight, he'd never been able to think of injections in any way other than as an intrusion into the body. There was a "before" and an "after" in the way he felt, a visceral sense that nothing could alter once he'd made the transition from one way of thinking to the next. He felt much the same way now: it was impossible to return to his perception of his own circumcision as a non-issue, impossible to shake a sense of penile nakedness. He'd explained that to Ruth the day she'd packed her things, thinking it would help her understand.

Sandy shuddered as he started down the stairs to the musty church basement. What would his father think, or his mother? What would his patients think if they knew that their admired, counted-on Dr. Sandor Waldman had attended a support group of men who were, by definition, obsessed with their own dicks? *Support* group, Sandy mused, like a jock strap! Did Sandy really want to spend an hour with these people?

Ruth wouldn't view it that way; while certainly skeptical of Sandy's absence-of-foreskin sensation, she'd never been a snob. Sandy actually felt he scored points with her when, in one of the earliest conversations in their relationship, he'd admitted to her that he wasn't some straight-ahead over-achiever; in fact, he'd come perilously close to getting thrown out of med school. Not that he'd wanted her to know the specifics. Carefully, he chose the phrase "drug bust," which he felt would offer less of an opportunity for a follow-up question than, say, "busted for drugs" or "possession." He hastily worked in the ambiguous word "stoned"—let it register on Ruth's face that he was talking about pot—before blurting out something about having been forced to go to twelve-step meetings. And he didn't mention his father's rescue of him.

"I was in meetings with some hardcore addicts," he'd gauged. The truth was, Sandy had felt a strong bond with the people in those rooms, had found it orienting to be in a no-bullshit setting with others who'd screwed up their lives. "You know, the kinds of people who'd lost their jobs because they were drunk all the time. People who were constantly, like, assaulting their parole officers, or whose kids had been made wards of the state. Not privileged students about to get kicked out of medical school."

Ruth had smiled at him and said, "What are you suggesting, that there should be twelve-step meetings just for brilliant medical students?"

"Oh, not at all, not at all." She thought he was brilliant?

"Because, I mean, wouldn't that kind of defeat the purpose? To admit you're out of control, to see that you're no better or worse than anyone else?"

"Exactly, exactly. Anyway, funny thing is, I liked a lot of those guys. It was kind of humbling, making friends with people from different socio-economic groups, different walks of life, and feeling this deep connection."

"Sounds like that was very grounding for you."

"Grounding, exactly. You're so intuitive."

How had Sandy and Ruth gotten to this place? Even now, in late March, several months into the new arrangement—and not having had sex since two times in December—Sandy couldn't quite believe the direction in which things had gone. When Ruth first left, he vacillated between self-reassurance that the situation was temporary, and abject terror. He used Xanax many evenings to quell his anxiety and help him sleep. He called Ruth every day, and on the few occasions when she came back to the house to pick up another pair of shoes or a forgotten sweater while he was home, he told her how amazing and rare it was that they still loved each other decades into their relationship, how there had to be a solution. Ruth wasn't unkind. It was worse than that—she seemed distracted, almost bored.

Sandy kept replaying the conversation they'd had while she was packing. So your penis feels naked, she'd said—how is that going to change? He didn't have a road map, he told her. Fine, forget the road map, give me a clue as to how our marriage is viable if you don't come to terms with your grief. But I *have* come to terms with my grief. So you continue to think there's no connection between losing your father and becoming fixated on—penile nakedness? Ruthie, all I know is that I'm sure, in every fiber of my being, that I have to explore this, in my own way. Well, I'm glad there's one thing you know. I didn't mean it like that. No? Of course not, Ruthie—I just think that if I explore all this—intellectually, spiritually, psychologically—I don't know, I guess things will shift over time. You guess? she'd said. And how long, exactly, is it going to take before you stop exploring your penis and start dealing with the real issue? Ruthie, come on, I love you. I know, she said. I can try to be more available to you. Really. I will try. Yes, Sandy, you'll be more available until the idea of our having sex comes up. And then your guilt and shame will kick in, don't you see? Ruthie, don't—Don't Ruthie me. Sorry. The point is,

Sandy, if you continue to gain insight about your penis, figure it all out with Ezra Kohn, we'll still be in the same situation. You'll still have been *denuded.*

Denuded, she'd said, almost snidely. His Ruth.

But she'd come around eventually, wouldn't she? For one thing, there was a built-in time limit at his parents' house. Shayna had advised that they postpone putting the place up for sale, claiming the residential real estate market was a little soft at the moment; Sandy suspected that aside from her ambivalence about selling, Shayna was protecting Ruth. But things couldn't go on this way forever. Shayna and Ruth both knew they needed the equity in that place for Belle's care.

Besides, once the cookbook came out in May, Ruth would need to do radio interviews from the telephone at the desk in her office at home. Sandy could see her leaning forward earnestly over the desk blotter as she spoke, her legs femininely crossed at the ankles behind her. She'd need to prepare for local book signings and maybe even a television talk show or two. She'd need ready access to her clothing, her files. And then too, Ruth would be excited when he told her he was preparing for his adult bar mitzvah. She'd call family and friends to make sure they came to the service. She'd make a beautiful spread for afterwards. Everyone would come back to the house to celebrate when the service was done...

Plus, Passover was coming up, something Ruth felt really strongly about observing as a family. Sandy visualized his parents' good dishes, which Ruth had brought home to their house not that many weeks ago. He could practically taste Ruth's roasted lamb, *charoses*, and hand-grated horseradish, see the party around the table: Amy, Shayna, Chris and the boys, Belle, Ruth's sister

Ellen. For the first time, no Abraham. He imagined Ruth storing all the leftovers in Tupperware containers after the seder, stacking them in the refrigerator. He tried to ward off thoughts of her then going back to his parents' house to sleep, his picking halfheartedly at the remnants for a couple of days before throwing them out. He'd never be able to make them taste as good on reheating as Ruth could.

Shayna wasn't being as sympathetic as Sandy had hoped. The other day, lonely and depressed, Sandy had phoned his sister, only to get an earful about how his visits to Belle were reactive and perfunctory, and would it kill him to ask, every now and then, how Shayna was coping with the loss of their father—or how she was doing in general? It was no coincidence, Shayna said, that all the women in his life were fed up. Sandy pointed out that recently, he seemed to be equally offensive to both genders. Shayna hadn't laughed.

Sandy tried to put all this out of his mind as he approached the landing at the bottom of the church steps and peered through the diamond wire grid in the window panel of the oversized yellow door in front of him. This was going to be tough enough without a lot of self-doubt.

If nothing else, he told himself, his attendance today would enable him to argue his case more effectively.

There was no natural light inside the room, and it looked as if one of the fluorescent bulbs was out. Two men were moving a folding conference table to the side of the room while three others arranged half a dozen folding chairs into a small circle. Jim had told him that Everett Peregrine, the facilitator of the group, was pushing seventy, and that it was only a couple of years ago that Everett had started his own foreskin restoration process (so it most certainly wasn't too late for Sandy! he'd enthused). But Sandy didn't see anyone who looked that old in the room, and for the first time he could remember, he felt self-conscious about his age. On the other hand, that would make it clear he was here mainly to gather information. He pulled the notebook and pen he'd brought out of his back pocket.

He suddenly thought of his mentor at Johns Hopkins, who would certainly howl at this spectacle; he was the kind of man who wouldn't just smirk silently when faced with absurdity; he'd belly-laugh. Guiltily, Sandy realized he was relieved the old endocrinologist was dead. His father, too. He took a deep breath in through his nose and tried to release it very slowly, through his mouth, as Ruth had taught him.

One of the men who was moving the table looked up and saw him, then put his end of the table down in place and approached. "Sandy?" he said, opening the door.

Sandy nodded.

"I'm Jim Horovich. Really glad you could join us."

Jim Horovich was taller than Sandy had imagined, and so self-confident in his Italian wool sweater, khakis, and polished tassel loafers that it was hard for Sandy to reconcile him with the fringiness he couldn't help expecting. When Sandy had "met" him in the chatroom and later e-mailed back and forth, he'd learned that Jim was a forty year-old gay trial lawyer, Jewish (though not particularly identified as a Jew), who had begun to be unhappy with his own circumcision when a boyfriend had confided that foreskins turned him on. Though he and the boyfriend hadn't stayed together, Jim had begun to think about his own circumcision differently from that time on, becoming more and more upset by the idea that without his permission, some doctor had forcibly (certainly without informed consent!) removed the healthy covering that protected the head of his penis. Jim had subsequently become a passionate legal advocate for the anti-circumcision movement, even taking on a couple of botched circumcision cases *pro bono*. Not that any of this was fringey, really. It was just that Sandy trusted iconoclasm in himself more than in others.

The slender man with whom Jim had been moving the table was approaching them, extending a bony hand. As he got closer, Sandy realized this must be Everett. Though his body was young and taut, his face was craggy. He had a thin ponytail of mousy-brown hair flecked with white, and a huge chain of keys attached to the back pocket of his light-blue jeans, all of which gave him the look of a custom wood cabinetry maker whose Berkeley hills clientele probably wanted to remodel their kitchens with all natural materials. "Sandy? I'm Everett. Jim told me you'd be joining us today."

"Nice to meet you."

"Guys?" Everett raised his voice a little. "Nicholas is out of town, so I think we're all here. Why don't we get started?"

The three other men joined Sandy, Everett and Jim as they sat down. "This is Martin, Plaid, and Tom," Everett gestured. "You already know Jim. This is Sandy, guys. He's checking us out."

Titters.

"Actually, I—" Sandy began.

"Welcome to our humble abode," boomed Tom, a muscular, cologned black man in his forties who was holding a rolled-up magazine in one hand.

"Okay, we're all here, so let's get started. Jim, could you get the curtain?"

Jim Horovich went over to the yellow door and pulled a thick curtain over the window in it, then sat down across from Sandy.

"Okay," continued Everett. "Does anyone have anything to share?"

Tom unrolled the magazine and held it up. There were two large capital letters on the cover—*FQ*.

"That's a porn magazine," objected Martin, a pasty thirtyish man who looked as if he were secretly hoping that in restoring his foreskin, he might finally get some woman to go to bed with him.

"There's some really good medical information in *FQ*," Tom insisted. The way he pronounced it, Sandy couldn't help hearing "fuck you."

"And lots of, like, intelligent letters to the editor," put in Plaid, a young redhead whose plaid flannel shirt was covered with political buttons. *Fuck Bush. Free Palestine.*

"Anyway, there's an article in here by Pickett about hospitals selling foreskin tissue," Tom said.

"Is that Dr. Noel Pickett?" Sandy asked.

"You know him?"

"I'm familiar with his anti-circumcision work. And he did his residency at the same place I did mine. As a physician, I—"

"Pickett is *so* cool," gushed Plaid. "At that protest at Westerly? He was like, *dude*, the Palestinians have rights, too."

Sandy had read about Pickett's latest escapade in the *Online Jewish News*. Though on the urology faculty at Westerly University medical school, Pickett was so well-known for his shenanigans that, as Anne Padway had said, he didn't have much personal credibility. A month ago, while passing by an outdoor student rally protesting Westerly's refusal to provide married student housing for gay couples, Pickett had grabbed the mike and shouted for five minutes about the evils of Israeli policies. There had been a suicide bombing the previous day in which six Israelis had been killed, and Pickett got huge cheers as he railed against the establishment that left Palestinians no choice but to engage in such tactics. Finally, a Jewish lesbian, one of the organizers of the event, had wrested the mike away from Pickett and pointed out angrily that the topic was gay housing, and that, by the way, in case Pickett was unaware, Israel was the only nation in the entire Middle East where gays had any rights whatsoever. By then, Pickett had stormed off, furious at having been interrupted.

Of course the Palestinians have rights, Sandy wanted to say to Plaid. *Like, the right to leaders who aren't thugs. Whose agenda isn't the annihilation of the state of Israel, but peaceful coexistence with the Jewish people. Who have their people's education and welfare in mind instead of making it their mission to manipulate them into becoming terrorists...* Why did so many lefties consistently refuse to acknowledge that there were bad guys out there in the world? Sandy clicked his ball point pen and glanced over at Jim, the only other Jew in the room, but Jim looked as if he were thinking about something else. Sandy wished he could get up and leave without calling more attention to himself.

"I thought we'd agreed to stay away from politics," Tom said irritably.

"Sorry." Plaid was meek.

"Anyway," Tom went on, "Pickett talks about how they use foreskin tissue for burn victims—"

"Which is all just fine," put in Jim, "except it's immoral to forcibly remove tissue from a perfectly healthy patient and then profit from it."

"And Pickett goes into that in depth," Tom said.

"It's certainly one of the best *FQ* articles I've seen lately," added Everett.

"Um—I'm sorry," Sandy interjected, his pen poised over his notebook. "What is *FQ*, exactly?"

"Oh!" Jim exclaimed. "It stands for *Foreskin Quarterly*."

Sandy gaped.

"We should explain," Jim went on. "There's a subculture within the gay community of—a kind of foreskin worship, I guess you might call it. Or obsession. One boyfriend of mine was really into—"

"Right, you told me about all that when we exchanged e-mails," Sandy said, wondering how anyone could lose track of which intimate information he'd shared with which Internet acquaintance.

"All right," Everett said. "If anyone wants a copy of that article, I'm sure Tom can photocopy it for you. We should all stay informed about what's happening on the medical and legal fronts. Okay, does anyone want to share about their month?" He looked around, gauging the enthusiasm of each participant. "Plaid?"

Plaid nodded like a schoolboy who'd been waiting impatiently to be called on. "Better sensation these last couple of weeks. Definitely."

"Great," said Everett. "Did the tape rash go away?"

"Pretty much."

"You know you're supposed to put the tape on your leg *first*, to see if you get an allergic reaction," said Jim.

"I shoulda done that," Plaid admitted. "But now I got a different tape that's, like, no-allergy. You know, cloth tape."

"I made the tape mistake, too, at first," Tom put in. "And it wasn't pretty."

"Why? What'd you try?" asked Martin.

Tom grimaced. "Regular cellophane tape."

"You mean, like, Scotch tape?" Plaid was incredulous.

"That can cut into the skin!" exclaimed Jim.

"Believe me, I know. And try taking it off."

The men chuckled.

"But then I got some of that clear plastic mesh that was moisture-proof," said Tom. "Micropore, I think it's called."

"I thought surgical cloth tape was the best one," said Plaid. "I just bought—"

"There are a lot of good options," Everett reassured him. "The important thing is to check first for a skin reaction. Then if there is none, you can go to a stronger adhesive."

"So tell us more about your progress," Tom said to Plaid, as Sandy tried to call up the neutrality he'd learned in medical school.

"Yeah, okay," said Plaid eagerly. "I'm for *sure* noticing a difference in the skin. It already started stretching and loosening up a lot. Cool, huh? And you guys know how at first I was kinda like, *no way*."

"That's great, Plaid."

"The only thing is, when I get ready to move into Stage II, am I supposed to use the same tape?"

"You might want to get self-sticking gauze for that," advised Everett. "You make a ring out of it, and then the tape sticks to that, not to the skin."

Plaid nodded. "Okay."

Everett paused, waiting for Plaid to say more. Sandy looked down at the blank page in his notebook. "Anyone else?" Everett said finally.

"Yeah, um, I'm having trouble with the tape strap," admitted Martin, who Sandy reasoned was probably the most recent addition to the group.

"You're in Stage I, right?" Everett asked Martin.

Martin nodded. "When I take the tape off, the head of my dick is so sensitive that rubbing against clothes is uncomfortable."

"That's because you're gaining sensitivity," said Tom. "I call that *success*."

"Really?" Martin looked skeptical.

There were vigorous nods.

"Then another problem I'm having," Martin went on, "is the skin is really hard to tape. It keeps wanting to bounce back up."

"Have you tried soaking in a hot bath first?" asked Everett.

"No, why?"

"It makes the skin more supple—much easier to tape. It really helps."

"Okay. I'll try it." Martin paused. "How long do people stay in Stage I, anyway? It seems like it's taking forever."

"When there's no tension any more," answered Jim, "that's when you go ahead to the next phase."

"It partly depends on how much foreskin you have to work with," added Everett. "Remember, some doctors leave practically nothing, and others don't take away as much skin. If you were lucky enough to have been cut by a *mohel* instead of a doctor—someone who left a little something to work with—it's going to be an easier process. I think Bigelow talks about that in the book."

Sandy was about to ask what book when Everett anticipated his question. "The required text for this course," he explained, looking at Sandy with a grin, "is *The Joy of Uncircumcising!* by Bigelow. Which is, unfortunately, out of print."

"Oh."

Everett pulled an oversized paperback out from under his chair and got up to hand it to Sandy. "Jim said a newcomer would be joining us today, so I thought I'd bring along my one extra copy. As a loaner."

"Umm, I really—" Sandy didn't want to appear rude. He took the book tentatively in his hands.

"Trust me, you don't want to have to go online and overpay because there are so few copies out there. I know I can count on you to return it to me when you're done." Everett turned to Martin again. "Anyway, I know of one case where Stage I took fifteen months of wearing the tape strap. But that was on someone who had practically no shaft skin to work with. You have a little more, right?"

"It looked like it," said Tom. Sandy wondered how Tom knew that.

"Well, it can also depend on how quickly your body generates the new skin cells," Everett pointed out, then looked at Sandy. "Just to make sure Sandy understands what we're talking about, Stage I refers to the part of foreskin restoration during which you wear a tape strap to stretch whatever skin you have."

Sandy nodded sagely.

"There's been shown to be a rise in cell formation activity in human skin during the process of tissue expansion," Everett went on, and Sandy realized with relief that Everett recognized his status as a physician. "The connective tissue underlying the penile covering elongates during the skin expansion phase. There's more mobility of the shaft skin. This leads to an increase in the number of cells. So with the stretching method, new tissue does eventually form, even though the skin thins at first."

"It thins all right," cracked Tom. "Mine *tore* a few weeks ago. Right after our last meeting." He looked at the group sheepishly. "I guess I overdid it with the weights."

Weights?

"Tearing is not an uncommon occurrence at the weights stage," said Everett. "Remember, you have to listen to your body. Go at your own pace."

Sandy swallowed. "What are the weights for?"

"In the first stages of stretching," Everett explained, "the glans and the body of the penis provide the necessary tension. But once you have a retractable hood of skin, various devices are needed to maintain enough tension on the 'foreskin' to keep growing it. Of course, not everybody bothers with weights. They're content just to have a bit of a covering over the glans."

"But how are the weights attached?" Martin wanted to know.

Sandy had to keep himself from gasping as Tom stood up suddenly and began undoing his belt. Involuntarily, Sandy's head turned to look at the door with the small window in it, realizing suddenly why Everett had asked Jim to draw the curtain.

"Don't worry," Everett reassured him. "No one's coming. It's just the janitor here this afternoon, and he always starts upstairs. We've never had a problem during show-and-tell."

"Hey, slow down," Martin said. "Sandy might not be used to this."

Everett turned to Sandy and smiled earnestly. "I know this might seem a little weird, Sandy, but we—well, we learn from each other as we're going along."

"Of course." Sandy laughed loudly. "Hey, I've been to medical school." He glanced around the group, but everyone's attention was on Tom as his khakis and underwear fell down around his ankles.

What Sandy saw immediately made him think of one of those bizarre getups featured in S & M magazines with chains, a whip, leather dog collar with chrome spikes. But the theme of this apparatus was bandaging. The head of Tom's penis had white surgical tape around it. From the end of the penis, suspended by more surgical tape and a little chain that resembled a fishing rig, dangled a chrome cylinder that looked as if it had been purchased from the ball bearing section of a hardware store. It was about the size of a small rubber ball, and shone and dangled like a Christmas tree ornament.

Sandy felt a little faint but, too embarrassed to put his head between his legs, he quickly stowed his notebook and pen in his pocket again, then leaned forward and put his chin in his hands, as if he had back trouble and were trying to find a more comfortable position. *Breathe.*

"See?" Tom enthused. "The weight just naturally pulls the foreskin downward."

"You've definitely made progress," Jim observed. "Last time it was hanging a lot more tightly. You look like you're ready to graduate to the next level."

"I don't get it," said Martin. "How is that thing attached?"

Tom was still standing up, his dark, muscular thighs framed by the bottom edge of his green silk turtleneck and the khakis that were down below his knees. "You have to put it together beforehand, with a snap swivel in place. See?" He pointed to the little chain. "Then you pull the skin forward, apply the strap, and then after that's on, you hang the 2-ounce sinker from the snap swivel."

"Awesome," breathed Plaid.

"It works great." Tom started getting his pants back on. "Of course you have to remove it to sleep and to bathe, and also to pee."

"After the phase that Tom's in," Everett explained to Martin and Sandy, "you get to Stage II. That's when you can use the weighted tape-ring. There's this latex cup *inside* the skin, over the glans. You can pee with it in place."

Martin scrunched his nose. "Huh?"

"The weighted tape-ring moves the process even further along. Here, I'll show you."

Sandy took his glasses off as Everett began removing his jeans to reveal sinewy thighs that looked anemic in comparison with Tom's. "I wear this thing for a few days until the tape ring loosens and falls off," Everett explained, showing everyone his penis as if it were no more attached to him than the foreign object he'd lodged inside it. "Then I start again."

"So lemme get this straight," said Martin. "The shaft skin is being held between the latex cup and the tape ring?"

"Exactly. You have to be sure to allow for blood flow to the tip of the foreskin, though."

"Where do you get a latex cup that's the right size?" Jim wanted to know.

"I used one of those nipples from a disposable baby bottle," Everett explained. "'Course, I had to check for latex allergy first," he added, winking at Plaid as he pulled his pants back up.

As Sandy hyperventilated, his glasses in his shirt pocket, his head in his hands, the "uncircumcising" book on his lap, he contemplated how best to give Jim Horovich the brush-off. In a nice e-mail, that was it. He'd enjoyed meeting everyone; he'd appreciated being included; it had helped him enormously in his research process. He'd gotten insights that would be invaluable in his taking on the medical community...

Sandy was leaning forward, considering his options, when something unexpected happened. For the first time in months, he felt it: the sharp, searing pain, right on the piece of anatomy in question.

CHAPTER TWENTY-TWO

SANDY HADN'T SEEN much of Anne Padway recently. He didn't usually bump into her in the course of a day; his office was two floors above hers, and like most of the other docs, they were too busy to have coffee or lunch together unless there was a specific reason such as a jointly authored research paper. Ordinarily they would have both been at last month's Quality and Utilization Management committee meeting, but Anne had been volunteering again at that clinic in Guatemala. Maybe it was just as well; Sandy had a sense that she'd be more sympathetic to Ruth than to him if she knew what was going on. When Anne happened to be in the elevator coming down from the library one afternoon as he got on it to leave work, Sandy found himself scowling.

"Hey, Sandy." She pressed the button for her floor. "Did you meet with that pale-and-frail I sent you?"

"Last week."

"Osteoporosis, right? Or just osteopenia?"

"Actually, Anne, besides having osteoporosis, that particular patient has osteomalacia." He pressed the "Lobby" button again.

"Rickets?" Anne was incredulous.

"Adult rickets, yes. Major Vitamin D deficiency. I can't even start her on Fosamax until we firm up her bones. You know that, right? Not to prescribe Fosamax unless you're sure there's no osteomalacia? We should be ordering Vitamin D tests every year, just like cholesterol tests."

"Don't patronize me, Sandy."

"Anne, have you said anything to Critch about me?"

"Critch—what do you mean?"

"You do see him at family gatherings, don't you?"

"Sometimes, sure. But what are you—"

"And of course you disagree with me about the circumcision issue."

"Sandy." She flung back her hair and smiled bravely as the elevator slowed down. He'd never noticed before how square and white her teeth were, small, like little Chicklets. "Whatever Critch might feel about you has nothing to do with the issue itself. It's more the fact that you've tended to be kind of—confrontational about it. But even so, I would *never*—"

"Let me ask you straight out, Anne. Has he said anything to you about me?"

"For God's sake, Sandy, we're not in junior high school."

As the door opened, Sandy wanted to pause the elevator, but the "open" and "close" buttons displayed those maddening triangles-facing-in, triangles-facing-out symbols, supposedly universal, that practically induced neurological damage if you tried to decipher them when you were in a hurry. Exasperated, Sandy blocked the door with his foot. *"Now*, Anne. I want to know now."

"Look, Sandy," she said evenly, "I can tell you Critch considers you reckless on the circumcision issue, or at least he did a few months ago. For one thing, it's not your area of expertise."

“But did he say anything about appointing Brett Ingersoll as second Assistant Chief?”

“Dr. Ingersoll?” She sounded surprised. “But I heard he’s never around.”

“Exactly. Something is really weird, Anne. Either Critch is losing it, or—”

“I don’t know anything about Dr. Ingersoll being made second Assistant Chief,” she said in a low voice. “He doesn’t have a very good reputation. Why would Critch—”

“Don’t you get it? He’s grooming Ingersoll for the Chief position!”

“Come on, Sandy, there’s no way he’d trade you in for Brett Ingersoll. Where’d you get that idea, anyway?”

But Anne hadn’t seen Dr. Ingersoll at the Quality and Utilization Management committee meeting. At his lunch table, where Sandy was also sitting, Ingersoll had told the group he was pretty sure he’d come up with a way to get all of them more time off. Sandy’s heart had sunk as he looked around and noticed several of his colleagues perking up, even those who’d had to deal with the man’s unreliability. Besides, people felt for Ingersoll; his wife was facing another round of chemo. And then there was the matter of Ingersoll’s beefy blond good looks. Sandy was reminded of a Shakespeare professor in college who had opined that the villain Iago ought not be played by a sinister-looking actor, but by an unassuming, sweet-looking one instead, creating a visual dissonance that gives Iago’s betrayal of Othello all the more impact.

“Anyway,” Anne pointed out, “if Ingersoll were being made second Assistant Chief, why hasn’t there been an announcement?”

That was true.

"Besides, the Chief appointment isn't just up to Critch. It's the colleagues who have to live with the appointment, and they're not going to want Brett Ingersoll." She stepped past him onto her floor.

He touched her arm. "You didn't tell him I was a lunatic?"

"Critch can see that perfectly well for himself," she said dryly. "Tell you what. I'll try to find out more about what Critch has in mind for the department. I'll e-mail you."

He knew she wouldn't.

"But try to lighten up, okay, Sandy? You're being kind of intense."

YOU'RE BEING KIND OF INTENSE—well, maybe so. Besides studying for his bar mitzvah, Sandy had started a modified version of *shabbat* observance. He'd attend Torah study at synagogue on Saturday mornings, followed by services in the sanctuary, and while he didn't refrain from driving or using the phone, he had stopped running around doing errands or catching up on paperwork. After Temple, he'd visit Belle, soothe her, make his presence known as a physician so the staff would be on its toes (this last part, though not so much in the spirit of *shabbat*, was at least consistent with being a better person). Then Sandy would go home and read, or go for a walk down along the Berkeley marina. A few times, he'd gone over to Cantor Traub's apartment to participate in a *shabbat* study group.

It wasn't so much spiritual connection Sandy sought; it was more a matter of his needing to take the edge off the tensions at work and the pain of the separation, and wanting to connect with a larger community—who knew, maybe find a path back to Ruth that way. After talking for years in the Children of Holocaust Survivors group about his own Jewish ambivalence, he was facing it now in a grounding way. He was learning the service. He was filling in knowledge of his heritage. He was saying *kaddish* for his father each week, no longer stumbling over that one thorny passage.

All of which was a little incongruous, Sandy supposed, in someone now actively in the process of restoring his own foreskin.

After scrambling out of Jim Horovich's group the day of the meeting—only realizing later that in his haste, he'd taken the copy of *The Joy of Uncircumcising!* with him when he left—Sandy had been, if anything, determined to distance himself from those guys, forget he'd ever attended. Though the pain had subsided within twenty minutes, Sandy popped half a Xanax as soon as he got home, another half that evening. He wasn't using it regularly any more, and the medicine knocked him out. But he woke up in a sweaty panic at 1 a.m. The pain had once again reared its ugly head, so to speak, in his dreams.

What is the pain about? What is the pain about? It was like the refrain of a song.

Sandy dragged his groggy body into the shower, thinking of all that had happened since that pivotal first event. He'd been buffeted about by physical and emotional reactions to it; engaged in intellectual and medical arguments related to it; immersed himself in Jewish inquiry in response to it. He'd lost his wife over it, at least for now. His father was gone; he was still scared of losing his daughter; his sister and his good friend were both fed up with him; his work life was unsettling. And he was still susceptible to the pain.

What did this journey add up to, so far, that was personal or concrete? Jewish thinking—did that really count? Had it brought him closer to God, for instance? Or did it amount to another going-through of motions, the way he'd worked the twelve steps so many years ago? Sandy revisited the thoughts he'd had just before today's foreskin restoration meeting: why so disdainful? *This is fine for other guys, but I'm above it*? One more way in which he was intellectualizing his problems instead of repairing the damage?

He toweled off, put on a robe and got online. There was a concerned, cloying e-mail from Jim Horovich to which Sandy didn't reply. He filled in some squares of an online *New York Times* crossword puzzle, then turned to his oversized pad of Post-Its and glanced at notes he'd recently scribbled. "In tradit. Jud., circ.= ultim. tang. act of devot. to God," one of them said. Tangible act, indeed.

Primum non nocere: first, do no harm. Already too late.

Tikkun olam: heal the world.

Sandy went back to bed and started reading the un-circumcising book.

A few days later, Sandy made his first attempt at the first step, taping himself. He'd never had great manual dexterity, and the tape was lopsided; when he tried to take it off, his skin got irritated. Ridiculous as it was to be using surgical tape on his penis, it was clearly far more so to fail at it. But Jim had e-mailed Sandy three more times since the meeting, and after the tape fiasco, Sandy finally answered him. Once he got over the initial distaste of confiding in Jim, he was glad there was someone from whom he could get practical advice. And Sandy was relieved to have something personal on which to focus his attention other than the family Passover at his and Ruth's house, which Ruth cooked for and participated in, yet seemed eerily absent from. She didn't know, yet, what he was up to.

Subtle results were apparent so quickly—within the first few weeks, Sandy swore there was a noticeable difference—that he soon stopped feeling squeamish. He was progressing. Already he had gained a little sensitivity at the head of his penis, and he allowed himself to wonder if and when he'd feel the difference in sexual pleasure that all the foreskin restoration literature talked about.

"WHY WOULD I DO a *bris* ceremony if the baby weren't being circumcised?" Rabbi Weinstein asked, walking swiftly across the courtyard as Sandy tagged alongside him one Saturday after services had ended. "It would kind of miss the point."

"I thought the point was entry into the covenant," Sandy said.

"You know what I mean." The rabbi fingered his hearing aid. Too bad he didn't have a *listening* aid.

"No, actually, Rabbi, I don't. *Bris* means 'covenant'—"

"Really. You don't say."

"—not circumcision. I mean, why can't the covenant be signified symbolically instead of literally? As it is for baby girls?"

Weinstein turned toward Sandy, his face red with barely suppressed annoyance—dislike, really, which obviously hadn't been mitigated by Sandy's recent steady attendance. There was a little white triangle of dried spittle in the corner of the rabbi's mouth, and he looked exhausted. "In a word, Sandy, *tradition*."

"Tradition—" Sandy intoned the word, then shrugged, "ehh," like Tevye in *Fiddler on the Roof*.

"Sandy, I'm in a hurry right now."

"All I'm saying is, there are young parents out there that want this kind of thing. Young families. *Unaffiliated* families."

Through Martha Berg, Sandy had been in contact with a number of expectant Jewish couples across the country who had decided to leave their baby boys intact, and he and Martha had been trying to compile a list of rabbis who would offer a ceremony without the circumcision. But of the few dozen rabbis who were known to have officiated at such ceremonies, Sandy and Martha had found only a handful who were willing to be "out" about it. It wasn't that Sandy expected Rabbi Weinstein to be swayed by his arguments, let alone agree to be on the roster. It was more that Weinstein's kneejerk dismissal of him struck Sandy as oddly inconsistent with his voracious membership-growing appetite.

Besides, there was already a strong precedent for the gender-rethinking of traditional Jewish liturgy, at least among the non-Orthodox. Gender-neutral prayer books (from which words like Lord, King, and male pronouns referring to God had been removed) were now in common use in most Reform and some Conservative synagogues. There were alternative *haggadot* for feminist Passover seders, wedding ceremonies for gays. More to the point, for decades there had been services welcoming infant girls into the community—services Weinstein himself had led. Was it such a leap to suggest that a Reform rabbi might consider offering that ceremony regardless of the baby's gender?

"You know, I wonder—" Sandy hesitated, but felt the need to seize the moment as an idea began to germinate. "Maybe we could have a panel discussion on circumcision. Talk these things through—leave out the medical issues entirely and just focus on the Jewish questions. Maybe you could provide the traditional viewpoint."

Rabbi Weinstein seemed taken aback, as if Sandy were asking him to chair a bake sale.

"And then we could have a *mohel*, and I could represent the—dissenting point of view, and maybe a Jewish feminist like Rabbi Kupferman-Adelstein could be part of it. Would you be willing to have the Temple sponsor something like that? For Temple members, but also for young families looking to join?"

"Personally, I wouldn't be comfortable participating. This kind of thing tends to attract hysterics."

"But isn't that all the more reason why a balanced panel is needed? A respectful discussion?"

"Classes and events at Temple are decided a year in advance. I suppose I could pitch the topic up at the Adult Education committee meeting in September."

"September? That's five months from now."

"For the following year of programming, of course." Rabbi Weinstein opened the door leading toward his office and let it shut in Sandy's face.

SANDY CONTINUED TO GROW his makeshift foreskin. One Wednesday after work, a month after he'd started the restoration process, he decided it was time to share the good news with Ruth.

Sandy didn't like dialing his parents' phone number to reach his wife, so he generally tried her cell first. Lately, he couldn't seem to get over the nervousness he felt in talking to her. There was some underlying impatience there that he'd never experienced with her before. Yesterday, she'd tried to end the conversation as soon as he started telling her about his progress with Vinod on the group they'd formed, Physicians Against Circumcision. In a mild panic at her coldness, he'd blurted out something about how there was a form of collagen derived from the cells of infant foreskins. "It's also one of the newer fillers they're using for cosmetic facial improvement, by the way."

"Why do you say 'by the way'?"

"Well, I—"

"Are you implying I need cosmetic surgery?"

"Of course not, Ruthie. I was just pointing out—"

"I have to go, Sandy." *Click.*

Now, picking up the receiver, it occurred to Sandy that there were two kinds of nausea. There was the purposeful type—the kind that resulted from food poisoning or chemotherapy, situations in which the body had good reason to try to reject the toxins invading it—and then there was the pointless type, like that brought on by morning sickness, or a winding car ride, or a migraine. Or anxiousness with an estranged wife.

"Ruthie?"

"Oh, hi, Sandy. Um, I'm kind of in the middle of something here—"

She sounded as if she were under water. Damned cell phones. "Listen, I'd like to see you. There's—something I need to talk with you about it in person."

"I don't know, Sandy—"

"Let me come over to the house."

"Please, Sandy, not now," Ruth said quietly, her voice echoing a little.

Sandy winced. How had he allowed Ruth to commandeer his parents' home, anyway? By abdicating, he reminded himself. By letting her handle the lion's share of the shit-work of clearing it out. "Look, Ruth, I need to see you. I just have to finish up a couple of e-mails, and then I'll be over."

Twenty-five minutes later, a few blocks from his parents' house, Sandy honked and waved to Critch, who was traveling in the opposite direction in his white Jaguar, but Critch didn't see him. One more sign of dementia: Critch driving aimlessly around in his new car, not even in his own neighborhood.

Sandy found himself knocking instead of using his key. He peered through the glass at the side of the door, and there was his wife, making her way toward him with the purposeful quick steps of someone being interrupted. She was wrapped in her yellow terry-cloth bathrobe and carrying a glass of white wine. Her hair was wet.

The house smelled of one of her white sauces—a cream sauce, that was it, with Chardonnay and grated Swiss cheese or Jarlsberg, or some combination thereof. Maybe she was making herself that wonderful gooey stuff with chunks of chicken and chopped celery and sauteed onion in it, served over wide egg noodles. There was something upsetting about the olfactory reminder that Ruth didn't need Sandy in order to make an elaborate dish. He glanced awkwardly over at the mirrored coat rack and fumbled with the keys in his jacket pocket. He'd given up foods that mixed meat with milk, anyway. Just as he'd stopped listening to Bach on Sunday mornings.

He followed her back toward the kitchen, slipping into the bathroom to jiggle the handle of the leaky toilet. In the kitchen, the commingled smells were more powerful. "You know, it's funny, that sauce almost smells like bourbon."

"Oh, I guess, umm. The—Gruyere has a pretty powerful—"

"—aroma." Sandy's stomach growled. He didn't sit down; he wanted to talk to Ruth in the living room, where they were on more equal footing.

"Hey, did I tell you I got this idea for a new project?" Ruth said brightly. "A how-to for college kids who've moved out of the dorms and are living on their own. Simple, nutritious stuff. My agent thinks it's a great idea."

It had never been Ruth's literary agent to whom she would pitch any new book idea; it was Sandy. Besides, he didn't like the way Ruth said "my agent," as if Sandy didn't know Honora's name. He steeled himself. "Listen, Ruth, I'm sorry about yesterday. I didn't mean to offend. I was just—"

"I know, Sandy," she said patiently. "Foreskins are being sold." Ruth put her glass down on the counter to take the lid off the pot. She stirred the food, banged the spoon against the rim of the pot and set it on a dish. "So Amy's coming over tomorrow. I think she wants those two small carpets from the back bedroom upstairs."

"Good. Does she need help schlepping them?" Sandy had been running into Amy nearly every Saturday at synagogue, between the end of Torah study and the beginning of services. Though he tried not to be obvious about it, it was the main reason he stayed after Torah study.

"Nah. We'll put her bike on the luggage rack of the Volvo and I'll give her a ride."

"Okay." Sandy was still standing. "Listen, Ruth, I want to talk with you about sex."

"Sex?"

"Sex, yes. Can we go into the living room?"

She covered the sauce, turned down the flame, and took up her wine glass. He led her by the hand and they sat down on the couch, Ruth with her back against the cushions, Sandy more toward the edge. "Ruth, I've had—a revelation, I guess you could call it. And—I want to show you something." He began to unbuckle his belt.

Ruth scrambled up off the couch. Her wine sloshed. "Hold it, Sandy. You said you needed to *talk* to me. So talk."

"But I—" He stood up next to her, holding the unfastened buckle in his hand. "Listen, Ruthie," he said tenderly, "I've neglected you sexually. And I know that's what's gotten us into this mess. It's put a weird torque on things. But now, I feel I can perform again."

She looked at him in a combination of bafflement and disdain. She never seemed as nice when she'd been drinking wine.

"That's been the problem, hasn't it?" he managed. "Sex?"

"Well, unfortunately, Sandy, that doesn't mean sex is the solution."

"But then—what is?"

"Um, talking, maybe? Caring about my feelings? Or, hey. Caring about really understanding yourself?"

"Okay, then, Ruth, let's talk."

"Okay then."

"But can I go first?" He reached out for her free hand and sat her back down on the couch. "I have to warn you that this is going to sound really weird, so please bear with me. I feel it's very important."

Ruth granted him a nod.

"Remember how at the very beginning when I was doing research on circumcision, I found that web site about support groups for men who want to stretch their skin? To mimic the function of a foreskin?"

"Yeah, those weirdos. I remember."

"Well, it turns out—that practice started nearly twenty-five hundred years ago. It dates back to the Hellenic period, when Jews were trying to pass as gentiles in order to avoid persecution, and also have access to education. That's when the phenomenon known as 'stretching' began."

"And?" She swirled the wine around in her glass.

He took her glass and put it on the coffee table, took both her hands. "See, originally, Ruthie," he said earnestly, "circumcision wasn't a very radical procedure. It was just the tip of the foreskin that was removed—that's what's mandated in the Torah."

"Yeah, so?"

"Well, there's historical evidence that the practice was made far more radical by the early rabbis, so that Jewish men couldn't reverse it. At least, not as—easily. And that more radical procedure is still in practice today."

She scrunched up her nose. "You mean to tell me that circumcision was more moderate in biblical times than it is now?"

"That's what I'm saying, yes."

"Well, that's certainly counter-intuitive. But I don't see what it has to do with—" Her eyes widened. "Sandy, you're not trying to—"

"Ruth, listen to me. I *am* trying it, and I'm telling you, it's helping."

"What do you mean, *helping*?"

"I mean I'm feeling more whole. And I think I might have a little more sensation. I want to show you what I'm talking about." He let go of her hands and undid the button of his trousers. The belt buckle clinked.

Ruth got up again. "Sandy, this is crazy. It's like chasing after some bizarre—why don't you have a penis enlargement, while you're at it?"

"*What?*"

"This is obsessive. It's narcissistic."

"Ruth, please listen to me." This certainly wasn't going as he had hoped. "It's making me feel better. Doesn't that matter to you?"

She looked down at him. "Have you ever considered that maybe one of your goals should be making *me* feel better?"

Sandy got up. "Of course I have. And that's exactly why I want to become more whole, Ruth! So that I can—"

"Sandy, this has gone too far. It's one thing to take a stand. But it's something else to associate yourself with a bunch of bizarre people who have nothing better to do with themselves than play with some flap of skin to see how long they can grow it. It's—sophomoric, is what it is. A pissing contest."

"Ruth!" Skepticism he was expecting. But not contempt.

"Or maybe 'circle jerk' would be a more apt term."

"Ruth!" he said again. Then, more quietly—"Actually, it's with the support of those *bizarre people*, as you put it, that I'm starting to feel more—"

She blanched. "Did you actually *go* to one of those groups?"

"Well, I—just one time, I—" He shuffled, hating the fact that they were having this conversation standing up.

"You met with men who want to do the same thing?"

"Okay, Ruth, it was kind of weird, sure, but—Ruth, this isn't like you at all. I mean, are you actually invoking Groucho here? That I shouldn't want to be a member of any club that would have me as a member?"

"No pun intended, I suppose. *Member*."

"Ruth, come on! You're the one who always thought I needed to watch my elitism."

"Elitism—what?"

Sandy re-buckled his belt, confused and frustrated. His wife was put off by the very thing he was doing to secure the hope of a future together? What was this, a grotesque variation on "The Gift of the Magi," with something more personal at stake than long hair or a watch chain? "You're the one who—I thought you, of all people, would disapprove of my tendency—my not wanting to associate myself with—riff-raff, as Margaret Dumont would say."

"What on earth are you talking about? Who's Margaret Dumont?"

"You know, my holding myself as superior."

Ruth looked at him impatiently. "Did you ever stop to think about your reputation, Sandy? Your credibility? What it could do to your career if anyone at work got wind of this—this childishness? This distraction from the real issue?"

Sandy furrowed his brow. He'd already confided in Vinod, and the two of them had even talked about collaborating on a research paper about foreskin restoration, in between all the legwork it was taking to get Physicians Against Circumcision off the ground.

"And anyway, what exactly does this entail? I mean, pulling the thing down for a few hours every day, like a yoga exercise or something?"

"Well, the actual techniques change as you progress. Initially—"

"Never mind. You know what? I really don't need to know."

"Ruth, I think—this is my choice and—I don't know why, exactly, but it feels right."

"Well, of course it feels right, Sandy. It's helping distract you from facing your truth."

"And what truth is that, Ruth?" Sandy's voice was raised. He had his limits. "I mean, how presumptuous! Why do you think *you* know my truth and I don't?"

"Because you don't see it!"

"Ruth, I'm trying to listen to my gut here. Go on my instincts." He started making his way toward the front door. Didn't she understand? Anyone could come to terms with grief over his father's passing. This, on the other hand! What more difficult truth could a man face than to recognize the wrongness of his circumcision, and then to set all dignity aside in order to try and fix it? This wasn't enough to restore his wife's respect? Fleetingly, Sandy thought of telling Ruth about the cocaine. Would that, finally, redeem him, make her understand how truly fearless he was about facing up to things?

"Sandy?" Ruth softened. "Look, I'm sorry. I don't mean to be dismissive about something that means so much to you." *Something that means so much to you*—how patronizing. "And you're right," she went on, "I've always wanted you to listen to your instincts more. Look, would you like some dinner?"

"No, thanks, Ruth. I don't eat *traife* any more." It came out more rejecting than he intended, so he smiled sadly at her, then started to leave.

"Sandy?"

He turned to her.

"Who's Margaret Dumont?"

Sandy gave another halfhearted smile. "She's that matronly woman in some of the Marx Brothers movies. You know, Groucho's foil." It was only after he left that Sandy realized he hadn't made sure Ruth had gotten her turn to talk.

CHAPTER TWENTY-THREE

THE FIRST SUNDAY OF MAY, the telephone-phobic contractor showed up with his truck to help Sandy and Amy cart the rest of the stuff they were saving to the storage unit. He was barefoot, but punctual, probably on some kind of medication. After insisting that he put his boots on, Sandy asked him to take a wrench and repair the leaky toilet in the bathroom on the main floor once and for all. From the front hallway, Sandy and Amy could hear little grunts coming from the echoey room, then one loud, long one. "Are you fixing that toilet," Sandy shouted, "or using it?"

"*Sandy!*" Amy whispered fiercely.

This was their last chance to go through the house before Shayna had it staged. Sandy and Amy had already spent hours doing a final pass through the books and LP records while waiting for the contractor.

Sandy and Ruth still hadn't discussed where she'd be going after the house sold. He tried to reassure himself that Ruth was ambivalent on the matter, but the truth was, his wife had given him no indication that she was considering coming home.

"Done," the contractor said, coming out of the bathroom. Hair had come loose from his long, scraggly ponytail, and he was panting a little. Sandy noticed he'd put his boots on without socks.

"Leak gone?"

"Yup. Hey, could I use your phone?"

Sandy winked at Amy as he handed him his cell.

The three of them loaded up the truck, chairs nesting into each other upside down, lamps placed between upside-down end-table legs, the whole thing an exercise in topology, like an obsessive-compulsive person loading a dishwasher. Then on the other end, at the storage unit, the same process. While they were unpacking, Sandy tore one of Belle's original oil paintings beyond salvation by accidentally dragging it across the sharp corner of the pre-amp from the stereo in the living room. Amy jumped to comfort him, but secretly, Sandy was relieved that the painting would have to be thrown away, the way he'd been feeling relieved lately when he neglected his non-circumcision-related e-mails for awhile and then went back through them and saw that certain deadlines had already passed: potlucks, charity events, due dates for endocrinology conference abstracts.

Afterward, Sandy and Amy were both in the mood for Gordito's, their favorite Mexican place. They brought their trays to a wooden table and sat down in view of the cars and pedestrian traffic along College Avenue. At the table next to theirs, a young mother strapped her happily babbling toddler into a wooden high chair, unaware that the legs were a little uneven. Sandy watched the drooly baby rock enthusiastically back and forth as the mother and father set down the trays of food, the mother's purse, and the diaper bag before the father finally tucked a folded napkin under the short leg. "Let's eat, little sport," the father said, and Sandy thought of how many times he and Ruth had brought Amy and her diaper bag to this place, how, when Amy got a little older, Sandy used to joke with her about whether ordering the Child Burrito made you a cannibal. How quickly Amy had moved into the phase when she rolled her eyes at that joke, and how now, it was possible the reference would evoke a tolerant chuckle.

Amy looked up from her food, not starting. "Know what I'm thinking of majoring in?"

Sandy was taken aback. He'd been very good lately about not bringing up the topic of school.

"Public policy."

"Really?"

"I don't know what specialty, though. There's a lot of stuff that's cool. You know, stuff like, if people don't have health insurance, how to get them medical care."

"A very important issue." Amy had done research into college programs? Did Ruth know? Sandy shifted in his chair so that the taped foreskin wasn't being pinched inside his underwear.

"And fuel efficiency. Like, if those hybrid cars they're working on are really going to help the environment, or not." Amy began to eat. "There's other stuff, too, like if the economy is bad, should you keep welfare programs. And the space program," she added, food in her mouth. "But, I'm not really about any of that."

This was almost provocative, as if his daughter wanted Sandy to know how useless he'd been in guiding her. "Wow, so you've started gathering information on what's out there. I really admire—"

"There's this one program? They let you get a bachelor's, and then it gets credited directly to a master's."

"That sounds great, honey." He picked up his fork.

"Yeah, whatever."

"Wait, why do you say 'whatever'?"

She shrugged. "You prob'ly don't think of me as getting a master's."

He leaned the fork against his plate. "Why not?"

"Come on, Sandy, don't act like I have the same genes as you." She shoveled a forkful of food into her mouth.

"Amy—" Sandy tried to focus on his breathing, the way Ruth was always trying to get him to do. He wished Ruth were there with them right now, effortlessly ensuring that thc discussion went in a positive direction. "You're from different genes, yes," he said slowly, "but you can do whatever you set your mind to. Haven't we always given you the message that—"

"See? *Set your mind to*. Like I couldn't do it unless I really tried."

"Well of course you have to try! Everyone does! And you're good at trying. You're a hard worker."

"That's so, like, condescending."

"It's the opposite!" Sandy raised his voice. After all the conversations they'd had, he and Ruth hadn't made a dent in this predictable, but nonetheless daunting, monolith of adoption-insecurity? "I believe you can accomplish whatever you want!"

"Then why are you always, like, *go to community college*?"

"Because you didn't apply to the U.C.'s or the state system in time! We reminded you about the deadlines—"

"*Duh*, why do you think I missed them?"

Sandy paused, his fork suspended in mid-air. "You deliberately missed those deadlines because you didn't feel you were good enough?"

"I guess." Amy softened. "Well, not exactly. It was more like—it's hard to explain. I mean, it's not like *you* ever had to wonder if you could achieve stuff."

"Amy, that's just not true. You have no idea how hard it was for me in medical school. I struggled, believe me. I worried that my parents—my father in particular—didn't think I had what it took."

"It's not the same thing," Amy said. "You had what it took."

Sandy leaned forward earnestly. "And so do you, my darling daughter."

"Whatever."

"Amy, you have a fine mind. We just—I guess—let me speak for myself here. I just never wanted you to have that feeling of needing to achieve in order to be loved. So if I ever gave you any message that—"

"I *want* to do important stuff, Sandy."

"I know you do. And I'm very proud of you for all you are doing and just for who you are—"

"It's all good," Amy said. "It's chill, really."

Sandy paused, unsure, as always with his daughter, whether they'd gotten anywhere.

"And hey, Sandy, I think it's cool what you're doing. With the whole circumcision thing, questioning it and everything."

"Well thank you, sweetheart. I appreciate that." She didn't know the half of it. "So you're thinking of applying?"

"Yeah, um—" Amy swallowed and wiped her mouth. "I already did apply. And got in. For the fall."

"You—what?"

"University of Colorado. Boulder."

"Wow. When did you find out?"

"Few weeks ago."

"*Oh.*" They'd e-mailed during that time. They'd talked on the phone. "D'you tell your mother?"

Amy nodded.

Sandy didn't want to know when. "So you're planning on Boulder."

"Yeah, in August. If you'll help."

"It's beautiful there," Sandy enthused. "Great for someone who loves the outdoors." The thought of living in Berkeley without Amy was terrifying, especially if it was without Ruth either. Besides, if Amy left for Boulder, what was to stop her from then going to Washington, D.C., and settling there? She could work for local or state government, but she could also wind up working for the E.P.A., or maybe the Department of Transportation. In a rush of shame, Sandy wished Amy would keep that going-nowhere job at the Botanical Gardens. "Of course we'll help. But I'm sure your mother already told you that."

"Thanks, Sandy." Amy grabbed another napkin. "Um, there's something else I've been—I wanted to—"

"What is it, honey?"

"I wanted to tell you, but—I talked to Ruth yesterday, finally."

"About what?"

"Well—I got this letter from Mick."

"*Mick?* You're kidding. When?"

"It's awhile ago. A few months."

"Oh."

"It took awhile for me to open it. It was like—I wanted to, but I didn't want to."

"I understand," Sandy said.

"You do?"

"Sure. Wait, so how did he—?"

"Through Corrador."

"Right." It was all starting to make sense. "So where is he?"

"In prison. Somewhere near L.A."

"Still? I thought his sentence—"

"Yeah, he was out for awhile, but then he was dealing cocaine. He's been in for around four years now, I think."

"Oh."

"He's not dealing anymore, obviously, and he's not using, either."

"Well, that's good."

"He said for this sentence, the one he's doing now, he got some time added onto it because of the Brenda thing. Which, he was all like, 'nothing can make up for my part in Brenda's death. Nothing can make up for my abandoning you at birth.' Stuff like that."

"Wow, sounds like he really poured out his heart to you."

"Well, see, he's been into recovery. He told me about how he's working on the program, and how he wanted to write to me because he was doing the ninth part of it."

"The ninth step?"

"Yeah, the one where you do amendments," Amy said.

"Amends. Right."

"Whatever. I guess you know the lingo."

Sandy wasn't sure what that meant. "So what else did Mick say?"

Amy shrugged, picked at the label of her soda with her fingernail. "Just stuff. He's in this training program at Lancaster to learn landscaping. Oh, and before, he was like, insane from coke use. He hit Brenda lots of times. Not just that one time at the end. I mean, I already knew that."

Sandy winced. Shayna had told her? Oh well, what difference did it make?

Amy laughed. "Sandy, don't look so worried! I'm not gonna start calling Mick 'Dad' or something."

Sandy grunted, collected himself. "Amy, I think it's great. It's something I never thought of—that Mick would contact you."

"Me, either. It's kinda weird."

"So are you gonna write back to him?"

"I'm not sure. Maybe. He was saying in the letter how he hoped he'd get to meet me someday, if I could forgive him, stuff like that. Actually, the letter was pretty chill."

"Well, sweetie, if you ever decided you did want to meet him, and you wanted us to go down there with you—you know we'd do that. Or if you wanted to do it alone—we'd support that, too. Of course."

"Well, yeah. Um, Sandy, you know Ruth's book is coming out next week, right?"

"Right." He'd gotten Ruth's mass e-mail regarding the publication of *Hypertension Life Extension*. For once, the publisher had chosen to keep the working title.

"There's gonna be, like, three bookstore events around here, after she gets back. First she's going to L.A. for the Barnes and Noble signings and the thing on cable. That's on Monday. Right after that, there's the thing here, at Campanile on Telegraph. And then two in San Francisco. So anyway, when she goes to L.A. next week—"

"*Oh.*" Sandy shifted in his chair. "You're thinking of going with her."

"Nah. Well, maybe. We'd have to set up an appointment in advance or whatever, and it has to be on a weekend. I mean, it might not happen—"

"You mean, visiting Mick in prison?"

"Yeah, Ruth looked on the web site, whatever."

Sandy struggled to keep his cool. Ruth had poked around a Department of Corrections web site and not said anything to him?

"So you wanna hit the Campanile thing together?" Amy offered.

"Ss-sure. Good idea."

Amy tore off a piece of the soda label and wadded it up. "Know what's weird, Sandy?"

"What?"

"You and I are both really affected by stuff that happened to us at birth. You with your circumcision stuff, and me with the adoption. I mean, the adoption isn't really a trauma, I guess," she backpedaled. "Just a big thing in my life that happened at birth."

"And what happened to you *in utero*—?"

She shrugged. "I don't think it really affects me. I mean, if I, like, remembered it somewhere, then wouldn't I be afraid of being hit or something?"

"You might. Or it might manifest itself more on a psychological level. Make you feel like you need protection."

"I really don't think it affected me. Except for hanging in, maybe."

"Hanging in?"

"I hung in, before I was born. That's something, right?"

"You're right, it is."

"Hey, Sandy? Do you think Brenda drank while she was pregnant with me?"

"Why do you ask that?"

Amy shrugged. "I mean, Denise drank a lot, right?"

"That's true. But according to Corrador—" Sandy paused. "Dr. Corrador always described her as pretty responsible. Not that responsible people can't be alcoholics and addicts. Of course they can. But—I just don't think of Brenda as someone who would have drunk to excess. She had chronic migraines, for one thing. Wouldn't she tend to avoid alcohol?"

Amy looked at him, her mouth open.

Sandy said, "I mean, when you think about it, a migraine attack is practically the same thing as a hangover. Head pain, light sensitivity, noise sensitivity, vomiting—and then the fact that Advil and ice packs and food and caffeine all help. Pretty much the same symptoms and the same treatments. D'you ever notice that? I read an article about it."

Amy gave him a long look. "So Sandy."

"Yeah?"

"You wanna come clean with me? About your getting busted for pot, back in the day?"

"Who told you that?"

Amy didn't blink.

Sandy swallowed hard and looked at his daughter. He waited a moment to be sure. "It was cocaine, actually. I got busted for coke."

NORMALLY SANDY SPOKE with Ruth every day, Amy two or three times a week, but he didn't call either one for the couple of days they were in L.A. In the conversations they had before Ruth left, Sandy had forced himself to sound casual, to let Ruth know he was aware of the planned prison visit without betraying how marginalized and anxious he felt. Now, his initial anger having subsided, Sandy almost relished the fact that Ruth was going through with the insult.

With Ruth and Amy gone, Sandy tried to focus on his sense of accomplishment about graduating from Stage I of his foreskin restoration to Stage II. Besides the fact that the extra tissue he was growing made his penis thicker and longer, Sandy hadn't had a single pain incident since he'd started "un-circumcising." Ruth wouldn't argue with any of it, once he was done with the process. Once she really understood.

Tuesday was the first day Sandy was scheduled to wear the weight full-time. The device consisted of two stainless steel spheres, each an inch in diameter, connected by a one-inch rod. One of the spheres sat inside Sandy's restored tissue, secured snugly by surgical tape on the outside, while the other sphere hung down outside his member. The thing looked a little like a miniature set of bar bells that functioned vertically instead of horizontally.

So far, Sandy had only worn the device around the house, and now, preparing to leave for work, he checked himself half a dozen times in the mirror, wishing Ruth were there to reassure him that the thing was undetectable. Hell, wishing she were there to call him ri*dick*ulous.

Why hadn't she phoned Sunday night, after they'd met Mick, or sometime yesterday? Or at least first thing today, now that they were back?

Should he choose a long jacket to cover himself up? But he didn't have one, not really, just that fake-fur-lined raincoat that was too heavy for a warm spring day. Finally he put on a tweed blazer, gave a final look in the mirror, headed out the door, then came back and grabbed a charcoal knitted Kangol hat that he didn't usually wear. That ought to distract anyone who might otherwise notice. Then when he got to work, he'd cover up with a lab coat.

Mid-morning, in between patients, having checked his cell half a dozen times for incoming calls, Sandy broke down and dialed. "Ruthie?"

"Hi, Sandy."

"Hi! How was the trip?"

"Fine."

"The cable show went okay?"

"Yes."

"And the signing?"

"Pretty well-attended. I think the TV exposure will help, even if it was an obscure station."

"That's great, that's great." Sandy was almost disgusted by his own forced perkiness. Reflexively, he pulled at the lab coat to make sure it was loose over his groin. "And Mick?"

"Yeah, we drove up to Lancaster on Sunday."

"Well? How was it?"

"An interesting experience."

"Okay, Ruth, could you be a little more specific?"

"I'm not sure what you're asking, Sandy. It was about what you'd expect. A real picnic. You show up in clothes that are completely non-provocative, of course, and then you give them your personal ID, fill out some form in triplicate—"

"No, Ruth, I mean—"

"—then you put your purse in these lockers—" Ruth paused. "Right, of course. You want to know about Mick. And how Amy did with all of it."

"Well, yes. She's my daughter, Ruth."

"I just thought you might want to know what you missed in terms of ambience."

"Ambience—Ruth, are you mad at me for missing the ambience?" He picked up his mug of instant decaf from the counter and took a sip, grimacing at the cold swill.

"Well, I guess I am. Yes."

"What? But you're the one—you didn't want me there!"

"Come on, Sandy, cut the crap."

"Cut what crap?"

"The passenger crap."

"Are you kidding me?" Sandy choked down rage, walked toward the window of the tiny exam room, where he was least likely to be overheard. "You exclude me from something that important, and then get mad at me for not being there?" He plunked the coffee cup on the sill.

"Look, since you called, Sandy—something came up while Amy and I were together, and I wanted to talk to you about. Because it's kind of odd."

"Wait, you're not going to answer me?"

"Hang on a sec, Sandy, that's my other line."

Sandy took his cup to the sink and poured the cold coffee down the drain.

"Are you there? That's Campanile Books, something about whether I need the P.A. system, how many people—I gotta take this. Sorry. You coming tonight?"

"Sure, Ruth. Wouldn't miss it."

"Okay, see you then. Gotta go."

That evening, Sandy wanted more than anything to ditch Ruth's book signing. But he still hadn't seen Amy, and he'd already called and told her he'd give her a ride. He didn't want her biking back to her co-op in the dark afterward, reflective clothing or no.

He wolfed down a store-bought whole wheat and brown rice burrito while standing up in the kitchen, put on the blazer and the Kangol hat again, and drove over to the co-op.

"Hey, sweetie!" he greeted her.

"Cool hat, Dad," Amy said as she climbed into the Mercedes.

Had he heard right? "Did you just call me—?"

She did her usual exaggerated sniff of the biodiesel smell. "French fries, *again*?"

Amy had called him Dad! This certainly wasn't on the list of Things to Expect After Daughter Meets Biological Father. Sandy resolved not to call further attention to it, or she might never do it again. He pulled out into the street, peering into his side view mirror. He did look kind of Continental in the Kangol.

Amy was snickering.

"What?"

"Just the hat. Like that's gonna impress Ruth."

"It's not—it's not what you think."

"Oh, I get it," Amy ribbed, "you suddenly went bald? Bald*er*?"

"So how was the trip?"

"Chill. We met Mick Sunday. We liked him."

We. Sandy glanced over at her. "That's wonderful, sweetie. I'm so glad."

"Yeah. He was really nice to Ruth, not just to me."

"That's great."

"I look just like him, too. We all joked about that."

"So what else?"

Amy shrugged. "I guess just, he loves being outdoors, so prison kinda sucks for him. Dude, prison sucks, period."

"Yeah, it must have been a pretty intense experience for you, visiting him there."

"Definitely. Really creepy, and the family lounge place smells really bad. Oh. He hates licorice, just like me."

"Interesting."

"You know what? I forgot to ask him how he parks his car, if he parks like me."

"Parks like you?"

"I mean, you know, I'm glad we met Mick and everything, but it's not like it really changes stuff. It's not like he's my long-loss dad or anything."

"Sure." Sandy tried not to smile.

"But it was cool. We're gonna stay in touch and get to know each other more."

They found a parking place in front of Restoration Hardware (whose name carried new meaning for Sandy). By the time they walked into Campanile Books, a small crowd had already formed around the author, who looked radiant in what seemed to be a new outfit. Shayna was next to Ruth just to the side of the podium, Ruth's literary agent Honora and her little dog behind her, a couple of neighbors and faculty members from the Cal nutrition department milling around nearby. The happiness that had flooded Sandy on the way over was replaced by the underlying agitation he'd felt all day.

When had Ruth gone shopping? In L.A., with Amy? Or had Shayna taken her? Sandy studied her in the silvery pantsuit, a look accentuated by a bold teal silk scarf and large dangling silver earrings he didn't recognize. She was even wearing silver pumps.

After coming up to give Ruth a kiss that barely seemed to register on her, Sandy retreated a few feet away while Amy disappeared into Campanile's music wing. Anne, Gina, Ellen, and a few people Sandy didn't recognize were milling around. Sandy rifled through nonfiction books in which he wasn't interested at a display table whose gleaming chrome corner brackets held together three-inch raw plywood lips that ran along the perimeter. What a stupid design; you could easily get a splinter.

Sandy reached toward the middle of the table for an oversized book on crocheting, thinking of his mother for the first time this evening. Over the last few months, Belle's health had declined to the point that he was confident no one had even discussed whether she should come to the signing. It was like being in the presence of a hard-of-hearing person and not noticing that you were talking loudly and exaggerating your annunciation until afterward, when you realized your throat hurt and you were generally exhausted. Everyone seemed to have made an unconscious adjustment to Belle's deterioration. Absently, Sandy wiped sawdust off his jacket.

Wait, was that the back of Critch's head? It was! When had he come in? And what was he doing here? Then Sandy remembered: *Hypertension Life Extension*. Of course. Critch had been studying hypertension in various populations for years, and had just recently published that paper—something about fat content inside the abdomen as a predictor of whether Japanese Americans will eventually develop high blood pressure. But did that give Critch the right to just show up wherever he wanted?

"Hey, Sandy, nice beret." Shayna was next to him, a huge black patent leather bag slung across her shoulder. "Mazel Tov. Aren't you proud?"

"Of course I am."

"Where's Amy?"

"Over looking at the rock CDs, I guess." Sandy felt like a teenager crashing a party. Not only was he here practically uninvited; he could swear that at this very moment, Critch, with his right foot planted on the floor, his left balanced on the ledge of the podium, was fawning over Ruth. Sandy's cheeks burned.

"Hey, what's this?" Shayna grabbed the crocheting book from Sandy, then started chatting with a woman next to her about the demise of yarn shops.

Sandy visually cruised the display table, scowling, feeling self-conscious about his apparatus.

Zev was coming towards him. "Hi, Sandy."

"Do you see who's over there?" he intoned, gesturing toward the podium with his chin.

Zev took a look over Sandy's shoulder.

"Critch!"

"Why is that—"

"Bad enough I have to work with that nut case, let alone run into him socially! At my own family function, I might add." Sandy glanced sideways and saw Ruth looking at him quizzically. He turned his back toward her and faced Zev. Despite their having drifted apart recently, Sandy realized he still thought of Zev as his best friend and ally. "Why is he standing so close to her?"

Zev eyed the situation. "Sandy, I think he's got some dementia."

"What, you're saying he'd have to be demented to find Ruth attractive?"

"Of course not, Sandy. Ruth is a beautiful woman, inside and out. I just mean there's something off about Critch, more than usual." Zev leaned in closer toward Sandy. "Gina stopped me this afternoon in the parking lot to tell me how concerned she is about him. By the way, did you know she had another run-in with Ingersoll about the on-call schedule?"

Sandy smirked. "You'll notice most of our colleagues seem to be tolerating Ingersoll's shenanigans just fine, now that he's managed to revamp the vacation policy."

Anne and Gina were coming up to greet Sandy and Zev, and Shayna, still chatting, shifted to the side to accommodate them, making herself smaller by inching closer to Sandy. What Shayna didn't seem to realize was that her massive purse had nowhere to go except into the small of Sandy's back, sending his crotch squarely and swiftly toward the corner of the table. Wincing, Sandy took a breath, then turned around uneasily and faced the women.

There was an unformulated question on the tip of his tongue.

Something was different now, that was it. A sound, almost: it reminded Sandy of the sensation of his cell phone ringing in his back pocket when it was on the "vibrate" setting. All at once, he understood that the surgical tape that held the little set of bar bells in place was coming loose.

Helplessly, he found himself glancing at Ruth just as she was mouthing, "Where's Amy?" So that was her quizzical look earlier. Not surprise that he'd show up here when their marriage was such a train wreck.

"Hey, cool hat," Anne said.

Should Sandy make a mad dash for the men's room, which he remembered was right behind the Psychology section? But that would involve crossing in front of Ruth and Critch. Did he have time to maneuver his way through the crowd, over to that folding chair about six feet away? Wildly considering his options, the back of his neck hot, Sandy had a split second to jam his thighs together, but it was too late. In one painful rip, the stainless steel device clattered loudly to the floor from the right leg of his khakis. There was a slight draft inside his boxers, air oddly circulating around too-loose surgical tape and insulted skin.

Sandy watched, horrified, as the device rolled quietly but unmistakably past Shayna, Gina and Anne on creaky wooden planks, right in the direction of Ruth's silver pumps. All conversation seemed to have stopped; all eyes, including Ruth's, seemed to be on the floor.

Critch turned around, bat-like, beady-eyed, to see why everyone had stopped talking.

Sandy forced a mad grin onto his face and lunged for the device, intending to swoop down and be back in an upright position in one swift motion. But suddenly he was sprawling on the floor, face to face with Critch's wingtips. It was only when he spied the little chrome device near the corner of the podium that Sandy realized that the Kangol had flown off his head. He'd tripped over it on the way down.

"Sandy!" Ruth exclaimed, rushing over to him. "You okay?"

Sandy stretched his arm out next to Critch's shoes and snatched the little chrome implement. "Of course," he smiled bravely, slipping the device into his blazer pocket and grabbing the Kangol as he scrambled up, mortified by Ruth's exaggerated kindness, grateful for the possibility that she'd only think he was an idiot for tripping over his hat. Forcing his hand onto Ruth's shoulder, he strained to keep the smile on his face. "Really, I'm fine. No problem. You go ahead and socialize." He winked at Critch, brushed the Kangol off with his hand, and put it back on his head.

He turned back to Gina, Anne, Shayna and Zev, all of whom were still looking at him in varying degrees of concern, bafflement and an odd skepticism. Anne seemed to be trying to determine whether there was some hardware missing from the corner of the display table. Shayna, on the other hand, narrowed her gaze at Sandy as if he were up to no good.

"Pocket must be t-torn," Sandy shrugged, mustering a helpless look calculated to make Shayna think *poor Sandy, Ruth used to attend to his clothing*.

"Doctor, are you all right?" Gina asked softly.

"Of course I am!" Sandy fairly shouted, freshly annoyed by Gina's spiked short white hair, too young a style for a woman in her fifties. He gave a curt wave to Zev and the others, turned and made his way toward the front of the store, his head down as the full weight of his embarrassment began to wash over him, the way pain floods in after the initial shock of a blow.

"Sandy, where are you going?" Shayna caught up to him.

"Can you give Amy a ride home?"

"Sure I can. But, Sandy—"

"I need some air, Shayna."

"But Ruth will be disappointed!"

"Phhh! She barely invited me in the first place."

"What on earth are you talking about?"

"Mass e-mail, that's what I'm talking about."

Sandy strode quickly up Telegraph Avenue, scorching with humiliation. Maybe he'd immerse himself in the classical music section of Criminal Records, try to find that new recording of the complete Shostakovich string quartets that he'd read about in the *Times*. No. Better to go directly to the car, get out of the neighborhood. He reached into his pocket, fingered the device as he kept going. He felt beaten. Misunderstood.

Ruth's white Volvo station wagon was parked right in front of Have A Hat, a dusty, dimly lit, floor-to-ceiling-stocked store that had been there since the sixties and was now in the final stages of its demise. *MOVING SALE*, said a forlorn sign in the window. It was moving all right. Sandy couldn't help slowing down. Involuntarily reaching up to touch the Kangol, he peered in the window, taking in the mostly empty shelves, empty cardboard boxes and packing detritus, the huge dark wood ladder on wheels that had been used to get hats down from the top shelves. Sandy and Ruth had bought matching black wool berets here just before getting married. *POIGNANT SALE*.

He heard the slaps of a woman's shoes on the pavement behind him. They got closer and closer until Sandy knew they were for him. *Ruth*? He turned around.

"What are you doing?" Shayna puffed.

"I'm—what are *you* doing? You're supposed to be inside."

Shayna waved her hand dismissively as she caught her breath. A few wisps had come loose from her pulled-back hair, and her eye makeup looked lopsided. "They're not starting yet. Some problem with the P.A. system. They weren't expecting such a big crowd. Anyway, I can go to the one tomorrow night in the city."

"But—"

"Sandy. Let's walk a little, huh?" Shayna tucked her hand into his arm. All the street vendors were gone for the day, and there was room for them to make their way up Telegraph without the usual heavy foot traffic. "I miss Daddy," she said quietly.

Sandy squeezed her hand with his arm. "I do, too."

"He wasn't nice to me."

"I know. Me, either."

"Yeah, but you were always the favored child."

"A dubious distinction," Sandy said.

"I miss him. Why do I miss him? He barely noticed me."

"Shayna," Sandy said plaintively, gripping the device in his pocket as if it were some kind of talisman. "How am I going to get her back?"

His sister looked at him with something more akin to impatience than he would have expected. "If you're really asking, Sandy, I think you're going to have to stop being such a doofus. Step up and make things better."

"But how? She doesn't need me," he whined. "She took Amy to L.A. to meet Mick without me."

"Yeah, why didn't you go with them?"

Sandy shrugged. "I didn't want to make Amy feel she couldn't do what she wanted. Besides, Ruth didn't even ask. She obviously didn't want me there. She doesn't want me under the same roof, and hey, maybe she's got a point. You know, Shayna, husbands and wives should live across the street from one another."

"Come on."

"You're right. Too close."

"Sandy, cut the crap. Did you ever think about how Ruth felt, being left to handle the whole Mick thing on her own?"

"That's *not* what happened. They—she—shut me out. It was presented to me as a *fait accomplis*. I still haven't really gotten a sense of how it went."

"Well, if that's the issue, I can fill you in a little."

"Okay." Sandy braced himself.

"I get the impression it was a bit of a letdown for Amy, maybe not quite as revealing or orienting as she could've used. The guy isn't much of a communicator. Admirable, working through all that. And a nice person. But ultimately, kind of mono-syllabic. You know. Not what our Amy is used to."

"Oh." Sandy leaned into the reassurance. Amy had called him Dad.

"Look, Sandy, you've got to stop neglecting Ruth, withholding sex—"

"I haven't been withholding sex, Shayna—not that it's any of your business—it's just that I'm trying to—" he stammered.

"Okay, spare me the details about the changes you're attempting to make to your personal anatomy. My point is, did it ever occur to you that Ruth needs your emotional support? I mean, just one example—she lost a parent, too. Did you ever think about that?"

"What?" Sandy was almost relieved. "That was two years ago." They were in front of Restoration Hardware now. Sandy rested against the Mercedes.

"Actually, Sandy, it's been three and a half years since Nadine's accident."

"So it's even less recent. Whatever. Besides, Ruth and Nadine didn't even—they weren't close."

"*What*? And you and Daddy were?"

"That's not the point! The point is—"

"Have you ever really *talked* to Ruth about what it was like to lose Nadine in such a horrible way?"

"For God's sake, Shayna, you're barking up the wrong tree. Ruth is over it. It was a horrible accident, it was a horrible relationship those two had, and it's done. And for your information, I *did* talk to her and comfort her. Of course I did, when it happened."

"Has she told you she's over it?"

"Shayna, we just lost our father a few months ago! How can you compare that to—"

"What, Ruth has to be on some timetable so her grief doesn't interfere with yours?"

"Look, what do you want from me?" He took his keys out of his pocket.

She sighed. "It's not what I want *from* you, Sandy, it's what I want *for* you. Some humility, for starters. I mean, I don't even know if Ruth's grieving over Nadine is a major thing. I'm just giving you one example of how you could be more sensitive to her. And how you could connect with her."

"Well, it's so obscure as to be practically—"

"If nothing else, Sandy, you know how important Daddy was to Ruth. It's an adjustment for her, too, to lose him. Did you ever think of that?"

"Not really," he admitted.

"And then your judgment, Sandy—like, what is this about telling Amy you got busted for cocaine? Why would you do that?"

"What? Shayna—"

"She's on her way to L.A. to meet her biological father, and you figure you should pile that on, so she'll be really freaked out that both her fathers have gotten into trouble with coke? What kind of a bullshit parenting technique—"

"Shayna!"

"What?"

"It's the truth. The coke story."

"*What?*" She gaped at him.

"I couldn't hack it in med school," Sandy shared miserably. "Had to keep going. Cope with the sleep deprivation. I started dealing to pay for it."

Her eyes widened.

"It was only that one time, really, the dealing. I was an amateur—that's how I got caught."

"Wait, are you saying—wait. Did Daddy and Mama know it was coke?"

Sandy sighed. "Dad did. He never wanted Mama to know. Swore me to secrecy."

"And then picked up the phone and pulled some strings for you."

"Exactly."

"Sandy, Sandy. Sharing that with Amy before you shared it with Ruth—that was a huge mistake, don't you see?"

"You're right. I guess I was just—maybe I was trying to get back at Ruth," he said weakly.

"Well, I think she's really confused by your behavior. From her point of view, either you lied to Amy for God knows what reason, or you lied to Ruth all these years about it having been pot. And me too, by the way. Your own sister."

Sandy hung his head.

Shayna softened. "Look, I've kind of dragged my feet about putting the house on the market. In fact, one thing I've really appreciated is—well, frankly, you've been too self-absorbed to push me on that. But now that we're moving forward—" She paused, then said gently, "Sandy, I can't quite put my finger on it, but Ruth just seems different somehow. You've got to do something. Before it's too late."

CHAPTER TWENTY-FOUR

NOTHING WENT AS SANDY intended with Ruth anymore. No matter what he said, she seemed to have a response he wasn't expecting in a tone he couldn't have predicted. He felt perpetually caught off guard, as if there were an unknown mathematical quantity informing every conversation between them. Something tiny but elemental. A hypothetical sub-atomic particle, a quark or something.

"But I don't get it," she said mildly at the other end of the phone. It was the morning after the book signing, and she'd just let him rant uninterrupted about the Mick visit (another strange thing, the non-interruption, with Ruth as emotionally detached as if she were observing a washing machine cycle: agitate, drain, rinse, spin). "Why would you tell Amy something like that, and not me?"

"I don't know, Ruth. It started out as—you mean, years ago? I guess I was always scared you'd think less of me."

"But you didn't think Amy would think less of you?"

"No. It was—I wanted her to know I could be open with her. Treat her like an adult."

"But by that criterion, you haven't treated me like an adult, right?" Matter-of-fact.

"Well, what I mean is—she's had enough doubt from me. What she needs is to feel I believe in her. In her capacity to be mature and make mature decisions."

"You know, Sandy, that makes perfect sense."

"It does?"

"Yeah. I can understand what you're trying to do there."

"Well, thanks for seeing it that way."

"Still," she said thoughtfully, "it was kinda awkward for me."

"I guess I did put you on the spot there."

Ruth laughed loudly. "Of course she thought I already knew!"

"Um, did you pretend to?" He figured she had; Amy would already have gotten on his case otherwise.

"You know, I did."

"Well, thanks for covering for me."

"For you? I was covering for myself. It had nothing to do with you."

"Oh."

"So do you think there's anything noteworthy about your having chosen to tell Amy such an explosive secret of yours just before we left on the trip?"

He wanted to deny it, but she had just let him go on that harangue. "I guess I was pissed off about the Mick thing," he said lamely.

"Well I'm still confused. Didn't you want to meet Mick with us?"

"What? Of course I did. Look, Ruth, I told you. It just seemed like I might do more damage to Amy if I interfered with how she wanted it. And besides, you never talked with me about going along. I keep feeling—you don't want me in your life."

"Hmm." Not a denial. "And that little ego bruise would keep you from participating in such an important family thing?"

This was exasperating. "I don't get it, Ruthie. Haven't you always seen me as relentless?"

"Definitely."

"But now you're saying I should be more relentless? Insinuate my way into a mother-daughter jaunt?"

"Well, *touché*, I guess."

There was a little silence. "Ruth, look, about the cocaine, can't you imagine how I might feel, revealing that stupidity to you, when I admire you so much?"

"That's hardly the point, Sandy."

"Really? Admiring you and loving you is not the point?"

"Huh." She sounded genuinely curious, as if she hadn't considered this before. "I don't know."

AFTER THE UNSATISFYING exchange with Rabbi Weinstein, Sandy had decided to host his own *shabbat* study group on the Jewish aspects of the circumcision controversy. It was too much to expect a Reform establishment figure like Rabbi Weinstein to go out on a limb. But that didn't mean Sandy couldn't set his sights on someone more viable—someone already sympathetic to the cause, who would be impressed with a balanced, thoughtful approach, who just needed a gentle push. Someone with an annoying hyphenated name.

Sandy got in touch with Avi Resnick, a local Orthodox *mohel* whose ads Sandy had seen in the *Jewish Bulletin*. Though Avi wouldn't drive or accept a ride on *shabbat*, it turned out he lived less than a mile away, and he said he'd be happy to walk over provided there was no *bris* to perform that day. Sandy added Martha Berg, who had just found out she was pregnant again, Cantor Traub, who said he was curious, and Jim Horovich, who if nothing else would make Sandy look less radical to the guest of honor. A week before the event, he e-mailed all the participants with a summary of what he'd learned in the last few months: the questions he'd been asking, the answers he'd been getting and not getting.

On Saturday, after attending Torah study, Sandy skipped services and went home to ready the house for the meeting. He laid out on the coffee table a copy of the Torah, some Jewish reference volumes, books about Jewish law, photocopies of various scholarly articles on circumcision, a book about *brit milah* within Reform Judaism, and another about the historical roots of Jewish circumcision. He'd marked the books and articles in advance with dozens of Post-Its so that he could refer to them quickly during the discussion.

Sandy had always thought of himself as competent in the kitchen, someone who abdicated his food involvement only because it was silly to pretend he wasn't married to an expert. But along with everything else that was difficult to do alone, Sandy found it an ordeal just to put a snack together. He brought a half-gallon of orange juice out to the living room, then realized he'd forgotten to purchase paper cups. He took some water glasses and two bottles of Calistoga bubbly water from the kitchen, but couldn't find the bottle opener. He brought the Calistogas back into the kitchen, then realized they were twist-off caps anyway. He brought them out again, along with a couple of packages of large, chewy Pepperidge Farm cookies. When he transferred the cookies to a serving dish, three of them fell out of the white paper cup they came in and landed on the floor. "Shit," said Sandy, bending to pick them up and trotting to the kitchen to throw them away. The five-second rule didn't apply to obsessive-compulsives.

A few minutes before three, while Sandy was still running around, the doorbell rang. "Are you Sandy?"

"You must be Martha," Sandy said, relieved to have the company. "Nice to finally meet you, have a face to put with an e-mail address. Come on in."

Sandy immediately felt comfortable with Martha. She was in her mid-thirties, tall, with an easy smile and a relaxed manner despite looking a bit green around the gills. Her thick dark hair was combed straight back from her high forehead and held in place with a tortoise-shell headband, reminding Sandy of Tenniel's illustrations of Alice in *Alice in Wonderland.* "How are you feeling?"

"Okay I guess." She smiled wanly. "Other than having to pull my minivan over and throw up in the gutter on the way over here."

"Let me try to find you something," Sandy said, trotting back into the kitchen to look for some soda crackers. "Or do you need some protein?" he offered under his breath, rooting around in the refrigerator drawer for a block of cheddar cheese. He wondered if he—if Ruth—had any ginger ale lying around. Come to think of it, his own stomach was jittery. Lucky the stainless steel device hadn't been giving him any trouble lately, and he'd gained confidence that it didn't show.

"Relax, Sandy," Martha grinned from the kitchen doorway. "I'm not ready to eat or drink anything just yet."

He led her into the living room. "You just sit on the couch. Or wherever is most comfortable. Have I left anything out?"

She sat down on the couch and surveyed the coffee table. "Napkins?"

"Napkins. Of course." He went back into the kitchen with a vague sense of futility, then remembered he'd run out weeks ago. He grabbed a roll of paper towels and started tearing off individual sheets as he came back out into the living room. "I'm not as good as my wife at keeping on top of things," he blurted.

"Oh. Your wife—"

"We're separated," Sandy confided without looking at her, sitting heavily down on the other end of the couch and continuing to tear off paper towels until there were too many.

"I'm so sorry," Martha said.

He looked at her glumly. "Well, I guess I've been kind of—obsessed lately. As you know." He'd begun to feel so comfortable with Martha via their e-mail over these past few months that at one point, he'd told her about his pain incidents. It was a little surprising to realize he hadn't mentioned anything about Ruth.

Someone was knocking. "Here goes," Sandy grunted.

"You'll do fine. *We'll* do fine. It'll be a great discussion."

"Let's just hope we can accomplish something." Sandy put the stack of torn-off paper towels on top of the study materials and went over to open the door. Jim Horovich was standing next to Rabbi Elizabeth, who was carrying a paper plate of cookies covered with plastic wrap.

"*Shabbat shalom*, Sandy," Rabbi Elizabeth said.

"Hey Sandy," said Jim.

"Hello, and welcome. *Shabbat shalom*." Sandy heard the gears of a bicycle. Immediately he thought of Amy, but it was Cantor Traub, tooling down the street and into their driveway. "Go on in," he said to Jim and the rabbi, gesturing toward the living room.

"What should I do with this?" Rabbi Elizabeth asked.

"Oh, wow, thanks for bringing something, Rabbi. Could you set it on the coffee table?" He raised the roll of paper towel. "I'll just put this away," he said, leaving the door ajar for the cantor and starting toward the kitchen.

Jim followed him. "How are you progressing?" he intoned, his Italian loafers tapping against the slate hallway floor.

"I think we're all set," Sandy said.

"No, I mean—"

Sandy gave Jim a puzzled look just as Rabbi Elizabeth reappeared.

"With the weight," Jim clarified.

"Weight?" the rabbi asked. "What, you're on a *diet*, Sandy?"

Sandy glared at Jim.

"Why is it always the skinny people who worry about their weight?" sighed the rabbi, putting the plate of cookies down on the kitchen table. "I'll just put these here for now," she explained. "You've got the table in there stacked so high, there's no room."

"Oh. Thanks," Sandy said. "Why don't you two go keep Martha company? I'll be right there." He started down the hallway toward the bathroom to collect himself. What had he been thinking, asking Jim to participate? *Clear case of LCS*, Ruth would have said: Loose Cannon Syndrome.

"Hey, Sandy." Jim was following him again. "I hope I didn't embarrass you there. I was only—"

"Look, Jim, I appreciate your concern. But this is not a foreskin restoration meeting, okay? We're here to focus on the Jewish issues."

"No problem," Jim said.

Sandy felt more relaxed as soon as all six of them were there, and were seated together in the living room. "Welcome, everyone," he said, looking at Rabbi Elizabeth, then Martha, Cantor Traub, Avi Resnick, and Jim. "I'd like to begin with the blessing for studying together. Rabbi, would you mind leading us?"

"*Baruch ata Adonai*," she chanted, "*eloheinu melech ha-olam, asher kidshanu be-mitzvotav, ve-tzivanu la-asok be-divrei Torah*."

"Thanks, Rabbi," Sandy said, "and thanks, everyone, for agreeing to be part of this study group. As we all know, circumcision is a hot topic. So I think it would be most productive if we limit our discussion to the Jewish issues." He paused and looked around the room. "We're all aware that there are medical reasons to question circumcision, and as a physician, I've been doing some work on that. But as you know, I've also been exploring whether there are *Jewish* reasons to question circumcision."

Avi Resnick looked skeptical. He was a massive, balding man, probably in his mid-forties, who had sounded accessible over the phone, but turned out in person to be rather dour. Sandy hadn't planned to ask him to speak, but quickly realized he needed to include Avi, the sooner the better. "Avi Resnick is here today to represent the traditional viewpoint," Sandy said to the others, pulling the copy of the Torah out of the pile on the coffee table and turning to the original passage, then handing the book over. "Avi, would you do the honors?"

"Well—of course," Avi said, and began reading aloud from Genesis 17.

> *This is My covenant, which ye shall keep, between Me and you and thy seed after thee: every male among you shall be circumcised. And ye shall be circumcised in the*

> *flesh of your foreskin; and it shall be a token of a covenant betwixt Me and you. And he that is eight days old shall be circumcised among you, every male throughout your generations, he that is born in the house, or bought with money of any foreigner, that is not of thy seed. He that is born in thy house, and he that is bought with thy money, must needs be circumcised; and My covenant shall be in your flesh for an everlasting covenant. And the uncircumcised male who is not circumcised in the flesh of his foreskin, that soul shall be cut off from his people; he hath broken My covenant.*

"Thank you, Avi," Sandy said, as Jim Horovich fidgeted. "Now if you're willing, Avi," Sandy continued, "I think we'd all appreciate hearing a summary of the significance of *brit milah* in Judaism so that we can bear it in mind as we begin our discussion."

Avi didn't try to hide his pleasure as he began to explain the history and meaning of circumcision in Judaism, the various components of the *bris* ceremony, and the connection with Jewish identity and commitment. Martha disappeared into the bathroom for a brief puke and Jim looked as if he wanted to jump out of his skin, but Rabbi Elizabeth was attentive.

Sandy glanced at his watch. "Thanks, Avi. You've given us a very good sense of the traditional perspective. I'd like to spend a few minutes now summarizing the reasons to question all of that, based on Jewish law and precedent." Watching the time carefully, and his tone, Sandy gave a rundown of everything he'd learned.

"Now, I know we could sit here and elevate our respective blood pressures," Sandy concluded. "We could spend the afternoon in a heated debate. But that probably wouldn't get us any closer to resolution."

"Then why are we here?" Jim wanted to know. He'd taken a cookie a few minutes ago but had yet to bite into it.

"Well—" Sandy was wondering how he'd gotten himself into this. "Maybe we could make this a more pragmatic discussion. I mean, try and address a very specific question." He paused. "Let's say a Jewish couple is expecting a baby, and they feel *brit milah* is unethical. So, are they Jewishly obligated to fulfill the commandment anyway, or—"

"We just read it," interrupted Avi. "The Torah clearly states—"

"—or are they Jewishly obligated, instead, to follow the admonition, 'what is hateful to you, do not do to your fellow person'?" Sandy finished.

"Obviously they shouldn't do it," said Jim Horovich, waving his cookie in the air. "Any enlightened person can see circumcision is an act of barbarity."

Sandy turned to him stiffly. "I'm not asking—"

"It's not as simple as that," Rabbi Elizabeth jumped in. "There's a larger context. Our tradition is thousands of years old. There's a big picture to think about."

"Jews have chosen to die rather than fail to perform *brit milah*," Avi said.

"That's not a reason to continue it if it's unethical," Martha pointed out.

"But who's going to decide whether or not it's ethical?" the rabbi said.

"What about the sexist aspect of the tradition?" Martha asked. "That alone is reason to question it."

"And we in the Reform Movement have made inroads over the past generation," the rabbi said. "As a feminist, I really believe girls need to be given equal fanfare at birth. And there are now some beautiful covenant ceremonies for girls."

"That has nothing to do with the issue," said Avi. "If this tradition dies, and our people continue to assimilate, pretty soon there's nothing distinctive about Judaism."

"Let's just look at one specific case at a time," Sandy suggested. "Suppose a couple is expecting a baby boy. They're intelligent and strongly Jewishly identified, and they're questioning the tradition in a thoughtful manner."

"Conscientious objectors," Martha put in. "Like me and my husband. We felt it would be unethical to circumcise our baby Seth, so we did our own ceremony."

"Your own ceremony," Avi repeated.

"Yes. We called it a *brit shalom*, which means 'covenant of peace.' And that's what other couples I've talked to want." Martha turned to Rabbi Elizabeth as if on cue. "Is this something you'd be willing to do?"

"You mean, officiate?"

"At that kind of ceremony, yes," Martha said. "Like, if a couple wants to use a girls' ceremony for their baby boy."

"Hmmm. I'd have to think about that."

"What is there to think about?" Avi was almost shrill.

"Wait, I don't get it," Jim Horovich said to the rabbi. "You described yourself as a feminist."

"Yes, I'm a feminist."

"Then you're against sexism, right?"

"Well, yes, but—"

"Yet you're hesitating to offer a baby boy the same ceremony you'd have no problem offering a baby girl?"

Sandy flushed with annoyance at Jim's tone.

"That's a specious argument," said the rabbi. "It sounds logical, it sounds fair, but it's a fallacy. You're taking a huge leap."

"There's no leap, really," Sandy said respectfully. "It's simply a covenant ceremony without the *milah*."

"Judaism is not a cola," retorted Avi Resnick. "You can't just order up a—a caffeine-free, low-carb ceremony and expect meaning."

Rabbi Elizabeth grinned nervously. "Tartar control, but with extra whitening power. But seriously, folks—"

"So I take it you wouldn't provide that service?" Martha asked Avi.

"Why would anyone call me for that? I'm known as an Orthodox *mohel*. I advertise in the *Jewish Bulletin* as a *mohel*."

"But let's say a couple approached you," Sandy said. "Let's say you knew them already, socially. How would you advise them?"

Avi Resnick shrugged. "I'd have to tell them I couldn't help them. Of course, first I'd talk to them at length about the significance of this commandment, and try to explain that they were making a serious mistake, something they would deeply regret."

"See, this is where I think you could help," Sandy said to the rabbi. "This kind of thing should be the subject of dialogue within the Reform Movement."

"It's not just providing a service," Rabbi Elizabeth pointed out.

"It's setting a precedent," the *mohel* agreed.

"It's a dessert topping *and* a floor wax!" the rabbi tittered.

"This is always an issue in Judaism," put in Cantor Traub, "or any modern religious observance. How much to turn your back on change in order to preserve valuable traditions, and how much to accommodate an evolving culture."

"Exactly," Rabbi Elizabeth said. "How much to accept assimilation, and how much to fight it."

"The main issue in Judaism," Avi said, "is that it's *disappearing*. Anything that's done to undermine tradition is just helping that process along."

"See, I'm not sure I believe that," said Cantor Traub. "I think Jewish life is thriving. Why else would there be a program just for Jewish physicians who want to become *mohelim*?"

Avi grunted. "That's not what I mean. I'm talking about intermarriage, assimilation, watered-down Jewish education—it's all contributing to the situation. If you start making changes to tradition, things fall apart even more."

"Oh, for God's sake," said Jim, finally taking a bite of the cookie.

Avi glared at Jim. "We *are* talking about God's sake."

"But isn't it worse for the future of Judaism if people don't join a synagogue because no one listens to their needs?" Martha asked.

"Well—" Rabbi Elizabeth hesitated.

"Look, if any rabbi offers people like that a *bris* ceremony without the circumcision," Avi said, "it sends a very damaging message. I don't care if it's a Reform rabbi or not. It's tantamount to the rabbi saying he agrees that the tradition is wrong."

Jim Horovich rolled his eyes and Avi caught him. Avi's chair creaked as he turned his large body toward Jim and looked him straight in the eye. "You know, I'm trying to understand what it is you're doing here."

"What I'm doing here?"

"Yes."

"Well, I'm an Intactivist."

"What's an in—tactivist?" asked Rabbi Elizabeth.

"It's an *activist* who's fighting for the rights of baby boys to have their penises left *intact*."

"Look, I don't care about your fancy puns," Avi sputtered. "Are you interested in studying together, or not?"

"I'm here because I'm a Jew against circumcision. Sandy and I met—"

"I think what Avi is asking, Jim," Sandy interrupted, "is whether you have respect for Jewish history and tradition, aside from this issue. Whether you're wrestling with this issue from a Jewish point of view, or whether you see yourself as an outsider in terms of Jewish life."

Jim Horovich shrugged. "I really don't see how my level of Jewish commitment or affiliation has anything to do with—"

"But it does," said Martha. "Look, I'm against circumcision, too. That doesn't mean it was an easy decision to make as a Jew."

Jim said, "You're talking about a completely irrational belief system. If you're asking me whether I buy into it, well, I'd have to say the answer is no."

"Come on, Jim, it's more complicated than that to be a Jew," Sandy said. "For one thing, Judaism is not just a set of beliefs. It's a set of actions, really. It's a religion, and a culture. And it's an ethnicity."

"Justify it however you'd like," Jim said. "Circumcision is still a savage act. And the violence of adults in the world will never stop until we stop perpetrating violence upon our children."

Avi looked as if it were taking his full effort not to get up and leave.

Jim went on, "Do you defend female genital mutilation?"

"Absolutely not," said Sandy.

"Right," Jim said. "We all see that as primitive and weird, and cruel. Well, why is that any different—"

"But let me ask you this," Sandy countered. "The African tribes that practice female genital mutilation—would you like to see them die out?"

Jim paused. "Of course not."

"Right. Because—well, besides being politically incorrect, Jim, that would be a loss for the world."

"But—"

"Well, that's what the Jewish people are facing, Jim—the *mohel* is absolutely right about that. There are only fourteen million Jews in the *entire world*. That's fewer than before the Holocaust—there were about seventeen million then." Sandy paused. "Now, you know I agree with you about circumcision itself, Jim. But there has to be some sense of a larger context. Some calibration about this issue, a recognition of the big picture. An acknowledgment that this is a complex issue. Not a slam dunk."

"I'm disappointed in you, Sandy," Jim said.

"Let's get back to the topic at hand," Sandy said, turning to Rabbi Elizabeth. "If you're a rabbi and you offer an alternative ceremony, you'd be responding to some people's personal ethics, their personal sense of what it means to be Jewish."

"It's funny," the cantor said to Sandy. "This, too, is in Korach. The idea that the individual is responsible for his or her own actions, rather than the entire tribe being on the hook spiritually."

Rabbi Elizabeth hedged. "I think what I would do is meet with the couple. Try to explain the significance of *brit milah*—"

"Look, I know a couple in San Francisco who would love to talk to someone about this right now," Martha said. "They're expecting a boy, any minute. They're not affiliated with any of the local congregations. In fact, they're looking to join."

"All you'd be doing, Rabbi," Sandy said softly, "would be honoring their well-thought-out choice."

The hyphenated rabbi sighed with an almost exaggerated weariness. "Look, I'm sorry, I can't. It just doesn't feel right to me. Not yet, anyway."

CANTOR TRAUB WAS THE last one to leave. "You did beautifully today, Sandy," he said as he and Sandy gathered the books and articles back into one stack. "You were very even-handed, and under tough circumstances."

I'm twice your age, Sandy thought irritably. "Well—thank you, Cantor. I didn't realize I came across as that neutral."

The cantor shook his head. "Not neutral. It's just that you have a reasonable perspective, and you presented it in a calm way. And please, after all this—call me Jay."

"The initial J? For Jeremiah?"

"J-A-Y."

"Thanks, Jay." Sandy began clearing the coffee table, laying the mostly-unused stack of paper towel squares back on the roll. What had he accomplished this afternoon? Rabbi Elizabeth hadn't budged. Amy was leaving. And Ruth wasn't there to lend an ear or help Sandy gain perspective.

"You know, Sandy, maybe you could give a *d'var torah* when Genesis 17 is read. In the fall. Usually it's within a month or so of Yom Kippur."

"You'd want me do that? Write something and read it to the congregation?"

"I'd have to check with Rabbi Weinstein, of course," Jay said, picking up an empty Calistoga bottle and following Sandy into the kitchen.

"Uh, don't hold your breath for *his* approval."

"Well, you're right—he may not feel comfortable having you state your views from the *bimah*," the cantor said thoughtfully. "*M*aybe *brit milah* would make a good topic for the Sunday lecture series I'm putting together for the fall."

Sandy gaped. "I thought all the programming was cast in stone. Decided a year in advance." As he said it, he realized how naive he sounded; of course the inner workings of an institution were never actually that rigid.

"Leave it to me." Jay waved the Calistoga bottle. "You know, Sandy, people don't generally call on a cantor to perform a ceremony."

"Yeah, I know." Comprehension dawned on Sandy's face. "Wait, are you saying—"

"I'm not saying anything. No one's ever asked."

"But you wouldn't rule out—"

Jay shrugged. "I wouldn't slam the door in anyone's face. I mean, I'd have to explain that I wasn't representing Temple Beth Isaac's policy. And I'm not a rabbi, even though I have quite a lot of religious training."

Sandy grinned. "Well, one thing's for sure, the music would be great at *that* ceremony." He paused. "So Jay, are you saying I should have Martha's couple contact you?"

"I don't know why I couldn't talk to them."

Later, maybe Sandy could ask Jay if he'd be willing to appear on the alternative *bris* provider list. For now, he'd leave well enough alone. "So I'm coming along on the bar mitzvah prep," Sandy said. "I think I'm on top of all the blessings and prayers."

"That's great."

"I'm still a little shaky on my part of the *parsha*, though."

"It'll come to you," Jay said absently, placing the bottle down on the kitchen table. "So Amy is going to Colorado."

Sandy nodded sadly. "I'll miss her like crazy." He hadn't quite believed Amy was leaving until last week, when she'd confided to him in an e-mail that she'd broken up with someone she'd been seeing, and that she was feeling free, and really ready to make a fresh start in the fall.

"You must be happy, though. That she's going to college."

"Of course I am. We are."

"I told her she could do it," Jay said.

"You encouraged her?"

"I didn't do much. Just held her hand through the application process. Figuratively speaking."

"Oh! I had no idea you helped. You did a huge mitzvah." How had Sandy failed to figure out that Jay was the "someone" Amy had been seeing—whose heart she seemed to have broken? That, *duh* (as Amy would say), Sandy and Ruth and Shayna weren't the only ones in Amy's life to whom she could turn for guidance or support?

"And I'm so glad for her about Mick," Jay went on.

"Mick, yeah." Not the traditional kind of name-dropping. "Amy enjoyed meeting him," Sandy said. "And it's good she took the time to go down there while she's between things. I don't know when she'll be able to get to L.A. again."

"Though I guess Mick could always visit her in Boulder," Jay said. "Or here."

"Wait—what?"

"He can visit her when he gets on his feet. Spare her a trip."

"Jay, you do realize Mick is incarcerated, right?"

"Of course. But isn't he getting out in about six months?"

"Oh—right." Sandy flushed angrily. It was one thing for Amy and Ruth to give him a sketchy report of their time with Mick; it was another for them to withhold a key detail from him while sharing it with a family outsider. Did they really think Sandy was so pathetic that he couldn't handle Mick's imminent freedom—the possibility that Mick might eventually play a larger role in Amy's life? Did Shayna know? Of course they told Shayna.

"You didn't know?" Jay said softly. "About Mick getting out?"

"Well—"

"I'm so sorry, Sandy. I just assumed—Amy talks about you like—well, she feels so close to you."

Sandy sat down at the kitchen table. "Amy says we're close?"

"Well, aren't you?" Jay pulled up a chair.

"We are," Sandy said. "In spite of some bumpy stuff, I think we really are." He paused. "What about you? When did you become so close to Amy?"

"We're just friends," the cantor said resignedly.

"You've stopped seeing each other."

"No, no—we never had that kind of relationship. She'd been seeing someone else."

Sandy picked at the label on the empty Calistoga bottle, feeling utterly superfluous.

"You know, there's something even worse than hearing 'I like you as a friend' from a beautiful girl," Jay observed.

"Yeah? What's that?"

"If she tells you, 'You're a really good listener.' Kiss of death."

CHAPTER TWENTY-FIVE

RUTH GOT A CALL from Amy on Tuesday morning, asking whether she was planning to go to Sandy's bar mitzvah ceremony that Friday. A few minutes later, Ruth's cell phone rang again.

"Ruthie?"

"Oh hi, Sandy." No doubt Amy had just phoned Sandy to prod him into calling Ruth himself about the service.

"I just wanted to let you know—"

"I know, Friday—"

"—I have some news, Ruth. Critch is dead."

"Dead? What do you mean?"

"He died. He's gone."

"*Gone*," Ruth repeated, sitting down on a padded chair in her in-laws' kitchen.

"Massive coronary at his desk, while he was catching up on some charting. Gina discovered him half an hour ago. Kept buzzing him, couldn't get a response, so she went in."

"God."

Sandy sighed. "He was a force to be reckoned with, that's for sure. One of a kind." He paused. "Ruthie? You there?"

"Of course."

"I wasn't sure if you were cutting out. Damned cell phones—"

"I'm here, Sandy."

"It must be weird for you, too. I mean, Critch was at your book signing just a few weeks ago. You were friends."

"Right."

"He'd really been looking bad lately," Sandy went on. "Apparently Gina and Anne had both been trying to get him to have a workup. Lorraine was worried about him, too. So was his son."

"So—what happens now?" Ruth managed.

"Well, as far as who's taking over, that's kind of up in the air."

Ruth stifled her irritation at Sandy's coyness; she'd never gotten a sense from Oliver that Sandy was anything but the heir apparent. "Of course you'll be made chief, Sandy," she said quietly.

"That depends on my colleagues. You know, morale has been low in the department. For one thing, Critch's alcoholism has been out of control. He'd gone more and more wacky these last few months. Years, maybe. It's affected things. Anyway, Dr. Pate—he's the Chief of Staff—"

"I know, Sandy."

"—he's interviewing everyone in the department over the next few days. So we'll see. I mean, I have good support. Maybe not from Dr. Ingersoll, but—"

"Ingersoll? Isn't he that guy who's been lobbying for better vacation and better raises for all the docs?" As soon as she said it, Ruth's heart fluttered. She had probably gotten the most recent information about Ingersoll from Oliver, not from Sandy.

"Right, he's the one we hired last fall. He's kind of a shirker, but for some reason he's been in Critch's good graces. I guess some of the docs feel he's looking out for them. But I can't imagine anyone actually respects him."

"Well, if people don't respect him—" Ruth said.

Oliver being about to die: how could Ruth have missed it? She'd been keenly aware of the dementia. On more than one occasion, Oliver had called her Becky, the name of his high school girlfriend. He'd repeated the same stories over and over. Alongside the cognitive impairment, there was alcohol; alongside alcohol, the headiness of their stolen time together. Three things for Ruth to experience, juggle. Now she had an odd sensation: that Oliver's having been at death's door would have been a fourth ball in the air, if only she'd known.

She was even more glad, now, for those bubble baths they'd taken together in her in-laws' oversized tub.

RUTH HAD ALWAYS THOUGHT of a bay view as someone else's selling point. She'd had other priorities every time she'd been in the market: great kitchen, good floor plan for entertaining, location. But as she stood at the oversized window of the 16th- floor apartment, Ruth realized how easily she could get used to this. She'd started taking smoking breaks on the balcony down the hall from her tiny office on campus, and had become more aware of the San Francisco skyline, the palpable sense of tranquility it offered from afar. Staring out now across the water, Ruth felt as if she were reclaiming a part of herself.

"They're going abroad for a year," the high-rise rental woman was saying. She was tiny, cat-like, old, with strange yellowish eyes and shoulder-length wavy yellow hair with white roots showing through. "He's a professor at Berkeley. Got a sabbatical starting in the fall, but they're traveling this summer. Indonesia, I think."

"Mmm," Ruth murmured, eyeing the Transamerica Pyramid. Oliver had talked about the lovely view from his house in the hills; wouldn't Ruth like to come over and see it sometime when Lorraine was out?

"Or Malaysia, maybe? Anyway, they'll be out of here July 1st."

Ruth had been in a haze since Sandy's call a few hours ago. After hanging up, she'd wandered through her in-laws' house as if looking for something. She'd cleaned up so well afterward each time Oliver had come over. He'd never left anything behind. No half-opened bottle of bourbon, no sleeveless ribbed white undershirt forgotten after a soak. There was nothing of his to bury her nose in, so Ruth went into the master bath, sat at the edge of the tub, and opened Belle's ancient bubble bath canister, the crystals somehow still fragrant after at least fifteen years, making her think of the Chanukah story: *there was only enough oil for one night, but miraculously, the oil had burned for eight instead...* Ruth noticed one of Oliver's curly white chest hairs in the tub. She bent down to pick it up, still sitting at the edge. She had the impulse to make a wish as if it were an eyelash. *I wish, I wish*, she thought. In *Lolita*, wasn't there a hair left in the bathtub that formed a question mark? Ruth blew the hair back into the tub without wishing, reflexively ran the water to wash it down the drain.

She'd left the house and driven up into the Berkeley hills, parking on Grizzly Peak and looking out toward the city in silence, smoking, not crying. Then she'd headed down to Trader Joe's in Emeryville, where she absently gathered a few items before abandoning her cart and leaving the store. She didn't want to go back to her in-laws' just yet and it was too warm to leave groceries in the car, so there was no point in purchasing them.

She'd always wondered about the one high-rise nearby, which reminded her of Nadine's last condo. She drove up to it and parked in the huge shadow that was gathering at its eastern edge. And now here she was with this elderly feline, enjoying a coveted western view on lush white wall-to-wall carpeting.

Ruth remembered the first time her literary agent Honora had come back to her with comments on the manuscript that was to become *Nourish Your Joints*. She hadn't realized that agents now did a lot of the kind of midwifery that in previous times had been the job of editors, so she wasn't expecting the level of detail Honora had provided—thoughtful remarks in the margins (*this recipe should go right after the explanation of oils!*) and, attached separately, several single-spaced pages of notes on the manuscript as a whole. Naturally the task ahead of Ruth had felt daunting; how would she synthesize Honora's suggestions into the book in just six weeks? But what had surprised Ruth was how *seen* she'd felt by Honora's critique. There was something grounding, intimate, about her work having been read so carefully.

Oliver: he had made Ruth feel seen. He'd made her feel more seen in their mediocre sexual encounters these past few months than Sandy, with all his personalized attention to her, his fully integrated—fully automated—understanding of her preferences.

Maybe Ruth was forgetting the satisfaction of intimacy with Sandy because she hadn't experienced it in a long time. Maybe she was exaggerating the joy of some awkward episodes with a man who was no longer there to disappoint her eventually. Or overestimating the delight of feeling so free from responsibility for Oliver's happiness that she had actually provided it.

If someone had asked Ruth whether she'd loved Oliver, she would probably have said no. If someone had asked who understood her better, Sandy or Oliver, she would have said Sandy. If someone had asked which was preferable, to hang out with an actively alcoholic, married, older man who could barely get it up, or to be hitched to a self-absorbed, eccentric but lovable Jewish neurotic—where was the controversy?

And yet, this matter of being seen.

The place would only be available for a year. Ruth trusted Sandy, and herself, to stay on good terms. There were Amy and Shayna and Belle to consider. There were decades of mutual respect and common experience and, yes, love. Ruth was still wearing her gold wedding band, and she realized with a start as she drove away from the high-rise that she hadn't thought to take it off. Hadn't noticed it, even while using her stretched-out left hand to steady the papers as she'd signed them with her right.

Stupid, to sign a lease while in shock, even if she did have a few days to cancel. Little stabs of panic rose in Ruth as she headed back toward Belle and Abraham's. What if Ruth hated the extra ten minutes it would take her to get to campus from the new place? What if, in these last few precious weeks before going away, Amy visited her less because Emeryville was further away from her co-op?

And what would she do about the place if Sandy were able to convince her to come home, prove to her that there was enough nourishment for her there? What if he could stop chasing his tail with this foreskin business and find some humility? Grieve, and move on? Not that any of that seemed likely.

Sandy's distant past had included a cocaine bust. But even so—and despite the self-conscious iconoclasm—Sandy was a goody-goody at heart. And goody-goodies were basically narcissists, weren't they, all that guilelessness revealing a certain self-centeredness? Sandy would never understand smoking, or drinking, or an irrational grief over the loss of Mother From Hell. He'd never understand an affair with an old codger. No, the kind of affair Sandy could understand was the kind a man could have with his own penis. It occurred to Ruth that there wasn't that much difference between obsession-over-the-appearance-of-his-dick Sandy, and plastic-surgery-hound Nadine.

Ruth would have to tell Sandy about the apartment, but not this week, not until his bar mitzvah was over. She'd be civil. No, more than that, she'd be genuinely loving. Go to his service on Friday night. That would set the tone.

CHAPTER TWENTY-SIX

AT LEAST DR. SEBASTIAN PATE had the courtesy to call Sandy into his office on Friday morning to tell him the news.

It had been a tough decision. A number of Sandy's colleagues had expressed strong support for him. And of course Dr. Pate was aware of all Sandy had done for Hyl. The priority he'd put on patient care. The years of loyal service.

The leadership, Sandy thought, hopelessly. In truth, Sandy hadn't fully prepared himself for this. He'd given it consideration only as a way of warding it off, like a hypochondriac who secretly believes he's covered his bases by thinking of every horrible possible outcome of a surgery beforehand. "So this is it," Sandy managed, shaking his head. "Dr. Ingersoll, Chief."

"Interim Chief," Dr. Pate consoled, furrowing his dandruffy white eyebrows. He was a rheumatologist who'd spent the bulk of his career at the San Francisco branch of Hyl, had come over to Berkeley eight or ten years ago, and had been named Chief of Staff not long afterward.

There was a saying that in the working world, first-rate people want first-rate people reporting to them. Second-rate people, on the other hand, want *third*-rate people reporting to them. What would become of the department now? Would Ingersoll be able to maintain its overall high caliber—would he be absent enough that these exceptionally smart and devoted physicians could just go about their business? Or would the bottom line be more and more in all of their faces, forcing the best and the brightest to leave? Even during the six-month interim period, Ingersoll could do a lot of damage.

"Well, I guess when you think about it," Sandy said, "I've always come up with ideas for making everyone around here work harder."

"Dr. Waldman."

"Time-consuming ideas," Sandy said bitterly. "Like more detailed communication with patients. Scheduling our staff meetings so that the poor schlubs in the waiting room aren't sitting there all day."

"Dr. Waldman, you know these choices are always—complicated."

Complicated? Apparently this one wasn't complicated at all. People vote their pocketbooks, their own personal interest. Damn it, do I have to spell it out? I'm the one who cares about our mission here! I'm the one who sees there's something more important than my own personal job benefits. I'm the one who cares about the truth. Isn't that enough?

But—it wasn't. Sandy slouched, his face flushed. It wasn't enough to be right about things and assume the rest would automatically follow. My God, he thought, I've turned into my father. So certain of himself, he saw no reason to consider the possibility that others might not just fall in line behind him. It was Sandy who had misjudged the respect of his colleagues as an entitlement, a wellspring of admiration and good will that would magically override everything else. It was Sandy who had misconstrued the love of his wife as a given.

How had Sandy missed it—that since his father's death, he'd taken on the man's basic emotional arrogance? Ruth, Shayna, Zev, Ezra Kohn—they'd all told him in one way or another. How had he failed to see?

"I'm sorry, Dr. Pate."

"Sorry for—"

"I shouldn't have sounded so—caustic, just then."

"Well, it's certainly understandable. You've put in a lot of time and effort, and vision. You're a fine physician, Dr. Waldman."

Improbably, Sandy smiled. "You know—I'm having my bar mitzvah this evening."

"Oh," Dr. Pate said, a little puzzled. "Well, congratulations—is that the right thing to say?"

"Sure. Thanks. It's something I feel very good about. I mean, my parents—they were Holocaust survivors. They wound up feeling ambivalent about Jewish observance, and I didn't have a bar mitzvah as a child."

"So you're doing it now." Dr. Pate was beginning to look worried, as if, in continuing the conversation, he might be incurring an obligation to attend the service.

"You know, I should go call my wife. Tell her everything. Just really level with her."

"It's good to have someone with whom you can share things like this," Dr. Pate soothed.

"Right. That, too," Sandy said.

∞

SANDY MILLED AROUND IN the social hall, waiting to enter the sanctuary. Rabbi Weinstein was chatting with a few of Sandy's classmates who were standing near the water cooler: a college girl with purplish hair; a woman whom Sandy knew from a couple of Sisterhood events Ruth had hosted; an Asian man in his thirties who was having his bar mitzvah as part of his conversion to Judaism; a tiny elderly Holocaust survivor whose colorful acrylic sweater reminded Sandy of his mother's endless gaudy crocheting projects.

Sandy loosened his tie slightly and straightened the green velvet *kipa* on his head, feeling edgy. It wasn't just stage fright, nor the thought of the *kipa* and *tallit* having belonged to his father, nor even the incongruent prospect of being on the *bimah* with a metal ball pulling down his foreskin. It had more to do with Ruth, who hadn't returned his call today. Would she show up? As he visualized himself walking out onto the *bimah* a few moments from now, being called to the Torah as a bar mitzvah, Sandy couldn't help imagining his wife glowing with pride and happiness on the occasion, wearing that new outfit maybe, seated in one of the front rows. His attempt to jolt her image out of the front row only made him think of her in the back row, or in the balcony, or in one of the side pews.

"Remember, everyone, this is not a performance," Jay said as they all gathered near the sanctuary's side entrance. "You're leading the congregation. There's no need to be nervous."

"What if I forget my part of the Torah portion?" giggled the college girl.

"No big deal," the cantor said. "Even in an Orthodox *shul*, if someone stumbles, the rabbi or cantor just corrects the stumble himself, as if he and the person chanting were leading the service together. Then the person who had been chanting takes it from there." Jay looked at all of them. "Just relax and enjoy this wonderful *mitzvah* you've chosen to do. This isn't a kid's piano recital. This evening's service is just that—a *service* you're providing, a function you're filling for the benefit of the community. You don't have to be perfect."

As the group prepared to go out onto the *bimah*, Rabbi Weinstein began shaking all of their hands—as if he'd been a key presence in their preparation these past few months.

Sandy was overtaken by a wave of sadness. His father probably wouldn't have understood Sandy's drive to become a bar mitzvah—let alone the chain of events spurring it on. But there was no question he'd attend the service. He'd show up for the occasion in a suit and tie, and would have insisted on bringing Belle in her wheelchair. He'd brush back his regal white hair with formidable hands, pull the wool *tallit* over his shoulders, clip the green velvet *kipa* to his head.

Sandy had learned through years of talking with other children of Holocaust survivors that many of the survivors rejected Jewish observance so thoroughly that they denigrated synagogue affiliation, put Christmas wreaths on their doors. But Abraham and Belle had always been respectful of Jewish life even if not actively engaged in it. There was no doubt in Sandy's mind that his parents would have been as proud of him today as they were at his medical school graduation. His eyes began to well with tears his father would have derided.

"It's time," Jay said, motioning to them.

Feet began to shuffle. They were moving. Sandy put his hand on the bony, acrylic-clad shoulder of the tiny old woman in front of him. She turned around and gave him a denturey smile, and he smiled back.

He straightened his *kipa*, glanced out into the congregation and gasped. Though they'd all been told to invite family and friends, Sandy hadn't done the math, hadn't anticipated the impact of the sanctuary filled to capacity. The attendance was more like Rosh Hashana or Yom Kippur than the usual turnout of several dozen for a Friday night service.

The first person Sandy recognized, toward the back and to the far side, was Vinod, seated next to his wife, who had brought both her parents as well as their children. Then Sandy saw that Gina, Anne and her husband had just entered the sanctuary and were trying to decide where to plant themselves. Not noticing Vinod, they made their way up toward the front to sit with Zev in the third row, passing by Martha Berg, her husband, and their little boy.

And there, suddenly, was darling Ruth in the fourth row, with Amy on one side of her, Shayna and Chris on the other. Ruth had those dangling earrings on again, and was dressed in a khaki skirt and what looked like a new form-fitting black top. Sandy squinted. Maybe it was just that she seemed to be wearing lipstick... absurdly, Sandy felt himself start to get an erection.

He smiled through tears. A boner—perfect—just as if he were a thirteen year-old bar mitzvah, about to die of pleasure that the girl he loved was there in the sanctuary on the day he was taking his place as a man among the Jewish people.

The metal ball tugged Sandy's penis downward, and he was spared any embarrassment. Ruth smiled up at him just as he was crossing the *bimah*, ready to take a seat along with the rest of his classmates.

ACKNOWLEDGMENTS

I AM DEEPLY GRATEFUL to my editor, Ruth Greenstein, whose steadfast belief in this project convinced me I had a story, and whose perceptive feedback provided the path. I'm also indebted to Mary Morris and my fellow Squaw Valley workshop participants, who saw an early excerpt and encouraged me to keep going.

Dr. John Rego generously shared his medical and HMO knowledge with me, as did Dr. Marc Anker and Dr. Rosetta Newhall. In other areas of my research, I was graciously guided by Lynne Fingerman, Judith Finn, Wayne Griffiths, Frederick Hodges, Mark Liss, Evan Moss, Neil Peterson, Dana Washington, and the inspiring Dr. Mark Reiss.

I greatly appreciate the support of Lynne Bosche, Deborah Braver, Rabbi Steven Chester, Barbara Cohen, Dr. Dean Edell, J. Edmund, Margo Braver Engels, Julia Holmes, Joy Jacobs, Bereni Karasik, Michael Kimmel, Nina Lesowitz, Michele Lieban Levine, Dawn Margolin, Eileen Ruby, Elisabeth Schlessinger, Rabbi Suzanne Singer, Anita Stapen and Anne Ziebur. Very special thanks to Liza Dalby and Erica Braver Gleason.

My husband, Mark Moss, always my first reader, has supported me with keen insight and tireless encouragement.

7035135R0

Made in the USA
Lexington, KY
13 October 2010